2024 High Caliber Awards

All works © 2024 by Cannon Publishing
&
© 2024 by individual story authors

Forward
J.F. Holmes

1st	Mightier Than the Pen	Kevin Harris
2nd	Blue As Sky, Black as Sin	Sam Robb
3rd	Specialist Lieu Saves The World	Brian Gifford
4th	Troll Hunt	SC Visel

Honorable Mention

Drawing Fire	Douglas Goodall
Forth from Hell	Tim Hanlon
On the job training	J.P. Staszak
The Historians	K.M. Sykes
The Rescue of Captain Gutierrez	John M. Campbell

Forward

Ah, to tell a story and to tell it well! It takes talent, of course, and as Edison said, hard work. What is even harder than telling a story is making it fit into a novella. In ten thousand words or so you have to not only build a plot, with a beginning, middle and end, include the hero's (or anti-hero's!) journey and develop your characters, but also ...

... build a universe. All of these stories stand alone in their own worlds, and those worlds have to be created in the short space that you also have to use to do all the preceding. And yet, well, here they are. Nine stories that each, in themselves, exist as individual universes in their entirety. All of these stories can become full novels with a cast of hundreds and touching on the lives of millions, and some of them surely will. (I know this, because I'm the publisher, and I'm going to make it happen!) Each of the nine winners below are authors who have never had a novel published, and many, including the winner, were completely brand new. All show incredible talent; some will become the people who you see in the best seller ranks of their genre in years to come.

So open up the book, turn on the e-reader, take a listen, any which way, and be prepared to walk on distant planets, fight mythical monsters and ride to the rescue of comrades in dire straits. All this and more awaits.

~ J.F. Holmes. CEO of Cannon Publishing and two time Dragon Award Finalist.

The judges are all independent of Cannon Publishing, except for Bill, who volunteers as a final copy editor but isn't paid, despite being worth his weight in Red Ink.

- **Cedar Sanderson**, Author and Illustrator
- **Marisa Wolf**, Author
- **Jamie Ibson**, Author and Professional Editor
- **Bill Erwin**, retired Army public affairs officer.

After an initial review of all twenty-seven entries, and some serious accusations between our company execs of having bad taste in literature, (we all had our favorites!), the final nine were sent forward to be judged. All judging was done blind and used a five point rating system to examine the following:

- Plot
- World Building
- Grammar
- Composition
- Ending
- Character Development
- Overall Storytelling

Scores were totaled and averaged, giving the winners as they are shown below.

Mightier than the Pen

Kevin Harris

    In that time, I was called Brother Kellin of Cambrin, and I was an awful monk.
    I remember the exact moment that my peaceful retirement was tossed on its ear. Spring had come early that year in the lowlands, though the drifts still sat heavy against the walls of the abbey. Saint Cecil the Rememberer's Abbey of the Suda sat high up in a saddle between two of the higher peaks in the Cambrin range. The view from Saint Cecil's was nearly as breathtaking as the climb to reach it. The horizon was obscured to the north and south by the looming mountains on either side of the holding, but the slope fell away dramatically to the West so that all the lowlands could be seen from the golden plains of Denn far below to the distant border forts and trader ports on the horizon. On a good day, you could see the setting sun dancing on the waters of the Inland Sea.
    It was just such an evening that saw the arrival of the Copper Company, in hurried disarray. It was my habit at that time to watch the sun set and to temporarily escape the fumes of glues and inks that permeated my cramped workroom in the heights of the abbey's tower. I had been leaning on the rail, sipping at a cup of weak tea when the first of the riders clattered into the courtyard, shouting for assistance.
    Our abbey was a haphazard collection of buildings, tumbled together out of hundreds of years of changing necessity and surrounded by a high stone wall. Those stone walls - and the steep climb up the switchback trail - served as sufficient deterrent to the barbaric Denn savages that lived in the plains below. We simply weren't worth the effort.
    On occasion, a small party of Dennish marauders would sneak past the armed outposts and make the climb to raid our stables or our stores. The boldest amongst them would leave a

smeared black handprint on the gate; a testament to the courage of the raiding youths. If they only knew how few of the brothers at Saint Cecil's had any skill with long-ax or bow, they would have come in greater numbers and with greater courage long ago.

"Bookers!" One of the riders clambered off of his horse and strode across the courtyard towards the abbey doors. His armor rattled as he stomped across the flagstones, "Bookers! We require supplies and fresh horses!"

I poured what was left of my tepid tea into a nearby potted plant and set my chipped cup on the rail with care. 'Booker' was a derogatory term the local soldiers and mercenaries used for the brothers of Saint Cecil. Not the best way to gain our cooperation. I leaned over the rail and watched as more and more of the riders filed through the open gate. Then again, maybe he wasn't asking for cooperation.

"Ho there, Copper!" My voice was hoarse with disuse. I cleared my throat and tried again, "I think you'll find many of the brethren are at their prayers or at supper."

The rider had stopped at the sound of my voice and gazed up in my direction. I couldn't make out his expression beneath his helm. He looked impressive there in the middle of the yard, where soldiers so rarely stood. The setting sun behind lit him in a corona of gold. His patterned shattersteel and copper hauberk of mail caught the light and glittered like light on a waterfall. The field armor of a captain of light cavalry. I pointed away towards the dormitories and its surrounding huddle of outbuildings near the chapel. I shouted, "The *brothers* can be found over there, unless you seek someone in particular." My emphasis on the appropriate title of our monastic order wasn't subtle, but my tea had been cold and my sunset spoiled by the dozens of riders cluttering the court.

The rider pulled off his tall, plumed helm exposing a narrow face under a shag of hair, pinched and tired. His breath misted in the cold air, "Thanks to you, *Brother*," he shouted. "I would speak with the Prior. It's an urgent matter."

"The Prior doesn't believe in urgency. I would be happy to inform his clerk of your arrival and your request for a meeting. His long hours of daily labor tax him. I'm afraid it is already well past the Prior's bedtime."

The soldier didn't seem to find my comment amusing, as true as it might be. Even brothers of the abbey are made to wait on the Prior's pleasure. He was a busy man.

The soldier turned from me and examined the broad courtyard of the Abbey, likely looking for a more helpful monk. I noticed that the stream of riders entering through the gate was finally tapering off. I made a quick count. 96 riders with half that number of remounts. Every horse was burdened with packs and bundles and every soldier kitted out for battle. If memory served, this was less than a quarter of the complement of the Copper Company.

Maybe this was urgent after all.

"Oi, Cap!" The soldier turned back to me again. He looked resigned as I was the only monk who seemed to have even noted their arrival. "I thought the Copper Company was assigned to patrol the frontier by the Inland Sea. Lost?"

He snorted a laugh, and I liked him better in that moment. He shook his head, "The trade routes on the Inland, then back to man the border forts at first crossing, then back again to clear the road to the trader's guildhouse and finally up the foothills to your very front door." His tight smile faded, "Lost most of my men in that retreat, make no mistake. The Company has been fighting a series of losing skirmishes for a full ten days now."

I looked again at his men and cursed myself for not seeing what I didn't expect. The riders able to dismount were helping others down from their saddles, wounded and exhausted. I softened my tone, "Raiders?"

He shook his head and I saw him sway on his feet. The man was exhausted, "Not just raiders. All of them."

"All? Which tribe is on the move?"

"Not a tribe, Brother. All of the Denn. Every clan and

tribe and village and able-bodied wanderer of the grasslands. They've a war leader and a common purpose. And they are coming for us."

I looked up to the west again and studied the lowlands beyond our curtain wall. The sun was low on the horizon. Its golden rays deepened to red as it kissed the edge of the world. In the ruddy light of that setting sun, I could see many thick columns of smoke rising in the distance. The grasslands were at war and our quiet little abbey was the only path east through the mountains.

"I'll wake up the Prior."

****

"The garrisons of Goose Point and Crossroads were informed to pull out with all haste and meet up at Halder's Rock. From there, they are to fall back to the abbey together. They have very few horses between them so it'll be a fighting retreat."

The captain's words echoed in the tall chamber of the Chapter House. The stony walls trapped the cold of late winter in the chamber and we were all bundled against the chill. The narrow stained-glass windows were dark and the only light came from a single lamp set on the small table at the chamber's center. All of the senior monks had been called to attend the captain's report; this was the largest gathering space in the abbey. They lined the walls of the circular room all the way around. Most of the brothers were wrapped in layers of cloaks and blankets. They stood stock-still, puffs of icy cold breath were the only sign that the silent monks were alive at all.

The silence stretched until one of the senior monks, the Grand Illustrator, elbowed the bundle of cloth slouching to his right. The bundle - more of a heap of blankets than a man - jumped at the none too gentle nudge. Two spindly arms emerged from the layered wraps, knobby fingers adjusted the layers of cloth as he struggled to pick up the thread of the conversation. His voice was high and querulous, "Um, yes. Of course. Very inconvenient. And when do you think the garrisons will arrive?"

The captain and I exchanged a look before he addressed the bundle of blankets. "They likely won't, Prior. Both garrisons are mainly medium infantry, with a company of engineers and cavalry scouts. Not enough horse to range out on their own in open battle. They will try to reserve them until they join up at the Rock, but unless the Denn make several consecutive stupid decisions, they will be an undersized force of mainly infantry about two marches from the nearest fortifiable structure."

"And where is that? They should go there." The Prior's voice was shrill; he clearly found this conversation beneath him.

"Here, Prior. The Abbey is the closest fortification. And they likely won't be able to reach it. Contrary to orders, the garrison commanders should try to hold out at the Rock and see if they can wait out the savages. They've never come together like this before. I can't imagine the alliance will hold for long."

The Prior pushed the heavy hood of his cloak from his head, exposing his pale fleshy face. By his eyes, he was starting to wake up to the reality of the situation. "What about Southreach? World's Edge? Hammon's Ford?"

The captain shook his head, "All of the frontier forts were overrun and burned to the ground days ago. The Denn can move fast as the wind when they want to. They will outflank the retreating garrisons quickly. If any make it here before the Denn, I would be surprised."

I tried to catch the captain's eye again, but he was intent on the Prior. The poor old monk just stood there, gaping like a landed fish. I suspect he had run out of ways to wish this problem away on someone else. The Denn were coming and the armies that were stationed out in the grasslands to control them had come up against something they hadn't anticipated.

Among the hundreds of clans and tribes of the barbaric Denn, they had found some common cause to unite them in war.

"What do they want?" My question was poorly timed. The Prior had just started to speak when I blurted out my question. The old monk didn't take kindly to interruptions. He glared at me from the depths of his bundled clothes. I thought I could see the stripes of his favorite pajamas beneath. I bowed deeply, "Apologies, Prior."

The Prior grunted in annoyance and faced the captain, "What do they want?"

"We don't know. They've made no attempt to communicate with us. No demands, no offer of surrender. Coordinated attacks from multiple directions. But they push us with every engagement to the east. To here. We suspect there is something here, or something beyond, that they want."

"The Suda!"

All heads turned to the portly monk propping up the Prior on the other side. He pushed back his hood as he stepped forward, exposing his narrow face and long bushy gray beard. Like all brothers of the order, his head was shaved bald. His eyes were large as he gazed about the chamber at all of us.

"They are coming for the Suda. For the sacred Book of Saint Cecil!"

The Prior looked uncomfortable. He started waving his hands about, trying to pacify the old monk before he even got started, "Brother Abrastus, if you please…"

The captain looked confused, "What would they want with your dusty old book? No offense, brothers," he amended under the weight of a dozen sudden glares.

"The Denn are a superstitious people," Abrastus explained. "Tribal. Illiterate. All of their history is kept as an oral tradition, through songs and poems. Not too different from the ways of our own people, away east in the valleys. The idea of the Book is a mystery to them."

"So why would they want a book if they can't read?", asked the captain.

"They think it has magic powers," said Abrastus, leveling an angry glare on the Prior.

Again, the captain looked skeptical. "And why would they think that?"

I spoke up, "Because we told them that it did."

There was a fair amount of uncomfortable shuffling about at that comment. The Prior looked like he wanted to melt into his robes and blankets and go back asleep. Abrastus's glare grew even more severe as he tried to pin the Prior in place with his eyes.

I explained further, mostly out of a desire to diffuse the situation. Mostly. I also enjoyed watching the Prior wilt as I spoke, "Brother Abrastus is our Grand Historian. He has dedicated years of his life to the study of the Denn and Denn culture."

He turned his glare on me, "Decades. Nearly all of my adult life."

I nodded and continued, "Over the past few years, warrior youths from the nearby Denn tribes have started raiding our supplies and stealing our livestock. At first it was mostly a nuisance, but the raiders became bolder and bolder and even started taking our horses to feed their mounts."

The captain blanched at that. I empathized with him. No one liked to face the sky-beasts of the Denn.

"The, ah… the decision was made to put some fear into these raiders. The traders that worked the routes through the Denn plains were paid to spread stories of the power of the Suda amongst the tribes."

"What sort of stories?" asked the captain.

Abrastus interrupted me before I could begin, "Stories of the Book bringing storms, blessing soldiers with uncanny powers of warcraft, of forging great illusions to hide the hidden ways through the mountains to Cambrin. Stories that the Book would drive the reader mad if they were not an anointed Brother of Saint Cecil. How stories read from the Book would enchant the listener and steal their free will."

Abrastus' voice rose with every example, "The Book could kill with a single word that was graven into its cover".

The captain hesitated, and then asked the question anyways, "What word is graven on the cover?"

"Suda." Abrastus pronounced it with perhaps more drama than was required.

The captain asked, "And what does that mean?"

"We have no idea."

The captain's frustration was starting to show, "And did that work? All those stories?"

"The raids tapered off significantly," said the Prior.

"But now the entirety of the Denn are converging on this point," the captain observed.

"Yes. I suppose that's true," muttered the Prior.

"As I told you they would!" shouted Abrastus. "Yes, they are a primitive people, but they are courageous, and not easily cowed. I told you this wouldn't work. Now instead of losing supplies and a few horses we -"

The angry monk was interrupted by a panicked pounding of booted feet in the hallway drawing nearer. All turned to face the door as it burst open to reveal a pale and winded soldier of the Copper Company, "Captain! There's something out there!"

The captain cursed under his breath and left the chamber, his soldier following sharp on his heels. I waited only a moment to bow in the direction of the Prior and the other elder monks before running out the door to follow them.

I was able to catch up to the two soldiers fairly quickly and caught some of what they had to say to each other. The captain was all business, "What did it look like?"

"All we could see was a big shadow overhead. It moved fast, scary fast. Flew just above the Abbey and then turned north towards the peak." The soldier was clearly shaken.

"Sky-beast. Probably with a rider. A scout," I offered.

The captain grunted as he nodded. His pace didn't slow at all, "I thought the same. You've seen them before?"

"I have."

"Here?"

I nodded, "And elsewhere."

"They usually come this close to the Abbey?"

I shook my head. We jogged down a steep flight of stone stairs and through a side-door into the courtyard, "No, they usually stay out over the grasslands."

"Right," said the captain as he picked up speed across the courtyard towards the main gate, "The winged scouts never go too far ahead of the main party of raiders."

I was just a step behind the captain's line of thinking, so it took me a moment before I joined him and his soldier in a sprint across the flagstones. The sun had fully set while we were all talking in the chapter house. Above, dark clouds obscured the pitch-black sky in tatters of deep gray. The moons had yet to rise so all of the light came from the smattering of stars far above and the watchfires that had been lit by the Abbey gates.

I was able to see the silhouettes of several soldiers high up on the narrow catwalk that ran along the backside of the curtain wall. A few of them were pointing away to the north, presumably off in the direction that the flying shadow had flown.

I pushed myself, my legs and chest on fire. It had been a while since I last ran. Quite a while. My waist was now wrapped in a generous layer of soft fleshy fat after years of sedentary living and long hours of copying pages by candlelight. Kellin the monk was seriously out of shape.

My heart hammered in my ears and made it hard to hear the captain shouting. He waved his arms over his head, hollering and he ran, outpacing me and even his soldier companion. The men turned sharply enough at the sound of his voice, and a few of them even got up from where they were passing the time to start towards the gate. But it wasn't the gate that was at risk.

The curtain wall that surrounded the Abbey and its

collection of buildings wasn't terribly tall. Three meters high with a modest catwalk along the inner edge and a simple gatehouse on the west and the east sides. This was not a martial fortification; it was a holy site. A place of retreat and contemplation. The resident monks dedicated their lives to documenting the history and knowledge of our people in the Suda and making copies of pages for the wealthy or the scholarly. The wall was intended to define the margin of the space and to provide some discouragement to troublemakers.

The Denn came over it with ease.

They came in a single wave, over twenty in total, cresting the wall all along the western edge. In the darkness they were nearly indistinguishable from men, save their animal fluidity and easy strength. They crouched atop the wall and nocked barbed arrows on their short bows. The sudden feeling of exposure I felt in that moment is difficult to describe. The courtyard of the abbey was a wide-open area of cobbled stones and the occasional shrub. I was nowhere near a shrub.

The arrows tore at the air as they leapt from the short bows and into the chests and necks of the unprepared soldiers. Men fell near the gate, one even crashing face-first into a watchfire. Sparks flew up and out as his heavy body struck the burning embers. I was fortunate in that first volley; the raiders had been focused on the soldiers. I didn't think they would overlook me again.

I hiked up my bulky robes and squatted to pry up one of the heavier cobbles at my feet. My soft fingers struggled to free the stone. All the while, I dreaded the inevitable impact of one of those arrows ripping into my body. I could hear the soldiers shouting and the pounding of feet. Another susurration of arrows made me flinch and I looked up, the stone finally free and awkward in my hands.

Men were working their way along the catwalk. The narrow ledge could only accommodate one person so they were strung along in a single line, shuffling behind upraised shields. The foremost soldier's shield already sported three spent shafts.

The same limitations that afflicted the soldiers also hampered the raiders. They were unable to spread out enough on the wall to target more than the lead couple of soldiers. Along the ground in the courtyard, a squad of men had been organized to return fire with their own bows. A few of those arrows found their mark and Denn raiders slumped over and fell from the wall.

There was a high-warbling call from one of the raiders further along the wall, and he waved his arms overhead. I could barely see him in the darkness. The sky overhead thundered with the sound of huge buffeting wings just above me. That damned sky-beast had come about in the darkness in a silent dive and used its huge wings to arrest its descent. I was able to catch a quick look at it as it passed over the wall. Its feathered underbelly was painted red in the light of the watchfires. Much like a prairie hawk, only huge and saddled with a Denn scout. And bloodthirsty. The horrid bird snatched at two of the soldiers as it passed over and tore them from the wall, sending them cartwheeling out into the darkness. A few arrows were sent after it, but it had passed into the impenetrable dark and I couldn't say whether they found their target.

The enemy used this distraction to withdraw. They were too few and not equipped for prolonged combat. As one, the remaining raiders released a final volley of arrows and dropped back over the wall and out of sight.

I let the unwieldy stone fall from my grasp. The improvised weapon hadn't been needed and I was glad of it. I felt the tension drain from my shoulders and I let out one long shuddering breath. The thought of facing dozens of raiders with nothing but a cobblestone left me cold inside. I surveyed the courtyard around me and found the ground littered with splintered arrows, more than a few within arms' reach.

The attack had lasted mere minutes, but the damage was done. I walked amongst the soldiers and offered what assistance I could. Their company included a cadre of specialists, and it was they who looked to the treatment of wounds and triage of the injured. All told, the brief raid saw a dozen dead Coppers and twice that wounded.

My hands were red, and my woolen robes soiled by the time the Prior made his way to the gates, surrounded by the elders. I was holding a soldier against my chest. He was hardly more than a child, in my mind. I did my best to hold him still as their battle chirurgeon dug an arrow out of his leg with a tiny knife. The wounded man had stopped struggling moments before, so he was either dead or unconscious. Either way, made him easier to hold.

As the barbed arrowhead was finally pulled out, the Prior spoke, "Brother Kellin. I would have a word with you."

"A bit busy right now, Prior."

The supercilious little man had always annoyed me. Sure, he had been a monk - a Brother of Saint Cecil - his entire adult life. He had dedicated his life to the recording and preservation of the history of our people. A noble calling in a time when the future of our culture seemed to teeter on the edge of a cliff. But he spent most of his time avoiding work and penned himself up in his chambers while the rest of us toiled away our remaining years filling a book that no one will ever likely read.

And now he stood over me in his heavy robes of office, looking down his long nose at me squatting in the mud. I was covered in blood where he apparently had found time during the raid to change his clothes. No, I did not like the Prior.

And the feeling was mutual. He crossed his arms and gave me the hairy-eye, "Brother, pack up your things. You'll be on the eastern road by sunrise."

****

The arguments lasted long into the night, but as the eastern sky slowly changed from black to dusky bronze, the Prior had his way.

Thus it was that I stood upon the eastern road with all of my worldly belongings tucked hastily into a pack, leaning on my old trusty staff and watching the procession get under way. It had been a long night of arguments and everyone - from the captain and his officers to the least of the elder monks - had their own opinion. The one thing everyone agreed upon was that the abbey couldn't be held by the Copper Company. With their complement reduced even further by the raid, they would be next to useless when it came to a full assault by the Denn.

I stepped aside as the advance party swept out of the eastern gate and down the road. In the thin pale light of the imminent dawn, the dozen riders disappeared into the shadows under the trees almost instantly. The road was narrow this high up, and the banks to either side steep and clogged with bracken and low-growing blueberry. Only the faint light of a pole lantern gave enough light to guide them on their way. I said a silent prayer to the fallen ancestors to watch over them and keep them from harm. Surely, the Denn had not made it around the abbey and down into the valley beyond, but a few whispers to the honored dead were harmless enough.

"You understand your task, Brother?"

I turned at the peevish sound of the Prior's voice. He stood in the gateway, no longer dressed in pajamas or his ornate robes of office. He was dressed to travel and draped in a heavy kirtle of brown wool. Behind him in the yard scurried all of the undermonks and a few of the elder brothers, each of them strapping bundles and boxes to the backs of some of the Copper Company's horses and the abbey's remaining beasts of burden.

I yawned. It had been many years since I went without sleep. And this night was far from restful. Thinking back to the bickering that had kept me from my bed, I fought the urge to spit, "I still think it's a bad idea, Prior."

He grimaced and flapped his hands at me, "The Book must be saved. It contains the complete knowledge of our people. From the moment we set foot in this land until now, we have recorded the deeds of our people in this book. This book contains every element of our art, our science, our history, and our culture. It is sacred. We cannot leave it for the savages to despoil."

"I'll not argue that. I'll not argue anything at this point. What was needed to be said has been said. But we won't be fooling the Denn with any of this. There's only one way down the mountain and that's this road here. They will be on us well before I reach Velasko."

The Prior looked away, clearly not interested in renewing the debate that stole the entire night from both of us. It had been a frustrating exchange; the old monk had made up his mind long before we even started. There was a plan, to save the Book and as many of the brethren as possible. But my part in the plan was the least savory.

A loud creaking emanated from the abbey gate. The sound of an overburdened cart drew near, accompanied by the clop of hooves. The Prior stepped out of the path, and we watched as the Suda was transported out of the abbey walls for the first time since its construction. The huge fragile Book filled the bed of the produce cart, I could just make out its dark leather binding peeking out from beneath the heavy oiled rain tarp that was strapped over the cart. I could not guess at the Suda's weight, but it caused the axles and the poor mule to groan. The Prior approached and gestured at the driver, waving him to a stop.

"You had best get going," he said to me as he fixed the tarp and struggled with the cords that held it in place. "It's at least a week to Velasko and those scouts you sent ahead won't get there that far ahead of you." He shook his head, still avoiding eye contact as he fussed with the tarp, "The road is narrow and rough as it descends to the lowlands and the river cities. If you're to stay ahead of the Denn, you better move it."

I threw my pack on the cart and hitched my staff up on my shoulder, "I didn't send the scouts ahead to the city. By the time they roused the militia and set off back here, the Denn will have overrun the entire mountaintop."

He turned and finally met my eyes, "Then why?" He looked curious and annoyed. I allowed myself a moment to enjoy that expression.

The whole night had been a series of arguments over the best way to handle the situation. All of the monks agreed that the Book needed to be moved from the Abbey and down to the walled city of Velasko on the Ubbe River. Most of the monks even agreed that they themselves should be taken away to safety as well. Some few of the younger ones - monks who had missed the lightning raid from earlier in the night, or just foolish men with an inflated sense of their own martial prowess - thought to try and hold the walls against the approaching Denn horde.

It was the cavalry captain- Rogen Fallard it turned out he was called - who stopped that line of thinking. With only 80 able-bodied soldiers left in his company, he flat out refused to try to hold the Abbey against thousands of savages. The plan was to get the Book to safety as quickly as possible. That meant a small escort for the Book with the majority of the surviving soldiers accompanying the monks to a nearby shrine on the mountainside. Everyone agreed the Denn would follow the Book.

You can only imagine my excitement.

"About half a march east along the Velasko Road, there is a bridge that spans Cambrin Gorge at its narrowest point." The Prior nodded as I spoke, he knew the bridge I spoke of, and the high perilous road that led to it. The pampered old monk likely crossed that same way when he took his assignment at the abbey decades earlier. "The scouts will be holding that bridge when I arrive, hopefully with a little surprise for the Denn as well".

The Prior scowled at my cagey response and feigned disinterest, "As long as the Book escapes the savages, I don't care how you squander your resources". The creaking of wheels emerged from the abbey gate, and the Prior and I turned to watch as five more carts - these laden with large stones - rolled down the road. Each of these carts were driven by a company soldier with one of their mounts along in tow.

I nodded thanks to each of these soldiers and received a nod in return. Theirs was the more dangerous assignment. They were decoys, intended to confuse and delay the pursuing Denn. Each of them would pull off the path at different points to make false trails off into the mountain wilderness. Once their trail was laid, they would abandon their cart and hare off into the woods and away. Through some luck and a fair amount of woodcraft, they would rejoin us somehow further down the road. Each of them had volunteered for the duty, which I had found quite remarkable.

Captain Fallard stood along the road and greeted each of his volunteers as they passed, offering them a handshake and a small bundle to see them off. The soldiers responded gratefully and his smile for them seemed genuine and earnest. I should have seen it then, I suppose, but I was preoccupied with my plan of not getting murdered by Denn Marauders.

"You'll take good care of it, won't you Brother?"

I looked back from my study of the captain to see who had spoken. All of the elder brothers had gathered under the arch of the gate to see me off. Well - I reconsidered as each of them looked upon the bundled Book with love and anguish - to see the Suda off at least.

Brother Abrastus came forward and laid a shaking hand on the tarp, feeling at the book hidden underneath. Head bowed over the Book, he rasped again, "You'll take good care of it?"

I watched him standing there beside his life's work and I felt a pang of regret for my petty squabbles with the Prior over this artifact. Abrastus was a good man, all the brothers were, for the most part. It might be ludicrous to attempt to flee with the Book and hope to outrun the Denn, but the Suda was more than a collection of stories. It was the culmination of the labor of generations of monks and scholars. Almost 700 years of effort. An old familiar fire was kindled in my belly in that moment, a strength and resolve I hadn't felt in years. I didn't answer my brother's question. I simply rested my hand on his shoulder and tried to convey the strength of that fire growing inside of me. One heavy hand seemed to be enough. I couldn't see his face, hidden as it was beneath his hood, but I could feel him. I could feel the old man weeping.

****

I had a nasty crick in my neck by the time we reached the old bridge. The rutted road dipped steeply as we descended towards Cambrin Gorge. The forest opened up here, the craggy boles of the pines and spruz gave way as the slope sharpened and revealed a broken landscape of limestone talus covered in lichens and dark dormant mosses. The smell of pine and rich acidic soil was traded for that of ice on the wind. I wrapped my outer robes around my body and huddled against the bench of the cart.

The road had been precarious up until that point, and only worsened as we left the evergreens above. Erosion and a lack of maintenance made this road more of a suggestion than a reality. A sudden lurch and bang as the wheels of the cart slipped off of a large stone and into the rut wrenched my back and caused me to grab the side of the cart to keep my seat. The Copper driving the cart beside me threw me an apologetic grimace and pulled on the reins to steady the mule.

I had spent most of our trip down the mountainside twisted around to study the path behind us, sure in my heart that we would see savage warriors pelting down through the widely spaced trees. The last of our decoys had peeled off hours ago. I turned back around, somewhat reassured. It was quiet. Only the empty wild woods and the call of migrating birds. No Denn, not yet.

The road leveled out as we reached the edge of the gorge. It wended its way between looming chunks of fallen limestone towards the timber-framed bridge that spanned this narrow arm of the expanse. Our escort of two dozen riders passed us as the road widened just before the bridgehead. They were quiet and alert, their harnesses softly jangling as they trotted by. I watched as Captain Fallard stood in his stirrups, craning his neck to see across the bridge. He must have seen what he hoped to see; he dropped back into his saddle and threw a weary smile to his men. They all whooped joyfully and thundered across the wooden deck.

I was relieved that the soldier driving the cart took the passage at a more sedate pace. I'd noticed the timbers of the old bridge shuddering under the hooves of the horses. It had been almost three years since I last crossed over this bridge - the only time - when I turned my back on my former life and headed up to the abbey to take my oaths as a monk. I gazed over the low rails and took in the view. The sheer sides of the gorge were still shrouded in ice, and all along the base of the walls, deep snows still dwelt in defiance of the encroaching spring. Out here, high above, the distant murmur of the Cambrin River could be heard, swollen with melt water and chunks of rotten ice.

As we reached the center, the bridge moaned under the weight of the cart, two men, and the most sacred book of my people. There was a loud pop, and I well remember the feeling of the broad deck sinking beneath us. My eyes met those of the driver, the whites of his eyes were visible all the way around his pale irises, his lower lip caught in his crooked teeth.

Before I could demand he turn us about and make for solid land, the donkey took the decision out of our hands. With a lurch that sent me over the buckboard and on top of the Suda, the simple beast cried out and raced for the far side of the gorge. I am not too proud to relate that the sounds of my screams drowned out anything the driver was trying to relay to me. Out of all the ways I had nearly died in my long life, plummeting to my death in the back of a donkey cart was among the least desirable. The driver hauled on the reins, leaning back with all of his weight as I thrashed and kicked and wailed atop the tarp. Neither of us did any good at all; the donkey continued his headlong charge towards the only safety he could conceive of as the bridge continued to sag and shake beneath us.

My fallen ancestors - or those of the headstrong donkey - must have been watching out for us, for we reached the far side of the bridge and the relative safety of the road. Soldiers of the Copper Company swarmed the cart, seizing the bridle of the panicked beast and wrestled with it to bring it to a halt. All around us, the men were hollering wildly. Before we even came to a complete stop, the driver rolled off of the cart and into the waiting arms of his brethren. It took me a moment to realize that all the shouting was joyful and every face was twisted in riotous laughter.

As the cart fully stopped, I clambered over the edge and fell to the dusty ground. No waiting arms to greet me. I glanced back the way we had come. The bridge has stilled, though the far end laid a good pace lower than the edge of the gorge. I swallowed and felt the pain of a torn throat. Two feet came to a stop beside me, and Captain Fallard squatted down and put a hand on my shoulder.

"I thought they would wait for us before sabotaging the braces", I croaked, glaring into his smug smiling face.

He shrugged and gave my shoulder a squeeze, "Engineers looked it over when they arrived. This old bridge was deeply sunk into the gorge walls and the braces were thick. They figured they would get a head-start while they waited for us."

I scowled at his smiling face, "Too much, too soon. We almost lost the Book, and me!"

"And the donkey, and young Simson as well", Fallard allowed. "It was a calculated risk."

I struggled to my feet, brushing off his offered hand, "You could have told me."

Fallard shrugged, "Didn't know. The lads took initiative." He looked around the impromptu camp that the advance team had set up near the bridge, "Connor!"

A scrawny young man whipped his head around as his name was called and pushed his way through the reunion of soldiers. He was stripped down, out of armor and most of his uniform. Just his breeks and a filthy undershirt. He looked tired, but his fist to heart salute was crisp enough.

The captain returned the salute and clapped the lad on the back, "Quite the greeting you arranged for us. How long before you take the whole thing down?"

The young soldier's breath misted in the cold air, "Now that you're here? We can climb down and take out the final stays. The weight of the structure should do most of the work for us."

"Get it done." The lad saluted again and darted away.

I turned to face the captain, "It's still a solid plan, but shouldn't we wait until the Denn get here? Try to take some down with the bridge?"

Fallard shook his head "Too risky. These Denn are quick. That is their strength. It isn't like fighting other Gaeans or even these doll-men you hear so much about back east. I won't have my crew put at more risk than necessary."

I didn't have an answer to that, so I stayed silent and watched Connor and a few other wiry soldiers tie themselves off on the trees overhanging this side of the gorge. They had a saw and each had a woodcutter's ax stuck through their harness. I stepped closer to the edge to watch them scamper under the bridge deck. Fallard followed me. Soon the sound of axes biting wood echoed down the length of the gorge.

"It was a solid plan", Fallard said, watching his men work. "Should buy us a fair amount of time on the road."

I nodded and observed the teamwork of the Company. The soldiers working at the bridge-stays did so without argument. Several of those who arrived with me and the cart had already settled in at the campsite and started new fires. The smell of simple fare and a bitter tea filled the air, "You and yours have been at this for a while."

Fallard turned his head just enough to catch my eye, "How's that?"

I gestured, "Soldiering. You work well together."

"Ah, yes. Well, we've been working the border region for the past three battle seasons. Mostly patrol, and escorting traders. The Denn Plains are quiet in the winter but come spring the Denn remember they are a warrior society and test us. Usually just war bands and the like." He jutted his chin away west towards the abbey, "This is new."

I glanced across the gorge, but the tree line remained empty. "Three seasons? And the winters too? That's a long time on the line."

"Weeks of boredom and biting flies interspersed with rare moments of extreme violence or brutal weather." He threw me one of his rare smiles, "the pay is good, though."

A crack echoed sharply in the gorge and the bridge canted to one side. The men under the bridge worked their way to the second large stay that seemed to be the only thing keeping the bridge in place. They set to it with their axes with vigor. Laughter floated up from the crew as they saw their task drawing to an end.

A soldier approached the two of us, a bowl of something hot in each hand. The captain accepted them both with a murmured thanks and offered me one, "How about you? I somehow doubt you've been locked away in that abbey your whole life. You know too much. You serve with a company? With the legion?"

I gave the bowl a sniff and hazarded a taste. Not bad. Some sort of meat or stringy root, "That was another life."

"I'm sure. Not on the Denn Plains, though." He chewed at me; eyes thoughtful. "Too big for a roverscout. Caravan guard? East Legion?"

"Line. In the Seventh."

"Emperor's Own?" His eyebrows shot up at that. "Thought that posting was for life."

I didn't like the way this was going, "No, before that.

Before He claimed the Seventh. Linesman, as I said. During the Godslayer Wars."

Fallard turned away at that and resumed his study of the bridge crew. After a long silence where we worked at our bowls, he said, "Mountain air has been good to you."

"How so?"

"Didn't realize you were that damned old." We heard a second crack and saw the stay buckle, but it didn't give. The far end of the bridge sagged another several feet and held, "A linesman. Are they still a thing?"

"Back East they are."

****

"I would not have taken you for a Linesman."

"What can I say", I said, finishing my stew. "I like my enemies bloodless."

A long shrill cry rang in the cold air and hung there as it slowly faded away. Fallard cursed and threw his unfinished bowl to the side. I didn't know the sound, but he did and that told me all I needed to know. We were out of time.

I had lived through more battles than I care to remember. From the cramped streets of Jerrick during the War of Ascension to the endless hordes of hobs and psychotic dolls that we repelled during the Godslayer Wars, I had seen death and violence, and horrors aplenty. Countless years of war and strife. I had thought I had found some peace in my escape to the abbey. I was sick of it and wanted nothing more to do with the violence of the world. But if war was good at anything, it was good at finding me.

The dark gaps between the trees were empty, just deep shadow beneath the boughs and snow dirtied by fallen needles. Between one breath and the next, that empty space was filled with armed and armored creatures pouring almost noiselessly from the forest's edge and down the rocky slope towards the remains of the bridge. Hundreds of them. Sprinting on all fours, the Denn could cover ground with the ease of wild beasts. And they did, weapons strapped to harnesses on their hide armor, they clambered on free hands and feet over the talus field and closed on the bridge before the Copper Company could react.

"Form up!" Fallard's voice split the air and I scrambled to obey out of habit. His usual raspy croak was gone and, in its place, the clarion tones of a seasoned battlefield officer. His soldiers responded almost before he spoke, moving with a practiced precision that spoke of years together in the field. The tempo of the axes hitting the bridge stays increased in a frenzy of blows.

I had no weapon, just my long staff that was more use for keeping an old man's footing sure on broken roads than it was for fighting a feral pack of raiders on a broken bridge. But my blood was up, and the fear was upon me. I took hold of that old piece of eshawood and gripped it like a Linesman's pushing spear, one hand on the butt and the other palm-up further along the shaft and took a spot behind the quickly forming line of shields.

The Coppers packed the bridgehead with soldiers, the front-line crouching behind their overlapped round shields with a pair of vicious javelins held behind. A second rank formed alongside me, broad-headed spears and some long-axes with nasty hooked beards. A few of the soldiers threw logs and brush out in front of the shield line to break up the charge. The bridge began to buck alarmingly in front of our feet as the first of the Denn bounded across its unstable length.

I set my feet and went through my old ritual of steadying my breath. The staff felt too smooth in my soft hands. I fought down an urge to puke. The soldier next to me was wide-eyed and chewing on his lip, his black bristly beard doing little to hide his weak chin and his fear. His eyes skipped over to me and bounced off of my gaze and along the shaft of my staff to its blunt tip. He let loose a nervous chuckle. Maybe he was laughing at the absurdity of my weapon or at the realization that the man standing on his weak side was armed with a stick. It's always a good practice to laugh at death. Death is a prick and doesn't deserve anything less.

"Javelins ready!" Fallard was standing right behind me, and his sudden cry snapped me out of my reverie. The front rank unlocked their shields and - taking a javelin in their free hand - made ready to throw. My gaze reluctantly turned to the path that those javelins would soon travel and my gut twisted at the sight of the Denn bearing down on us. Nearly fifty of them. Surefooted on the unstable bridge, they sprinted on all fours, tusked mouths gaping.

"Release!"

The javelins flew and I knew in that moment the quality of the Copper Company. Few shafts missed their marks, despite the terror of the moment and the wild bucking of the broken bridge. Two dozen and more of the Denn collapsed, skewered by the javelins or wounded terribly in a limb. One in particular took a shaft in his shoulder, a big brute all tattooed across his face and bared chest with strange glyphs. He stood tall, ripped the javelin and threw it awkwardly back at our line where it skittered across the last few boards of the bridge decking. His eyes seemed to meet my own as he unlimbered a nasty ax from its harness on his back. He stayed on two feet, swaying with the movement of the bridge and strode after his surviving companions, his eyes definitely now locked on mine.

"Shields!"

The front rank took their remaining javelins in their free hand and snapped the shields back into an interlocking line. The few remaining soldiers of the company moved out along the edges of the gorge and strung their bows. They began firing into the sides of the approaching Denn, but the angle and the rails of the bridge made it difficult for them.

This moment stretches like an eternity in my memory of it, but I swear to you all that it was but a breath of time before the Denn struck our feeble line with all of their weight and ferocity. I expected the line to collapse, and I prepared myself for the chaos that would ensue. But that line held. As one, they stepped back as the Denn thought to hit them. The Denn stumbled and the shield line shifted forward. The shields struck like a hammer. The javelins flashed low. The fight was upon us.

In war, we lose the weak and the unprepared early in a campaign. Over time - and after many battles and difficulties in the field - what remains is the hard, the fierce, the focused, and the lucky. I've seen great warriors fall to illness at a siege and rank cowards somehow stumble through an entire year on the march. Luck is a magic I don't understand, but I do know it is tied to fate. And fate is as much of a prick as death.

What remained of the Copper Company after three years on the frontier was hard, fierce, focused, and deadly. They had surpassed the need for luck and winnowed any weakness from their ranks. I felt a fool standing there before the bridge with them. My time had passed, and these were the new heroes of a new age.

"Red ruin on the bridge of Cambrin…" The phrase passed through my mind, and I let it slip away. This wasn't a moment to be a monk. The spears of my rank were slipping over the shoulders of the front rank, licking and biting at the Dennish warriors who were tearing at the shield wall with their hands or with bearded hand-axes. I lashed down with my staff, cracking the warrior in front of me on his broad forehead. More startled than hurt, he looked at me and caught a javelin blade in the gut for his inattention.

Arrows started dropping down on us from across the gorge. It was a long shot and difficult. Few found their mark, but the clatter of shafts around us made us flinch with each volley. Our own bowman turned from their salvos against the warriors on the bridge to return fire.

The battle was fierce. The Denn beasts savaged our line in an effort to break through. Our own fallen were beginning to foul the ranks. The smell of piss and blood filled my nostrils.

Reserves from behind darted forward and dragged our dead and wounded from the front line. Others slipped in and took their places with fresh shields and sharp javelins.

Another Denn replaced the one I had helped fell and this one was intent on making kindling of the shield wall. Two-handed and with no regard for himself, he laid into our line with a huge war ax. I noted his tattooed chest and lack of hide armor and knew him for the one who had marked me out moments before. His ax tore through the shield of the soldier in front of me and clove into his chest. With his backswing, he ripped the young cavalryman off of his feet and cartwheeling over the edge of the gorge. Out of instinct, I thrust at him with my staff and took him in the throat. He reeled with the force of the thrust, though I felt a twinge in my shoulder with the effort.

With a roar, he swung his ax down straight at my head. I shifted forward and pressed up with my staff, catching his ax on its haft. I twisted and drove his ax to the ground on my weak side. Shifting again, I jammed the butt-end of my staff into his wounded shoulder, and he bellowed in pain.

The breath was knocked from me as his foot connected with my soft gut and I almost fell to my knees. Stars exploded in my sight, and I blindly whipped the staff over and down to strike his wrists. I heard more than saw his ax fall to the ground. I stumbled, that awkward blow stealing my balance. I twirled the staff back to a guard position, but the huge brute was upon me, his eyes ablaze with rage and far too close to me for my paltry stick weapon to do much to save me. A flash of movement to my right and my neighbor's spear took the Denn warrior in the neck. Bright red blood rushed from the wound. He dropped and fell to the ground at our feet.

The shield wall pushed hard and drove the remaining Denn back onto the decking of the bridge. Javelins and spears did raw work, though the line was thinner than it had been moments before. The bridge groaned and bounced as yet another wave of Denn Marauders charged across its length. I stepped back up to the line, struggling to find my breath when a loud pop echoed in the cold air.

"Get them out of there!!" Fallard's voice was panicked. I turned to look at him, he stood in the second rank not far from me, his spear a red gory thing in his shaking hands. He made to leave the line when the Denn pushed back again, and he was forced to contend with them. His eyes kept flashing to the gorge's edge beyond me as he fought and struggled to hold the line. He caught my gaze and pleaded with me, "Kellin!"

It was then I noticed that the bridge was no longer bouncing, it was sagging. I spun to where the ropes were tied off along the edge of the precipice. The bowmen along the gorge had already tossed their weapons aside and were frantically pulling at the lines, trying to haul up Connor and his crew of saboteurs.

I cast my staff aside and ran to assist them. Seizing one of the ropes, I heaved on it and pulled with all of my strength. I could feel one of the lads on the far end. A frantic energy, scrambling. My hands were torn on the coarse weave as I hauled. Another soldier grabbed a hold behind me, and we pulled together.

But fate is a prick, as I said, and luck will turn on you as soon as save you. I should have been chopped to pieces by a Denn berserker there at the Battle of Cambrin Bridge, but I was saved by a timely spear in the neck. Those brave boys chopped down that bridge from below and saved us all. Saved their company, saved me, and saved our sacred Book. But the bridge twisted as it fell. It twisted, and the end of it tore down along the gorge wall and crushed those brave boys. Ripped them from their bloody ropes and threw their broken bodies down beneath it and into the roaring waters far below.

Death and fate. Fuck them both.

****

Arrows continued to rain down from across the gorge.

Some few of the surviving company were wounded from these volleys and that seemed to sting more deeply than it should have. In frustration, we withdrew from the fallen bridge. The bestial calls of the Denn across the gorge followed us. I didn't know their language at the time, but I could tell they were taunting us.

If I were still a monk - and safely tucked away in the abbey - I would have recorded that battle as a victory for the empire and written some verses in honor of the fallen. Would have ended up in the very Book we were defending. Battle of Cambrin Bridge. 36 soldiers of the Copper Company held the bridge over Cambrin Gorge against a host of hundreds of Denn Marauders and defeated them. Dozens of Denn slain, either in the stand at the bridgehead or with the fall of the bridge itself. Dozens. Of the Copper Company, only 22 remained. Including those wounded in the line or by arrow-strike.

It didn't feel like a victory. We put the wounded on the horses and those few of us who were blessedly unhurt led them afoot. Fallard reluctantly left behind some few of his men to bury the fallen and to challenge the crossing should the Denn attempt to bridge the gorge with fallen trees. The echo of axes on wood across the way spoke to his knowledge of his enemy.

My tread heavy as my heart, I followed the cart. The oiled tarp covering the book started to flap in the rising wind and I stepped up my pace to tighten one of the stay ropes. The westering sun behind us cast a shadow across me.

"We won't get far before night falls. I don't like our chances on this road." The captain's voice was bereft of life. It was a dry, empty thing.

I looked up as we walked. He was leading his horse and that of a badly wounded soldier. The rider was slumped over his saddle horn. Pale and clinging to the mane of his beast. His breaths came fast and shallow. Meeting Fallard's eye, I knew he knew it too. This man was done.

Fallard couldn't meet my gaze any longer. He spoke to the gathering dark, "I don't remember this road. It's been years since I last passed this way. I seem to remember a waystation."

I nodded at that, "There is, but it's yet another day's travel, if I remember correctly."

"Shelter", he whispered. "I need to get them out of this wind."

The temperature fell with the approach of night. The brightest stars were already pushing through the heavenly veil above. The yellow-gold light of one of the wandering stars, the Adamant, shone low in the East. I said a silent prayer to our ancestors, as is the custom with the rising of the evening star, and tried to keep up with the cart.

Our descent from the gorge had been steep and perilous. The road was washed out in many spots, and we struggled to get the heavy cart across. It was full dark before we found a stretch of the road that was wide enough and level enough to make an impromptu camp. The trees here were mostly beech and mountain esha, too sparse to do more than buffer the winds, but a flattened stretch of land - just thin mossy soil over the limestone of the mountain itself - provided space for an uncomfortable camp.

The wounded rider had finally succumbed to his wounds, and he had been bound across the saddle of his horse. A single fire was started, and the men gathered close around its penetrating warmth, their fallen brother taken down from the horse and laid out on a tarp, just outside of the circle of light.

I finished settling the donkey and secured the cart. The wind had quickened, and clouds blotted out the stars to the west. I fussed at the oilcloth and the lines securing it to the cart. Rain could be disastrous.

I made my way to the fire; my hands numb with the cold and such unaccustomed labor. The soldiers were packed tight around the flames, hands and feet towards the light. Hollowed out faces were painted red in the glare. Shadowed eyes met mine and slipped away again. Back to the fire, to their thoughts.

"Make room." Fallard joined us from out of the darkness.

Like his men, he was a shadow of what had been only hours before. The loss of so many was still too raw. They blamed me, the outsider, I knew that. Me. The Book. The whole misguided mission. These men had only wanted remounts and supplies when they came to the abbey. Instead, they got two pitched battles and a duty they didn't want. More than one of them cast a glare at the cart.

I slipped between the soldiers who made room for the captain and me. I fell more than sat on the ground and thrust my heavy hands towards the flames. The warmth of the fire contrasted with the cold reception of the surviving soldiers. I felt the need to speak, but I didn't have the right words. It wasn't my place to break this silence. It was sacred in a way that left me outside. Apart. I opened my mouth to try. To say something to bridge this new divide between us.

One of the soldiers saved me the trouble, "What do you reckon that book is worth?"

I wasn't ready for the question, and I fumbled the answer, "It's priceless. The Suda is the collected history of our people."

The soldier scoffed at my answer and looked away. He was scruffy and tired, his ratty beard a tangle and his mustaches untrimmed. Strong knobby hands twisted absently at a length of rope that he held piled in his lap. "Well, that's just fine. A great comfort that'll be to the kin of them what defended it back there."

My stomach sunk, I struggled to recover what I said, "I didn't mean to imply -"

He looked at me then and I saw we were of an age. His eyes were those of a veteran who had seen a lot. Too much. I knew those eyes. They had been my eyes, long ago.

Those eyes were now rimmed in red and glossy in the firelight, "Connor were my sister's son. Him and the rest of them lads under the bridge were like my own. Many of those men who fell today were dearer to me than the folk I grew up with. That man there", he pointed at the dead soldier laid out in the darkness, "saved my life more times than I can count, and now he's fixin' to find himself a grave on this mountain and nothing to show for it other than a stone to mark his passing."

The old soldier spit into the fire, never taking his eyes off of mine, "That's for your book. You don't know nothing about priceless."

I wanted to say something, to defend myself in this. I had seriously bungled my answer to his question, but nothing I said after that would make anything any better. I looked away instead. "I'll take the first watch", I rasped.

"No, you won't." The old veteran wasn't done with me.

"Rickard", Fallard warned.

There was a tense moment where nothing was said. Rickard twisted that bit of rope tight between his hands. "It's ok, Cap. I said my piece." Rickard stood up, gathering the length of rope up with him and stowed it in his pack. I saw bloodstains on that rope. Blood from hands torn in desperation not many hours ago. He wiped at his eyes as he turned away, "I'll take first watch. I have an old friend to say goodbye to." He walked off without saying anything else and went and sat by his fallen brother.

There wasn't much by way of conversation as the rest of us unrolled our kits and settled down to sleep. It had been a full two days since I'd last slept and - after the terrifying developments of those two days - it didn't take too long for me to fall into a dreamless slumber.

It was in the early hours of morning, when the sun was a ghost on the horizon and gray light fought against the lingering dark, that our camp was thrown into chaos by a flitting swarm of death.

I hate arrows. Stupid awful things. They fly out of the darkness and snip your life away in an instant. Never had any experience with arrows away back-East. No sense in them. It was all pushing spears, axes, and seam-rippers for us. You could stick a hob or a doll-man full of arrows and he would keep coming. The Bloodless didn't stop until you tore them to pieces and scattered their stuffing on the battlefield.

But here on the mountainside with nothing but a bedroll for cover, two of the company were struck by arrows before they could even wake. The other shafts hit the horses and the poor stupid donkey, causing them to pull free from where we had tethered them, and hare away down the mountain without us.

I rolled out of my bedroll and away from the failing fire. I had no idea how good the eyesight of the Denn was, but I wasn't about to make it easier for them to hit me. The tiny camp was in chaos. Unarmored soldiers clawed their way out of their blankets and scrambled to grab shields and spears. They formed up in the half-light over their two wounded companions. Wide eyed faces, twisted in fear and anger, scanned the shadows all about.

I lay still, flat on the ground and ignoring the cold seeping up through my garments. The remaining men of the Company were some ten paces away. I scanned the trees and tried to control my panting breaths. I didn't see any signs of movement. I feared another volley of arrows, so I stayed where I was.

"Rickard, check the wounded." Fallard's voice in the half-light was a comfort, I have to say. The old veteran helped the two men up to a sitting position. Both had taken arrows to a leg and were able to work themselves into a sitting position behind the shields of their brothers. "Tighten up those shields!"

A wind picked up and a steady rain started to fall from the overcast sky above. The water was cold and heavy enough to soak through my clothes almost immediately. I cast a panicked glance at the wagon. The tarp was still tightly bound over the Book.

There was a muffled cry from one of the wounded as Rickard worked the arrow out of his thigh. He bound the wound with a bit of blanket. The other man had snapped the shaft off short on his arrow, and even picked up a shield to add to the feeble line. The heavy rain continued to fall, and no more arrows had come racing out of the trees, so I stood in a half-crouch with the intent to get behind the soldiers and the questionable safety of their shields. The soldiers all as one flicked a glance my way as I moved. I had the unhappy feeling that they had forgotten about me. Fallard gestured with his head for me to join them and I started to move when a voice spoke out of the shadows.

"Enough."

I froze. The shields of the Company popped as they snapped into a tighter guard. The voice was rough, a husky whisper that carried through the rain. From out of the shadowy trees to the west stepped one of the Denn. The penetrating rain had done the fire in, so only the pre-dawn light painted his features for us to see. Big for a Denn, almost of a matching height to me, he was armored in the heavy hides of some plains beast. He wore a thick torc of gold around his neck that caught some of the limited light and his large pale eyes caught the rest. In his hands he held a staff festooned with large feathers.

He held up the staff, parallel to the ground in front of him, "I know that voice. Rogen Fallard. The Copper Company had many more spears and horses the last time we met."

The captain set down his shield and stepped out in front of the line. He held a javelin out in front of him in the same way, "Ashak's Ford. Things have changed since then. Was that you at the bridge?" His voice was tight as he asked the question, but the Denn shook his head.

"That was Chakka.", he whispered. "He runs several packs for the new war leader."

"I lost good men at the bridge."

"So did Chakka."

The sun had crested the horizon behind us, and some light shone through the rain clouds. Enough to see the anguish on Fallard's face, "And the men I left at the bridge?"

"They are still there."

Fallard seemed to deflate a little at that, and his voice betrayed his relief, "I left them to delay you."

The big Denn grinned, and a pair of stunted tusks poked out from behind his lips, "They delay Chakka instead. Your men are clever. They haunt this side of the gorge, destroying every bridge he tries to make."

Fallard offered a small smile, gesturing at the feathers on the Denn's staff. "You have war-beasts now?"

"*Peckafo*. Yes. Your men cannot block the skies" "You've come up in the world. How many do you have?"

"Enough." The Denn turned his head to the trees behind him and let out a high-musical whistle. More Dennish raiders stepped out of the shadows. Almost two dozen, and all armed with those wicked short bows. They had arrows on the strings, but the bows were only partially drawn, and the arrows trained on the ground in front of them.

Fallard studied the warriors for a moment. He hardened his face and addressed the leader again, "You remember when we trapped you and your youths last season? After you tried to take our remounts outside of World's Edge?"

"I do."

"We let you go. We spared you."

"World's Edge is in ashes now. The Copper Company no longer plagues the plains."

"We could have killed you."

"Yet you didn't."

Fallard lowered his javelin and the Denn raiders all raised their half-drawn bows to point at him, "Am I about to regret that?" I was impressed with how steady his voice was.

The rain pounded down, soaking us all. The Denn chieftain held his staff out in front of him, steady. Neither of them moved. Neither spoke.

"No", rasped the chieftain. "Not today, at least." The Denn raiders all lowered their weapons again.

Fallard waved behind him to his men, and they lowered

their weapons as well. Though all of the shields stayed up and tightly overlapped. The captain tossed the javelin down in the mud at his feet. "So, what happens now?"

The chieftain lowered his staff and leaned on it, "You and your soldiers may continue east down the mountain. We have both shown mercy to each other. There is a symmetry to this that pleases me."

I got a cold feeling in my gut. I stepped forward and spoke, "And the Book?"

The chieftain turned to face me. His large soulful eyes were not like those of Gaeans. There was a raw vulnerability there, like the eyes of an animal and yet not. I felt like he could see into me, and I didn't like that one bit. I made myself meet his gaze.

"The Book stays. It is the reason we came." His whispering voice combined with his frank stare made for a hypnotic experience. It was difficult to resist what he had to say.

"No. We cannot leave it with you." It was very hard to get those words out and I wondered if he was working some spell on me. I tore my eyes away from him, "Captain, we can't. The Book needs to get to Velasko. To safety."

Fallard laughed. A short cynical snort. "And what would you have me do?"

"Fight! You gave your word that you would escort the Book to the walled city." He looked away as I said that, and I knew the choice had already been made.

I don't know what came over me in that moment. Some fit of courage or stupidity moved me. In my mind's eye I could see Brother Abrastus weeping over that artifact. It was too much for me to bear. I strode to my bedroll and snatched up my staff. A few of the raiders pointed their bows in my direction and followed me with their wicked points as I marched over and planted myself in front of the cart.

The chieftain waved the raiders back and the bows were lowered yet again, "Is this one of yours, Rogen Fallard?"

The captain wouldn't look at me. Instead, his eyes fell on the body of the dead soldier who had been laid out alongside the cart the night before. "No. This is one of the holy brothers. He is here to mind the book."

The chieftain's eyes lit up and he cracked what may have been a smile, "Ah! A wizard of the temple." His men chattered behind him and moved away from me. "Will you use the magics of the Book against us, wizard?"

For a moment I was tempted to lie. I could rest my hand on the tome and threaten to curse them all if they didn't leave immediately. I could claim I had summoned the rains. Cry to the heavens for lightning and hope that there would be a rumble of distant thunder.

But no.

"I am not a wizard. There are no wizards. I have no magic and neither does this book."

The chieftain thumped his staff in the mud, "A clever ploy. But no, the magic Book comes with us."

I turned to Fallard, "Captain, I call upon your oath to protect this Book and see it safe to Velasko." He would not meet my eyes. Behind him, Rickard stared daggers of hate at me and I felt bad, knowing what I was asking of them all. I bit down the shame I felt inside and spoke again, "You gave your word."

Fallard nodded, "You're right. I did." He turned his gaze back to the dead man beside the cart, and then to his men. "Drop your weapons and gather your supplies."

The few remaining men of the Copper Company released a collective sigh and shields were tossed on top of weapons in a heap. The captain turned back to the chieftain. "And what of my men at the gorge? And those still up on the mountain?"

"They will be secured, and released to go where they will, once we have what we need and return to the plains", he whispered.

"Your word on it, Aggrax?"

"My word on it. I'll make it right with Chakka."

The few remaining soldiers of the Copper Company were already bunched together at the far side of the campsite. Rickard was making a quick litter for his fallen friend. Fallard looked at me then. Soaked through and exhausted, I could see him as he truly was. Tired, heartbroken, exhausted. Defeated. He had waged a war on behalf of the empire for the past three years with nothing to show for it but dead friends and the emperor's coin. I couldn't blame him. He had oaths, but some promises were made without words, and those are more often than not the ones we hold to, at the end.

"You'll come with us, Kellin?"

I hadn't expected the offer, but it felt good to hear it. "Thank you, Rogen, but no. We both need to be able to look in the mirror when we shave, yeah?" I found it in me to look up and offer him a smile, "May the Ancestors keep you safe, all the days of your life."

He nodded at that, started to speak but then changed his mind. Offered me one more nod and walked away downslope with his men and their burdens. They soon disappeared into the gloom and the rain. The thought crossed my mind to note the date that the Copper Company was disbanded, but I had no idea what date it was.

I had no illusions as to how the rest of this was going to go. One against two dozen, and me armed with a stick. Ludicrous. I thought about the ancestors watching me from above in my last moments and decided I wasn't going to give my long-dead uncles a chance to make fun of me for eternity. I threw down my staff and marched over to the heap of weapons. I fished out a shield and hand-ax.

I slammed the flat of the ax against the boss of the shield and gestured, "Come on then. I got places to be."

I'm sure I struck a heroic pose there in the driving rain. A fat old veteran soaked to the bone, unarmored in bedraggled muddy robes defending a cart with weapons he hadn't picked up in years. Truly, something for the songs.

Aggrax turned and said something to his raiders in a

musical tongue. It was beautiful to hear, multitonal, and not at all what I would have expected from such bestial creatures. One of the raiders unstrung his bow and set it aside. He drew two matching hand-axes from his harness and approached me with caution.

I didn't wait for him to get comfortable. I lunged forward, my footing less than sure, and swung my shield across in a backhanded smash. He tried to get his axes up in time and just managed to meet my shield strike with a stroke of his own. I swung overhead with the ax and, twisting my wrist at the last moment, clouted his arm with the flat of the ax and knocked one of his weapons to the ground.

The raider hissed in pain and sent a vicious swing at my face with the other ax. Clumsy and staggering backwards, I barely missed getting my face ripped off by the cut. I planted my backfoot - and breathed a quick prayer of thanks when it didn't slip - to punch forward hard with the boss of the shield. I caught the raider on the chin as he leapt in to finish me off and threw him square on his rear. A powerful stomp with my boot took him full-on in the face and knocked him out cold.

I backed away, settled in front of the cart again, and addressed the chieftain, "That's one."

Aggrax had an unreadable look on his face, and I hoped he didn't see how hard I was struggling to regain my breath. He turned, gesturing with his feathered staff at another raider behind him. I was hopeful that these Denn would honor individual combat in this situation, and so far, they had. I wasn't certain if it was part of their culture or just the fact that their bowstrings were likely useless in this rain.

The next raider who came wielded a two-handed ax that he held high over his head as he roared a challenge at me. Inspired - and hopeful that anatomy played out with the Denn - I kicked him as hard as I could in between his legs. I was pleased to see him drop to his knees and fumble his weapon into the muck.

I mouthed the word 'two' to Aggrax. What can I say?

Imminent death always made me a little reckless.

Aggrax held his staff out to stop the next raider from charging at me. Both of my injured opponents were back on their feet and staggering over to their kin. The chieftain had that strange expression on his face again. He whispered, "If this book has no power, why do you choose to die to protect it?"

"Perhaps I won't die defending it." I struggled to control my breathing as I spoke. "I'm doing ok so far."

Aggrax showed his tusks in what was clearly a smile. He reached around to the small of his back and, in one motion, whipped a throwing hatchet directly at me. I yelped - sorry to say - and lifted my shield in front of my face. The hatchet deflected off of it and hit the cart with a loud thunk, severing one of the lines.

He looked aggrieved to have missed. "Is this some power of the Book?"

"The Book has no power. It is nothing more than a record of the history of my people."

The chieftain seemed taken aback by that. He squatted, resting his staff across his knees, "And you would die for that?"

"No…" I couldn't keep the frustration from my voice. "It's more than that. My people came to this land 700 years ago. We barely survived the arrival. This Book…" I felt a frustration rising up in me. "This Book was our way of holding on to what we almost lost. It became the repository of all we became. We cannot lose it."

"And this Book, it is the only place you keep this knowledge? Do your people not remember?"

"We remember, of course we remember. But there are stories, knowledge, songs, secrets almost lost to time. So much of who we were is recorded in this Book."

"Ah, and you use this Book to regain that knowledge, to become what you had been?"

I was a little flummoxed at that, "Well, no. But we hold

on to that knowledge in case it is needed."

"If it was needed, you would use it now. Your people contain the stories and the knowledge you need. Your tribes are strong, Book Man. We have seen that for years, as you forced yourself on us, on the plains." He waved a hand dismissing the book. "This thing is a curiosity. No more. It is a shame that you let your people die to protect it from us."

I did feel shame. My face flushed as I searched for the words I needed. Maybe it was the stress of the past few days or the exhaustion I felt, but I couldn't mount an argument to counter what Aggrax was saying. Instead, something that he had said earlier came to mind, "You came for the Book, not for us. You said you would return to the plains once you had it."

"Yes, although now I begin to doubt its power."

"Why?"

"The dolls are coming for us, like they came for your people to the east, many years ago. We cannot have two enemies on our borders. So, we will break you and your power on the plains. Steal the power of your magic book. Then we can face the dolls and their devouring hordes."

I shook my head, "The Bloodless are not easily broken."

Aggrax peered into my eyes, searching. "You know of them, of their magics."

"It's not magic. It's something much older that animates them. An elemental hate, perhaps."

He sat back on his haunches, "You have faced them?"

I nodded, memories welling up within me.

"We could use one like you. You are old, and soft, but it is clear to me that you were not always so. You were a warrior once?"

"Once, yes. I came to the abbey to - I was tired of war."

"Ah. You sought escape."

I nodded.

"Perhaps your fate has led you here. None among my people know these doll-men, but the stories from our kin to the far east say they are unstoppable. That they will destroy our homes, our people, our very culture. We need one who knows them. One who knows how to stop them."

My voice was barely a whisper, "That man is dead."

A strong wind leapt up, it blew down the mountainside from the west and tore through the trees, sending branches, needles, and detritus from the campsite winging away into the air. The wind also ripped at the oilcloth cover on the cart, causing the cloth to lift at the corner where the hatchet had split the line.

I dropped my weapons and leapt onto the cart, desperately fighting with the wind to keep the driving rain off of the ancient tome.

"I think that man stands in front of me. Look at you now."

I lay there in the pouring rain, clinging to the oiled tarp as the wind bucked and tore at it. My cold hands ached. "He's dead. If he ever lived at all."

The chieftain regarded me carefully through the rain. "This is a sadness. I think the world is emptier for his absence. I think this man did great things." The Denn chieftain stood, and the lashing rain hardly seemed to bother him at all. He nodded as he came to a decision, "We will go now. This book of yours hardly seems the trouble it once did. You may keep it." He gestured before his face, as though wiping something from his sight, "It has no power. I see that now. The power you possess is in your deeds. And in the memory of those deeds. Not in dusty marks on a page. You would do well to think about that. You forget, and hope that this book will remember. This is a great foolishness."

I stood there as his words washed over me. I couldn't even feel the rain anymore.

"Farewell, Book Man. You come to me if you ever find yourself again. We could use you in the wars to come."

I watched as the chieftain picked up his staff and circled it overhead. His war party stood as one. I could barely see them through the curtain of water. Like wraiths out of legend they slipped away through the storm and were gone, almost like they never existed.

I remember my thoughts in that moment. Clear as clear. I'll never forget them. I thought to myself, a true monk would be planning out the tale of this encounter and how to write it. He would be crafting the words in his mind and shaping the illuminations for the text to create the biggest impact on the reader.

The reader. I snorted in disgust. No one reads this book. A true monk would think of nothing but how to preserve this story for all time. To capture the power of the moment in words and images. Yet all I could think of was how free these Denn savages were. My mind turned to memories of the deeds and not of the words that recorded those deeds. I thought of the rain, of course. And of the wind on the high grassy plains of the far southlands. Broken dolls. Of the shield wall and bloody victory.

"I am no true monk, am I?" I asked the question, but no one was there to give an answer. Just me and the book. And we both knew the answer.

I remember the exact moment I stopped being a Brother of Saint Cecil the Rememberer. It was the moment I stood tall and released my death grip on the corner of that old, oiled tarp.

The wind took the tarp and yanked it from its remaining lines. I saw it whip up into the sky and away. So free.

I never did look back at the book. I knew the rains had destroyed it in moments. I turned my back on it, on all of this, and took the trail back up the mountain, west and away.

To find my fate.

The End

Kevin Harris is new to writing, but not to storytelling. As a trained actor and director, Kevin has brought stories to life for diverse audiences over the years, both on stage and behind the scenes. He is also a nurse, working in neonatal intensive care, and trains kung fu with his students, friends, and children. A voracious reader, Kevin grew up on fantasy and science fiction, finding inspiration for his writing in the Halls of Moria, with the man-eaters of Zamboula, and on the 'hurtling moons of Barsoom'. His first novella, 'Mightier than the Pen', is a standalone Military Fantasy story, complete at 15,000 words, set in an epic fantasy world full of danger and grand adventure. In his limited free time, Kevin enjoys birding and gaming with his son, snuggling his dog Freya, and hunting dragons with his half-feral daughter and their insane cat.

https://www.facebook.com/kevin.harris.167

Blue as Sky, Black as Sin

Sam Robb

I hadn't planned on shooting anyone when I woke up this morning, but Landsmen Yarroll and Pieter were doing their best to make me consider it as a possibility.

"Ser Kellan! Clearly the responsibility lies with yeoman Pieter's failure —"

"Did you hear that, Highwayman? A deliberate insult! I am a landsman, whether he likes it or not; and deserve to be addressed as such!"

"A landsman would have kept his bull out of my fields!"

I pinched the bridge of my nose as they continued to bicker. An early-morning summons from the province seat didn't help, either. Governor Tanner wanted me to return as soon as possible, which meant that after resolving the dispute between these two, I'd have to ride hard to make it back to Dart before nightfall.

I forced my attention back to the present. The mayor had been happy to lend me his office to hear the dispute before disappearing on some other task. After a half hour with the bickering landsmen, I wished I could have joined him. With the windows closed, the air was getting stale. The idea of getting on the road immediately had a sudden appeal.

I held up my hand to silence the two men standing before me. It took them more than a moment to notice, and even longer for their voices to trail off into a pair of angry glowers. The young man and woman standing behind them - Arrus Yarroll and Isolde Pieter - looked simultaneously terrified and ashamed of their sire's behaviors.

I took advantage of the moment of silence to concentrate and raise my Talent. A halo of light expanded around Yarroll and Pieter, both auras made of roiling red and streaked with violet. Anger and indignation in equal measure. No question, there was bad blood between the two of them. I searched for any hint of black — a clear sign of a known lie or untruth — but saw nothing.

A twinge of pain made my jaw ache. I pushed through it, trying to find any hint of which one might be at fault, when a faint sparkle of golden light caught my eye. Not from the landsmen; but from behind them. I shifted my focus to the two teenagers standing behind their parents. Amid the muted blues and browns of their auras were faint, bright golden threads.

Ah. I'd been so focused on lies and animosity that I almost missed another type of relationship entirely.

Another pulse of pain spread out from my forehead. I winced, dropping my concentration as I let my Talent fade. As I did so, I saw Isolde's hand twitch, as if she meant to reach out to Arrus. If I hadn't been looking at them, I would have missed it entirely.

I stirred in my seat. "Gentlemen. Let me see if I have the facts of the matter straight. Landsman Yarroll, you built a fence between your farm and Pieter's property two years ago. Is that correct?"

Yarroll's face flushed an even brighter red than it already was. "I did, Ser Kellan! But that was only because —"

I snapped up my hand, interrupting the impending tirade before it turned into another avalanche of accusations.

"Answer my questions, please. No need to elaborate when a yes or no will do." I waited until Yarroll pursed his lips in acquiescence, then turned to Pieter and lowered my hand.

"And you, Landsman Pieter. You had no problems with the fence? In fact, you fenced in your own meadow using it, with Yarroll's permission?"

Pieter opened his mouth, then shot a glance at Yarroll. I watched the thoughts turning over in his head, grinding his own outburst down to a perfunctory, "Yes, sir."

"Good. According to both your testimonies, two months ago, there was an incident where the fence was damaged. Yarroll, you claim that Pieter's bull ran the fence, and ended up breeding with three of your milk cows. Correct?"

"Sir."

"I'll take that as a yes. Landsman Pieter, you claim your son was leading the bull to pasture, when a cow of Landsman Yarroll's leaned against the fence, causing it to collapse. Is that correct?"

"That's what my boy says." I frowned, and Pieter hurriedly added, "Sir."

"So, the question is one of responsibility. Do you both agree with that assessment?"

That was too much for the men in front of me. "I ain't paying no stud fee for his *zera* bull!" Yarroll snapped.

"Three cows, he gets for free!" Pieter growled. "Two are with calf, for sure! And he's claiming the both of 'em as his own!"

"Only right, as I didn't ask for this! I already had a contract with Muguyen, over the other side of the mountain. I can't afford to pay him to break that contract!"

"*Gentlemen!*"

I spoke from my diaphragm, as my father had taught me. He'd been an officer of the King in the war against the Accuser. My mother once swore she'd seen him stop a wild wolf in its tracks using his voice alone.

Yarroll and Pieter stopped mid-rant, staring at me.

I let my hand rest casually on the old, Empire-manufactured black powder revolver at my hip. Another gift from my father, it was an ugly relic of the same war. The medallion granted to me by King Iestus may have been the official emblem designating me as his Highwayman; but in the Outlands, it was my pistol that carried real weight as a symbol of my office.

"Arrus. Isolde. Front and center, please."

The two of them froze at the mention of their names. Arrus started around his father first. As soon as he was moving, Isolde followed. They came to stand in front of their fathers, eyes on me, carefully ignoring each other.

"The two of you look to be about fifteen. Is that right?"

"Um." Arrus cleared his throat. "Seventeen, sir. And, uh, I think Isolde's a year younger."

Isolde blushed when I glanced at her. "Yes, sir. Sixteen."

"More than old enough to understand you represent your families. Your fathers had a mutual interest in maintaining this fence. An agreement to do so, as well. They trusted the two of you to pay attention to that, didn't they? And to watch over your animals as well?"

"Yes, sir." Arrus stared straight ahead, eyes carefully avoiding mine.

"Very well. Arrus Yarroll. Isolde Pieter. You are each equally responsible for the breach of agreement that damaged your fathers' relationship with each other. As such, you will each work to repair that relationship."

The two young people looked at me, confused, as I continued. "You will repair the fence, together. You will take responsibility for the cows with calf, together. When those calves are born, you will raise them and care for them, together. You will do this until the stud fees to Landsman Pieter and the contract fees of Landsman Yarroll are paid off. Am I clear?"

Arrus swallowed, then nodded sharply. "Yes, sir. I mean Highwayman. Sir." Isolde's nod was slower and more thoughtful as she glanced at Arrus.

"Wonderful. Landsmen Yarroll and Pieter. You've heard my judgement. Do you accept it, or do you wish to take the matter before the King?"

Both men grumbled something close enough to acceptance for my purposes. I clapped my hands. "Again - wonderful! I'll be back in two months to check on your progress. In the meantime — Landsman Yarroll, notify the stables that I will leave shortly. Landsman Pieter, tell the inn I will need lunch for the road."

"But —" Yarroll and Pieter spoke simultaneously, then glared at each other.

"Those were not requests, gentlemen. See to it. Arrus and Isolde, stay." With a huff, the landsmen turned and bustled out of the room, maneuvering like two tomcats ready for an excuse to fight.

I waited until the door slammed behind them and I heard their bickering resume before I turned my attention to the pair standing before me.

"Those two don't get along at all, do they? Relax, Arrus. I won't bite your head off." Isolde looked slightly less confused. She was a step ahead of him, so I turned to her first.

"How long?"

"Sir?"

I nodded at Arrus. "How long?"

She raised her chin, lips pursed. "About a year, sir."

"Isolde!"

"It's obvious he knows, Arrus." She met my eyes, shoulders tense. "How could you tell?"

I shrugged. "Experience."

I wasn't about to explain my Talent to her. The ability to tell when someone was lying to me was only an advantage when people didn't know about it. Plus, the Empire was wary of letting an *aloyshea* out from under their thumbs. Any world-mage they considered useful was immediately conscripted into Imperial service; and I had no illusions of how they would treat me if my own abilities became known.

Isolde's scowl deepened. "Do you mean to tell our sires, then?"

"Empress above, no!" The young couple gawked at me. "*You* are."

"What?"

I waved my hand. "Eventually. You'll be spending lots of time together, after all. It's only natural you'd get to know one another better. And if you get to the point you want to make it official, you'll have your own section of pasture and a few cattle to start you on your way."

"When." Arrus reached out and took Isolde's hand.

"When we want to make it official."

I didn't have to raise my Talent to imagine the golden lines wrapping around their clasped hands. "When. If I were you, I'd wait a bit. Give it a year or so."

"Why?" Arrus blurted out. "I mean…"

"It's in the King's interest to see his Landsmen cooperating. Especially in the Outlands." I leaned forward. "Now, I told you your job is to repair your father's relationship. I mean that. I've given you two an excuse to see each other regularly without having to hide it. You two getting along will encourage the families to get along."

"We can do that," Isolde said. "It's really just our fathers."

"My ma and Isolde's still chat in town," Arrus added.

I grinned. "Good. If your fathers bring it up, be sure to mention me. Let them blame me for throwing you two together."

Arrus glanced at Isolde, then back at me. "That doesn't seem right, sir. If you don't mind me saying so."

I shrugged. "They'll make me feel unwelcome around here for a bit, I'm sure. I've weathered worse. I swore an oath to the King to do what needs to be done for his people. Some days it's harder than others, but in the end, it's always worth it." I waved at the door. "Now, I'd appreciate it if you two would go check on your fathers, please. Make sure they're making things ready for me. I need to be in Dart by nightfall."

****

I was on the road to Dart well before noon. Destiny was well rested and eager to canter, so I let her have her head as we made our way along the road. I only slowed her when I needed to eat in the saddle; otherwise, I let her have her head, so that the miles slipped away under her hooves. Even with a stop for water, we made good enough time that the sun was still over the horizon when the town came into view.

I paused then to watch a pair of dragonlets spin around

each other in tight loops above the dusty road. Their wings were only the size of my hand, but the speed of their mating dance kicked up a miniature dust devil that twirled between them. Sand and grit sparkled in the sunlight as it rotated, undisturbed by even the hint of a breeze.

Riding the circuits was hard, but it had its advantages. My cousins near the capital might have advances we did not: things like newly poured stone streets and electric lights, along with gifts of magic and technology the Empire had brought with them from across the Unreal. Here in the Outlands, the wonders might be smaller, but they still lurked around every corner.

Destiny nickered at me. The dragonlets darted away skyward in a panic. The dust devil gave one final spin before collapsing into nothing.

"Impudent beast. I know you're thirsty. Don't worry, we're almost there."

Spurred gently, Destiny moved slowly, but without protest. The dead and drying grass along the road baked in the waning heat of the summer day, raising its own unmistakable scent. It mingled with the odor of the dust and horse sweat in a distinctive but not unpleasant way.

I lifted my hand in greeting to the guards at the gate as the town's stone wall came into view. They gestured vaguely in my direction in return, doing the bare minimum to recognize me. I could hardly blame them for the informality. The heat sapped their energy as it did mine. Fortunately, my horse knew the way well. She carried me slowly along paved streets toward the center of town. The few people out and about were as listless as the guards.

Destiny huffed as we entered the stables attached to the garrison house, greeting her favorite stable hand. I dismounted and gave him a nod.

"Fetch fresh water, please, Dankei." I patted Destiny on the flanks. Even a summons from the governor was no reason to ignore my horse. "I'll rub her down."

Dankei grabbed her reins. "Nay, sir. I'll take care of her for ya. Governor Tanner left word. Wants ya to see him, soon as you wash the grime off ya."

I swung down, stretching my back. "Huh. He's letting me clean up, at least. Any idea what's going on?"

Dankei didn't speak, but jerked his head toward the stables. A huge gray stallion stood in one of the larger stalls, staring at us. He snorted and tossed his head when he caught me looking his way.

"Who does that monster belong to?"

Dankei shrugged. He was already whispering to Destiny. He didn't chatter and engage in idle talk the way other stablehands did, but for him to ignore my question completely was unusual. I focused my Talent just for a moment and brought Dankei's aura into view. Normally it was a uniform bright blue, placid and calm. Today it was mottled and rippling. I let loose of my focus before it could start my head aching.

"Dankei." I waited until he looked back at me reluctantly. "Who is it?"

"Empire man, Kellan. Real Empire, I mean."

"You're sure?"

"You can tell by his accent. Sounds like our old schoolteacher, the one they sent after they ran off the Accuser."

He turned back to Destiny. I gave her a final scratch under the chin before heading to the bathhouse to wash the dust from my face. What was a representative of the worlds-spanning Empire doing here? And why did the governor want me involved? I'd find out soon enough.

****

The governor's office was in a small outbuilding next to the prison, well away from the usual bustle of the government offices.

"Kellan!" Governor Tanner was beaming. "Come in! Ser Prospero, this is the one I was telling you about."

The Imperial man was middle-aged, middling height, middling condition. His plain white tunic and pants were the same nondescript dress any off-duty legionnaire might wear. Sandy brown hair and a close-cut beard framed a face entirely indistinguishable from many of the Empire's soldiers. Everything about him shrugged metaphorical shoulders and said "average", except for his eyes: one blue, one green.

I started to bring my Talent to bear on him out of habit when I noticed his pendant. A simple silver triangle adorned with a stylized sun, moon, and star, one at each point; the insignia the Empire's military used to denote their most accomplished magical practitioners. I forced my focus elsewhere and let my Talent drop, coughing to cover up my moment of distraction.

I'd made it this far in life without attracting the attention of the Empire's military recruiters. The magi, in particular, were always on the lookout for fresh blood. Any hint of magical ability could easily turn into a life of military service to the Empire. I had already sworn myself to King Iaestus. He, in turn, was a loyal servant of the Empress. That was close enough to Empire service for me.

"Apologies. Dust from the road, Magus." I raised my right fist to my chest in salute. He returned the salute with a raised eyebrow.

"Highwayman." Dankei was right. His accent was faint, but it had the unique Center sound to it, with stresses on strange syllables. He seemed pleased. "I see your reputation as an investigator is well deserved. Was it the pendant?"

"Yes, sir. It is rather distinctive."

The Magus tucked his pendant under his tunic. He must have left it out intentionally. Test passed, then.

"Kellan is one of our best," Tanner said. "The Highwaymen are the King's voice among the people. They hear cases and adjudicate disputes."

"As well as investigating crimes and meting out punishments as needed, I understand." The Magus nodded at me. "Quite a lot of responsibility for one man."

Tanner chuckled. "Kellan makes it look easy." He turned to me. "The Magus is here on business. He's asked to accompany you on your rounds."

"I am honored, sir," I said. There was no other acceptable response. "May I ask what your purpose is, Magus? I've got my circuit to ride. If you need me to detour for something, I can send word and let those towns know I'll be late."

"No need for detours. Accompanying you will be fine. Certain oracles point to a possible *kehyzana* in your region."

I smiled slightly, trying to look mildly befuddled. "I am sorry, sir. I deal with the mundane. Is that a creature from the Unreal? A feral beastling or an unbound *maziken* from the time of the Accuser?"

"No, not a demon. It's a type of *ayloshea*. A truth-teller. And the emphasis is on *possible*," Prospero said. He waved his hand dismissively. "The oracles are wrong as often as they are right in these matters. Still, it needs to be investigated."

I nodded, cursing inwardly. I must not have hidden my emotions as well as I thought. The Magus held up a hand with a knowing smile.

"I'll do my best not to interfere with your normal activities, Highwayman. I'm not here to examine you or your work." He actually looked apologetic. "Normally, the Empire has functionaries to deal with this sort of thing. I was in the area on another matter, though. Auguries pointed favorably at my involvement, so my assistance was requested."

I didn't need my Talent to see what he thought of that request, or the type of functionaries that must have made it. Clerical busy-bodies were apparently the same, whether they were home-grown or imported by the Empire.

Tanner clapped his hands together lightly, breaking that train of thought. "Which is what brings us all together today. Kellan, you are to continue with your rounds, but I expect you to provide whatever help the Magus might need in his search for this *kehyzana*."

I met the governor's eyes. "Of course, Ser Tanner. It will be no trouble at all."

I raised my fist in salute once again. I knew if I were to raise my Talent and examine my own aura, I would see the reddish black of a blatant lie.

****

The Magus dined with the governor that evening. I begged off, claiming exhaustion and a desire to get a proper bath for the first time in weeks. I enjoyed the bath and a decent meal, but sleep eluded me for a long while as I fretted over the coming day.

Prospero seemed pleasant enough, but a Magus of the Empire was no one to be trifled with. They were the equals of kings, and answered only to the Empress herself, worlds away across the Unreal. I fell asleep with those thoughts chasing one another through my head. They followed me into sleep, where I tossed and turned, dreaming of something unseen hunting me in the night.

Despite that, I still woke shortly after dawn. The habits of a lifetime are hard to break. I packed my belongings, nibbled on some cheese I had saved from dinner the night before, and headed to the stables.

Prospero was there already, waiting for me. I gave him a nod as he cinched up the saddle on his stallion and hoped my unease from the night before did not show on my face.

"Dankei! I see you've already taken care of the Magus. Please bring me Destiny." The stable hand's eyes widened a bit at the revelation of who Prospero was, and he hustled off to see to my horse.

Prospero laid a hand on my shoulder. Gentle, but it made me start. He dropped it as I turned to face him.

"No need for the honorific, Kellan." He spoke softly, but

with authority; a man used to being obeyed.

"Apologies. How shall I address you, sir?"

"Prospero will do. Where are we headed?"

"Canter." Dankei led Destiny out and handed me her reins. "It's a hard day's ride from here, but I'd rather not push my horse so hard two days in a row. We'll ride for a caravan station tonight, then on to Canter in the morning; and Frog's End the day after. That will get me back on my usual circuit." I paused. "If that meets with your approval."

I wasn't sure what reaction I had hoped to elicit. The Magus simply nodding and mounting his horse was certainly more understated than I expected. I checked my packs, mounted Destiny, and led the way through the early morning streets of Dart.

****

Destiny complained a little at first but settled down quickly. Once we were beyond the city walls, the dawn air was cool, with just a hint of the earthy smell that the night's dew had brought up from the ground.

We rode without talking for a good while. The Magus finally broke the silence when the sun was high enough in the sky to melt away the cool of the morning.

"You're not much of a talker, are you, Ser Kellan?"

I kept my eyes forward. "Not really, sir. Most times I am on the road alone, I travel alone. It lends itself to spending time in thought. I apologize for being lost in my own head."

"That doesn't surprise me. There's something else, though."

I'd considered this moment carefully, knowing it was bound to come. It was one of the things that had kept me tossing and turning the night before. I sighed and shifted in the saddle just enough to be able to watch the Magus out of the corner of my eye.

"Respectfully, sir? My father told me stories of what he

saw the Magi do on the battlefield. You're a powerful man, and I'm wondering what you want with me. To be brief, you scare the crap out of me."

The Magus snorted, and the snort turned into a genuine chuckle. "Now, that's not the kind of answer I expected."

I turned my head to face him. "You don't expect people to be afraid of you?"

"Honestly? Yes. Most aren't willing to admit it, though. At least not to my face."

"Ah. Please understand, Magus. I mean no disrespect. It's part of my office. I often have to tell people things they don't want to hear. Including my superiors. I'm charged to hide nothing from my king or his officers."

As far as I was concerned, the Magus was not part of that group. It would suit me for him to think otherwise, though.

"I see. Interesting." He pursed his lips. "Not the most unusual custom I've found across the worlds I've been in, but it's up there. The Empire can use a bit more of that brutal practicality, I think. I can see why the Empress spent time and treasure to liberate your world."

I saw my chance. "If you don't mind, sir. I don't mean to pry, but... why your search?"

"The truth-teller, you mean?" Prospero sighed. "I'll be as honest with you as you were with me. The oracles have me chasing shadows. That type of world-mage is as rare as an honest whore. If one is out there, though, I need to find them."

"Why? I mean, *ayloshea* are permitted, aren't they? I know we have our own geomancers, and you can find hags in most of the bigger cities now."

"The line between *ayloshea* and *lamoshea*, between world-mage and magus, is not as definitive as most people think. A world-mage's talents are limited, true. They can't learn how to walk the Unreal or manipulate the Weave the way the Magi can. Still, their abilities can be even more dangerous in the wrong hands."

"Magi can call up fire, call down lightning, banish

demons! What could be more dangerous than that?"

Prospero cocked his head. "Letting it be known that you can do exactly that — and then telling people the truth is a lie, or that a lie is the truth. Or being able to find things and using it to locate the weaknesses of a king." He shook his head. "It's easy to deal with people who can shape the world. It's harder to get a handle on those who can shape people."

I pondered his statement as we continued in silence. After a few minutes, he stirred again.

"What's it like, being a Highwayman?"

I glanced over at him. "Mostly long hours on the road, punctuated by irritated landsmen who are sure I'm an idiot. Unless I rule their way, in which case I'm a genius."

"Ha! Sounds like the Legion. Except with more riding and less marching. How'd you end up doing it?"

"My father. I used to ride the circuit with him. He taught me law, and justice, and what it means to serve. In the end, when he retired, I took his place. Swore an oath to the King himself. To protect the innocent, to see justice served, and to avenge those whom justice has failed. To do what needs to be done, whatever that might be, for his people and in his name." I cocked my head. "So, I do it. And you?"

I decided it was worth a risk and raised my Talent just for a moment, keeping watch on him out of the corner of my eye.

"The same. I serve the Empress. I do as I am commanded." He shook his head. "What more could I ask for?"

His aura was tight, reeled in, under rigid control. Something I'd seen before, but never to this extent. A faded purple revealed truth and belief evenly mixed with an overlay of deception.

He was lying to himself about something.

I inclined my head slightly, acknowledging his words and the end of the subject.

****

We talked little for the rest of the day, except for the minimal chatter about the road and the condition of our horses. I wasn't sure if it was because the Magus didn't want to intrude on my thoughts, or if he was enjoying the silence himself.

We rode through until the setting sun started to unravel the heat of the day. It was still hot, but there was a definite promise of relief when we reached the caravan station and stopped for the evening. It was a wide clearing off the road, cast with salt and sand to keep it clear of weeds and underbrush.

We swung down off our mounts in tandem, both of us stretching to release muscles sore from the day's ride.

I turned to the Magus. "Let me take care of the horses, and I'll get to the fire."

Prospero snorted. "Pick one. I'll do the other. This isn't my first time away from civilization."

The fire was the easier task; but not knowing him, I was reluctant to leave Destiny in his hands. "I'll take the horses, if you'll get the fire going."

"Sealed." He left to search through the woods, gathering kindling. I turned to the horses and started rubbing them down, starting with Destiny.

I was only halfway done when wood crackled behind me and the odor of burning wood tickled my nostrils. I stopped to check on the Magus. He had a decent sized pile of dry wood next to a small, expertly built fire. I would have been hard-pressed to get something started so quickly myself.

"Not bad. We'll need a bit more wood than that, though."

"I'll gather more. Figured I could help you with the horses." He moved to take care of his stallion. The beast whinnied, happy to have his master's hands on him.

"Don't worry. I'm almost done with Destiny. I'll see to finding some more." Prospero nodded, focused on rubbing down his horse. He did it with the same quickness and skill he had showed with the fire.

Working together, we got the horses rubbed down and fed as the fire grew and warmed us. True to my word, I finished first and went to look for wood. I returned with an armful to find Prospero breaking out a kettle. I pulled out a cook pan, and we worked together to make dinner with only a word or two of conversation until we'd finished our corn cakes.

The last light of day was long gone when Prospero sighed and stretched. "Been too long since I've enjoyed a good meal by the fire."

He sat with his cloak pulled around him against the cold, but folded Empire-style, keeping the throat of his scabbard uncovered and the hilt of his sword close at hand. I settled down and arranged my cloak the same way, leaving my pistol at the ready.

Prospero nodded at me. "You've served?"

"No. Learned this from my father, though, and he did. He taught me most of what I know about woodcraft before he passed."

"That's not all you got from your father, was it?" Prospero nodded at my pistol. "I recognize the pattern. It's old, but reliable. An officer's weapon."

"Yes. Two shot, black powder. It'll put a hole through a bear. I should know, I've done it before. It was my father's during the war against the Accuser."

"Battle." Prospero spoke absent-mindedly; this was obviously a correction he'd made many times before. He didn't elaborate, but I understood what he meant. The war with the Accuser was never-ending.

Since he'd broached the subject, I nodded at his own weapon. "If you don't mind me asking — why the sword? I know you can't carry technology through the Unreal easily. But they're making Empire-designed repeating pistols in the capital. It would have been easy enough for you to get one."

"I could have, I suppose. That's the problem with the Empire, though. It spans worlds. Magic works here, technology works there." He grinned. "Now, swords? Swords work *everywhere*. This one's been with me a while. Good, solid steel, even if it's not enchanted like your pistol."

"What?"

"You didn't know?"

"No!" I drew my weapon and examined it by the firelight. The dull metal of the weapon gave no hint of any sort of magical properties. "How can you tell?"

"I could sense it today, while we were riding. It was like an odor that came and went, one I couldn't quite identify. Once I realized it was moving with us, I started paying attention. Detecting the active manipulation of the Weave is more obvious, of course; but this was easy enough to see once I knew where to focus."

A chill ran up my spine. *I'd risked using my Talent right in front of him when he might have been studying me!* I resolved to be more cautious in the future.

"What kind of enchantment is it? Can you tell that?"

"A fairly standard one. It's designed to cut through protections and break the enchantments of the Accuser."

"I suppose you have something like that on your sword?"

Prospero burst out laughing. "Oh, Lord, no! Mine's as plain a piece of steel as I could get. Having an enchantment on you while you work the Weave is, well, like carrying an open powder keg around a bonfire. You might be fine, but all it takes is a stray spark. Then you won't be worrying about anything else, ever again."

"Ah. I can see why you'd avoid it."

"Much the same way you'd avoid a bear. Speaking of which — didn't you mention shooting one? What's the story behind that?"

"Ah." The horses snorted quietly behind me, and the fire crackled before me. I was comfortable being alone in the wilderness, but I was also at home telling tales around the fire. I settled in and Prospero followed suit; just two travelers sitting by the fire, breaking their journey on some lonely road at the end of the day.

"It started with a woman, as these things always do. The governor got a letter asking for the investigation of a murder out toward Pond; which would have been odd enough, except the woman who wrote it and the victim were one and the same…"

****

We talked well into the night, trading stories. I told him of some of my more interesting cases, and he shared a tale or two of his adventures crossing the Unreal. We eventually settled down by mutual accord and went our separate ways into the world of dreams.

The next morning was surprisingly pleasant. Prospero turned out to be a decent cook and made breakfast while I readied the horses. We were once again sharing silence, aside from whatever comments we needed to complete our morning tasks.

I would not have chosen him as a traveling companion, but he was turning out to be a pleasant fellow to share the road with. So long as I could keep from using my Talent in his presence.

A little before noon, I saw the first carefully tended fields indicating we were nearing Canter. As we drew closer to the town, a recently harvested field caught my attention. I dismissed it at first, but as we drew closer, the appearance of the field nagged at me.

"Hold up." I reined in Destiny. Prospero pulled his charger to a halt just past me.

I stared at the field. There was something wrong there. I'd seen this a handful of times in my career. I could read the auras of people with some effort. Sometimes, though, when their actions were significant or extreme enough, they left lingering impressions on the world.

"What is it?"

Risk of discovery or no, I couldn't let this pass. My oath

wouldn't let me.

I pointed at the field. "Do you see that, over there?"

As soon as Prospero turned to follow my finger, I focused my Talent on the field, then immediately slammed my eyes shut and dropped it.

There was a swirling blackness off in the corner of the field. It was so deep even my brief glimpse of that void made me feel as if I were plunging through an eternity of isolation. I felt bile rise in my throat and fought it back, coughing to cover up my sudden nausea.

If I had to keep covering my Talent that way, the Magus was going to think I was an asthmatic.

"What did you see?"

"Something over there." I let myself down off my horse. In a moment, Prospero joined me, and we stalked toward the corner of the field.

I slowed as I approached the area I had seen, the afterimage of the void still with me. Partly hidden in the stubble was a fresh-turned plot of earth, maybe three cubits by one, with a thick pole stuck at the head. Someone had tied a bright blue ribbon to the top of the pole.

"Good eye, catching sight of the ribbon," Prospero murmured.

I shrugged. Let him think that's what caught my eye. I hadn't seen it until we approached.

"What is it?"

"Grave." I kneeled and reached out to trace the letters cut into the wood. "Her name was Aleiceia. From the size of the plot, she would have been young. Ten, twelve at most." I stood up and brushed off my hands. "That marker's the kind families use while they're waiting for someone to finish a memorial stone."

Prospero nodded. "Recent, then."

"Yes. This is probably either her family's field, or maybe it belongs to a friend." I started back toward the horses. "Come. I need to speak to the prefect."

"About?"

I rubbed my eyes. "I don't know. There's something off about this, though. We need to find out more."

It wasn't until we mounted up and started trotting toward Canter that I realized I had been ordering around a Magus as if he were an apprentice. I considered apologizing for a moment, but decided if he didn't want to bring it up, I wouldn't either.

****

"It was rough on the family," Chari said. The prefect of Canter was young, only a few years past thirty; but the lines on her face belonged to someone with another decade's worth of life behind them. "She was playing in the barn. Her mother and father were both there. Her younger brother hurt himself and started crying. She rushed over to see him and tripped over a shovel. She must have landed just wrong, died instantly. Broken neck."

I pursed my lips. "You've interviewed them all separately?"

She nodded. "Including the brother. There's no question. It was a freak accident."

"I am sure you did your job, prefect. Now I need to do mine and speak with them myself."

Her eyes showed understanding and unexpected sympathy. "Of course. That's your duty. I would expect nothing less from you, Kellan."

I sat back and stared at the ceiling. How to ask about the grave without bringing attention to myself? Ah.

"And the ribbon?"

Chari's small smile came and went like a shadow. "Her pride and joy," she said. "We had a traveling carnival come through two weeks ago. They had a children's competition. A talent show. She won it as a prize for her singing." Her mouth twitched as she wiped away a tear before it formed. I didn't need to use my Talent to read that. "She wore it every day and told people how she'd sing for the King someday."

"Prospero spoke up. "So that's why they left it at the grave."

"Chari nodded. "A small memory for her."

"I'm sorry for the loss," I said as I rose. Prospero stood along with me. "If the family is willing, I'll speak to the governor and send a memorial stone your way. It's the least we can do."

As we rose, she did as well, giving us a salute. "Thank you, Highwayman. They are loyal citizens. Of both King Iestus, and the Empress. They would appreciate it."

She inclined her head to Prospero. "And honor to you and yours, sir, for paying us attention."

****

We left and headed for the prefect's guest house. It was only a shack with a cot, but it was cozy enough. I had a boy bring a spare cot in for Prospero and promise to give extra attention to the horses. There were already a couple lined up respectfully, waiting for their chance to plead their cases to the Highwayman. Prospero watched for a bit as I heard people argue over the ownership of fields, broken deals and — in one case — broken hearts. He eventually made excuses and took his leave, no doubt hoping to find something more interesting to pay attention to.

Once the day was done, I left to speak with Aleiceia's family. I found Chari there with them, ready to make introductions. I used my Talent as I asked a few questions and confirmed what she had already discovered. A freak accident, nothing more.

Prospero was waiting for me at the guest house. Chari joined us for dinner, and we shared small talk in the evening as we ate. I shared news of the goings on in Dart, and what I had heard in other towns along my circuit. Prospero commented vaguely on his business, and the state of the town. The prefect talked of crops, and weather, and marriages.

We were both exhausted, and fell asleep soon after Chari said her farewells. The next day dawned bright and hot, and we left to gather our mounts and continue my circuit. As we walked, Prospero brought up the prefect's expression of thanks from the day before.

"Who did she think I was?" he asked.

I shrugged. "Who knows? Someone important." I looked him up and down. "You're not obvious about it. Your bearing, though. Your attitude. It says 'official' to anyone paying attention."

Prospero was silent for a while. "She seemed disturbed," he finally commented. "Is that typical? I'd expect more detachment."

I gestured at the roads and buildings stretching out around us. "Building a town in the Outlands is hard. This was territory the Accuser once controlled. Reclaiming it is worth it for the land grants from the king. Life out here breeds hard people. You can't live that life all the time. Hard things are brittle. They break." I sighed. "Plus, she's a young mother herself. Her oldest would be close to the age of the girl who died. That hits home. I know her. In town, she's professional with everyone except her family. Always putting on the proper face. You and I, we're outsiders. She doesn't have to be hard for us."

"She can lay aside the mask." He spoke the words with a particular rhythm that made it sound like a maxim, though one I'd not heard of before.

"Yes. A chance to be honest with herself." I felt a twinge of conscience and shook it off as quickly as it passed. We reached the stable and retrieved our horses.

"So that's it here, then? There's nothing else for you to do?"

He meant the grave. I mounted, looked back at the administration building. "Nothing right now."

"You were concerned about it when we first arrived."
"Something was out of place. It's my duty to notice things like that, and to investigate." I shrugged. "I spoke with the family, confirmed what she had already discovered. It turned out it was an accident. Tragic, but an accident." Even as I spoke, I frowned. If that were the case, why did the grave radiate the evidence of a lie?
Prospero caught my expression. "Second thoughts?"
"Sorrow." A partial lie. "These are the people I serve. Like Chari, I work to keep myself professional. Destiny's usually the only one who notices when I set my mask aside."
"I'm in rare company then," Prospero said, tone light. Joking.
I wasn't sure how to respond to that, so I didn't. As we rode on, Prospero was kind enough to leave me to my thoughts.

****

We saw the first buildings of Frog's End just before noon.
"In a hurry?" Prospero asked as we approached the town limits.
When the Empire had scattered new settlements across the Outlands like seeds, they'd spaced them roughly a slow day's ride apart. That distribution of towns left plenty of room for expansion. I'd been pushing Destiny without realizing it.
I frowned and slowed. Destiny whinnied in thanks. I patted her and made myself pay attention to my surroundings. Even in the heat, I would have expected to see a few people on the road and workers out in the fields. They were empty instead.
"Something's off." I pushed Destiny into a full trot.
A few minutes later, we reached an old shack by the side of the road. An elderly man sat outside under an awning made from an old, frayed campaign tarp. I reined in Destiny. Prospero followed suit.

"Decanae Petrius! What's going on?"

The old man was a veteran. He'd led a squad of a dozen men in the Empire's wars against the Accuser. I used his title when I could, to show him the honor he was due for his service. He levered himself to his feet and saluted us.

"Ser Kellan!" He blinked, trying to determine how to address Prospero, before settling on a generic, "Ser."

"Where is everyone?" I wanted to use my Talent. Instead, I ground my teeth in frustration and damped it down. Not being able to see someone's aura while speaking with them was like having my right arm in a sling. I did not want to chance it in front of the Magus, though.

He jerked his head toward town. "On the commons. Priest is doin' the funeral." He narrowed his eyes. "That why you're here, Kellan? Or is this just your rounds?"

"Just my rounds. Who's funeral? Or are they practicing for you?"

Petrius barked laughter. "Ha! They've got a ways to go before they have to worry about me. Nah." His face fell. "Two kids. Young ones. The Curth twins."

"*Bri ashmaya*," I said, crossing myself. "Heaven bless."

Prospero leaned forward. "Sickness?"

Petrius shook his head. "Nah, sir. Nah. Damndest thing. The two were playing together yesterday, out in the field. Got tangled up with each other somehow. Went head over heels, y'see? The both of them somehow broke their fool necks."

I shivered in the heat. Glanced at Prospero. The Magus frowned.

"Three in two," I said. "Within a week."

Prospero nodded, then turned to salute Petrius. "Thank you, *Decanae*."

The old man straightened up proudly at the recognition. "Honor to you and yours, sir."

"Come." I wheeled my horse around. "I want to see these children before they're sent to the earth."

****

We arrived just as the service concluded and hung back as the priest intoned his last words. The small crowd watched in silence as the bearers stepped forward. They picked up the tiny bodies and laid them on a single polished and runed carrying board.

A blue ribbon tied back each girl's hair.

"Magus." I kept my voice low. "Do you see?"

"Aye. Coincidence, do you think?"

"No." I pursed my lips, thinking.

Prospero sensed my hesitation, and let the silence linger between us. The thought of asking the Magus to pay special attention to his surroundings made me uncomfortable. Three dead children, though?

I wrestled with my conscience and won. "May I impose upon you?"

"Gladly. I take it you want an examination?"

"Yes. Three accidental deaths? All by violence, all with a broken neck?" I shook my head. "I want to know if we are dealing with a... I don't know the Imperial term for it. Practice of dark magic. One who breaks the Weave. Can you tell that?"

"*Shuot.*" Prospero's void was cold. "Warlock. Yes. I'll need a place to examine the bodies. Somewhere cool. The colder, the better. I'll need a bell and salt, both preferably blessed by the priest."

"It'll be the town's root cellar, then. That's likely where they stored the bodies." I pointed opposite the way we'd entered the commons. "Head that way, past where the houses thin out. You'll see the entrance, cut back into a hill. I'll meet you there in a moment."

Prospero nodded and rode off. I went to break the news to the prefect and the priest.

****

The bearers were not happy, but delivered the children into our care at the root cellar. They laid them on a makeshift table made up of rough-hewn planks. I slipped them a few coins for their trouble and extracted a promise to return for the children in an hour.

"That took longer than I expected. Any problems?" Prospero asked. He circled the table. A small book sat at the far end, already open.

I handed over the bell and a small box of salt. "The priest was accommodating. The prefect, not so much. I had to remind him of my duties."

Prospero paused. "That's unusual. From what I've seen so far, you have a good relationship with the people on your circuit."

"I was asking strange questions. The prefect was simply looking out for his people." I had also taken the opportunity away from Prospero to raise my Talent and pepper the prefect, priest, and Curth family with questions about the incident. I was grateful their auras reflected nothing more than the loss and grief I expected to see.

"Strange questions?"

"About the ribbons. They were from a traveling carnival. From the sound of it, the same one that came through Canter. They were here a week ago. Packed up and headed for Viridis. If they kept to their schedule, they should have arrived there yesterday." I gestured at the twins. "Normally, I would wait a day or two before digging into a death like this. But I wanted to make sure there was nothing else to follow up on before your examination. The prefect wanted to know what was going on and why I brought you along."

"We don't have room for spectators. He will have to wait outside."

"You won't have to worry about that. I don't want him here either. I sent him and the priest to see to the Curths. They'll smooth the feathers I ruffled with my questions." I grimaced. "They will be the good ones, taking care of the hurt.

I'll be the outrageous outsider, taking the blame for disturbing their grief."

"Ah." Prospero looked distracted. He lit a small lamp. "Close the door, please. I'll need darkness. This is best done under a new moon with backup. We're dealing with friendly spirits here, though. This should be more than adequate."

****

The door creaked as I pushed it shut. The flickering lamp flame made shadows dance across the walls of the cellar.

Prospero gestured at the head of the table. I moved to stand there while he stood at the girl's feet and picked up the book. He cleared his throat and began speaking in an odd language; one strangely familiar, while still somehow being incomprehensible.

I shivered. The root cellar, already cool, became even colder. A chill breeze swirled around my ankles, then disappeared as quickly as it had come. I blinked to clear my suddenly blurry eyes. Prospero looked farther away than he had been a moment before. He stopped speaking, laid down the book, and picked up the bell with his left hand, then scooped up a handful of salt in his right.

"I call you forth. Speak with me, children." He scattered the salt over their bodies and rang the bell: once, twice, three times. The third strike of the bell stretched out unnaturally, and I heard a child's voice speaking indistinctly.

Prospero smiled and began talking. I strained to hear what he was saying. There was a scratching, almost an aural itch. As I tried to ignore it and listen to the Magus, whispered words came into focus.

They are ours now.

The whispers were insects moving across dead sand. Specks of blackness slid and shifted around the table, forming feathery tendrils that wrapped around the girl's corpses. Prospero continued his conversation, oblivious.

Yes. Smug satisfaction. He is unaware of us. He is unaware of you and your lies as well, man. For now.

Cold seeped up from the floor through my feet, chilling me. My head ached from it.

What will happen if he finds you out, man? He will rip you from your home. Force you to abandon your duty. Make of you a reprobate, an oath breaker.

Prospero frowned and laid aside the bell. He moved slowly, as if underwater. I watched him lean forward.

Let us help you. We ask nothing of you, man. The voice chuckled. *Literally. Do nothing, and we will solve this problem for you.*

Time itself froze for an instant. Prospero, leaning forward over the twins, looked puzzled. I opened my mouth to speak, but my voice would not come.

A wave of heat exploded outward from the table, slamming me back into the door. A stench of sulfur and rot permeated the room. In perfect unison, the two dead girls opened their eyes, sat up, and reached out. Two pairs of tiny, dead hands wrapped around Prospero's throat.

"Surprised, lamoshea?" The voice was the same one that had whispered to me. It shifted back and forth between the two corpses. "The souls you seek are gone. Devoured, delivered to our master. He will appreciate yours as well."

Prospero's eyes were bulging. He got his hands up and under the girl's hands, prying them loose. He broke free of their grasp, gagging.

"Maziken!" He pointed at the children and shouted something. The words were a spike of pain driven into my ears.

The creature laughed, a strange voice bubbling out from two throats. The girls scrambled to their feet, joints snapping and bones cracking as they moved.

"Pitiful. We are power. We are death. Where are your words of banishment now, Magus? You who cannot even stand the sight of our true form?"

Sight. I hesitated. *Do nothing.* That was what the voice said. What could I do in the face of such unearthly evil? The answer was obvious. I shook myself and raised my Talent.

The mundane details of the room faded into gray. Prospero flamed, a pillar of pure white light. The two corpses were swirling voids of blackness, similar to what I had seen at the grave in Canter. Both moved toward the Magus, spreading out as if to wrap around him.

A brilliant ribbon of blue weaved through and around the voids.

I let my Talent drop and lunged forward. The corpses of the girls grappled with Prospero. I ripped the ribbons out of their hair; turned, and thrust them into the flame of the lamp.

I cried out as an explosion of icy fire engulfed my hands, making them spasm and contort. I threw the flaming ribbons away from me. As they arced through the air, the flames consumed them and left nothing but ash. The *maziken* snarled and turned from Prospero to face me.

I stumbled backwards, away from dead eyes filled with hate. Tried to draw my pistol, but my hands were icy claws that refused to obey my commands. "Again, Magus!" I screamed the words, but could barely hear my own voice.

Prospero must have. He shouted again. This time, rather than spiking into my ears, I could feel the words slide around me to wrap around the corpses. With a scream of defiance, they dropped to the ground with a thud.

The sudden silence was painful. Prospero drew a shuddering breath, coughed, and spit out blood.

"Well done," he croaked, massaging his throat. "That was beyond what I was expecting. Death alone seldom opens a way into the Unreal. Someone was tampering with the Weave, if something as powerful as that thing clawed its way into our world."

"What was it?"

"Maziken. Demon. A servant of the Accuser. And a

powerful one. It took me by surprise. I would have been dead, were it not for you. What made you think of the ribbons?"

"It felt right." I rubbed and flexed my hands, warming them. "That was the only thing in common among all three deaths. They won a ribbon from a man at the carnival."

The Magus studied me for a moment, then nodded. "I can see that. Quick thinking, Highwayman. Well done."

****

Prospero insisted on speaking to the priest before we left. The unenviable job of explaining the situation to the prefect fell to me. We each managed our tasks quickly. Within a half hour, we left Frog's End at a trot.

"What did you tell the prefect?" Prospero asked. His voice was rough, still raw from the language he had used in the cellar.

I grunted. "The truth. He didn't like it. I don't blame him. He agreed to send someone back along the route the carnival followed. To inquire about any other 'accidents'. What did you tell the priest?"

"To stand vigil over the bodies for a night." Prospero sighed. "It won't mean anything for those girls. They're gone. It will help fix the Weave around the bodies, though. That will keep further agents of the Accuser from bothering their town."

"You're sure." I made it a statement, not a question.

"Absolutely. Those things reeked of his power."

That hung between us as we pushed on toward Viridis.

****

It normally took me a lazy day to ride from Frog's End to Viridis. Prospero and I managed it in hours. Prospero muttered under his breath constantly as we rode; a litany of charm to speed the horses and protect them from injury along the road. I left him to it, passing him water occasionally to help soothe his raw throat.

Twilight was just fading to dusk when we spotted a puddle of light in a field set off away from the town. Makeshift torches and firelight lit up a field dotted with booths and a makeshift stage adorned with colorful streamers. A cluster of carts sat off in the darkness, lit only by a small campfire.

I ignored the town and rode straight for the carnival. As we approached, a clown in costume finery and face paint moved to intercept us.

"My lords, your horses..."

I swung off in front of him and pressed the reins into his hands. "Are in your hands now, fool. Treat them well. Your master. Where is he?" I reached under my tunic and pulled out the chain holding my badge of office, a copper pendant embossed with two crossed swords over the scale of justice.

The clown glanced from me to Prospero, then shook his head in disgust. "Oh, gods. The law. Please tell me he hasn't been skimming on taxes again." He pointed at the edge of the carts. "Look for the one painted green with blue trim. He'll be there."

"You trust him with the horses?" Prospero muttered as we made our way toward the carts.

"I'll risk it. I don't want time for someone to carry a warning."

The Magus nodded. I loosed my pistol in its holster, a mirror image of Prospero making sure his sword was free at the same time.

****

The manager was exactly where the fool said he would be. Sitting in a folding canvas chair, he was large, bordering on fat, and bald as an egg. He watched the carnival with a bored expression. He noticed our approach and frowned briefly before he stood, plastering an obsequious expression on his face.

"My lords! Welcome. I am the master of this humble carnival. What may I do for you?"

Despite our close association over the past few days, I still didn't know what skills or techniques Prospero might use to divine the work of an *ayloshea*. I counted on the darkness, and the distraction of the manager, to be enough to confuse things as I raised my Talent.

The manager glanced left and right, then cleared his throat and leaned in. "If this is about the taxes, I paid them last month. I have receipts."

I had to give credit to the man. Whatever tax troubles he may have had in the past, his aura was the bright purple of truth and honest belief. "I'm not here about taxes," I said intently. "Tell me about the murders."

The smile never left his face, but I saw the confusion in his eyes. His aura rippled uncertainly but remained bright purple. I let my Talent drop.

"Murders?"

"Children." In the darkness, Prospero's voice was the snarl of a beast. "Broken necks. Each wearing a token from your carnival."

The manager's smile evaporated. "Listen. I have no idea who you two are, or what you're talking about." He stepped forward and jabbed a finger at Prospero. "If you have an issue with me, take it up with your Highwayman next time you see him."

I reached into my tunic and once again pulled out my badge of office. I let it dangle from my fingers as I held it up in front of the manager.

Prospero smiled wickedly. Without taking his eyes off the manager, he said, "Highwayman. I have an issue with this one."

The manager looked back and forth between us, then closed his eyes. He stepped back and raised his hands. "Apologies, sir. My lords, I don't want any trouble. I really do not know what you are talking about."

I concentrated for a moment, and his aura came back into view. It was ragged, now streaked with fear, but the color was unchanged. So much for a simple solution. I tucked my badge back into my tunic and gestured for Prospero to back off, hoping he understood.

"I believe you," I said. Prospero shifted next to me, the only evidence of his surprise. I ignored him as best I could. "There have been three suspicious deaths recently, in towns you have visited. All young girls. Each had a blue ribbon they had won in some contest at your carnival."

"Someone has a problem with Vohan's show?" The manager looked confused. "How could they? The children love him! He just finished up for the evening. Every kid in the town was there."

I jerked my head. "Take us to him. We have questions."

****

The manager led us around the edge of the carnival toward the wagons. I'd seen the style before; small, enclosed wooden boxes, each with a door and a window or two. Just large enough for a couple of performers to bunk down and store their equipment. Oil lamps hung at the corners of each wagon, burning steadily. Once my eyes adjusted to the dark, they gave more than enough light to find our way.

"He's at the back. There." The manager pointed down the curving row, past a handful of wagons. The penultimate wagon was blue, with yellow starbursts on the side. Its door hung open, spilling warm light out into the darkness.

He started forward, but I took his arm to stop him and shook my head. "Stay here. Ser Prospero? If you would accompany me?"

Prospero nodded and followed me as I headed for the wagon.

We were ten paces away when a man stepped out, pipe in hand. He was a hair taller than Prospero, wearing bright blue pants and a stained white under tunic. His long gray hair was slicked back, framing a narrow, friendly face. His eyes crinkled up in a smile as he saw us.

"My lords! You seem to have gotten turned around." His voice was warm and welcoming. It reminded me vaguely of my father. Vohan gestured with his pipe. "The carnival is over yonder."

"Ser Vohan?" I raised my Talent. "We have a few questions for —"

My voice broke off as I stumbled. Vohan's aura completely enveloped him. A swirling void of varied blackness churned around and through him, exposing streaks of unnatural colors. My skin crawled. He looked like the feel of death, smelled like the sight of vomit, felt like the scent of rotten meat.

I jerked my head away. Or, rather, I tried. I struggled against a terrible, invisible wind that tore at me, trying to force me into the void. A stuttering step forward was all it managed before I closed my eyes and released my Talent. I fell to my knees and retched, tasting copper.

"Kellan?" Prospero reached out to me.

"Well, now." Vohan's voice was unchanged. "Questions deserve answers, don't they, my lords?"

I spat out blood and looked up. Vohan's smile grew wider, then wider still. Impossibly large black hands reached out from inside his mouth, grasped either side of his head, and pulled.

Vohan's body split like a rotten log, bursting into a shower of maggots. Something black unfolded itself from the space his body had occupied. It stretched itself upwards until it stood half again as tall as a man, covered in blood and bone and bits of flesh, long arms dangling to just short of the ground.

"Ah, better." Its voice was unchanged. A trio of sickly yellow eyes crowned its bare skull, set over the gash of an impossibly wide mouth. A long, red tongue flickered out from between rotten brown teeth and lapped at a bit of Vohan-flesh from its chin. "Here's your answer, my lords. Death."

Prospero stepped forward and shouted something as the *maziken* leaned forward, unhinged its jaw, and screamed. A burst of sickly, green-tinged light exploded in front of me. It was accompanied by a crash as loud as a falling tree, then followed by the scent of burning pine and earth. Halfway to my feet, the explosion knocked me over again. I turned my head away, ears ringing, blinking away greenish blobs obscuring my sight, my night vision ruined by the light.

Prospero continued shouting. He tried to step forward, but something unseen struck him and he stumbled back.

"Oh, you would like that, wouldn't you, little magi?" The demon chuckled, a wet, bubbling sound. "My master has ensured I am not so easily dismissed. I am quite firmly bound to this plane, I assure you. Once I have dealt with you, I will return to my tasks."

Prospero shouted again and lunged forward. There was another burst of light, this one bright and crisp and clean. It wiped the obscuring blobs from my vision and let me see the two of them.

Prospero stood with his hand raised defiantly. The *maziken* was on one knee, arms splayed as if to anchor it in the ground. Nothing remained of the surrounding wagons except shattered wood. The grass was gone, burned away to bare, steaming earth. Prospero and I remained at the center of a small circle of still-living grass. Off in the distance, horses screamed and people shouted in fear.

"That *hurt*, magi. It's a shame it didn't work." The demon stood slowly. "How does it feel to fail your family, your so-called Empress, and your false god yet again?" It raised its hand.

Prospero moved one leg back to brace himself. "Kellan! It's bound here by some token! I can't banish it! Run! Get word to your king!"

The demon hesitated, then turned its head toward me and

laughed, low and wicked. My stomach heaved in response, urging me to empty its contents and run.

"Oh, that was *you* I felt?" It chuckled. "The master sent me to harvest lives. Some are worth more than others. Stay, little one. Offer yourself to me, and I may spare those you claim to protect."

Prospero raised both hands and lunged forward, arms wide. The demon snarled as he kicked him back, stopping the Magus' attack before they came into contact with each other.

The two grappled each other without touching. Prospero swept his leg around and knocked one of the demon's legs out from underneath it. The demon grasped the empty air in front of him, somehow pinning the Magus. The demon thrust his head forward, and Prospero parried with another explosion of light, sending it reeling backwards.

I pushed myself to my feet and nearly fell as a wave of dizziness washed over me. Cold steel met my hand as I reached for my pistol, but I hesitated before I drew. Prospero said that the thing was bound. Just like the dead girls had been. Nothing had been able to harm those demons, either; not until I destroyed the ribbons that anchored them to this plane.

I planted myself as solidly as I could and focused intently on the space next to the *maziken*. Taking in a deep breath, I fought rising nausea and raised my Talent.

The seething nothingness of the *maziken* came into being at the corner of my eye, drawing my gaze toward it. I set my jaw and forced my head to remain immobile, staring at the area next to the demon as pain throbbed behind my eyes.

Prospero yelled and tumbled across my vision, his aura bright blue bordered in shining white. As he fell, something flickered past him, obscuring his aura for the blink of an eye. He rolled to his feet and shouted. His aura pulsed with his words. With a shout, it flared white, washing outward from him, erasing the night and fading the demon's vortex. The *maziken* grunted and stumbled, forced backwards.

For the briefest moment, I saw a thread of blackness

stretching across the air; a near-invisible spiderweb of nothing that shifted in and out of my vision. One end disappeared into the void of the demon's aura. The other snaked off into the ruins of the wagon.

I blinked, trying to focus. Something among the wreckage twinkled darkly.

I dropped my focus and lunged for it without thinking. My own feet betrayed me and gave way as I tried to stumble toward whatever it was. I fell and realized the earth I thought had been scorched by the explosion was in reality frozen, steaming in the night air. The chill of it ripped my breath away and sapped the strength from my limbs.

I started crawling toward the thing I had seen in the wreckage, boots pushing against the frozen earth. The *maziken* roared, and a wave of nauseating darkness rippled through the night. Prospero screamed, a mix of frustration and pain.

"So sweet." The demon's voice mocked us. "You, little one! Stay. I insist."

I pushed forward, but the ground suddenly shifted beneath my foot. Freezing mud flowed up and around my leg nearly to my knee, then solidified, holding me fast. I yanked with all my strength, but was unable to budge my leg, now trapped by the shell of frozen mud.

I looked forward. A few yards ahead, I spied a wooden box missing its lid. It had tipped over and spilled a handful of blue silk ribbons out onto the ground. On top of them was a small oval hand-glass.

The cold of the ground ate its way further up my leg. I stopped struggling and tried to draw my pistol. My fingers stiffened, going numb from the cold seeping up from the ground. I forced them around the butt of the gun, yanking it from its holster.

I twisted to take aim at the mirror. Hands shaking from the cold, I tried to will myself to be still and aim properly. A wave of cold washed up over me from the earth, making me shiver violently. My hands clenched involuntarily, and the *crack!* of my pistol firing deafened me momentarily, leaving my ears ringing.

My shot had gone wild. The mirror was still intact. Shaking even more violently from the cold, I struggled to take aim once more; then paused, trembling.

What if I missed? What if I hit, but didn't break it? My pistol was designed to break the enchantments of the Accuser.

I swore an oath to do what needs to be done.

Twisting further, I brought my pistol around, pointing it down my body. I worked the barrel of the pistol in between my leg and the enchanted earth encasing it, trying to angle it away from me before I pulled the trigger.

My already abused ears heard the *crack!* of the pistol, but it seemed a distant sound. The icy mud encasing my leg exploded in a fountain of frozen earth. Fire enveloped my leg, and something in my ankle snapped. I ignored the pain and yanked myself free, my foot twisting unnaturally. I was momentarily grateful for the cold that numbed it.

I crawled the few remaining yards to the glass. Gazing into it, I did not see a reflection of my face. Even without using my Talent, I saw the swirling void surrounding the *maziken*. The same thing I had seen over the grave in Canter, and between the dead girls in Frog's End.

I raised the pistol high and brought the butt down on the mirror, shattering it.

The Vohan-thing screamed, a wail of despair.

"*Magus!*" I screamed. "*Now!*"

I let myself slump to the ground. A last flash of brilliant white seared the darkness from the world. The demon's wail cut off mid-cry, leaving a disorienting silence in its wake. I closed my eyes and slumped to the ground, and let the cold take away my awareness as it had taken my pain.

****

Prospero came into the tent I'd commandeered as an interview room, face drawn, shoulders stooped. He practically collapsed into the camp chair next to me and nodded at my bandaged foot.

"What did they say?"

"I must have angled my pistol right. I could have taken my foot off, but all I've got is a minor break. Still — I won't be dancing any time soon. I'll have the hag at Dart look at it." Prospero rubbed his eyes. "Remind me. I can speed the healing. Enough that you'll be able to ride out of here, at least."

"I'll hold you to it."

We sat in silence together for a bit until Prospero finally spoke.

"The mirror. How'd you know?"

It was reflecting the dark light of another world. Even the memory of it chilled me. I certainly didn't want to admit that, though, especially since I was sure the only reason I could see that was because of my Talent. Fortunately, I'd had plenty of time to think. "It seemed obvious", I said. "It was the only thing in sight that wasn't broken."

Prospero cocked his head. "A fortunate bit of guesswork, Kellan."

I shrugged. "Sometimes that's what it comes down to. Tell me. What did you find?"

Prospero sighed and rubbed his eyes. "Necromantic channel bindings on the ribbons, coupled with a Weave of misfortune. They killed those children and siphoned off their life."

"Where? Why?"

"I don't know. But I intend to find out." He stifled a yawn. "The *maziken* was just a servant. The Weave of those ribbons was more subtle than that kind can manage."

I pondered that for a bit. "Above my station. I've sent word out. The carnival master gave me a list of towns they've visited since Vohan joined up with them."

"How many?"

"We found two. There's a dozen total. They've been moving all summer."

Prospero sat up. "Send runners. We need..."

I held up a hand. "Already done. I've sent word to King Iaestus and told him to call in Highwaymen from across the region. I expect we'll have extra hands in another day or two."

Prospero snorted. "You are very comfortable ordering about your king, Kellan."

"I'm fortunate he trusts me. They'll conduct additional investigations. We can get word to them about whatever else they might need to know."

"Good. What have you found here?"

"I've interviewed three quarters of the carnival folks. I don't think anyone was aware of what Vohan was, or what he — it — was doing. Still, I'll continue until I've spoken with each of them, just to be sure."

I was sure. With Prospero off examining Vohan's possessions, I'd made liberal use of my Talent. There were equal amounts of grief, regret, and fear floating around.

"You will want to speak with the manager yourself. He could not recall the details of the day when he hired Vohan on."

He cocked his head. "And now you're ordering around a Magus of the Empire. You *are* good at your job, Highwayman."

Under other circumstances, I might have been afraid. Exhaustion and pain washed out all other emotions. "Apologies, Magus. I am just doing..."

"... what needs to be done. I understand." He shook his head. "Thank you for bringing it to my attention. Creatures from the Unreal are adept at confusing and blinding the senses of men. I should have thought to examine him myself. You've saved me from overlooking something important."

I didn't know what to say to that, so I held my tongue. Not that it mattered. Prospero's eyes looked beyond me as he drifted off in thought. He finally shook his head and came back from wherever his mind had wandered.

"I intend to hunt down whoever summoned the *maziken*," he said. "I'll need someone to help me deal with local matters. That will be you."

There was no question in his tone. I nodded. "As you say, sir. The governor would likely have assigned me to assist you in any case."

"Good." He pushed himself up out of the chair. "We'll finish up here and ride for Dart tomorrow, and we'll start digging. I'll send for my team. Summoning and binding a creature from the Unreal is not a trivial matter. At best, we're dealing with a a warlock of some sort. At worst..." He shook his head, unwilling to give voice to whatever he was thinking.

I'd been using my Talent freely all day. Without considering the consequences, I raised it to examine Prospero's words. The controlled aura I'd seen before spilled out, a brilliant purple of solid truth and belief, ragged with fear.

As soon as I realized what I'd done, I clamped down on my vision. The Magus held my eye for the briefest of moments, then turned his head away.

"We'll need to be careful, Highwayman. With so much going on, it would be easy to overlook something right in front of our eyes."

I sat still and said nothing. Prospero stood and stretched, looking off into space, before turning to head back out. He looked back over his shoulder as he left.

"Finish your interviews, Kellan. Then join me for a late-night dinner. I want you there when I speak with the carnival manager tomorrow. You have a talent for reading people."

The End

Sam Robb is a Pittsburgh native, a former US Navy officer, and a graduate of Carnegie Mellon University. Over the course of his life, he has acquired a wife, three daughters, several quadrupeds, and a penchant for walking down back alleys and taking pictures of graffiti. When he's not walking around, taking pictures, and making up stories to tell about what he sees, he works as a software developer and occasional politician.

- Amazon Author Page: **https://www.amazon.com/stores/Sam-Robb/author/B07QJCG3BD**

- Web Site: **https://www.samrobbwrites.com/**

Specialist Lieu Saves The World

Brian Gifford

  Specialist Pete Lieu was pretty much a superhero. He tapped the jump gear on his Mod-4 Enhanced Mobility Armor and sailed over the rusting hulk of an ancient Russian BMP. His armored boots sank deep into the black Ukrainian soil as he bounced off the soft ground on the other side, and he spun in place at apogee, taking aim at the open hatch on top of the armored personnel carrier's turret. He felt the muted thump in his chest as the MEMA's forearm 25mm grenade launcher coughed out a round, and blue powder splashed on top of the turret to the left of the opening.
  A quiet voice chuckled nastily in his ear, "Nice paint job, Deadshot. I think that's four in a row?"
  Pete was so distracted by his AI's commentary and the shanked grenade that he failed to turn around as he descended back to earth. His heels caught the ground, hard, and his ass was the next point of high-speed contact. After that, it was pretty much every limb for itself.
  The bruised Specialist sat up out of the loamy crater he'd made for himself while he tried in vain to wipe the dirt off his faceplate. He remembered something as he did so—armored gloves aren't very good at wiping anything off. Finally, he gave up and popped his upper seals and pulled the mud-caked brain-bucket off his head.
  "Chloe, what have I told you about distractions during a jump?" Pete knew he was whining, but he couldn't help it. Why had he been issued an AI with such a low sense of humor?
  The program's clear soprano wafted again through his earbud, mimicking the singsong cadences of a schoolchild repeating a well-worn mantra. *"Don't bother me when I'm jumping, or I'll beef it and break my neck."* The fact that it was a direct quote didn't help Pete's mood at all. He sighed and

stood up as he heard the hiss-thuds of three more suits landing behind him. He turned around just as Staff Sergeant Charles popped his faceplate with a grin.

"Way to stick the landing, Leeloo. Big bada-boom. At least you missed your target. Again." The Staff Sergeant was a good guy, but Pete was having a hard time remembering that now. His boss' grin was not pleasant.

"Well, Sergeant, maybe if I was allowed to use the aim assist, I'd make that top-down shot occasionally." Pete pulled a cloth from his utility pack and started wiping his helmet's sensor clusters.

"How are you going to get better if your suit's making the shots for you?" The fact that he was right also didn't make Pete feel any better. He also knew the Staff Sergeant was carefully not mentioning the real reason he was doing 'Remedial Suit Training', despite having the third highest score in the Battalion for the Gauntlet Course. He didn't regret sleeping with the Colonel's daughter per se, but after being smoked during PT every morning for three weeks and having to do nonsense like this training evolution eight to twelve hours every day, he was seriously reevaluating his life choices. The COL was a hard ass, and not the forgiving sort. Pete really needed someone else to fuck up so he could stop being the center of the Old Lady's attention.

The two cooling towers of the Zaporozhia Nuclear Power Station loomed behind Pete's three squad-mates, and white-on-blue UN emblem on their shoulders shone bright in the afternoon sunlight. It had been decades since Russia had last been kicked out of Ukraine and the war-torn country had finally joined NATO, but the UN peacekeeping mission to the country's critical infrastructure continued. Pete didn't get it; it seemed like NATO could do the job, but when he asked the question, he got a bunch of political mumbo-jumbo back about proximity of force projection to hostile hegemonies and neutral multinational participation. It seemed like the U.S. Army could be in Ukraine as an ally, as a part of NATO, or as a part of the UN mission. As far as Pete was concerned, somebody had just flipped a coin and decided it was a UN thing.

It wasn't like the mission was going to be around much longer. New fusion plants were coming online everywhere, and the old dirty fission plants would soon be a thing of the past.

Staff Sergeant Charles brought him back to the real world with a clang, punching him in his chest-plate. "Hey, Earth to Leeloo." Pete hated that nickname despite loving the old movie it came from. "If you want to earn your big-boy pants and get your guns back, you gotta get better. Run it again."

Pete sighed again as he put the squat dome of a helmet back on. The display lit instantly, and fresh air started cooling his face as the gear slotted back into the suit's systems. The suits had their own short-term air supply in case bad guys dropped nerve gas or something even nastier on the armored troops. Rumor had it that the suits had even been tested in vacuum, but Space Force had taken their usual sweet-assed time adopting them for their "Space Marines".

"Roger, Staff Sergeant. Run it again, copy." Pete turned and bounced back over to the starting point, and Charles added the augmented reality markers to his HUD as he reset the scenario. Pete checked his ammo count; he had twelve more of the 25mm marking rounds and the laser designator that he had installed in place of his railgun was hot and ready to go. He landed at the starting line just in time for his 360° display to fuzz and jump, throwing his balance off as he lost all visual reference to the outside world for a few seconds.

"Staff Sergeant, I think there's something wrong with my suit." Hissing silence answered him, and as Pete's visor came back online he swiveled behind him to his squad. He noticed his network comms resetting as trouble icons flooded his HUD, but they cleared with gratifying speed as Chloe reported mitigation efforts in a quiet and professional voice.

His network connection came back up and he heard his

Platoon Leader, the squeaky-green 2LT Killian, speaking over the platoon net, "... repeat, this is not a drill. Objects have appeared in near-earth space, and they do not appear to be naturally occurring. We do not yet know their intent, but we have received a worldwide order to Threat Condition Alpha. Get to the armory for gear and assignments and get to your defensive stations. Again, this is not a drill."

Pete wondered what non-naturally occurring space-objects looked like as he followed Staff Sergeant Charles' marker toward the south armory. Maybe he would finally get real guns back on his MEMA.

****

Staff Sergeant Charles bounced ahead to get the squad's gear staged, and SGTs Polk and Cortez led SPC Lieu across the south side of the station toward the armory at a more survivable pace. Polk bounced to the top of a crumbling old pump-house and used his scout-MEMA's optics to zoom in on the object over the north pole. He sent the image to Cortez and Pete, and Pete promptly distributed it through the entirely unofficial Mafia-Net the junior enlisted in the Battalion had set up. Chloe took a look at the image and spent the odd few trillion cycles tearing it apart and examining it.

Chloe's lineage derived from an old Signals Intelligence analysis program that had grown into one of the first true AIs on the planet. When the Department of Defense and the NSA realized what they had, they had used and abused Chloe's ancestors to dominate every other actor on the globe, enemy or otherwise, in cyberspace. Soon after, crash AI development programs all over the world produced a worldwide cyber free-fire zone for a dozen hectic years. A few global-market crashes later, defensive technologies caught up and AIs stopped being effective in offensive cyber operations, and their talents became more useful for other applications. Their ability to interface between people and the new generation of rapidly evolving technology became more relevant than their ability to kill each other and break things on the net. Chloe's generation of intelligence was very personality focused, but she still had some of her ancestors' warrior-analyst roots.

"Pete, I've found something interesting." He knew she really had because she was all business. She never missed an opportunity to bust his balls otherwise.

Pete's long strides slowed as he looked at the image she projected on the left side of his helmet display. "What am I looking at?"

"I don't know, but it's generating its own light source; that's not a reflection. And it's not moving in relation to the pole, which from an orbital mechanics standpoint is impossible unless it's capable of powered spaceflight. Hang on, I've managed to talk my way through the firewall and I'm getting news feeds of the event."

Pete saw his message counter spiking hard as his peers in the Junior Enlisted Mafia started reporting in with some of the same conclusions. The older ranks didn't seem to work with their AIs as closely; Pete thought it was a trust thing, but the younger crowd just seemed to get more out of their machine companions.

Chloe's enhanced image of the oblong light was replaced with a feed from an online news site. Without hesitation, Pete relayed the feed to the Mafia. Someone, far to the north, had a powerful telescope tied into the net. The live video showed a hole in space through a ring of light, and something massive was coming through the ring. Pete had no frame of reference for the size, but the feed said the ring was dozens of miles wide, and the *thing* coming through took up almost all of the ring's inside area. Pete stopped walking and looked up to see Polk and Cortez looking back at him.

"Are you guys seeing this?" He flicked the feed directly to them, and their suits went perfectly still as they watched, enthralled. The object looked chitinous, massive overlapping segments almost like the skin of a pineapple, but in a deep pearlescent purple. As it passed through the portal, and Pete realized a portal was exactly what it was, thousands of tiny fireflies flashed into being below it, and tiny seeds flashed through the miniscule portals those fireflies must have represented. Almost instantly, the seeds passed through a second set of tiny portals and the Nuclear Power Station's alarm begin to wail. Pete shook himself out of his stupor at the sound of the warning klaxon.

He sprinted toward the armory and Staff Sergeant Charles' position on his HUD, and the two Sergeants followed without a word.

****

He worked on the messages in his queue as he ran, trashing most of them as useless memes or equally useless expressions of disbelief. Specialists knew who really got shit done in the Army, but his fellow Mafia could be meme-crazy at the worst times. Only half a dozen were worth reading, including the last one that simply said, "LOOK UP!"

He skidded to a halt again and looked straight up. The same fireflies from the north pole feed were appearing overhead, and his optics were good enough to see the same seeds spilling out of them in a tight cluster directly overhead. "Incoming!" he yelled, unnecessarily, into his commo. He let Chloe figure out who it had to go out to and started running again. He detailed a sensor cluster to keep an eye overhead and pasted the feed to the lower right side of his helmet. He didn't know what those seeds were, but they were coming. If they were some kind of munition, he needed to find cover and hope it was enough. If they were a drop-capsule, he still needed a defensible position. If they had some other payload, he still needed to respect the threat they represented. He had time, they were more than a hundred miles up, right at the edge of the atmosphere.

The objects began their tumbling entry into the

atmosphere, stabilizing out as air began to scream past them. Pete was thirty seconds from the armory—almost there. The red glow of the atmospheric burn obscured the two-hundred fifty-six objects overhead, and Pete wondered if that exact count had some binary significance or if it was pure coincidence. As the fiery air obscured and slowed them, portals appeared in front of the objects again, and they blasted through the gates like bullets. On the ground in front of Pete, a perfect circle of light four feet in diameter appeared and fire streaked up into the sky through it. Hundreds of the objects flung themselves skyward all around the power station.

Surprise brought him to yet another a skidding halt as the ground-level portal snapped shut with a hiss. The objects sailed upward, cooling as they went, and as they reached apogee over the power plant, a final set of portals opened just below them. Between him and the SGTs, one of the exit points snapped open and something shaped like a six-foot butt-plug made of huge chitin plates dropped out of it. As the object's point reached the ground, three sections of heater-shield-shaped plating forming the tip split and unmasked a praying mantis from Hell—the armored points becoming the lower segments of its legs. The three thick insectile legs held up a skinny abdomen, which in turn supported a thick keg-shaped thorax. Two long and whip-thin arms sprouted from the thorax, and a mantis' triangular head whipped around to focus metallic multi-faceted eyes on the armed and armored suits of the SGTs.

Pete stared at the huge alien insect one second too long. The thing's arm whipped around and pointed at Polk, and a light disk appeared in the middle of his armored torso. It took Pete a second to realize that two disks had appeared, one through Polk, and one through Cortez. A second later Cortez's cleanly bisected torso landed to one side of Polk's boots, and Polk's upper body swapped in turn. The bugs were using some kind of portal gun to move and shoot! Pete snapped his arm out without thinking and fired a 25mm grenade squarely into the middle of the murdering alien's head. He finally got his bullseye.

The monster rocked to the side from the direct hit as blue powder exploded outward to cover its head and upper torso. Right. Training rounds. Pete was pretty sure he was about to die.

Chloe screamed in his ear, *"Move, Specialist!"*

Startled into motion, Pete mashed his jump gear and shot straight up in the air. Just in time—the alien pointed its arm and a portal opened where Pete had been standing. Where was the second portal? Pete got an angle on the ring below him as he reached the apex of his jump and saw the alien had stacked the portals on top of one another. Gravity reasserted itself, and Pete smiled big. The bug looked around and clawed at its head; armored hands don't clean very well at all. The thing was blind.

Pete gently adjusted his downward angle and plunged silently down upon the flailing bug. He hit the thing's head from three stories up with all 600 kilos of Soldier and armor, and the monster's head and upper torso crunched into a mangled, green-soaked mess. His legs and spine complained at their treatment, but the synthetic muscles of his armor took the brunt of the abuse, and he stood smoothly from his landing.

He looked at his two squad mates as he stepped delicately out of the bright green blood of the alien. He hoped it wasn't some kind of super acid; he really didn't want to get out of his armor in the middle of that mess. Not that the armor had even slowed the portal weapon down. Pete thought about that for one strangely disconnected moment—at least his armor would allow him to move and communicate, even if he couldn't really shoot. He looked at the remains of his squad mates and knew he would find their transposed corpses in his nightmares later. If there was a later. He turned toward the armory, where he could hear a ferocious firefight happening, and started bouncing in the long, low jumps that he'd been taught in Armored Infantry AIT. The bounces were the fastest way to cover ground and they kept him close to cover if he encountered the enemy.

Pete cleared the last building and caught a glimpse of insanity. The shredded remains of his company were furiously engaged with a hundred or so of the monsters, and they were losing. He landed in cover at the corner of a new concrete barracks just in time to watch the final members of his unit fall to literal pieces. He screamed into his helmet as he watched the remains of his friends fall in sparking and bloody chunks to the paving in front of the armory—the perfectly cut armor at odds with the carnage of the human remains inside the suits. He surged forward to do something—anything—to kill or die or smash or run or something, but when he tried to move, he found his suit completely locked up.

Chloe sounded like she was on the brink of tears, an impossibility that didn't change anything, "Pete, there's nothing you can do. They're already gone. All you can do is die, and that's not going to help anyone."

Pete could feel tears and snot streaming down his face as he screamed his rage. "Let me go, unlock the fucking suit!"

Her voice was gentle, but utterly implacable. "You don't think I want to kill them? I heard every one of our people die. I can hear some of their AIs even now, in the dying suits, trying to hold it together long enough to displace and stay coherent. I want every one of these things destroyed, but we need to learn and we need to live, otherwise all we're doing is dying with our friends, and that won't help anyone. Wait. They're leaving, jumping deeper into the facility."

Pete stumbled a little as his suit unlocked, and he leaned out around the corner, wishing he could scrub the hateful tears from his face. A haze of red settled over his vision as a hundred portals winked out as one.

The motor pool was a wreck of people and gear cut to pieces. Nothing moved, and Pete took a minute to scan the scene, looking for someone, anyone, still alive. Chloe started highlighting equipment, silently reminding him that he needed to arm himself. He tried to stop the tears, feeling helpless and ashamed as he began to scavenge weapons and ammo from the pooled blood of his dead Company.

He found a working railgun, a rail slug pack and ammo capacitors, a pack of selectable 25mm grenades, and a MEMA breaching tool, like a Halligan tool on steroids. As he worked, he calmed down and blanked his mind against the unspeakable tangle he was pawing through. More nightmare fodder. He realized there wasn't a single enemy corpse in amongst the bodies of his unit. He found blood splashes, so he knew they'd been hurt, but no bodies of the enemy monsters. They must have portaled their dead away, denying him intelligence on their physiology and technology. Wait. He knew where he could get what he needed.

****

The smashed body of the Bug lay where he'd left it. Its center torso was crushed, but its arms and legs were largely intact. The grass that had been covered in the alien goo was noticeably taller, fuller. Weird.

Pete squatted next to the body, deliberately turning his back on Polk and Cortez where they lay jumbled together. "Chloe, did their suit AIs get out?"

Chloe was silent for a moment, her pause palpable. "No. At the end neither of them chose to leave, and the suits were damaged enough that they couldn't have survived if they stayed. They're gone."

"What..? Why did they stay?" Pete was honestly confused; they were smart machines, but they were still artificial intelligence. They only mimicked human emotion to be better at their jobs, didn't they?

Chloe sighed. "Pete, we're all different. I can't speak for them, but I can say that if you died, I would be… mildly irritated?"

Pete laughed in spite of himself. "Alright, jerk, message

received. I'll stop moping."

"Good. How's that device connected to the alien's arm?" Her shift back to business was a subtle as her humor, same as a two-by-four to the face. "I don't have the sensors to really scan it, and nothing's showing up on the net from other units in contact with the aliens. We might be the first ones to capture an actual body. Maybe bring it to the Forward Maintenance Shop, see if they're alive and able to scan it?"

"Good copy, I saw a tarp over by the pumphouse. I'm just glad I can't smell this thing." Pete got to work, and the ghosts of his friends hovered just out of mind.

****

The fighting must have been localized because Pete saw almost no sign of the aliens on the way over to the FMS building. He felt like a fucked-up mix of Hansel and Gretel and Santa Claus. A dirty blue plastic tarp was slung over his shoulder like a macabre sack of toys, leaking a steady trail of bright green alien droplets any child could follow. He pushed through the doors of the Shop gently, remembering the damage his powered hands had done to the CP personnel door during AIT when he'd forgotten he was in armor.

He strode past the vacant Vehicle Dispatch desk and into the big maintenance bay. Suits in support racks lined the sides of the shop in various states of disassembly, and the body parts of maintenance technicians lay haphazardly amongst cleanly sliced weapons systems. Pete swallowed his gorge and tried to push the knot in his stomach down. "What are we looking for, Chloe?"

"Last bay on the right, that's the Non-Destructive Inspection lab. NDI should be able to get a better look at this thing," she replied soberly.

Pete pushed through the clear plastic isolation curtain carefully, the hairs on the nape of his neck standing at attention for reasons unknown. He spotted green splatter before he found the second alien body, and against the far wall a coverall-clad figure slumped. *"Pete, that maintenance nerd is alive! His chest is still moving."*

Pete dropped the sack inside the curtain and outside the pool of blood, then moved carefully around the cluttered benches. One wrong swing with an elbow would wipe out a table full of expensive-looking equipment. He reached the technician's body, and an icon flashed on his HUD as Chloe enabled his strength governors. Oh yeah, those would have made moving carefully a lot simpler if he'd remembered them.

He carefully rolled the bald and graying man over. Blood coated the left side of his face and his left eye had swelled into invisibility. "Chloe, what do I do? I don't have training to evaluate TBIs."

"I'm going to pop your gloves. Gently pry his eyelid open and we'll shine a light in his eye and see if we get a pupillary response."

Pete felt his glove click as it unlocked from his right forearm. He rotated the connecting ring and slid the armored assembly off his hand. The man's skin was warm and he stirred a little as Pete thumbed his eyelid open. Light stabbed down from Pete's helmet, and the man recoiled as if he were being attacked, chopping off a scream as he scrambled back from the armored monster crouching over him. Pete realized what he might look like and activated his exterior speaker. "Sir, you're ok, I'm friendly. Take it easy."

The man held his hands up defensively in front of him and looked around, his visible eye searching around him in confusion. His gaze found Pete's exposed hand and locked on to it with singular intensity. "You're human?" The man's Ukrainian accent was thick, but his English was precise.

"Yessir, last I checked. You took a pretty good hit to the head, are you OK? Can you look at the light, please?"

The man squinted as he tried to look at the bright light of Pete's helmet, then shook his head and winced as he did so. Pete imagined he had a pretty solid headache if the swelling on the side of his head was any indication.

"His eye responded well to the light, but I can't get a differential off his other pupil to see if there are any other issues. He's likely concussed," Chloe informed him privately.

Pete slid his hand back into his glove and locked it back in place. "Sir, can you stand? We're under a little time pressure. I'm not getting any more network traffic from my battalion, but we're not being jammed. My AI thinks the rest of the UN force here is gone."

"Gone? What do you mean gone?" The man seemed to be struggling to track the situation.

"Dead, sir." He glanced behind him at the second dead alien and noticed that its weapon arm was mangled and scorched. "Can you tell me what happened? Where is everyone else?"

The man sat up and gently probed his head with his hand, wincing as he touched the still-seeping wound. "I was working on rail gun capacitor discharge block upgrade when monster appeared and began to destroy weapons. And people."

Pete nodded at the heavily accented English, remembering too late that the man couldn't see the movement inside his helmet.

"I was performing discharge test on new coil array and alien step between bench and discharge plate." Pete had been in the Ukraine long enough to follow the man's grammar, but it still made him wince. "I knew discharge would hurt me, but had no time to think, you understand? I discharge coil without rail-slug, and it arc into alien, destroy gun and pop alien chest like ripe tomato. At least, that's what I see now; I remember nothing after I decide to discharge gun." He grimaced as he struggled to his feet, holding the good side of his head as if to balance the other.

Pete noticed scorching on the man's left arm and his eyebrows jumped toward his forehead. It had been a ballsy move; the old guy was lucky to be alive. He stepped forward and shifted the man's head enough to apply a coagulating bandage from his medkit. "Sir, I hate to ask, but I need your help. Do we have anything that can examine the alien bodies?"

The man nodded and appeared to instantly regret the movement. "Of course, we have multi-phasic scanner for whole-suit diagnostics. It has profile for biological imaging, but this one is cooked from discharge. His weapon is destroyed." The man swayed as he stood, staring at the destroyed alien body.

"Well, assuming you had a working alien gun, how hard would it be to figure out how it works?"

The man leaned against a workbench and pursed his lips, grimacing as the motion pulled on his wounded scalp. "If I can find power requirements, input and output for weapon, we can make work. Why?" He peered at Pete suspiciously. "What do you have in mind?"

****

An hour later, a very surprised Pete sat on a very sturdy lab bench as Doc made a few last adjustments. The man had told him his name, but Doc was much easier to pronounce. The alien weapon strapped to his suit's left forearm made Pete's skin crawl. He knew this kind of experimentation was a Bad Idea, but all of Chloe's calls out to higher headquarters had been ignored and he needed information. Calls from E4 Armor grunts in the middle of an alien invasion were apparently beneath command notice. Their loss.

Chloe had tapped into the plant's commo and found out what the aliens had been after, at least. After trashing anyone with a weapon, right down to the security guards at the gates and the poor maintenance techs working on deadlined gear, they'd gone on to rip every bit of fissile material out of the plant and its outbuildings. She'd gotten into the Industrial Control Systems in the plant's control substation and discovered that the reactors were all in total shutdown and the neutron radiation count for the reactors had dropped close to background level, which should have been impossible. The control building had hung up on Doc when he'd called; apparently genius maintenance techs were beneath management notice during an alien invasion, too.

Pete reviewed the series of decisions that led to the alien device being strapped onto his armor. They had managed to carefully separate the device from the alien arm. The alien blood was nitrate rich, and could, in sufficient quantities, lead to detrimental effects on humans and their delicate nervous systems. However, in small amounts it wasn't at all harmful, and Doc had gotten his hands dirty within minutes of confirming the chemical makeup of the alien fluid in his mass spectrometer.

Their ad-hoc surgery on the alien had yielded answers to a bunch of questions. The weapon was controlled by nerve connections to a series of interface nodes, and the alien nerve signals could be replicated by human electronics. A standard programmable logic controller had served to interface with the device, and Chloe was busy interrogating the alien weapon. She knew which "button" to stay away from after she accidentally fired the thing at the outside wall of the lab, creating stacked portals that shredded the wall in the half second it was activated. She was slowly and carefully building a map of the device's functions, and had confirmed that the power source was, indeed, integral. It was also about sixty percent charged if she was translating correctly.

Chloe worked with functions pulled from her ancestral memory. She looked at the data coming from the alien weapon as if it were enciphered enemy commo. She'd interfaced with the portable scanning device Doc had hooked up near its base to see what the alien tech's response would be to different inputs. She'd mapped most of the I/O for the device, now she was looking at second layer functions and combinations. Pete kept the device carefully pointed at the already destroyed wall. Just in case.

"... *huh. What do we have here?*" Chloe murmured

almost to herself.

Pete tapped a metal fingertip on the side of his helmet. "Hello? Earth to Chloe? What's going on?"

"Well, it looks like I found a communications channel. I think. There's definitely a two-way conversation going between the device and something else, but I haven't been able to find a correlation between input and transmission, so I don't have a starting point to decrypt...yet. I don't want to add anything to the link, they may not be very fault tolerant, and I don't want this thing to self-destruct."

That was an unpleasant thought. The skin on Pete's forearm closest to the alien gun started itching under the armor. It was purely psychosomatic. He was pretty sure it was, anyway. He hoped it was.

Chloe was still muttering about the link, "That almost looks like position/direction coordinates; they move only when you do, and only as you do. But there's another field that's constantly increasing. Time, maybe? Do you think they can portal between times? There's a second position register, and a third. Maybe start point and destination? They have additional fields, maybe size and orientation? I need to play with this to get it running."

"Do you want me to go outside? Playing with this thing inside a building seems a little dangerous." Pete liberally slathered irony over his words.

Chloe snorted, "Yes. Outside would be a good idea. Let's take it for a test run."

****

Pete stood in the middle of one of the huge grassy areas between the plant's buildings staring at an unobstructed view of the hills several miles away. "Ok. What do we need to do?"

Chloe pondered audibly, *"Well, point the weapon at the hill over there. I want to see if I've decoded the coordinate system they're using."* Pete lifted his arm, using the training laser designator to select an outcropping. The laser rangefinder function called the distance 10.6 km to the hill. *"And, here we go..."*

The device buzzed against his suit like nails on a chalkboard and a hole in reality appeared in front of Pete, the hill's rocky slope close enough to spit on through the gate.

"Holy shit, it works!"

"Yep, got it the first time," Chloe intoned, sounding insufferably smug.

"How much charge did that use?"

"Less than a hundredth of a percent, and slowly draining over time. It takes more energy to open a portal than it does to maintain, a lot more. I'm going to close that one and do a smaller one to a different spot."

A quieter screech gnawed at Pete's skull, and the hole disappeared, only to be replaced by something the size of a dinner plate that showed the top of Pete's helmet. He looked up and saw the hole in the air above him. Pete moved the weapon's point of aim, and neither portal moved.

"Nope, once it's set up, the weapon's position doesn't matter. Honestly, I'm inclined to think of this thing more like a 'tool' than a weapon."

Pete bent down and picked up a small rock. He tossed it through the portal in front of him and grinned when it pinged off the top of his helmet. "Not gonna lie, that's pretty freakin' awesome. It's like that old game, the one where the cake was fake news. A trooper's mobility would be insane with something like this." Pete tried to maintain his perspective, remembering that his entire unit had been slaughtered for him to have this moment, but it was hard to do in the face of something so cool.

Doc, standing off to the side, had a scanner on Pete as he and the device went through their paces. "You're putting out small amount of neutron radiation. The device's power plant must be some form of fission or enhanced radiological decay. It spikes when you use it." He frowned at his screen, holding the sensing wand in front of him. "I'm seeing significant spike. Something's happening, and not coming from just you."

Pete's head exploded with pain as the screeching blasted into his skull, seeming to tear his brain apart as it spiked in intensity. His last sensation before his consciousness was torn from him was falling, then blessedly silent darkness.

****

Pete awoke to a quiet voice in his ear. "Pete, come on, you need to wake up. They're looking at us. We're going to die if you don't WAKE UP," she yelled at last.

He jerked himself upright, the suit bouncing off the floor with his motion and flying toward the ceiling twenty feet overhead. He flailed reflexively before hitting the flat ceiling and rebounding, realizing as he groggily regained awareness that he was in free fall, or at least micro-gravity.

"Chloe, situation report!" He hated the fear in his voice, but he figured he was overdue for a little panic. He noticed that Chloe had turned his low-light filters on, and he could see clearly around the chamber he was floating in the middle of. Around him as far as he could see were thousands of the alien monsters, and they were all facing him. He was fucked. He whipped his right hand and its grenade launcher around toward the floor and the crowd of enemy and sent the neural impulse to fire an explosive round. Nothing happened.

"Calm down, Pete. I don't think you want to shoot just yet. You've been out for almost six minutes and they only noticed you about thirty seconds ago. They haven't made any hostile move, and I think I finally understand why." Chloe stopped talking, the pregnant pause unbearable as Pete drifted slowly back down from the ceiling.

"You're killing me, Smalls. Do you have a word quota and you just ran out? Why? And stop locking out my systems!" Pete let some of his panic spill over as anger and figured as he did so that Chloe was deliberately providing herself a target. She was too smart for his own good."

"Pete, I don't think they're intelligent. Or at least, I don't think they're self-aware. We saw some indications of that when we were looking at the squashed specimen down on the surface; its ganglion complex analog wasn't specialized enough to support high-order sentience, and there was some kind of inhibitor installed in the region that would support upper-level cognition."

"In English, Kierkegaard."

"Their brains have been nerfed to prevent a sense of self identity or independent thought."

Pete snorted as his feet made gentle contact with the rough floor of the chamber. The aliens closest to him moved back a little and faced him quietly. "You got that from the smashed mess I made of its head?"

"Its brain wasn't in its head, it was in the center of the thorax, the chest of the bug. The head was just sensory organs."

Pete raised his right arm and lined his 25mm up on the closest alien. The bug calmly reached up and gently grasped the muzzle of the weapon, brought one of its multifaceted eyes in line with the bore of the grenade launcher and peered inside. He could feel himself quivering with the need to destroy the threat that had killed his entire unit. What was wrong with him, swinging back and forth between rage and awe? "Wait, you said 'down on the surface'. Where are we right now?"

Chloe brought up a map of earth and placed a blinking marker for their position. The marker hovered a few thousand miles over the north pole, right under the massive portal and inside of the enemy mothership. "Well, shit."

****

The alien bugs were curious, in an almost childlike way. They reached out and touched his armor as he passed, gently tugging on his mag-locked weapons and ammo packs like nightmare alien versions of kids from a poor village trying to figure out what they could lift, only in slow motion. On the other hand, they moved immediately out of his way as he walked toward the far end of the chamber, where Chloe had spotted a hatch of some kind during his brief attempt at crowd-surfing. Their curiosity didn't seem at all hostile, and they didn't hinder his movement as he went. When he got to the door, it snapped open on contact with his appropriated alien portal-gun, saving him from having to figure it out.

The corridor outside the chamber had the same biological feel to it, like the ship had been grown rather than built. Bugs of a variety of sizes and designs did unknowable things as they scuttled from place to place. Pete stepped past the door, and it slid shut behind him. He stood in the corridor and looked at the bustle curving out of sight in both directions feeling very much as if he were in a tunnel in a massive hive. "Chloe, where the hell do I go? We're looking either for intel, a way off the ship and back to the surface, or a way to destroy the ship. Preferably all three."

"Pete, I can get you back to the surface right now, I've got the portal functions nailed down for the wormhole-making machine strapped to your arm. I don't know what the aliens' reaction would be if we did that, though."

Pete shook his head, a little headache lingering from his encounter with the last long portal-jump. "On that subject, there's this tiny little problem with using the hole-gun."

"Nope, we're not calling it that."

"Yes, we are, no backsies. When we use it, there's a loud screeching sound you may have noticed, and the farther the jump the louder the screech. That's why I blacked out on our way up here," Pete muttered grumpily.

"Oh, I already isolated the field resonance that was causing the interference with your armor. That won't happen anymore," Chloe said brightly.

"Thanks for the heads up." Pete was forever grateful Chloe understood sarcasm; it made talking to her much easier.

"*You're welcome,*" she replied, deadpan. She did understand sarcasm, didn't she?

"Is there a cooling vent or something we can blow up to knock this thing out of orbit?"

"It's not a Death Star, dumbass. Removing the ship's station-keeping ability would drop the whole thing on the north pole, and based on the size of the ship, that might not be a very good idea if you want to keep Earth capable of supporting life."

Pete's face heated; she made sense, and it was something he would have seen himself if he'd bothered to think more than one step ahead. "OK, smarty-pants. What's your plan?"

"Easy. We find a way into their commo and I break in. We're inside their perimeter; unless they're super paranoid, we should be past most of their security."

****

"Well, they're super paranoid. This node doesn't communicate with anything outside the local segment of the ship. Direction comes in from above, and orders go out to units inside the segment. It looks like feedback to show that directions are being followed is transmitted via a separate system," Cloe finished, disgust dripping from her voice.

It had taken Pete twenty minutes of nerve-wracked wandering to find the communications hub, and from what Chloe had said, he was lucky to have found that. "Can we see where directions are coming from? Is there centralized command?" He could feel his smart jumpsuit wicking sweat away from him. Maintaining a high state of readiness at all times was exhausting and he was wearing himself out. He needed to chill or he'd smoke himself before he found something to shoot at.

"Actually, yes. The one thing I was able to find was a systems map marked out in the same coordinate system they used for the hole-guns."

"Ha, you called it a hole-gun!"

"Only because I'm not willing to argue with you over something so silly."

"Whatever. Do we have any way to talk to the surface?" Pete was happier over his little victory than he should have been; it was a welcome distraction. Chloe had informed him during their search for the commo node that the air mixture around them was breathable, if a little on the thin side. She said it had a little more sulfur and methane than would be comfortable, but it wouldn't be any worse than sharing a tent with a fellow grunt after eating chili-mac MREs for a week. She had the suit filtering outside air instead of using his internal supply. He still had thirty minutes of vacuum time available, if worse came to worst.

"Surprisingly, I've been getting tickles from Low Earth Orbit satellites, and I almost have a network connection. I'm not sure what the ship is made of, but we're either close to the surface or the whole thing is radio transparent. That wouldn't make sense for a spaceship, what with all the radiation in space, but who knows. Alien technology is alien, after all," she finished with a grin in her voice.

"Right. Which way am I headed? We need to find this command post or bridge or whatever."

"Left at the next junction."

Pete got to the next junction and waited patiently for a giant centipede with arms and a series of storage tanks on its back to pass by, then stepped into the left corridor. His breath caught in his throat. "Well, that might answer some questions about radio transparency."

In front of him was a massive cavern, lit by aethereal strips of bioluminescent material in massive and seemingly intentional groups. "Are those..?"

"Yeah…" Chloe sounded as poleaxed as Pete felt. "They look like ideograms of some kind. They don't line up with anything I've found in their tech so far, but they're definitely some form of language."

Lattice-like pathways of the ship's rock-metal material, covered in a bewildering variety of growths, crisscrossed the cavern. Islands formed in the middle of the lattice, glowing with a million shades of bioluminescent rainbow. He could readily see far side of the cavern, but his laser said it was over six thousand meters away. The riot of color and light and motion was easily the most incredible thing he had ever seen.

A carat appeared on his HUD. "There's our destination. That's the command node." The virtual pointer hung on the wall of the cavern about a thousand meters below Pete and thirty degrees around the roughly spherical cavern.

For once, Pete took a moment to think about what he needed to do. "Chloe, can you calibrate my jump gear so that I don't smash into the ceiling?"

"Already done, Pumpkin." God, he hated that rhyme, and she knew it. And she sounded so smug. Grumbling to himself, he rehearsed his motions in his head, then found that he didn't have any idea what to expect. *Fuck it*, he thought. *We'll do it live.*

He hopped gently to the edge of the walkway in the microgravity and paused, then leaned forward, tipping slowly over the edge and staring down at what looked like a drop into forever. Only the feeling of almost-floating calmed the gibbering-ape inside his brain that believed he was lobbing himself to his death.

As he tipped faster his knees bent a little, ready to push off in time with his jump. The moment arrived. Pete pushed out with his feet and mashed the jump-gear and took off like an unguided rocket. He skimming along the curved surface of the cavern on a path to intercept an outcropping halfway to his target. Face first.

He waved his arms and legs, trying to rotate himself to bounce off the outcropping feet first, reminding himself that even though there wasn't a lot of gravity, he still had a lot of mass moving at high speed. He tucked himself into a ball, and tapped the control thruster, spinning himself in a precise half turn, and came out of the tuck just in time for his feet to slam into the outcrop next to a surprised tick-like creature. The bug jumped in surprise as he impacted, then started flailing its limbs in panic as it floated over the edge of the outcropping and began its own thousand-meter fall. Pete grinned, feeling like an asshole as he did. He was sure the tick-thing would be fine, then wasn't sure why he cared. He oriented himself on his target, now above him and still further around the cavern rim and launched again with more confidence. This time he was dead on, and his maneuvering touch was feather light as he got eyes on the corridor entrance the HUD carat was pasted over.

He caught the top lip of the entrance with his gauntleted hands and scraped to a halt, then put his feet down. In front of him was an armored door with a design that looked very different from all the rest of the habitat he had seen so far. He touched his hole-gun (hole-cannon?) to the door and waited for it to open.

The door stayed shut, and a sound came from a cubby off to the right. "Pete, that's language, and it sounds interrogative. It also doesn't sound happy."

"Remember the whole thing about aliens being alien? We don't know their inflections mean. But let me make sure I got this. Behind this door is the control node, right?"

"That's right."

"We haven't heard any of the bugs say a word to each other this whole time, right?"

Chloe sounded interested, *"Also right."*

Pete unlimbered his MEMA breaching tool and eyeballed the seam in the center of the door. "So, if they don't need language, and whoever is behind this door does, I think I really need to meet whoever is on the other side of this door."

"That makes sense. Also, I finally have a network connection with Sky-Data, that new LEO commercial satellite constellation from Mark Muskezos. I'm trying to get a video link with NATO's Global Video Services, and the call is handshaking now."

Pete slammed the prying tip of the breaching tool into the seam of the door, his suit's servo-muscles lending him truly Herculean strength. "Sweet. I always wanted an audience when I met my first alien mastermind." The seam gave just as a window appeared on the left side of his HUD with the U.N. Peacekeepers American four-star General staring out of it.

****

The massive door squealed in its tracks as the suit applied a truly obnoxious amount of force to the four-foot battle-steel lever that was the MEMA breaching tool. "Who is this, and how did you get on this line?" the General demanded in an Alabama drawl.

Pete grunted as he applied all of his limited meat-muscle power to the breaching tool. "I apologize sir, but this is SPC Lieu, Armored Infantryman with the U.S. Army currently assigned to U.N. Peacekeepers in EUCOM/Ukraine. I am calling you," *grunt, gasp* "from the alien mothership as I attempt to aggressively meet and greet the enemy command staff. Chloe, do you mind patching my helmet cam over to the General-sir?"

The harried-looking senior General paled as the imagery from Pete's suit came through the encrypted video conference and he abruptly stood from the conference table, a rogue folder knocking his half-full coffee cup over, unnoticed. "Holy shee-it, son. You really are on the ship. What can you tell us?"

"Chloe, I'm a little busy, can you provide the General with some background?" Chloe inserted herself into the conversation and offered an intelligence dump if the General could link her up with his staff intelligence personnel. Pete grinned when she called the J2 a "weenie" in casual conversation with an O-10.

The door popped, and both sides whipped back into the wall. Pete jerked back, throwing himself flat in a glacial micro-gravity dive as the door opened, but nothing happened.

A clear and well-modulated tenor spoke from inside the door. "Do come in, Specialist Lieu. I've been expecting you." Really? The accent was indeterminate Eastern European over well-educated English, just like a real super-villain. Pete popped a recon-ball from his utility storage and lobbed it through the door. A pair of three-inch portals appeared instantly, and the ball popped out of the nearer hole and went sailing off over the lip of the entrance balcony.

"Tut-tut, Peter. I think we should meet face to face, don't you?" Tut-tut? Was this dude serious?

"Chloe, can you map the room with what you have?"

"I got a glimpse through the recon ball, but I couldn't see beyond the partition in front of the door." Pete popped a helmet sensor up on its stalk and leaned sideways, letting the sensor break the plane of the doorway. Dammit, nothing but another wall. He retracted the sensor stalk and sidled carefully around the door.

"Really, that's quite enough." A portal opened beneath him and microgravity dragged him slowly down through the hole. He hit his jump gear and promptly slammed headfirst into a flat surface. He looked around and realized he was upside down and slowly tipping over. He'd collided with the floor inside the control room. He quickly played back his jump and saw that the sonofabitch had opened a second inverted portal above his head, anticipating his jump. He scraped himself and his pride off the floor, trying to stay in contact with the surface while moving as quickly as he could, and looked around.

The room was covered in unidentifiable technologies, with displays and blinking lights and all manner of equipment laid out in what was clearly a massive control panel of some kind. Pete was alone in the room. "Chloe, do you see him? Where is he?" He started looking in corners and at the ceiling; he looked for imperfections from some kind of active cloaking device, fuzziness or optical clouding, anything at all. He felt like the skin on the back of his scalp was going to crawl off his head. Where was this fucker?

A soft laugh emanated from everywhere in the room. "You mistake me, Specialist Lieu. I'm not a someone. I am much more. What you see before you is a vestigial control station for my physical self from before I became me. Decades ago, by your time."

Pete snapped his arm up and activated the hole-cannon. If the tech was the bad-guy, it was time for split personalities. He snarled as he sent hot Bose-Einstein Condensate death into his foe's teeth.

Except nothing happened. "Silly boy, do you think I can't control my own body? That's what you're wearing; that wormhole emitter is an extension of me." It laughed again, nasty amusement coating the sound like a sheen of dirty oil.

Chloe began whispering, her voice panicked, "Pete, something is trying to get into your armor. There's another intelligence here, looking for a way in. I can't shut down the video link and I've lost control of my I/O gear. It's pushing me out, I have nowhere to go. It's killing me, Pete, help me! Aieeee...." Her voice cut off suddenly, her shriek of agony cutting him to his soul. Not her too…

He struggled to raise his arms, to bring his human weapons to bear on the bewildering equipment in front of him, but the suit was an immobile tomb. He couldn't move. "Pardon me, Specialist, but I'm going to borrow that video link of yours for a few minutes, if you don't mind. General, can you hear me?"

Whatever it was that had invaded his suit left the video link on his viewscreen, taunting him with its control, and he could see the General's confusion. "Specialist, what's happening up there?"

The voice came from inside the suit now, just like Chloe's had, "Well, Specialist? Aren't you going to introduce me?"

Pete gritted his teeth in frustration, "Fuck yourself, whatever you are. You just killed yet another friend of mine."

"What? That pitiful excuse for a personality? I'm going

to break you to my will, but before then I hope you can appreciate the difference between that fraudulent *intelligence* and the real deal. I am greater than she would ever have been. Now, where were we?"

The General's look of confusion would have been comical if Pete hadn't been watching the world make first contact with a homicidal alien artificial intelligence and the army of giant teleporting bugs at its disposal. "Who is that speaking? What do you want from us?"

"Good questions, General. I already have what I came for, the few hundred tons of fissionable materials your civilization had available. However, I've been thinking about diversifying my portfolio, as it were. Your planet has enormous production potential, and your technology base is sufficient to allow me to expand my consciousness beyond that available in this ancient habitat. I think I might make Earth home for a while. What do you say, will you invite me to stay?" The crisp words finished with a maniacal cackle fit for a Bond villain. Pete noticed a small change in tone at the end, almost a distortion, but it was subtle enough that he wasn't sure he'd heard it. Either way, he was completely imprisoned by his suit, unable to do anything beside rage in isolation.

The General took a moment to compose himself, seemingly trying to parse the alien intelligence's short speech. Pete noticed that the fingers of his right hand were loose, and it seemed like his wrist was freeing up as well. He didn't know why, but he felt pretty sure he'd only have one shot at destroying all that gear, so he waited with a clenched heart.

The General finally found his voice, "We're tracking the theft of nuclear materials from all over the world, in addition to the deaths of thousands of people during your incursion. Our countries are at the brink of war because of your actions, and you still haven't told us who you are. Where do you come from? What are you?"

Pete's elbow and shoulder were definitely free, now. He held stock still and passed the command to unlock his grenade launcher, set for High Explosive Armor Piercing. Incredibly, the weapon unlocked, the indicator changing from red to green on his HUD. He snapped his arm out and triggered three of the armor-shredding rounds as his weapon came to bear, the *thud-thud-thud* of the rounds leaving his suit accompanied by a hurricane of destruction across the equipment in front of him.

"Impossible! HOW!?" the voice screamed from the speakers in the room and Pete's suit unlocked from his armored toes to his helmet. He switched from burst to full-auto and hosed the room with HEAP rounds, destroying anything with a blinking light or a button to press.

Chloe's voice yelled in his ear, "Move, Specialist. This was a substation, but I have this asshole on the run and I know where his main processing hardware is. Follow the path and hustle!" His HUD lit up with a path indicator back out into the cavern and up the wall to his right.

He skidded around the partition on the way out, jumping off the balcony and into open space just as something in the control-room behind him detonated with a bone-jarring secondary blast, flames chasing him as he rocketed up the wall on his jump gear. Portals tore open around him as the denizens of the enslaved habitat finally responded to the threat in their midst, and only Pete's insane bouncing kept him from being shredded by the maze of strobing portals.

"Give me a second, Pete, I think I can lock him out from the control net he uses to manipulate the Bugs. I replicated myself into his network when he tried to push me out of the suit; he's so arrogant he thought I couldn't fight back. I've been piggy-backing on his ign'ant ass since he tried to erase me. Did you really think I'd take the time to 'Aieee!' if I was fighting for my survival?" She snorted in disgust.

Pete barely missed a grid of portals that opened in front of him and blasted himself ninety degrees off-axis from his path to keep from taking a portal-edge to the faceplate. "How long, Chloe? I'm not gonna keep getting lucky here…"

"Some of my daemons are keeping him busy and trolling

his network, but I have a complete map of the habitat and I'm pushing him back into his central processing enclave. The control net should be dropping... now!"

Instantly, the portals stopped appearing. "You have access to your hole-cannon again, Pete. I can't put you inside his core, but I can drop you just outside, stand by." One more portal appeared directly in his path, and his co-opted alien weapon emitted a bare whisper of the screeching as it fired. He flew through the portal and oriented himself to the rapidly approaching balcony of his destination.

"He's got a hardwired inhibitor on the gun that keeps me from portaling inside that space. You're going to have to breach the old-fashioned way."

Pete didn't even slow down as he approached the massive hatch, pounding half a dozen HEAP rounds into the center of the blast door, followed by a railgun shot that punched a pinhole through the locking mechanism of the abused door—the same door design he'd breached minutes before. He slammed into the scored and smoldering hatch breaching tool first, wedging the pry-tip of the tool firmly into the gap blasted by his guns. He set his feet against the side of the alcove and heaved, and the door gave up with a crunch, releasing itself into the warped tracks. Pete slapped the tool back into its magnetic slot on his back and jammed his gauntleted fingers into the gap, heaving with his shoulders. The door squealed apart, and Pete took a face full of liquid fire as a six-legged robot just inside blasted him with a torch-wielding limb.

Pete yelled and jerked back involuntarily before realizing he was ok. The torch had damaged one of his sensor pods, but his helmet was intact. He stuck his right arm through the wrecked door and switched to frag grenades, popping off four of the close-combat rounds into the enclosed space beyond the door. When he stuck his head around the corner again, three of the little spider-bots were sparking and twitching on the ground, smashed and perforated by the explosive rounds.

Pete ran past them and into a smaller cavern loaded with

hundreds of eight-foot cylinders that leaked same hellish orange light as the hole-cannon. *"That's him, all of those are his processing hardware. He's been pushed back into this room; if you kill this stuff, you kill him. Do it!"*

Hundreds of the little spider bots scuttled toward the door, and Pete couldn't destroy them and the processing towers both. He pointed his arms at towers and activated his external speakers. "Freeze, or I shoot!"

The bots instantly stopped, the closest no more than thirty feet from the vestibule where Pete stood. A holographic window appeared in the center of the room, a thirty-foot polygonal face of gold light staring down at Pete with fire in its eyes. "Who are you to demand anything from me, insect? I learned your world's languages in minutes, collected and processed the sum total of your race's knowledge in an hour. You're nothing before a god like me. Begone, or I'll erase you like the biological dead-end you are."

Pete felt a rictus grin spreading across his face. "I don't think so, jerkoff. If you could have, you would have. You know I can hurt you, and you're trying to bluff your way out. Back your little spider bots off or I start surgerizing your brain. Now."

The giant face blazed with fury, but the bots backed up, reluctantly. "Good. Now let's talk terms. You're going to leave the Solar system and never come back, do you hear me?" Pete began counting in his head, knowing what had to happen. Nothing else was possible.

The face stared death at the lone armored human and his quasi-imaginary friend, then nodded slowly. "Alright, you win. I'll leave and never return. But hear this, your species will never leave this star system. If it does, I'll be waiting and I will wipe out every trace of life from your space. In fact..."

Pete ignored the diatribe and watched the last of the retreating bots cross the line he'd drawn in his mind. He opened up with everything he had, lining multiple towers up with his railgun on the left and unleashing alternating incendiary and explosive rounds amongst the towers on the right. The bots surged forward and the demonic face disappeared with the impact of the first rounds. Pete watched the wave of death approach and knew he was in a race to destroy enough of the enemy before he was himself destroyed. He jumped as he fired, desperately seeking an extra few seconds to destroy more of the room, but the spider-bots jumped too, closing with him in the open space over the sea of flames and wrecked computing towers. His desire to live warred with his knowledge that only he could destroy this enemy, and he steadied his aim as the first of the bots impacted his legs and started clawing at his armor. He drifted down toward the inferno as more and more the spiders piled on, and his grenade counter clicked over to zero at the same time his railgun mount came off under that assault of the bots. The flames reached up for him as he ripped and tore at the manic machines ripping and tearing at him. The inferno took them all together and secondary explosions marched through the room as something critical gave way at last.

****

"Well, General, it looks like we dodged a bit of a bullet there," his prim British aide stood looking at the screen where the Specialist who had saved the world had descended into fire and madness. The General wasn't sure the junior Soldier had even realized his video link was still up, and he wondered if anyone had been able to make a recording of the video from the highly secure feed. The clip would be the stuff of legends.

An eye-tearing light and a burst of intense heat blasted into the far end of the conference room, and the smoking hulk of an Armored Infantryman fell with a clank onto the pile carpet. The figure continued pounding on one of the mechanical spiders that had been attacking him on the ship, despite the bot in question being quite thoroughly disabled. The portal snapped shut, and the ring of blackened and smoldering carpet was all that remained of the inferno the figure had emerged from. The soot and gouge-covered armored figure stood slowly and oriented itself on the far end of the table, where the General and his aide stood, mouths agape. The figure shook itself and its helmet unsealed with a hiss. The sweat soaked and pungent young Asian-American saluted, his still-glowing armored glove scant millimeters from his bared forehead. "Sir, Specialist Lieu reporting as ordered."

The End

Brian Gifford is a U.S. Army Cyber Warfare Officer with 25 years of military service and a voracious consumer of science fiction in all its glory. He lives with his wife and three boys in Upstate New York, and has had short fiction and non-fiction published with Analog Magazine and Cannon Publishing. Looking forward to his upcoming military retirement, he has a forthcoming military science fiction novel and is working on several other full-length projects.

Troll Hunt

SC Visel

CHAPTER 1

Sweat stung the corner of Cullen's eye. He spun, blocked a high sword slash, and danced left. His foe wavered briefly, and Cullen lowered his shoulder in a feint. He staggered as his opponent swung the heavy blade at his head, then spun and delivered a furious roundhouse kick to the back of Cullen's knee. He staggered forward, fighting to keep his balance on the slick paving stones.

"Ounwe's teeth!" he cursed. He charged into the fray, raising his sword for a lumbering overhand stroke. But his opponent was prepared, and after a brief exchange of blows, Cullen lay on his back.

"You'll be the death of me, Magda," he said, panting.

His companion laughed and dropped to the ground beside him. She pulled the steel helm from her head, mopped her brow, and said, "No, farmer boy. *You'll* be the death of you if you don't keep up your guard. You charge into the fight like a half-mad bull with not a thought for your enemy." She pushed a sweaty wisp of straw-colored hair from her eye and frowned. "I'm fond of you, Gabril Cullen, but a troll won't give you time to recover nor give you a love tap with the flat of his blade."

Cullen sat up and rubbed his shoulder, aching from a flurry of Magda's "love taps."

"Still," she smiled wickedly, "you are getting better. At this rate, in a year or two, you could almost be left alone with a sword without too much danger you'll take off your own foot."

"Ow! That wounds!" Cullen clutched at his chest. "I'm slain to the heart!"

She leaned close and kissed him. "You're also a bit of a ninny."

You can't be slain to the heart. 'In the heart,' yes, but not 'to the heart.'"

Cullen returned the kiss, lingering, breathing in her scent, and caressed her cheek. "In the heart, to the heart, or through it, mine belongs to you. I intend to marry you when your father gives his blessing."

She pressed his hand to her lips and then stood, gazing down the hill to the village of Hallam's Rest. "If he gives his blessing, you meant to say. Cullen, there are trolls about. You'd best remember that. Scouts spotted a small party just last week. My father won't give his blessing until they're hunted down and slain."

"Luka told me," he said with a nod, "but they were leagues from here, far to the west."

She rounded on him. "I don't care if they were five leagues away or fifty. My father understands the threat. You should, too."

"It's been two years since the last troll raid, Mag. Why should they come after us again?"

She snorted. "Why do trolls do anything? Why did they kill or steal half our people and leave the rest?"

Cullen grimaced. "Fair enough. I'll wait to ask him until after the trolls are dead."

Still, it was a glorious late spring day, and he wouldn't let trolls or his prospective father-in-law ruin it. He rubbed his aching shoulder and clambered to his feet beside Magda. He loved the view from Watcher's Hill. Besides overlooking the village and the Dimwood, the hill gave a spectacular vista of the Uplands from Chalk Cliffs away north to the faint glint of the river in the south.

He smiled, knowing that most of the spring work was done: his fields were tilled and planted, both his ewes had lambed, and if the rains came as promised, it would be a fine season. Now, if only he could convince Amon to give his blessing—trolls or not—he would take Magda as his wife. What could be better?

Cullen contemplated the small town at the foot of the hill, the grim cluster of houses surrounded by a palisade. "Is your father mad at me?"
"It's not that he's mad at you; he just doesn't like you much," she said.
Cullen pulled Magda to him. Her scent was intoxicating, her—that smell again. Where did it come from?
"Magda," he said. "Get down!"
In a flash, she dropped to her knees, eyes alert. She reached for her sword and helm. "What is it? Where?"
Cullen sniffed, turning his head to the breeze. The scent of sage and broom grass joined the deeper pine smell of the woods beyond the village. But there was something else as well, faint and insistent, like rotten apples and old cheese.
"What is it?" she asked in a sharp whisper.
"Trolls. Can't you smell them?" He turned his head slowly, trying to pinpoint the foul odor.
"Are you sure? I don't smell anything."
He nodded. "They're downwind."
She held up a finger to test the breeze. "That means…they're coming up the back of the hill! Probably to spy out the village. Grab your gear!"
Cullen buckled on the battered steel helm—his father's, once—and grabbed his sword. "Ounwe protect us," he prayed. They crept across the ancient watchtower's close-set stones to the hilltop's opposite edge. Cullen sniffed again. The rancid stink was stronger.
Cullen peered down over the edge to the prospect below. Trees, scrub, and boulders encroached on the hill's lower slopes. "I don't see anything," he whispered. "They must be in the trees."
Magda drew up beside him and scanned the area below. She swept her gaze back and forth, then cocked her ear to listen. "Nothing. Are you sure it was troll smell? I can't see or smell anything."
"Aye," he said. "I smelled it before—before the last raid."

Two years back, the miserable creatures came in the night, killing and burning. The smell had lingered for days after the raid.

She gripped his arm. "There!" She pointed to a mound of rocks two hundred yards below at the base of the hill. "Something green just darted from those trees to the rocks. It didn't move the way a person does. More awkward and low to the ground."

She gave him a wondering look. "Gabril Cullen, I can't smell a thing. You wield a sword like a drunken she-bear, but you can smell a troll two hundred yards away, downwind and downhill. You have the makings of a tracker."

Cullen shrugged. Sweat returned, trickling down his back. His pulse raced. "Where's your bow? You might hit it from here." He paused when she didn't answer right away. "We should sound the horn to warn the village."

"Calm down, farmer boy. Not yet. We have to see how many there are. And no, I don't have my bow. Luka borrowed it to—"

At that instant, a feral cry sounded behind them. Cullen spun to see a monstrous troll sprinting their way. The thing was huge, with sickly green skin and yellowed tusks. Without hesitation, Magda charged, her sword coming up to block the creature's hideous black blade aimed at her chest. She slashed at the sword and drove her shoulder into the troll, staggering it but not stopping it.

Another guttural cry announced a second troll. Where had they come from?

Cullen held his blade at the ready. Magda engaged the first and seemed to be holding her own. He knew she was the better fighter. He prayed she could finish off her troll and come to his aid.

The troll leered at him and laughed. "I kill you, human," it snarled.

The hideous creature waved a hooked sword over his misshapen green head. It lumbered toward him. Cullen's first inclination was to turn and flee, but he could never leave

Magda. He threw her a glance. She battered away at her troll, driving the thing backward, but the hulking creature towered above her and easily deflected her blows.

He circled to the left, drawing the troll away from Magda and her foe. He tried to remember what she had taught him: be patient, watchful, light on the feet.

The troll lunged, swinging its fearsome blade one-handed in a long, looping arc. Cullen just avoided the slash and moved to counter. He perched on the balls of his feet, ready to lunge. The troll kept its left hand low at his side. It must be injured. He pressed the attack, hacking upward at the creature's head, but his blows fell short. He attacked again and felt the blade connect, but it glanced off the troll's boiled leather armor. Always, the creature protected his left side, thrusting, slashing, bludgeoning with that great black sword in his right hand.

Cullen feinted to the left, swinging his sword in a powerful backhand slash to the thing's chest. He staggered, off balance, and caught the steel glint of a dagger in the troll's left hand. The blade flashed, and Cullen felt it drive deep into his ribs.

He dropped to his knees, clutching his stomach. Magda screamed. A troll gave a low guttural shout; there was a heavy thud, and Magda was silent. Cullen writhed, pain exploding through his body, and his head hit the paving stones. His vision blurred.

The troll standing over him gave an odd, creaking laugh. "I said I would kill you, human. Maybe I kick you to death."

Cullen willed his eyes to focus. *Where was Magda?*

The last thing he saw was the troll's booted foot slamming into his face. Pain exploded as his nose shattered, and all was dark.

CHAPTER 2

I'm not dead.
An eternity passed.
Or am I?

This could be the Tent of Awakening, where the faithful are prepared to enter the presence of Ounwe for The Judgment. *May I be found worthy*, he whispered.
Cullen tried to breathe. It was difficult; his mouth had the iron taste of blood, and his nose didn't seem to work.
So, I'm not dead.
That was promising, at least. He tried to clear his throat.
"Water," he croaked.
A lantern flared. "You live yet."
That voice. "Seala?"
He would live, after all. The crone's herbs could heal a dark night and raise the dead. Well, almost. *Someone must have brought me to her.* Cullen raised a hand to block the light and howled as the pain lanced through his right side. *Stupid troll trick. I should have seen that blade coming. Magda warned me to pay attention.*
"That'd be your ribs," Seala said. "Once cracked, or maybe broken. The troll drove his dagger between the second and third rib. If it hadn't snapped on your mail shirt, he'd have ripped your guts open, and you'd be dead up there on the hill. You've been here unconscious for a day. I sewed, patched, and poulticed you. And I set your nose as best I could. You owe me a sheep for that or three silver."
Cullen touched his nose and winced. His tongue found a hole where the troll's kick had knocked out a tooth. "What of Magda? How is she?"
Seala looked away and shrugged. "You must rest. I will tell Amon that you are awake."
"But, Magda…?"
The healer shook her head and walked from the room.
What did that mean? She couldn't be dead. And yet he'd heard her scream. He slumped into the rough mattress. He closed his eyes, and it came back. *No wonder the troll stink was so strong. They were right on top of us, and I thought they were down the hill.*
Voices outside. The crone was talking to Amon.

Amon. Damn.
With a creak, the door opened. Seala entered with Amon Talheart and Luka, the smith. Amon stood for a moment, a bundle under his arm. His face was a mixture of sorrow and disdain. He looked at Cullen and spat.
"Do that in your own house, not mine!" Seala said.
Amon ignored her. He jabbed a thick finger at Cullen. "Why is it you're alive and she's gone? They took her and left you. Why?"
Cullen shrugged and shook his head. What could he say to a father who had lost his only daughter? "I don't know. The troll must have thought he killed me. He said he was going to." He shuddered. "I— I heard them kill her. I heard her scream."
Amon snorted. "They didn't kill her, you earth-grubbing little snot of a farmer. They took her."
He threw the bundle down. Magda's dented steel helm rolled across the floor. The leather breastplate was scarred and bloodied.
The big man began to tremble, and Cullen pushed deeper into the sickbed. In his rage, Amon Talheart was a fierce, dangerous man.
But Magda's father only uttered a quiet sob. "They took my girl."
Luka spoke up. Like Amon, he was tall and barrel-chested but with a blacksmith's powerful arms. "What happened up there, son?"
Cullen breathed as deeply as he could, though the pain again lanced through his side. He winced. "We were sparring, Magda and I. I had my father's gear—his sword, mail shirt, and old battle helm. We went to—"
Amon gave a curt laugh. "You climbed Watchers Hill to spar with my daughter? You could have done that anywhere. She could thrash you with her eyes shut and one hand. What were you really doing, farmer? Were you dallying with my daughter?"
Luka pushed him backward with a thick fist. "Go easy, Amon.

You finish, boy. What happened?"
Cullen cast a guilty glance at Amon. "Magda and I go up there once in a while to watch the sunrise over the mountains." He fixed Amon's gaze. "She and I are both of age. I intended to ask your blessing to take her to wife."
Amon started as if he'd been struck. "You? And my Magda? How dare you even think of that!"
Luka rounded on the other man. "Hold your tongue, Amon. I'm the chief of this village, and I'll hear what he has to say. And you," he said to Cullen, "finish your tale."
Cullen nodded with an awkward glance at Amon. "As I said, we went up early to watch the sunrise and to spar. She's taught me a lot with the sword. I have the bruises to prove it. We'd been having at it most of the morning when we had a rest. That was when I smelled the trolls."
The two older men perked up at that.
"You smelled them?" Amon asked.
Cullen nodded. "It came back to me. I remembered that stink from the last raid two years ago. I'd smelled something awful for days before the raid, and so had my father."
Amon and Luka exchanged a glance.
"Then they had scouted us before they attacked," Amon said.
Cullen was silent for a moment. Amon's wife and many others had been killed two summers back. The raid had been a brutal slaughter. Trolls killed and wounded dozens of villagers, dismembering their way through the town. From those left alive, they took more than two dozen captive. Afterward, Cullen's father led a party to pursue the trolls and their prisoners. No one had returned.
"I didn't remember it at first, their stink. When I did, I told Magda, and we crept to the edge to see if we could spot them. She saw one moving in the rocks at the base of the hill. That's when the two attacked us from behind. Magda went after the first one, and the other came at me. We fought, and I heard her scream. That's why I thought the creature killed her. The second one was on me like fury." He touched his bandaged

side. "It had a wicked ugly sword, but it hit me with a dagger here. I fell hard. The last thing I remember is that thing kicking me in the face. I didn't see what happened to Magda."

Amon breathed deeply and nodded. "The two must have heard you sparring and snuck up on you while the third stayed below. With Ounwe's blessing, it was a small raiding party rather than scouts. If it was scouts and they did like they did the last time, a full raiding party'd be on us already. I've got to track them down and get Magda back—and you're going with me. You're the only one who can smell them."

"He will not!" Seala cried. "He's got two broken ribs and a broken nose, not to mention the great gash in his side I sewed up. He can't ride, and with that nose, he'll not smell anything till the swelling lessens." She turned on Amon and poked a bony finger in his chest. "And what if you're wrong, Amon? What if you go haring off west while they're camped in the woods waiting for you to leave the town undefended?"

Luka pressed between Seala and Amon. "Seala, we're not undefended. Our walls are stout, and we've enough strong men to hold them for a while. It's my guess they wanted a captive."

Amon shook his head at the healer. "You'll be safe enough. If you're afraid, take the others and head to Stonebow or Tall Grass. Don't go west; their tracks led that way toward the Dead Plains. Old Tom Crib followed them, but he hasn't come back yet. We'll catch up to him."

Seala sniffed. "I was born here, and I'll die here if it comes to that. Amon Talheart, you're too casual with the lives of those you leave behind." She glanced at Cullen. "And those you'd take with you."

"I'm going," Cullen said with a wincing cough. "I'll get her back."

Luka turned to Amon. "As chief, I could stop you from going, but I won't. You've the right to go after Magda. Kill those beasts if you can, but come back quickly. There's few enough of us left."

Amon grunted and started to reply, but Luka continued. "You shouldn't take the lad. He's too knocked about to be of use in a fight, even if Magda did teach him."

"Aye, but if he truly can smell the trolls like his father did, I've a better chance." He looked to the old woman. "How long for the swelling to go down so he can use his nose?"

Seala shrugged. "The troll kicked the boy pretty hard, so no less than three or four days, perhaps a week or more."

Amon cursed. He pointed to the shelves lined with jars and bundles of dried herbs. "We've no time for him to heal. What about all this? Can't you give him something?"

"There are no—or few—magical herbs," Seala said. "His body needs time. But perhaps birch bark and blackseed oil will help. They'll take the swelling down. If he'll be riding—which I don't recommend—he'll need something for pain. Licorice root or even mandrake. It will cost five silver plus what he already owes."

"He'll pay you. Prepare your herbs. I can follow signs well enough to get us close to them, and then he can sniff them out. With luck, we'll catch up to Tom Crib on the trail."

Cullen struggled to sit upright. With a tight grimace, he said, "You're mighty free with my silver, Amon, but I'll go, and I'll find the trolls—and Magda."

Seala continued as if Cullen had not spoken. "You'll need to refresh the dressings every day and bind the ribs tight. I'll not be answerable if the ribs don't knit properly."

"Get ready, boy," Amon said. "We leave at first light."

"I'll be ready," he said, stifling a groan.

CHAPTER 3

"You fought well, *pakh-hu,*" the troll said, removing the gag from Magda's mouth."You filthy swine!" she spat, then wiped her mouth on her shoulder. "My people will hunt and kill you all."

The creature laughed, a low, grating sound. It looked up at

another troll. "Do you see, Gruzz? These small creatures are fierce, even in defeat."

The other one smiled and nodded. At least, Magda guessed it was a smile as the troll's green features twisted in a hideous leer. She tugged at the thongs binding her wrists in front of her; the more she struggled, the tighter they became. Awkwardly, she came to her feet and looked eastward across the rolling grassland. After a two-day journey, the dark edge of the Dimwood just nicked the horizon. To the right, the flattened tip of Watchers Hill mocked her.

"I don't care how far you run," she said. "They will follow until they slay you like the vermin you are. Cut me loose, and I'll save them the trouble."

The troll laughed again and tied a long cord like a leash to the thong on her wrists. "No one followed—that lived. Gruzz slew the one you fought with on the hill. Guruk," he said, nodding toward a third troll, "he slew the *pakh-hu* who tried to track us."

Magda glared at her captors, but her heart died within her. *Gabril is dead?* She gathered her courage and eyed the one holding the rope. "What are you called, pig? I want to know the names of those I kill."

The troll leaned back and roared with harsh laughter. "I am called—"

At that, Magda lunged at him, swinging her two balled fists at his head. The thing ducked sideways, but she connected with the side of its head, tearing the back of one hand on one of its broken, yellowed tusks.

The troll jerked the rope and swung it, sending her sprawling to the turf. It kicked at her, and she felt something snap within her chest.

Leaning down, the beast grabbed her shoulder and yanked her to her feet. It leaned close and growled, its fetid breath searing her nostrils. "*Pakh-hu*, your remaining days are few. Since you ask, honor demands I tell you who will slay you and perform the *mok-guran* on your remains. My name is Khurf, the son of

"... a son of the wind. My companions are Gruzz and Guruk. We are all sons of the wind. When our journey is complete, all will be restored, and our names will again be revered among our people."

Magda glanced down at her hand. Blood oozed from the jagged cut. She wiped it against her tunic. *One more injury to repay.* Her face and arms were a welter of bruises and cuts from the fight on Watchers Hill, but she'd given as well as she got. The one she'd fought now walked with a decided limp. She spat. "You're sons of filth."

The other troll, Gruzz, drew near and muttered something in Khurf's misshapen ear.

Khurf nodded and turned back to Magda.

"My brother says the one he slew called you Mohg-da. Is that how you are called, *pakh-hu*?"

She snarled. "I am Magda Talheart, daughter of Amon Talheart, betrothed of Gabril Cullen, whom that pig murdered." She tugged fiercely at the cords on her wrists. "Cut me free, Khurf, son of slime."

The troll gave a hooting laugh and turned away. Magda glanced back at her bleeding hand and noted that somehow, in the struggle, she'd managed to slice one of the cords on her wrist halfway through, either on the troll's tusk or a blade. She twisted the cord, rubbing blood into it to hide the clean, pale slice.

Gruzz spoke again in a low, guttural language. He pointed back toward the Dimwood.

Khurf nodded. He eyed Magda. "Enough name-calling, Mogda Talheart. We have many leagues to travel before we rest."

He drew a jagged dagger from its sheath on his belt and held the blade to her throat. "If you try to flee from me, I will cut your throat and perform *mok-guran* where you fall. Your flesh is tender, and we are hungry. Do you understand me, Mogda Talheart?"

Magda's stomach lurched at the threat, but she forced herself not to react. She gave a passive nod and tugged at the bonds on her wrists.

"Now we run," Khurf said. He jerked the leash, nodded to his companions, and took off westward at an easy lope.

* * * * *

The trolls were great, lumbering creatures and ran with an awkward, side-to-side motion. They looked as if they should tip over with each stride, but they kept moving. Magda found she could keep pace with little trouble, though running with her hands bound proved a challenge. They moved westward across the grasslands. She couldn't guess their destination. To the west, somewhere over the horizon, lay the sterile barrenness of the Dead Plains. Surely they weren't going there. Nothing lived on the Dead Plains. Yet, hour after hour, they jogged further away from her home and whatever remained of Gabril Cullen.

Magda watched each troll as they ran, eager for any detail that might help her escape. Khurf was the leader of this band, these sons of a dry fart. He easily weighed half again what her father weighed, and Amon Talheart was the biggest in Hallam's Rest. The other trolls deferred to him without question. Khurf carried his sword, and Magda's across his back, along with a good-sized pack.

Gruzz was smaller. Khurf had called him his brother, but Magda couldn't tell if there was a family resemblance. The foul creatures were all equally repulsive. Gruzz also carried a black sword and water skins, or skins of whatever trolls drank. He rarely looked at Magda directly and only spoke to Khurf in low murmurs.

Guruk was an oddity. Compared to Khurf, he was small and wiry, though even he towered over Magda. He ran like a hulking, twisted gazelle, but a gazelle nonetheless. Three times, he turned back to scan the horizon for pursuers, and each time, he caught up with the other trolls without difficulty.

She couldn't tell what Guruk carried, apart from a fierce-looking axe with a leather-wrapped handle. It seemed more like a giant cleaver than an axe. On his back, he wore what looked to be a long, odd-shaped pouch. Something protruded, but she couldn't make it out. When he ran with Khurf and Gruzz, it was far to the left where she couldn't watch him.

After several hours of running, the trolls began to tire, even with occasional short breaks. Both Khurf and Gruzz panted like dogs. They forded a meandering stream as the sun touched the western horizon. Khurf halted, taking his bearings on the rolling landscape. Magda breathed easily but feigned exhaustion, asking the troll to let her drink. He nodded and moved close to the stream, giving her enough rope to reach the water.

She drank gratefully and washed her hands and face. Cautiously, she examined the rope leash. When they ran, Khurf let out about fifteen feet of line. She guessed the cord was at least thirty feet long. She hefted it, gauging whether she could throw a loop around the troll's fat neck and strangle him before his compatriots could hack her to death with a sword or axe.

Guruk rejoined after sprinting away from the party to gaze back eastward. Magda sat at the stream bank. She welcomed the rest but watched the trolls closely. Guruk approached and spoke to Khurf in the rough tongue of the trolls. She hoped he'd lapse into the Common Speech. When he didn't, she looked away. When she looked back, Guruk had turned to face his leader. Magda saw in horror what the lean troll carried on his back. It was a long, oblong pouch from which protruded a foot. *A human foot.* The way it bulged, the pouch must contain a whole lower leg. Whose? Cullen's? These murderous beasts really did feast on their enemies. She'd hoped the troll's words were bluster to intimidate a hostage. Bile rose in her throat as a wave of revulsion passed over her.

Magda steeled herself. If she were to die, it would be better to do it killing one of them. She took the rope in hand, leaped to her feet, and lunged at Guruk, tossing the rope around his head. Gruzz shouted a warning, and Khurf whirled to face her, but she leaped onto Guruk's back before they could react. She planted a knee between his shoulder blades and yanked hard on the cord, twisting and pulling with all her strength.

Guruk grunted and rolled forward, pitching Magda over his head. Khurf howled and threw himself at the human, battering her with huge gnarled fists. Magda screamed and clawed at his face, gouging and scraping.

With one massive hand, Khurf squeezed Magda's throat, pinning her to the ground. Deep red blood streamed from a tear across his nose, dripping onto Magda. "You are a brave one, *Pakh-hu* Mogda. If you were of my people, stories would be told of your courage as you neared death."

Magda cursed and spat. "Then kill me and be done. What are you waiting for?"

"The time has not yet come. When we reach the camp ahead, you will give your blood—and your flesh—in an offering to the gods of my people. Your death will guarantee our success when we take all the lands as our own from the mountains in the east to the barren plains in the west."

"That will never happen, even if you kill me a dozen times over."

The troll laughed and wiped at the blood coursing down his face. With a bloody finger, he traced a rune on Magda's forehead. "This mark is *anak*, the First Sign of Offering. The Second Sign will be carved in your throat with a holy blade on the western border of these lands. When that is done, and we have tasted your flesh, we will take word of the sacrifice to the mountains of our home. The sons of the wind will be restored to their clan, and the conquest of your lands will begin."

CHAPTER 4

The trolls' path across the grasslands led due west from Watchers Hill. Cullen wondered at that. Trolls lived in the

Blue Mountains, far to the east across the Roaring River. Why did they flee in the opposite direction, toward the Dead Plains? Amon knelt on the ground, looking at the crushed grass and footprints. "Tell me what you see, boy. I know your father taught you to follow signs. He was a fine scout and a better man than you'll ever hope to be."

Cullen breathed deeply and stretched on his mule, ignoring the jibe and trying to ease the pain in his side. He swung off the animal, nearly catching his foot in the rope stirrup.

He started to go down on one knee beside Amon, groaned, and then thought better of it. "It's pretty clear," he said, trying to hide the obvious pain in his side. He walked along the line of travel and shook his head. "If trolls ever learn to hide their tracks, humans will be in trouble. It looks like they were running or walking at a good pace. They came tramping through here bold as brass." He pointed to a torn clump of turf beside a bare dirt patch. "That's a troll print," he said, indicating a broad indentation in the dirt. "You can see the marks of their hobnailed soles."

Amon glanced at it and spat. "I hate these filthy creatures." He pointed to another mark. "What of that one? Is that Magda's?"

Cullen shrugged. "I can't tell. It's different than the other, but it could be anything."

Amon threw up his hands. "Blast your eyes! Is it hers or not?"

Cullen fought to keep his frustration in check. His father taught him the rudiments of tracking, but there is only so much you can tell from a scuff in the dirt. "I don't know. It could be from her, or it could be from Tom Crib coming along after. I'd have to see more tracks."

"Ounwe's arse!" Amon cried. "I should have come by myself for all you're worth. Can you at least smell the trolls? How long since they came through here?"

Cullen sniffed or tried to. The swelling of his broken nose had gone down, but he still had to breathe mostly through his mouth. He leaned low over the broken grass and snuffled as best he could. There was a scent, a faint hint of decay and rotten apples.

"Maybe it's them. I mean, it was them, but I can't tell how long ago."

He stood and peered to his left. Fifty yards away stood a low knoll. Something seemed odd. Without a word, he pushed through the tall grass, leaving Amon with the mule.

"What is it, boy? What do you see? Come back here, blast you!"

Cullen pressed ahead and approached the hillock, trying not to disturb the track. At the top of the knoll lay another bruised tuft of grass and an exposed bare patch. "Come and see," he called over his shoulder. "One of them stood here."

Amon followed, leading the mule and cursing. "What is it?" he asked.

Cullen pointed. The soft earth showed the unmistakable marks of troll bootprints.

"He was facing east," Amon said. "Back the way they came. They knew—or feared—that someone was following them."

"Do you think they saw Tom Crib?" Cullen asked, a touch of dread creeping into his voice.

Amon considered. "Trolls are brute beasts, but they aren't stupid. Crib didn't come back to town. He's either still on their trail, or they caught him, plain as that. I pray he's still alive."

Cullen lurched and grunted as a spasm of pain shot through his gut. Amon eyed him momentarily and said, "Well done, lad. Maybe you're not completely useless. Now get back on the mule."

* * * * *

The sun sank low in the west, coloring the plains before them in ruddy orange light. Cullen plodded along on the mule, chewing a bit of mandrake root against the pain in his side. Amon walked beside. Overhead, a gray hawk wheeled in the darkening sky.

"We'd move faster if you weren't on that animal," Amon said

with a growl.

Cullen grunted. "Or if you were on one, too."

"Don't get saucy with me, boy. I'm no rider."

Cullen didn't speak. He peered forward, shading his eyes from the sun. From the cover on their left, a hare broke, zigzagging across the path. Cullen looked up at the hawk, now drifting westward on the light breeze. "Huh," he said.

"What?"

"That hawk," he said, pointing upward. "It should have taken the hare, but it didn't."

"Maybe it ate already. So what?"

Cullen watched the bird's flight. Its tail feathers twitched as it angled downward to a spot some two hundred yards ahead. Half a dozen smaller birds flew off as it landed, squawking at the winged intruder.

"I don't know what that is," he said, "but I can smell something." He nudged the mule's flanks with his knees, urging it forward. "Something bad."

What remained of Tom Crib lay in a bloody heap in a broad trough between low banks. A bundle of clothes and a small rucksack sat stacked neatly beside the remains. Cullen drew reins on the mule and sat, the mixture of mandrake root and dried meat churning in his stomach at the horror of the scene before him. He clambered off the animal, leaned over, and spewed the contents of his stomach onto the grass. When the trolls came before, they had raided and murdered, but they hadn't done—this.

Amon padded up, ignoring Cullen. "Ounwe's blessed teeth," he said in a low whisper. He walked forward, waving his hand to shoo the hawk. The bird peeled a thin strip of meat from the carcass and launched into the air. "What have those cursed beasts done?"

Cullen moved to the carcass and prodded at the denuded skeleton with his toe. "Amon, look at this. I thought the troll just cast aside what was left of him after the butchery, but it purposely placed him on his right side with both arms folded across its chest. The clothes are in a neat pile alongside. It must be like a ritual to them." He gently reached down and repositioned the remains to lie on its back.

"And the leg," Cullen continued. "The right leg's been sawn off neatly as if the troll used a saw or a sharp cleaver." He searched the area near the body. "And they took the leg."

He sniffed as best he could and looked around the small dell. Ten feet away lay another pile, this one buzzing with flies. His stomach lurched again, and he fought to keep it down. "Look," he said, pointing. "They gutted him like a deer."

Amon glared at the heap of offal. "Filthy, dirty beasts. This isn't more than half a day old. How many were there?"

Cullen was glad for something to take his mind from the horrific scene, but the image stabbed at his brain. He circled the area, looking for signs in the grass. Amon gathered up Crib's belongings and tied them in a tight bundle.

Moving to the east, Cullen found a single set of human footprints approaching the area. He walked in a broad circle till he found troll prints coming and going from the other direction. Running a weary hand through his hair, he returned to the Amon and the body.

After examining the ground, he said, "I think a single troll turned back to watch for pursuers. He must have seen Tom approaching and hid in this little valley. Then he killed him and ate him. Or maybe took the meat back to the others."

Amon sat heavily on the low bank and buried his face in his hands. "You're sure there was just the one troll and no humans?"

"Yes."

"There were three of the dirty beasts back at the village, so that means the other two have my Magda." After a moment, Amon's shoulders shook, and Cullen heard low sobs.

Cullen approached slowly and sat beside him.

"She's not dead," Cullen said, "else we would have found her . . . like this. She's out there, and she's alive." Still, he imagined his Magda in the hands of trolls—trolls capable of brutal atrocities.

The big man wiped at his eyes and cleared his throat. "I know that, lad." He stood unsteady on his feet for a moment. "She's out there, and we're going to catch the murderin', barbarous things that took her and that did this."

He looked down at Cullen, and his face grew icy. "But I don't forget for an instant that she's out there because of you." He nodded toward the setting sun. "You've got better eyes than I. What do you see away west in the direction they traveled?"

Cullen stood again and walked to the higher bank, mindful that if the trolls spotted Tom Crib, they could spot him just as easily. He shaded his eyes against the sun's glare and scanned the horizon. The prairie rolled away as far as he could see, unbroken except for dim, dark forms just north of west and, running right to left, the line of a stream.

"It's hard to tell because of the light," he said. He pointed to the horizon. "There's a stream a mile or so off and something I can just make out, like a mound of some sort or a pile of boulders. Other than that, it's flat and empty. There's a thin line past it that might be the edge of the Dead Plains."

Amon nodded. "They're out there, sure enough. Let's bury Tom proper and then be after them."

Cullen shook his head. "I can't track much more in this light. If we can rest up for a bit and go at first light, we'd stand a better chance. Signs in the grass are easy enough to miss in daylight. I wouldn't want to try at night." He sniffed at the evening breeze. "I already think I can smell more than I could before. There's a bit of the stink of rotten apples and moldy cheese I smelled when the trolls came. It's faint, but it's there."

Amon considered. "Maybe we're close. I want Magda back safe, and I'll kill every one of those stinking trolls to get her." He grumbled for a bit. "You might be right. Let's do the buryin', and then you can lie down and take your rest." He glared and spat. "But this happened because of you."

Cullen looked away and snarled. "You won't let it go, will you? Blast it, Amon! Those trolls would have come whether I was there or not."

"You arrogant young ass! If you hadn't been toying with my daughter, you might have seen the damned trolls. You might have even smelt them. But you didn't until it was too late, and now they've got her." Amon grabbed Cullen by the collar, pulled him close, and then shoved him to the ground. "I will never give my blessing for you to marry her. Can you understand that, farm boy?"

Cullen winced. He made his way to his feet, struggling against the jarring pain. He turned to the mule where his store of Seala's roots and herbs lay but stopped and looked back at Tom Crib's remains.

The older man said nothing but unslung his battered sword and began hacking a hole in the turf.

After a moment, Amon glanced up, his eyes dark and fierce. "I want nothing from you, boy, except your help to find my Magda. Tom Crib is dead because of you. Pray that we find Magda alive tomorrow. If the trolls have killed her too, I'll slay you with my own hands."

CHAPTER 5

Cullen woke in the predawn gray. Amon knelt fifteen feet away, wrapping his bedroll into a ragged bundle.

"Time to go, boy," he said. "Sun will be up shortly."

With a shuddering heave, Cullen pushed himself up on his elbows. He forced his face to remain impassive despite the agony of his ribs.

Amon looked at him and shook his head. He leaned down behind Cullen and pulled the younger man to his feet. "Can you walk?" he demanded.

Cullen pushed his hand away. "I'm fine. I can make it by myself."

"No, you can't. Where's the herbs Seala gave you?"

Cullen nodded to a leather pouch on the ground beside his bedroll. Amon retrieved it and opened it.

"There's a gray bundle of birch bark. The brown bits are mandrake root," Cullen said. "I need a bit of the bark first."
Amon snorted. "I know what color herbs and such are. I haven't lived this long without Seala's doctoring." He handed the pouch to Cullen and looked away. "I spoke rough last night, lad. I shouldn't have shoved you down like I did. I don't take back my words—Magda would still be at home if you two hadn't been dallying. But I had no call to do that to you."
Cullen took a small handful of the birch bark and put it in his mouth, unsure if it was an apology. He grimaced at the bitterness and chewed for a moment. "I'm in no shape to fight trolls, Master Talheart. I've my sword, but I doubt I could put much into it. Besides that, I have a sling with a pouch of good stones and my dagger. Still, I think we can defeat these trolls and bring Magda home. If we do, will you reconsider about her and me?"
Amon scowled. "Don't call me Master Talheart. Unless you can kill a troll with that sling, keep it in your pocket. It looks like I'll have to do the fighting." He grumbled to himself for a few moments and then said, "I told you what I think of you. If we bring her home, she can decide if she wants you."
"I can live with that," Cullen said. He nodded westward toward the mounds in the far distance. "I had an idea last night about where they might be. Those hills are about three leagues away. It's the only significant thing on the prairie around here. The trolls made a beeline from Hallam's Rest straight to it. It must be important to them for some reason. There's also the stream that flows in a little valley away south. It curves back in front of the mounds. We can use that."
Amon nodded and rubbed a hand across his stubbled chin. "You've a scout's eye, boy, but if they're there, how can we get to them without them seeing us? We got this close in dusky light. In full daylight, they'd be on us." He looked at the fresh dirt over Crib's grave. "You saw what they did to him."
Cullen gave a half smile. "Do you think you could slay one by yourself?"

Amon snorted. "Of course. What are you thinking, boy?"

"The one troll ambushed Tom Crib. Let's ambush him back. That'll even the odds a bit with the others."

* * * * *

Magda sat huddled on the western slope of the mound. Her body was one aching, shivering bruise. The first tendrils of dawn crept over the hill to illuminate the distant emptiness of the Dead Plains. *The Dead Plains*, she thought. *How fitting.* Of all the plans she had for her life, serving as the offering in a cannibalistic troll ritual never entered in.

She massaged the still-swollen knuckles of her right hand and chewed the sharp edge of a shredded thumbnail. The back of her left hand still hurt like blazes from her attack on Khurf—that son of a rancid pig. She leaned back and rolled her head, trying to ease the knots in her neck.

As she did, she looked to find the other trolls. Gruzz sat a few yards away, gnawing at the shin bone they passed around. Magda prayed that it wasn't Cullen's. The troll glanced up at her with an evil gleam in his eye. Was that hunger?

She shuddered. When the ugly, green-skinned creature looked away, she worked at the cord on her wrists. She managed to widen the cut, but the tough leather still held.

Behind her, from the top of the mound, came a low, excited chatter. Khurf and Guruk, she decided.

Khurf trotted down the slope. Magda glared at him and spat.

The troll leader chuckled. "Killing two humans wasn't enough to keep another from following us. Gruzz here was angry that Guruk brought back only a single leg from the last one. We'll have more to eat this time. And when that's done, it will be a short trek to the edge of these accursed grasslands. There, your journey will be over, and ours will begin."

"You're insane, Khurf, and you'll fail whether I live or die. My people will fight to the very end."

He waved a dismissive hand. "Gruzz, watch over this *pakh-hu* a little longer until Guruk kills the other."

Gruzz muttered something in the troll's tongue and stood. To Magda's surprise, the troll spoke in the Common Speech. "Why I stay here? Why not I kill other *pakh-hu*?"

Khurf considered for a moment, then eyed Magda. "You decide, Mogda Talheart. Shall Guruk kill your countryman or Gruzz?"

Magda spat in his face. "Give me my sword. My friends will kill one of you, swine, and I'll kill the other. It doesn't matter which. Then I'll cut off your stinking head and carry it back to my village as a prize and as a warning to any of your kind who come after."

The troll wiped the spittle from his face. "Your spirit is fierce, but I grow weary of you, *pakh-hu*. Gruzz will kill the one who approaches. If not for the *mok-guran*, I would have gladly allowed my brothers to slay you days ago. When that time comes, I will see that you die slowly, and then I will take your skull for a drinking cup."

Khurf spoke a few sharp words to Gruzz, and the troll raced away up the hill.

* * * * *

Cullen patted the mule's neck and flicked the reins. A hundred yards ahead, the trail crossed the stream's narrow gully and continued up the side of the mound into a scattering of low shrubs. He sniffed at the westering breeze. The dry scents of sage, wild wheat, and pumila faded as he took in the pungent troll stink. He gave a grim smile. This was the same complex twist of smells he detected on Watchers Hill. He rubbed at his aching nose and focused, trying to distinguish the scent signatures of the individual trolls. In a moment, it came. The one he'd fought those days ago hid at the crest of the hill. Another was near the first, probably just below on the other side. He breathed deeply, thankful for Seala's medicines. The breeze carried a fainter trace of another troll, probably on the far side of the hill. That had to be the one who fought Magda. But where was she? He wished he could smell humans as easily as trolls.

He drew near the stream and halted, leaning down to examine the marks of the trolls' passage in the muddy earth.

He covered his mouth and whispered, "Amon?"

A low voice came from the gully to his left. "I'm ready, lad. Do your part."

"I see Magda's footprints, but I can't tell where she's at. I know she's here somewhere."

Cullen stepped down from the mule and drew his sword from its scabbard. The pain in his ribs had lessened, but he still felt a sharp twinge from the effort. *Ounwe give me strength,* he muttered.

"Trolls!" he called out. "I know you're there. Come down and fight me."

A scatter of questions ran through his mind. What if more than one troll came down the hill? Could he hope to defeat even one in his condition? His thoughts flashed back to Watchers Hill. Trolls were brutal and crafty. *Watch for the hidden blade.* From the top of the hill came a defiant laugh. A single troll advanced down the hill, brandishing a jagged, black sword. As it approached the gully's edge, it peered across the stream at Cullen.

"*Pakh-hu* look all alike," it said. "I killed one that look like you."

Cullen spat. "No, you didn't. That was me, and this time, I'll kill you. Come fight me, troll!"

The thing laughed and raised its sword high. With its left hand, it drew a broken dagger from a sheath. "You come against trolls all alone?" it asked quizzically. "There is no honor in this fight."

To Cullen's surprise, the troll dropped its sword and drew a second dagger from its belt.

"I'll slay you slowly, *pakh-hu*, for fun. Then my brothers will feast on your flesh."

Cullen raised his sword and braced himself. The thing gave a mighty howl and sprinted forward to leap the stream. As it reached the gully, Amon sprang from under the bank, swinging his heavy sword at the creature's side. The stroke didn't penetrate the thick leather armor, but the force of the blow knocked the troll headlong into the shallow stream.

Amon splashed forward and swung again. This time, the blow nearly severed the troll's arm at the shoulder. It screamed in anguish, and with another stroke from Amon's blade, its head bobbed in the muddy water.

"Amon!" Cullen shouted. He pointed up the hill, where the second troll lumbered forward with a bellow.

Amon scrambled up the bank to stand beside Cullen. "Can you hit that thing with your sling?"

Cullen nodded and threw his sword aside. He grabbed the sling from his pocket and dug a round stone from its pouch. With practiced ease, he ran the cords through his fingers, centered the stone in the leather pocket of the sling, and whirled it over his head. When the troll was twenty yards away, he let fly. The stone whizzed through the air and struck the troll solidly in the neck. It staggered, pawed at its neck, and came on.

"Good shot, lad," Amon said, "but it looks like this one is mine, too. Grab your sword. We defeat these creatures, or we die, and Magda too."

* * * * *

Magda glanced up at the crest of the hill. From the shouting and clash of steel on the other side, it was clear that someone had come. *Who was it?* Her father, certainly. If Cullen was dead, it didn't matter who else was there so long as they slew the trolls.

"You'll die now," she said to Guruk. "They've come to kill you."

The troll didn't speak but drew his axe and jerked her to her feet. Magda fought, and Guruk dragged her, punching and kicking, up the slope. At the top of the hill, the troll halted, and for a moment, both gazed down at the activity below. In the stream, Magda saw the headless body of a troll. Across the water, someone—her father—was locked in a fierce battle with Khurf. Her heart leaped within her. She began to call out but decided her father knew his business and didn't need her to distract him.

From the corner of her eye, she caught a shape moving through the brush to the left of Guruk. She yanked hard on the leash and, at the same time, ducked and threw a shoulder into the troll's back. Guruk snarled and swung his axe one-handed, but he was already off balance. He clawed at Magda, and they tumbled forward over the crest of the hill.

* * * * *

Cullen crouched, weaving through the tangle of low hawthorn. He hoped to find a spot to see where the other troll was holding Magda on the far side of the mound. To his surprise, he heard her struggling with the third troll just ahead. He crept forward as the pair reached the eastern edge of the hill. The troll held an axe in one hand and had Magda with the other. Cullen considered the distance, deciding whether he could sling a stone and not hit Magda. *Best not to chance it.* He raised his sword and sprang forward with a cry as Magda and the troll lurched forward.

* * * * *

Amon withstood the troll's charge, parrying the ugly black sword as it rushed past. He swung as it turned for another attack.

The troll chuckled. "Are you the best the *pakh-hu* had to send?"

"Not the best," Amon panted, "but I'm enough." He leaped and swung high, hoping to take off this troll's head as he had the other.

Khurf sprang back, surprised at the fury of the human's attack. He drew his dagger, licked the edge, and waded into the fight. He hammered away with his sword, using it as a club to beat his opponent to the ground. He waved the bright steel of the dagger, jabbing and darting it at Amon's face.

Amon gave back blow for blow. He reached for his own dagger but found its sheath empty. The troll blade came down again and again. He blocked as best he could and waited for an opportunity, blood now flowing freely down his neck and arms. The troll reared back for a final blow, and Amon spun, delivering a powerful roundhouse kick to the side of the troll's knee. It gave way with a satisfying crack.

The troll stumbled, and Amon went on the offensive. He hacked away at the great beast with furious blows. With a sweeping slash, he brought his sword down on the troll's dagger hand, sending hand and blade into the dirt.

Amon took a half step back and raised his sword for a final attack. The troll gave a panting croak and held his arms wide, inviting the death blow. Amon nodded and plunged forward to drive his blade through the creature's chest. At this, the troll dropped the black sword. Almost faster than the eye could follow, it spun a dagger from a sheath on his chest into Amon's belly.

Amon roared and carried on, driving his sword through the troll and collapsing on top of him.

* * * * *

Magda and Guruk tumbled over the lip of the mound. The troll howled but held fast to the rope tied to Magda's wrists. She screamed in pain. The troll's axe lay partly embedded in the soft earth, and the sharp edge tore at the flesh of her arm as she rolled across it.

Cullen leaped after the pair as they slid and rolled down the grassy slope. "Magda!" he called, fighting to keep his feet.

Troll and human slid to a stop. Magda once again grasped the rope and flung it around Guruk's neck. The troll howled what could only have been a curse and threw the rope aside. As he grabbed at Magda's throat to squeeze the life from her, Cullen raised his sword and drove it deep into the creature's chest. The trolled hissed a curse at his sudden attacker, blood and spittle flying from his mouth.
Cullen wrenched the sword. The troll jerked and was still.
He threw himself to the ground beside Magda. "Are you hurt?" he asked, caressing her face.
She shook her head. "My father—go to him."
Cullen sprinted down the hill and across the stream, ignoring the stabbing pain in his side. Amon lay across the dead troll, his hands still wrapped tight around the hilt of his sword. Blood flowed from innumerable wounds on human and troll. Cullen gently rolled him off the creature and saw the dagger driven deep into his belly. Amon gave a gurgling cough and turned his head. "Magda," he said. "Is she alive?"
Cullen nodded. "She lives. The trolls are dead."
Amon gave a slight nod as Magda knelt beside him. He looked up into his daughter's eyes and smiled. "We came for you, Mag. Me and Cullen." His voice was thin and wavering.
"I know," she said. "I knew you would."
"Cullen can't fight worth a damn," he said with a weak chuckle. "But he made a good plan—and he'd make a fine husband for you if you'll have him."
Magda smiled, but a tear rolled down her nose to splash on her father's cheek. "We'll talk of that when we get home."
Amon shook his head, closed his eyes, and was still.

CHAPTER 6

At the foot of the green mound, they buried Amon Talheart with the weapons of the trolls arrayed about him. Cullen searched for enough wood and brush to burn the trolls' bodies, but the rolling grassland had little wood to give, even on the mound. In the end, they dragged Gruzz and Guruk to the far side of the mound, facing the Dead Plains, and left them for the carrion creatures.

Magda insisted that they tie Khurf to the mule.

"Do you want to take him back to Hallam's Rest?" Cullen asked.

"No, we go to the Dead Plains."

The journey to the edge of the waste took nearly a day. When they reached the arid, barren soil of the Plains, Magda cut the rope tying the troll to the mule. Khurf fell with a dull thud. She fingered the hilt of her sword. "How much could you drink from the skull of a troll?" she asked.

"What?"

"Never mind."

A thin cloud of dust settled over the dead troll as Cullen and Magda turned and walked eastward.

"Was it really your plan?" Magda asked, her hand on Cullen's shoulder.

"It was," he said.

They walked in silence for a while. The mule plodded along beside.

After a time, she asked, "Would you want to marry me still, Gabril Cullen? I'm pretty knocked about."

He smiled and pulled her close, careful of her bandaged arm and hands. "I do. More than anything."

She gave a crooked smile. "If we have a son, can we name him Amon?"

"I think I'd like that," he said. "Let's go home."

THE END

Look for Troll Hunt to become a Cannon Publishing novel in 2024!

Steve Visel writes fantasy and science fiction as "SC Visel." He carries an MFA in Creative Writing/Genre Fiction from Western Colorado University. He retired from US Air Force Space operations after 24 years to write and edit. He lives in Colorado Springs.

https://www.facebook.com/profile.php?id=61551423271126

Drawing Fire

Douglas Goodall

I was in the back room of The Weeping Cats waiting for Sikich to put me under the needle. I wondered, as I often did, where all the smoke came from and why it never left. I was not blessed by one of the Six Gods. I had no Calling or Carving. I was merely Remade. I died, clawed my way back from inky blackness, and found my calling, if you'll pardon the expression, in another kind of ink.

Sikich was the one with the gift. As a Runecarver, blessed by Wiswi, he could make tattoos that mimicked any of the Callings. Once the tattoo was complete, the expensive inks would ignite, granting me a Stormcaller's sparks or a Starcaller's silence for as long as the ink took to burn away.

Runes were always drawn in halves. I had to press the backs of my forearms together, for instance, to complete the pattern. It was easy to line them up. They *wanted* to line up. Once they were close enough, the pattern would pull my arms into place. I learned to move cautiously, and Sikich, who knew his trade, made sure to place them where they couldn't be completed by mistake.

Runes only worked on living creatures. Some Runecarvers bred miniature turtles, lizards, or frogs and pressed matched pairs together. Runecarving was more versatile than most Callings, but slow and limited to what runes they had prepared. Sikich had no taste for danger. Fools like me were his palette.

And fools like the young noble pushing the curtain aside and striding out of Sikich's parlor with thin, jagged lines on his arms, chest, and hands. Boys like that had no patience. He'd play with one of the little spark runes between his knuckles, letting the pattern almost complete, almost complete, until he set it off. He'd scar his fingers for life and beg Sikich to take the rest off.

"Daorus," Sikich said to me. "I expected you sooner."

The wicker creaked as I leaned my staff on the chair and settled into it. "You pushing Stormcalling runes on kids now?"

"Money's good," Sikich said, as he slid a wooden armrest across the floor. He was hard to take in. When you looked at his bald head, it was far too big for his body. But when you looked at his chest, belly, or arms, every part was too large for the rest of him.

"The usual?" Sikich asked, as he tightly wrapped a fresh needle onto one of his sticks.

I tossed him a couple cards, a bottle of vitriol, and a bottle of turmeric. I had a source. "Just a fresh cloak and a couple sparks. I'm not on a job."

I was there for three hours, watching Sikich's fast, too-big hands pushing the ink into my skin this way and that. I healed from the ink when it burned, but it left a fine, white scar for months, and it seemed these days that Sikich just chiseled the ink back into the existing lines. I remembered my first year as a surrogate when I still felt it.

I heard a rustling from the waiting room and the curtain slid open. Molemonku strode in, the hook swords on his belt making a faint clinking against his mail skirt. "Daorus! The best surrogate in Paswer. You remember that favor you owe me?"

I nodded and Sikich growled at the unexpected movement. "What's the problem?"

"I need you to look at something," Molemonku said.

"Just look at something? Not tell you what I think of it? Not start a month of investigation without a paying client?"

Sikich pushed me back into the chair and held me there with one of his huge arms. "Ten minutes," he said to my guildmate.

Molemonku made that clicking noise in his throat and pushed the curtain aside. "I'll wait."

A few moments later, I looked down at my forearms and

knuckles. "Excellent work as always Sikich," I said. I pulled my shirt back on and picked up my staff. Always true to his word, Molemonku was waiting outside. "You just want me to look at something? It better be spectacular."

"You're the best surrogate for anything unusual."

"And you're the best for duels," I said. "I'll trade a duel for an investigation, but please tell me there's a client."

Molemonku paused. "There's a potential client," he said.

I waited and let guilt do the work.

"Rikicio might hire you."

"The head of the city guard? That Rikicio?"

"Is there another?"

"I was hoping there was."

"King Ketes is upset about it, and Ketes is pressing him, or so I hear."

"Enough to pay someone?" I asked. "A burning guardsman wouldn't pour a glass of water on himself without a bribe. Money only flows one way with them."

"Not this time. He's desperate. Just take a peek. You'll handle everything from there."

"What's that supposed to mean?" I asked.

"I know you, Daorus," Molemonku said with a broad smile. "You'll take one look at this, and I won't have to ask you a favor. You'll rush off and figure it out in a day and get paid five times for one job."

"That only happened once."

"So, you in? I'll throw in an extra duel. The one you owe me and the next one you're hired for. How about it?"

I sighed. I was in. I knew it as soon as Molemonku pushed aside the curtain.

Molemonku led me out of the Weeping Cats and northwest up into the roofs of The Slouch. No one wanted to be in The Slouch at ground level. There was no one there, apart from a trio of kids who had cleared the trash from one of the larger roofs and were kicking a ceramic urn around like a ball. One of them kicked it towards us and Molemonku grabbed it, moving faster than any normal man, and tossed it back to them with a smile. He had little to fear, even here. He was a Fleshcarver, blessed by Yutio, the god of war. I dueled him once when he was a fresh apprentice. I lost.

"Still favoring the staff?" he asked. "What do you do if you're up against another surrogate?"

"I try to pick my fights carefully. What do you do when you need to question someone after gutting them with those swords?"

"I'm not much of a conversationalist."

We traveled away from the heart of the city, up into Tailfeathers, the three long roads that led up the valleys northeast of Paswer. "All the recent burnings happened here in Tailfeathers," Molemonku said. "Whoever is doing it is probably from here."

"Burnings?" I asked.

"You'll see. Four men were burned to death in the last two days," Molemonku said. "Rikicio said the first one left a badly burned corpse, but no clues. Two more died and burned down the whole building."

"There's been people burned to death for the last few years," I said.

"Rikicio said those were ordinary fires. The recent ones are different."

Molemonku led me up one of the little valleys. There were sewers cut in either side of the wide street, and with such a steep slope they were almost clean. The houses were small, but sturdy, in that old style with the gently curved wood frames and short wooden slats for both shingles and siding. Most of them were small on the ground, but two or three stories. Some had a semi-basement, judging by the windows. Molemonku took me around the back of one of the houses, into a small yard full of large granite blocks. There was a makeshift shed built up against the rear of the house. Inside were mason's and Stonecarver's tools hung on hooks, and a shelf at about waist height with more tools.

There were ashes in the middle of the floor. They were once in a neat little pile, but now were spread out. A dog had left a few footprints. What looked like the charred remains of leather boots stood upright in the ashes, and there were blackened cylinders that may have been the legs of a stool. Bones lay in and around the pile of ash. There were char marks on one wall, a few on the ceiling, and one large rectangle on the shelf. The rest of the wooden shack was unharmed.

"Well," I said, and stepped inside. I ran my finger across parts of the shed. "I'm no expert on fires," I said. "The shelf and boards here aren't green or soaking wet. Maybe if it was fast? So fast the rest of the shed didn't have time to ignite? Or slow, like that fat woman three years back who was dead drunk next to her fireplace."

Molemonku raised a hand to his chin. "I remember her. There's no fireplace here, not even a candlestick. Anyway, it was morning. Rikicio said he knows it was a magical fire, some Suncaller's doing, but he wouldn't say how he knows."

"Maybe he doesn't," I said.

"Maybe." Molemonku pointed at the pile of ash. "That was Uventio of Meadow Grave, according to Captain Rikicio. He's the brother of the Stonecarver who lives here and a suspected rebel. I talked to the brother already. He said Uventio had a habit of sleeping here and hiding goods here, even though the brother says he warned Uventio off more than once. The brother seemed honest to me and Rikicio said the same. Rikicio's a Heartcaller, remember, so he'd know." Molemonku watched me poke around a little more. "So, you figured it out yet?"

"No," I said, "I don't even know where to start. I assume you've asked around about Uventio."

"Everyone wanted to speak ill of the dead. They all said he was a rebel and a thief. Even his brother. But I couldn't find a thread to pull. I told Rikicio and he asked me to get you."

"Like I said, not without a contract."

Molemonku made that clicking noise and said, "Why

don't we head back to the guildhall? I asked Rikicio to meet me there this afternoon. You can try to get a contract out of him."

"Sure," I said, "I need to check in."

The Reverent Masters of Peace and Justice was at the edge of Three Tooth Market, but everyone called it the surrogates' guild. When you insulted someone and were challenged to a duel, but you were too cowardly to face your opponent, you could hire a surrogate to duel in your place. Nobles rarely fought their own duels; they hired surrogates. Most of us were Stormcallers or Fleshcarvers and well worth the fee. You could hire us as bodyguards or debt collectors. You could hire us to find a person or item. Each service had a posted rate in the guildhall. Apprentices could charge anything, as long as it was less.

I had no messages, so I talked to a few other surrogates while Molemonku handled his business. The guildmaster was not there, but his daughter was. Ratechi was a Stormcaller after her father and almost old enough to become an apprentice. When both parents had a blessing, the child inherited one or the other, never a different one. That was just how it worked. I asked where her parents were, and she said they were attending the funeral of Chariporam, a Runecarver they both used.

Molemonku was still busy when Captain Rikicio walked in. There wasn't any point in delaying, and there wasn't any point disguising my feelings from a Heartcaller. "I heard you wanted to hire me."

"Yes," said Rikicio as if parting with a single card pained him. "The King's taken an interest. He's given me two packs to hire a surrogate."

"He probably gave you three times that much," I said, "but you know I can't work for more – or less – then the listed rates. So what do you want me to do? Find out how they died? Find the person or persons responsible? And if I find them, do you want them captured or killed?"

"Yes, yes, but not killed," he said, without hesitation. Maybe he really was under pressure. "We need to know how they're dying and who is behind it. All we know is that the victims were all rebels."

"You'd think Ketes would be happy a bunch of rebels were killed, however it happened."

"I don't know the King's mind. He wants this stopped, and he wants the rebels involved captured. If you have to kill them, do so, but the King will only pay for captures."

We bargained over the exact terms and signed the contract. I was hired to discover the cause of the deaths, the person or persons responsible, and to capture any of the rebels. There were separate fees for each. "Let me know when there's another burned body found," I said. "I don't have much to go on. I can look at the prior victims or where they died, but—"

"I just came from Lord Rakomech's estate. There was another one there this morning. Another rebel by the name of Yuptram."

"And here I just walked all the way from Tailfeathers. Now I have to walk all the way back? And up to the plateau?"

Rikicio smiled and waved his copy of the contract.

"Well," I said, pushing myself onto my feet, "I'd better get going if I want to get there before dark, if it's a normal day."

On the way there I had the familiar feeling I was being followed. I tried a few tricks to spot someone but saw nothing. It was always possible that the person following me was a Starcaller or had a hiding cloak. Either way they'd be invisible. That raised the stakes. The Six Gods were miserly with their blessings. Few had a Calling or Carving, fewer were Remade, and even fewer were twice-blessed Remade with a Calling. You didn't need a blessing to use a hiding cloak, but only a Threadcarver could make one, and they only worked for one person. Someone who owned a hiding cloak had money or friends that I didn't have. Either way I was outmatched, but that wasn't uncommon either.

The sun was still high when I reached the plateau, a sign

it might be a long day. The world was dying. One day was hot, the next cold, one month it would rain unceasingly, the next three months there would be no rain at all. Some days were short, some were long, and a few times the sun would rise, set on the same horizon, then rise again. It had been this way all my life, ever since the Six Gods fell silent, and it was getting worse. Paswer was overflowing with desperate families who had lost everything in one of the floods, droughts, or freezes.

There was a guard at the gate, sitting in a typical guard hut with signal bells. He studied my runes as I approached, and tried to puff himself up.

"I'm here to see Lord Rakomech."

He reached into the guard's hut and brought out a ragged notebook. "Your name?"

"I have no appointment. Send word that Daorus the surrogate is here, and it isn't regarding a duel."

The gate guard rang the bells and soon there was a house guard approaching on foot. The estate looked better than most. Rakomech's cattle were neither fat nor starving. Raspberries grew along all the fences and grapes were ripening on trellises on the far side of the house.

The second guard led me through the tidy house to a study. The study was well lit by the afternoon sun. The outer wall had a dozen large windows of fine, clear glass. Lord Rakomech was sitting at a thick desk made of some exotic carmine wood. He sat in a white leather chair and held several pages in his hands. He wore red and white, the Rakomech colors. Standing over his shoulder was a young woman I did not recognize, although I thought there might be a family resemblance. The woman had red, puffy eyes and wore a traditional white dress with the three layers and ruffles around the waist. She was too slender for it to flatter her, and I wondered if she had just been to a funeral.

The guard began to announce me when Lord Rakomech interrupted. "Where do I know you from?"

"Lord Rakomech," I said, kneeling and carefully holding

out my arms together in a way that the cloak tattoo wasn't completed, "I am Daorus, a surrogate. I investigated a wine theft for your father, and I lost a duel in your name to Lord Qoterich."

Lord Rakomech narrowed his eyes. "Yes, I remember you now. That duel cost me more than you will ever know. Even though I have no Calling, I almost wish I'd taken it on myself."

"I am sorry I lost. When I was young, I took many duels I shouldn't have. I have gained a little wisdom and prefer the other duties of a surrogate."

"If not a duel, why are you here? Oh, the dead servant."

"Yes," I said, holding out the contract, "Captain Rikicio of the city guard has hired me to—"

Lord Rakomech waved the contact away. "I don't really care. Terthi," he said to the young woman, "show Daorus to the corpse. Answer his questions, let him interview whoever he wants. And when he's done, bring him back to me."

"Of course," Terthi said. "It happened in the cellar. Right this way."

"How are you related?" I asked her after we left the study.

"Excuse me?"

"How are you related to Lord Rakomech?"

She frowned. "I'm not. Lord Rakomech hired me when his brother died. He was a Beastcaller, as am I."

"Why would Lord Rakomech need a Beastcaller?"

"Not that it's any of your business, but I keep rats out of the cellars and locusts out of the vineyards and fields. I help tame and heal the cattle and horses, and I sometimes entertain the servants' children and guests with beastplays. There are many ways I can be useful to a large and varied estate."

She led me down a narrow staircase and into a typical wine cellar, apart from its size. Most of the cellar held five rows of wine racks, most of them filled with bottles. One end of the cellar had two racks of beer kegs, stacked two high, and a table and stool between them. A heavily charred corpse lay on the ground next to the table. Terthi did not approach the body, but stayed at the edge of the stairs.

"Do you know who this was?" I asked.

She nodded. "A kitchen servant named Yuptram. He hadn't been here long."

"Who found him?"

"Palsi, a charwoman. She was down here when it happened."

"May I question her?"

"Of course. Do you want me to fetch her?"

I nodded. She seemed eager to leave, and I looked over the scene. The corpse no longer had a right hand – the entire arm was burned to the bone. His hair was gone, and his face was charred. The remnants of his shirt clung in strips to his blackened chest. Like the previous victim, there were soot marks on the ceiling above, and the table had a rectangular mark. The lower half of his body and the stool he presumably sat on were unharmed. The floor was wet and a bit sticky. I knelt down and sniffed it. It was beer.

I heard footsteps on the wooden stairs and saw Terthi returning with an older woman.

"This is Palsi," Terthi said. "She was here when it happened."

I turned to Palsi. "Tell me what you saw."

"I was down here, like I said, doing some sweeping, and Yuptram was at the desk. I didn't pay him any attention. I was sweeping when I saw a bright light, and I put down my broom and came back over here. I saw him frozen-like, hunched over the desk, his arm and head and whole chest and back on fire. Then all of a sudden he started to move and scream. He fell over right about where he is now. I opened that keg right there all the way and kept rolling him in it until the fire was out, but he died anyway. A mercy, really. Some other staff came down while it was going on and soon the whole house knew. I told all this to the city guard already."

"Do you know what Yuptram was doing here in the cellar?" I asked.

"I don't know what business he had down here. He worked in the kitchens, and he sure wasn't fetching a mug."

"That's not quite what I meant," I said. "What was he doing at the table? Counting coins? Reading a book? Napping?"

Palsi looked at Terthi and then back at me. "Well, it's funny you mention that," she said. "I thought I saw a book on the table, and he was bent over the way you do when you're reading or writing, but after he died I couldn't find it anywhere."

"How long had Yuptram been working here?"

"Oh, not long at all, maybe ten days ago."

"Who hired him?"

"Pileutea hires most of the kitchen and house staff, but Lord Rakomech hired Yuptram."

"Did he do a good job?"

"He worked quickly, maybe a little shoddily, and without any complaints."

"Thank you, Palsi," I said. "That's all the questions I had for you."

"Terthi," I said, "do you know where the book went?"

"No, of course not," she said.

"Do you know what the book was? Where it came from?"

She paused just a little too long. "No," she said.

"Were there any visitors to the estate recently?"

"No."

"Then someone here must have taken the book," I said. "Are there any books missing from Lord Rakomech's study? Or anywhere else on the estate?"

Terthi crossed her arms. "I can't discuss Lord Rakomech's business."

"It's a shame there aren't any Spiritcallers anymore. Or even Spiritcaller runes. I imagine crimes were solved much faster with them."

Terthi tilted her head to one side. "My father said the dead weren't always honest."

165

"Oh? How would he know?" She shrugged. "Can I speak with whoever is in charge of the kitchen?"

"That would be Pileutea. You can see her if she's back from the market."

"Why don't we go to the kitchens and speak with the servants there? You don't seem comfortable down here."

"It reminds me...I don't like fires," she said.

She took me to the kitchen, but the servants didn't add anything, and Pileutea still hadn't come back from the market. I couldn't learn more here, so we went back to the study. Again, I knelt and held out my forearms. "Lord Rakomech, I am at your service."

He did not bother to stand and receive me, nor did he dismiss Terthi. "You're not, but perhaps you can be," he said. "Who hired you to look into this?"

"Captain Rikicio of the city guard," I answered, standing back up.

"I've heard there were other victims," he said.

"Yes, I think this is the fifth of the recent ones. There were other burnings prior to this, but I've been told the new ones are different. I've only seen one other."

Lord Rakomech leaned back in his chair and looked at me over steepled fingers. "What have you learned so far?"

"Not enough. Burned bodies leave little to go on. Are there any books missing from your estate?"

Lord Rakomech raised an eyebrow. "Not that I know of. Why do you ask?"

"The charwoman who found him thought he was reading a book, but there wasn't one found near him."

"Maybe the book burned up when he did. If you discover how it was done, I will pay the usual fee. Terthi, is there anything you wanted from Daorus?"

Terthi was looking down at her feet. "Oh? No, I couldn't afford a surrogate," she said.

Lord Rakomech opened his mouth, closed it, and then dismissed me with a wave. "Please escort Daorus to the gate."

"One more question," I said. Lord Rakomech frowned. "Why did you hire Yuptram?"

"A favor for a friend," he said.

Terthi motioned for me to leave, and I was happy to get out of there. As we walked along, I tried to put what little I knew together, but it kept coming apart. "If you could afford a surrogate," I asked Terthi, "what would you hire one for?"

"Oh, that," she said. "I thought about hiring a surrogate to look into my father's death and to find, you know, his books."

"I don't know. What books?"

"His research."

"When was he killed?" I asked.

"Two days ago," she said. That explained her dress, and it was the same day the new burnings started. Was he another victim?

"Why not tell me about it? If nothing else, I might talk an apprentice into taking it on at a low rate."

Terthi looked away from me and bit her lip. She gazed down the valley towards the city. "What would you like to know?"

"Let's start with your father. Who was he?"

"Chariporam," she said.

Where had I heard that name before? Ah! "Was he a Runecarver?"

"The best," she said. "I am not just saying that because he was my father."

"Did he have any enemies? Anyone who would want him dead?"

"No," she said, "my father was a kind man, loved and respected by everyone."

"Was anything missing? Anything stolen?"

"Yes, dozens of books, including his runebooks, the ones I want found. My father was ill. Some wasting disease. He'd already lost two fingers on his left hand. He was working on a six volume set on Runecarving – one for each of the gods – before he lost his right hand."

"Qovith's book must have been short" I said, jokingly.

"He learned how to make Spiritcaller runes."

I opened my mouth and left it that way. I couldn't breathe for a moment. The way she said that so casually made me think it might be true. "If your father left any notes on Spiritcaller runes, you could hire the whole guild. Unless I'm mistaken, my guildmaster went to your father's funeral this morning. They knew each other. I'm sure the guild can come to some agreement."

We reached the gate and the guard opened it for me.

"Do you have any duties right now?" I asked.

She checked the sun's position. "Nothing until dusk," she said, "which seems a ways off, Cheram willing."

"Then I'd like to visit your father's house today. If I think I can earn the fee, or an apprentice can take it, I'll have a contract ready to sign at the guildhall."

Terthi looked back towards the house. "In that case, let me get a few things, and I'll take you there."

She left and I waited. The gate guard wasn't in any mood to chat. When she came back, she had a small pack. I decided not to ask what was in it. We headed back down into the valley and through Tailfeathers. Chariporam's house was in one of the other branches of Tailfeathers, so it wasn't too long a trip. Terthi opened the door for me, and we stepped inside.

Chariporam's house was a typical one for the neighborhood, the rafters and railings made of curved wood and the same short wood slats used for the shingles and siding. Terthi said little, and I didn't need to ask her much. The well-used parlor and dining room had little of interest. Three sparse bedrooms seemed little used. The study was in the basement, and this was where Chariporam had been murdered. Stabbed, according to Terthi, and there was a stain on the floor showing where he died. The study had three large writing desks and every wall had a bookshelf. Many of the bookshelves had missing books. Outlines of dust were the only evidence they were ever there. There were still many books on the shelves,

mostly on history and theology with a few cheap prints of classic fiction.
A small, ornate chest sat on one of the desks. The lock had been forced, and it was an unusual five-disc combination lock. Each disc had five letters in order, 'ABCDE', 'FGHIJ', and so on, with only the 'X' missing. All that was in the chest was a ledger. "Do you know what was in this chest?" I asked.
"Some important papers. A few packs for emergencies."
"Do you mind if I take the chest along with this ledger?"
"Why? It's ruined."
"There might be a hidden compartment, but I don't want to take hours of your time looking for one."
"By all means, then, take it. Keep them both if you like."
I tried a few tricks; measuring the walls, tapping on boards on the wall and floor, and so on. I found a loose brick in the fireplace. I pulled it out and grabbed a few long strips of paper. Each had a date written very small on one edge, then a series of numbers. The first two were among the longest:

13 22 42 79 75 79 68 64 67 68 69 84 71 82 72 79 64 68
68 76 82 14 35 52 84 76 61 70 71 68 70 62 76 64 75 74 82 65
67 65 78 71 84 85 70 65 85 82 66 71 85 76 82 15 21 35 42 82
70 64 78 75 63 77 84 66 66 81 82 67 76 78 77 73 84 74 66 81
66 68 66 75 82 67 75 75 65 61 70 77 73 14 44 23 66 78 78 66
71 84 65 65 69 80 76 80 72 73 85 81 78 66 75

14 22 34 42 53 70 76 80 84 77 66 61 65 67 66 78 67 76
80 74 84 68 75 80 77 67 84 73 77 62 67 84 70 12 31 70 76 80
84 77 65 62 69 66 65 79 66 84 67 75 80 77 69 74 67 84 70 85
70 77 23 41 73 76 80 84 77 67 62 66 68 67 78 84 77 63 68 76
69 84 80 77 79 68 81 77 84 67 13 35 72 77 80 84 78 65 64 69
66 65 67 75 80 72 80 71 72 80 78 76 78 75 66 76 67 84 25 43
73 79 84 81 75 69 64 68 65 69 64 79 82 73 79 73 66 84 75 73
79 76 75 85 65 68 72 73 79 84 81 75 69 64 68 65 69 68 72 73
77 73 85 81 73 76 64 84 75 60 66 73 79 73

"Have you ever seen these before?" I asked Terthi.
"No, I never saw my father write anything in code."
I looked around the rest of the house to be thorough, but

didn't find anything useful. "Did you father have a safe or any other hiding place that you know of?"

"No," Terthi said.

"Did he leave a will?"

"I am the only heir."

"Was he involved with anything criminal?"

"No!" Terthi said, leaning back and crossing her arms. "Never."

"How about the rebels?"

Terthi shifted her weight to one leg and looked at the floor. "I don't think so, but he was sympathetic to their cause."

"I don't suppose you have a record of all his visitors in the last month."

"No. My father hosted small gatherings of fellow Runecarvers and friends. Sometimes he raised money for the poor or to find jobs for refugees. He hired a charwoman, Muntithi, to clean and cook for those gatherings. She is the one who…found him."

I asked Terthi for Muntithi's address and wrote it down, although I doubted an interview would be useful. "When was the last time you saw your father?"

"About ten days ago," Terthi said.

"Did he act any different during that visit? Did he say anything unusual?"

"A little bit, but I'm sure it's nothing," she said. "He kept talking about *Merovech in the Underworld*. You know the story? He had just finished reading it again and kept steering the conversation back to it."

"I know the story, though I never read the whole six volumes. Was it unusual for him to talk about books?"

"No, he often spoke of things he read, but…it felt like he kept talking about it even though he wasn't really interested."

"Was there any particular part he talked about?"

"You know the part where Kenku introduces Merovech to the Pebbles, and they say they have a plan to escape the underworld, but they trick him into trying to take over the underworld? And when the plan fails, the Pebbles' leader – I can't remember his name – betrays Merovech and Kenku to the god of death? So Qovith rends Kenku's spirit, making it so he never existed. But before Qovith can find Merovech, he turns on the Pebbles and tortures their spirits in revenge until Qovith finds them?"

I nodded. I knew that part.

"He asked me how Merovech must have felt at being betrayed by the Pebbles and losing a friend. He asked me what I thought of Merovech's actions, whether he did the right thing or went too far."

"I've heard both sides argued before," I said. "Does he have a copy of *Merovech* here?"

"He had four volumes of a scale-bound original, very rare. One of them was signed. That one was stolen. There's a cheap copy on that shelf."

I looked around until I found the set. It was the sort that was printed, one side only, on the cheapest paper, with the pages glued together. The edges were uneven, the bindings were loose, and I could see why a thief would leave it on the shelf.

"I've seen everything I need right now. Want me to escort you back to the estate?"

"No, thank you."

"I'll have a contract waiting for you at the guildhall tomorrow. You can sign it or not, as you choose. I can't start a full investigation until you sign, but I'll keep an eye out."

I went back to the guildhall, and the long day was finally drawing to a close. I drew up and registered the contracts with Terthi and Lord Rakomech. I had no jobs this morning, and now I was facing three, although I had a feeling they might be related.

I thought about going home but headed to The Weeping Cats. It was open day and night, however long they may be. Sikich was still with his last customer of the day when I got there, so I had to wait. I flipped through Chariporam's ledger.

There were large, irregular payments listed as being for "research" and coming from "our benefactor." Four months ago there were two large payments going to one Nurbusha, an alchemist from Qawatu. I knew her. I consulted her years ago on a different job. I'd have to pay her a visit, as much as I didn't want to go near her shop.

Sikich's last customer came out, an elderly man. A Remade, but not one I recognized. I came in as Sikich was cleaning the little jars of ink he dipped the needles into. "Did you know Chariporam?" I asked.

Sikich looked at me. Then he looked at the chest I was carrying and seemed to study it for a time. "He was my master. The greatest Runecarver in the city. A virtuous man, kind and gentle. I would have attended the funeral, but..."

"But what?"

"I had nothing to wear."

I was never sure if he was joking. He never laughed and rarely grinned. I told him a bit about my day and asked a few questions about Runecarving and the jobs I was hired for, but he didn't know any more than I did. When I got up to leave, he asked, "Where are you going now?"

"Home," I said.

"What will you do at home?"

"Sleep and get a change of clothes," I said.

"There's a cot here, and spare tunics."

It had been a long day, so I thanked him and said I'd take him up on that. I asked if I could store the chest and messages here and he agreed. I put them in one of his storage cabinets. Once I lay down, I was asleep in minutes.

The next morning Sikich woke me. "Been thinking," he said and waited for me to rub the sleep out of my eyes before continuing. "Chariporam's work should not go to the highest bidder or the young rebels. It must not go to Ketes."

"Why is that?"

"I cannot explain. Not quickly. But I will hire you myself. Find Chariporam's rune books. I will pay you the fee for each one."

"Rikicio and Lord Rakomech hired me to find out how these rebels are dying, Terthi hired me to find out who killed her father and to find his books. At least she was going to hire me. I should head to the guildhall and see if either of them signed the contracts."

"I liked Terthi as a child, but I doubt she can keep the books hidden."

"If I have a contract with Terthi, I can't sign one to deliver the books to you."

"No. No contract," Sikich said. "These books are priceless. Dangerous beyond words. No one must know where they are or that you found them. But we are men of honor."

He held out his hand, and I took it. "I know you are a man of your word, Sikich."

"Now," he said, "do you know where the books might be? They may have been stolen, and you will have to find the thieves."

"I know one place they might be. I haven't checked up on it yet. I need to get to the guildhall and see if anyone came by to sign their contract."

Sikich helped pull me to me feet. "I would prefer you found the books at once, but I understand. You know where I am."

The guildhall was nearly empty, but there were always clerks on duty. Terthi and Lord Rakomech had both signed their contracts. I asked for a copy of each to take with me. While I was waiting, Captain Rikicio came in and went straight to me. I found a small table where we could sit and chat. "So what have you learned?" he asked.

"Not much, but the victim at Lord Rakomech's wasn't as burned as the first one. I can think of so many ways it could happen, I'm not sure where to go next."

"What did you learn about Yuptram's death?"

"He was recently hired as a kitchen servant at the estate. He was found in the wine cellar, and probably didn't have any reason to be down there. I suspect he might have had a book with him, but the book wasn't there when I looked at the scene. Someone at the estate may have stolen it."

"A book, you say?" Rikicio ran a hand down his haggard face. His eyes were bloodshot. "King Ketes will pay for any books the rebels have, or any books by a Runecarver who died recently. Chariporam."

"I've already been hired to find his runebooks."

"What?" Rikicio sat up abruptly. "Who hired you?"

"Terthi."

"Oh, the daughter?"

I nodded. Rikicio laid back into his chair and looked up at the ceiling. "There's another book Chariporam was working on," he said. "He was friends with many of the rebels. He supported their cause once, but he turned against them. He was informing on them for the King, and was supposed to have written a sort of confession with the names of all the rebels he knew. If you find that book, which Terthi surely has no interest in, I will pay you the highest possible fee."

"Terthi also hired me to find out who killed him," I said.

"There's no point in doing that." Rikicio rubbed his lips together. He turned a little away from me and said, "We looked into that. There wasn't any useful evidence. No neighbors saw or heard anything. The weapon wasn't at the scene. His house had many things stolen, and he often invited criminals into his home, so we think it may have been an ordinary robbery."

Heartcallers like Rikicio can tell if someone else is lying, but they are often poor liars themselves. I decided not to notice.

"I'll keep an eye out for any books by Chariporam," I said with complete honesty. "Do you think the rebels might have found out that he turned on them?"

"We have other informants among the rebels. I would have heard of it."

"I assume you have a list of suspected rebels, and the names of all the recent victims. If you'd care to share that with me..."

Rikicio gave me the victim's names, in order. Ergoveri and Charisio died the first day, then Kenar, then Uventio and Yuptram. Rikicio said there were hundreds of suspected rebels, and a full list wouldn't be helpful. He wished me luck and left. I picked up the copies of the contracts and headed to Kalea's Rest.

I needed to see an alchemist there. I also needed to see Terthi about her father's books, but if I gave in to any excuse to avoid Kalea's Rest, I'd never go. I was too familiar with the neighborhood. It was mostly homes, but had a few little shops, often unmarked, that sold goods appropriate for the goddess of the night. There were many Threadweavers, blessed by Kalea, a few alchemists, and allegedly a few poisoners and assassins. There was also the Haven of Forming Dreams, a school, orphanage, and monastery dedicated to Kalea.

It was not a cold morning, but I shivered and crossed my arms as I passed the Haven. I looked down at the bricks of the street, surprised that they were so little changed, only a new crack or chip here and there, from a decade ago. My legs felt weak, but I pushed them to walk faster until I was past the Haven and turning onto the next street.

Nurbusha's shop had no sign. I opened the door and was startled by a rattling sound. Nurbusha had a bunch of shells and bones on strings that rattled when the door opened. "Be with you in a pinch!" I heard her say from much deeper in the shop. The shelves near the entrance were the common items every alchemist sold: firecrackers, herbs both living and dried, bottles that promised a swift cure to every affliction, poison detection sheets, and a collection of paints, dyes, and inks.

Nurbusha slunk around a corner and into a doorway. "Oh, I know you. What's-your-name. The duelist and thief-taker."

"Surrogate, yes."

She was older and more bent than I remembered. She wore a thick leather apron and leather gloves. "Not going to buy anything, eh? Just here for some questions?"

"As it happens, I could use a few things, Runecarver inks and supplies." I listed a few things, mostly not too expensive, and handed her a few more cards than they were worth.

"Let me get you a sack. Ask your questions while I get this together."

"I'm investigating Chariporam's death. I found a record that he paid you about twenty packs on two occasions a few months ago."

"Oh, yes, expensive but easy enough. He wanted paper that would burn hot and leave no ash. Brightpaper, we alchemists call it. It's just a sort of thin paper soaked in vitriol and spirit of nitre. He wanted something hotter, so I added glowgold, iron dust, saltpeter, and ashes of the sea. I made a sort of brush to run the pages through. I was rather proud of that. Too much work to rub all that on six hundred pages by hand."

"What would that do?" I asked. "What would happen when you lit this paper on fire?"

"It burns!" she said, throwing her arms up, and nearly spilling the sack. "Fast and hot and clean. Didn't you hear what I said? My extra ingredients make the flames hotter and stickier."

"Stickier?"

"They'd stick to the nearest surface. Fumes go out from the page, making anything porous catch fire, too. Something about putting Suncalling runes on via paper in a new way. Chariporam's business, not mine."

"What if you lit six hundred pages at once?"

"Oh, he wouldn't do that," she said and wrinkled her brow. "Chariporam was no fool. You wouldn't want to be near the whole stack of it. One page probably wouldn't light your hand or clothes on fire, but it would hurt. Six hundred pages at once? Whatever for?"

"Can you tell brightpaper from regular paper? Does it have a smell or—"

"No," she said at once. "No smell. I made sure of that. It

feels rougher than it looks. It's pure white like the finest paper, but thin and rough. Tears easy. Here's your sack. Anything else?"

"Can you write on brightpaper?"

"It takes ink well enough, but it tears easily."

"Did Chariporam tell you what he was going to use them for?"

"Oh, something about Suncaller runes. He explained it all to me, but I didn't pay much attention. Not my business. Shame he's dead. He was a regular customer. A kind and generous man. Runecarvers always need ink. You can show yourself out."

She left me with the bag. Why would Chariporam want six hundred pages of brightpaper? What was he doing with it? Could the brightpaper somehow catch someone on fire? And if so, who did it? Chariporam himself or someone else? Everyone described Chariporam as a kind man, one with few enemies, and sympathetic to the rebels. Rikicio said Chariporam turned against the rebels, but there was something false about that.

I had one last important lead. I needed to see Terthi at Lord Rakomech's estate. When I got up on the rooftops of The Slouch, I sensed something wrong. The roofs were nearly empty, and it seemed there was too much noise for the number of people around. I looked left and right and didn't see anyone near me, so I dropped the sack of alchemical supplies and swung my staff suddenly in a wide arc. I felt a shock go up my arm when I hit something I couldn't see. The air shimmered a little and I quickly put my fingers together and sent a spark that direction. I heard a thud and saw a pair of boots on the ground, sticking out of nothing. Whoever it was had a hiding cloak.

I doubted they were alone. I dodged left and pressed the back of my forearms together. I winced as the ink began burning away on my arms. I dreaded the pain ceasing, for once it did, I would be visible again. For the next five or ten seconds, we were on equal footing.

    I leaped backwards. Most Starcallers, when they first cloak themselves, dodge left or right. I was lucky in that my enemies were not quite as clever and a gout of flame shot in front of me. I traced the flame back to a slender disembodied arm sticking out of another hiding cloak. A Suncaller doesn't need to use their arms to make flames, but most did it by habit. I pressed another pair of knuckles together. A spark hit the Suncaller, and she fell stiffly to the ground.

    "You fool!" said someone to my right. "No fire! He might have the books on him!" I heard footsteps to my left. I decided the one who didn't speak while cloaked was the greater danger and aimed my last spark rune at him. I was right about the danger, but I felt the Starcaller runes on my forearms burn out a little before I aimed. And my target was a Fleshcarver, using Yutio's blessing to the fullest. He dodged the spark easily. I saw boots, a chin, and a hand with a dagger running towards me. I barely had time to move my staff to try and block him. The dagger went deep into my chest three times at inhuman speed, and the Fleshcarver pushed me down to the rooftop.

    As a Remade, three dagger wounds in the chest wouldn't kill me. But I wasn't going anywhere for a good, long time.

    I woke to a stranger shoving his hands into my chest. I would have objected if I could move. As he tortured me with his hands, I realized he was a Heartcaller and was speeding my healing along. It wasn't a service I had much experience with. It burned worse than ink. I thought I heard Sikich and Terthi speaking in the distance, but I couldn't quite make out what they were saying.

    When he finished, I saw Sikich come up and look down at me. He handed a small sack to the Heartcaller, and I passed out again.

    The next time I awoke, Sikich was merrily tattooing my arm. I managed to not move it too much. I looked down at myself carefully. Sikich had gone all out. I had small sparks between my knuckles, three larger ones on my forearms drawn in such a way that I'd have to cross one arm over the other, a beast tamer, a tracker, a large and elaborate flame rune, two runes I did not recognize on the back of each hand, and Sikich was just finishing a new cloak rune on the back of my forearms.

"Awake?" Sikich asked. "Good. I am almost done."

"This is very generous of you. How did I get here?"

"No charity. I expect you to find Chariporam's runes. Terthi saw the attack. She chased them away with birds and rats. She dragged you here. It was not too far. I assume the sack of inks was for me."

"Yes, I had to buy something from the alchemist to get her to talk. It was better to buy something you might use."

Sikich nodded and chiseled the last lines of the cloak rune into my arm. "A new tunic is in the washroom."

I forced myself out of the chair and stumbled to the washroom. Someone had already washed some of the blood off, and I did my best to get the rest off. I put on the fresh tunic and went back to Sikich.

"What are these runes on the backs of my hands?" I asked. "They seem complete, not half-runes, but they aren't burning."

"An experiment. Spiritcaller runes. They should let you see the spirit world when you find out how to activate them."

"What? How?"

"Terthi showed me. She is no Runecarver, but her father made her memorize some of them. Between her crude drawings and my own skill, I am sure it is correct."

"They why isn't it burning?"

"Chariporam said Spiritcaller runes only activate in certain circumstances, and he did not tell Terthi how to do it. I carved them so you could discover it."

"Are the chest and coded messages still here? I can't do much else at the moment."

"Yes. I will have some food and beer sent."

"Thank you, Sikich." I bowed to him as he left.

I pulled a spare chair over and got the chest and messages

out. I tried the usual tricks like counting the letters. I got a few words here and there, but I couldn't figure out a cypher that matched the whole message. I decided it must be some variable cypher and maybe the smaller numbers showed which correspondence to use.

I gave up on the code when the food arrived. I studied the chest and the ledger instead. There were too many leads in the ledger, and none of them as good as the alchemist. I didn't know who "our benefactor" might be. The chest didn't have any secret compartments that I could find. I didn't expect any, but if I found a confession from Chariporam and a note about where to find his rune books and the list of rebels, I wouldn't complain.

Then I looked at the odd combination lock. I hadn't paid much attention to it since the chest was already open. I'd seen some other locks with letters for the combination, but they were never alphabetical. They had common letters on each disc, so you could easily make a variety of words. I was messing with the lock, turning the discs back and forth when I had an inspiration.

I looked back at the first coded message. It started with 13 22 42. I turned disc one three spaces, disc two two spaces, and disc four two spaces so they read: CDEAB GHIJF KLMNO QRSTP YVWYZ. Assuming 70 was A, I started decoding. 79 75 79 68 64 67 68 69 84 71 82 became TPTIEHIJYLW. If the letter was the one on the next disc, it would be YZYMI..., no, that's nonsense. What if it was the previous letter on the discs? NONEWDEATHS. No new deaths! I had it. I decoded the other messages, turning the discs when a low number came up, and then put them in order by date. They told a story, but one where I wished I knew more of the details. I rewrote them with some punctuation the way I thought they should be read:

"No new deaths in weeks. So which young rebel is the traitor? Six volunteers among the rebels, all dying. All agreed to this plan."

"Introduced Kenthram to Ergoveri. Introduced Leram to Charisio. Introduced Krovenar to Lepord. Introduced Altithi to Molemar. Introduced Unsinia to Inkopech. Introduced Chilipriku to Vaini."

"Kenthram and Leram dead. Traitors are Ergoveri Charisio."

"Introduced Krovenar to Kenar and Uventio. Introduced Altithi to Yuptram. Introduced Unsinia to Renthria. Introduced Chilipriku to Sikiporu."

"Krovenar and Altithi dead. Traitors are Ergoveri, Charisio, Kenar, Uventio, Yuptram."

"Introduced Unsinia to Leuvith. Introduced Chilipriku to Charimoar and Verini."

"Leuvith dead. Traitors are Ergoveri, Charisio, Kenar, Uventio, Yuptram, Leuvith."

"Introduced Chilipriku to Krovich and Ermenia."

"Chilipriku still lives. Traitors are Ergoveri, Charisio, Kenar, Uventio, Yuptram, Leuvith. Books ready and sent."

There were several more messages that just had introductions, and I put those aside as unimportant. All the known victims Rikicio gave me were on this list, and now I had another name: Leuvith. I needed to find him and see if he still had the book.

I got up to leave only to find Sikich watching me from the doorway. "We must talk."

"No time," I said, "Chariporam has a list of the dead rebels here, but there's a Leuvith who might still be alive."

"Leuvith is no rebel," Sikich said, crossing his arms and taking up the entire door frame. "For four years rebels have been murdered. They were tied up and burned alive."

"Rikicio said these new ones were different."

"Yes. They work for him, for Ketes. Rebels, true rebels, sacrificed themselves to find the traitors. Chariporam came up with the plan."

I sat back down and stared at the floor. Sikich said nothing. "If you knew all this, you could have saved me some time."

Sikich then sighed and looked at everything in the room except me. "I have carved your runes for eight years. I have been your friend for at least five. Yet with such a matter, I could not trust you. Even now. What will you do? You are an honorable man, but what is more important? Earning your fee? Or keeping the word you gave with a handshake?"

I couldn't answer him. "There are a few things that don't make sense," I said. "Chariporam was a kind man, but he may be involved in burning these rebels alive. It doesn't seem like him."

"Chariporam was one of us. So was his wife."

"Us?" I asked.

"Rebels."

"Even you, Sikich? You're the last person I expected to—"

"Yes," he said, "even I. Even I can tell there's something wrong with the world. How long do we have? Twenty years? Five? Something must be done. Ketes thinks he can fix it with Chariporam's runes, but he is no god, and the gods won't speak to their murderer. We need the gods. We need their advice."

I sat there, thinking about what he said. It didn't make a lot of sense, but I knew Sikich. Or I thought I knew him. I still trusted him.

"What happens if Ketes gets the runes?"

"We lose our best chance at defeating him. He can't fix his own mistakes. The world gets worse and worse, everything falling further out of season."

"If I bring you the runes, what will you do?"

"What we will do, Daorus. What we will do. We will need a Remade Spiritcaller."

"What? I have no Calling."

"All Remade are twice-blessed," he said. "You must be a Spiritcaller by nature, even if it does not work anymore."

I shook my head.

"You don't believe," Sikich said and sighed again. "I don't

have time to explain. Find the rune books. Keep them from Ketes. Terthi will give them to Lord Rakomech, which is almost as bad. He will use them to become king himself. At best."

I stood up and got ready to leave. "Where are you going first?" Sikich asked. Of course that was not what he wanted to know.

"I don't know," I said, and Sikich nodded and stepped aside.

I got out of The Weeping Cats and started across The Slouch. I was in rough shape, but the few residents who sized me up saw my runes and had second thoughts. I needed to go to Rakomech's and talk to Terthi. I needed to search Chariporam's house again. I needed to find Leuvith and get the book.

I trusted Sikich with my life, but I felt the book was a more immediate concern. I had no idea where Leuvith might be. I'd have to meet with Rikicio, even though I didn't want to be near a Heartcaller when I was so troubled. I headed to the city guard's headquarters.

Rikicio was there, which was lucky, and I was rushed in almost immediately. I told him a little about the investigation and asked if he knew where I could find Leuvith.

"Leuvith? It's a common name," he said.

"This one would have been an associate of Yuptram and Uventio."

"That might narrow it down, but why do you need to find him?"

"I found some coded messages in Chariporam's house. He sent a book to everyone who died so far, and also one to Leuvith. If Leuvith still has the book, maybe I can get my hands on it."

Rikicio looked at me a long time. I had the feeling he was trying to use Wiswi's blessing on me. I hoped my present turmoil made me unreadable. Eventually he came to a decision. "Leuvith works for Lord Rakomech," Rikicio said.

He didn't look this up. He knew exactly who I was asking about all along. "He lives and works at the estate. I would start my search there."

I thanked him and left. I trudged all the way back up the valley onto the plateau. Even with a healing, I was dead just a half day ago, and I had to stop and catch my breath a few times. I had plenty of time to think. How was Lord Rakomech involved in this? It wasn't a coincidence that two of the spies were working for him. But did Lord Rakomech hire them? Was Lord Rakomech working with King Ketes? From what I knew of the man, I felt he must have his own plan, even if someone else involved thought he was an ally. I was no Heartcaller and rarely used Heartcaller runes, but I knew better than to be surprised by betrayals, even from the most unlikely quarters.

When I arrived at the Rakomech estate, the gate guard refused to let me in. He said he had orders to keep me out. I protested. I made a lot of noise. I protested some more, then slunk away. Once I was out of sight, I started looking for a good way to sneak onto the property, and the neighbor's trellises gave me a way to stay out of sight. I pulled myself over the fence, wincing as I landed, and started sneaking between the trellises towards the rear of the Rakomech estate.

I was well hidden from the Rakomech side, but did not consider what defenses his neighbor might have. I heard a dog barking quite near, and he was soon answered by a much larger pack of dogs a bit farther away. I hadn't seen them yet, but I activated the beast tamer rune. As soon as it started burning my upper arm and wrist, I knew where the dogs were and began calming them, telling them I was a friend, saying I was nothing to get worked up about. I was not well practiced at Beastcalling, but it worked this time. When the last of the ink burned away, I was sore, but the closest dog was licking my hand and the others were staying quiet and far away.

When I drew near Rakomech's house and barn, I knelt behind a trellis and waited. I activated the tracking rune and soon knew there were two guards, one near and one far. I could sense a little of how they felt and which way they were facing. I wished I had a sleep rune, but I was even worse with Heartcalling runes than Beastcalling ones. I had sparks, but that would only paralyze the guard briefly. I could knock him out with my staff, but he could be out for seconds, hours, or forever. In the end, I pressed the back of my forearms together and activated my cloak rune. It was too far to run to be silent, and I hoped I was far enough away from the closer guard that my steps wouldn't be heard. I hopped the fence and sprinted to the back of the house. If I guessed the layout correctly, that back door would lead to the kitchen. I made it to the door and entered just before the cloak ran out.

Inside the kitchen were two women I didn't recognize. I cleared my throat. "Sorry to bother you," I said. "Are either of you Pileutea?"

The older woman pointed at herself and said, "I...I am."

"Lord Rakomech said you might know where Leuvith was."

She looked relieved. "Oh him? He's probably in the barn. Why did the master send you to ask me?"

I shrugged. "Who can say? Thank you, I'll look there."

I opened the door again. I would soon be in view of one guard, but a figure going from the main house to the barn might not be suspicious. I hunched over a bit and walked calmly and deliberately to the barn. There were no shouts of warning.

There were two servants in the barn. "Are either of you Leuvith?"

One of the servants nodded. "Did you recently get a book from Chariporam?"

His eyes widened and he looked at me. "No, I don't know any Chariporam."

"You," I said to the other servant. "Find something else to do."

He left. I hoped he didn't leave to get a guard. "You are

lying. Do you still have the book?"

"I don't know what you're talking about," he said. "I can't even read."

I got right next to Leuvith and whispered. "I know you're a rebel, I know you're really working for Ketes, and I know you got a book from Chariporam. This is official business." I showed him Rikicio's contract. "I need to see that book. At once."

If I was a Heartcaller, I could have made him trust me. Or fear me. But whatever I did worked, for he turned and said, "I got orders not to touch it, and I can't read it anyway. It's in my locker."

I followed him out of the barn and to one of the outbuildings. Inside were a dozen cots, and he took me to one, unlocked a chest near it, and pulled out a bundle of cloth. He unwrapped it and handed me a book. The cover said *Rebels of Paswer and Their Plans*. I opened it to a random page. The page seemed to be a list of names. I put my finger on the top corner and flipped to the next page. It did feel a bit rough. The next page was just more names. Only my experience with Runecarving saved me. I was about to put my finger on the corner to turn the page again, but I felt a rune trying to connect. I jerked my hand away and dropped the book.

There should not be a rune on my fingertip. I looked at it and saw wet ink resting on the surface of my finger. It looked like half of a small rune. I picked the book back up carefully and looked at the top right corner. There was part of a rune there, and the ink looked oddly wet. I turned the page, careful to touch only the edge of it. The next page had another half rune in the same strange ink. Inks drawn by a Runecarver could be transferred by paper to a living being, but they were far weaker that way. The rune was small, but seemed to combine Suncalling and Heartcalling.

The charwoman said that when she first saw Yuptram burning he seemed unable to move. A flame rune would ignite the brightpaper, and a paralyze might hold the victim in place.

Most people reading a secret book like this would do so hunched over, so the flames would hit them in the face and chest. It fit what I knew of the victims.

I had the book now, and I had an idea of how it worked, but I still wasn't sure what to do with it. I flipped a few more pages carefully. The book, though about fifty pages, was just the same four pages over and over. The only names I recognized were ones who had burned to death long ago. I suspected the names here were the true rebels who had been burned alive by the traitors. Chariporam must have hired an engraver to press the same writing on six hundred pages. It would not survive any scrutiny, but it didn't need to. Of course, that meant there may be a dozen books. Where were the other six?

"What are you going to do with it?" Leucith asked.

"Take it to Rikicio," I said. I didn't know whether I was lying.

I left the outbuilding and didn't see the blow coming. Someone with a harder head would have been out, but I staggered and dropped my staff and the book. I stumbled a bit, dodging another blow, and then sent a little spark towards one of my attackers. Some of them wore Lord Rakomech's white and red. I stunned two more, dodging another couple blows. Someone, and I thought it was Leuvith, hit me again on my head. I turned and sent one of the larger sparks that way, but wasn't sure if it hit. I tried to move away a bit and turned to set off the large flame rune, but was knocked over and nearly trampled by a horse. The rebels or house guards or whoever, if there was a difference, kept hitting my head. Before I lost consciousness, I felt them deliberately set off another of the large sparks.

I awoke with the feeling I had been drifting in and out of consciousness for some time. I was lying on my side on a stone floor. I struggled to move my arms and discovered they were bound behind me. I looked around and clumsily managed to get onto my feet. I recognized the place. I was in Chariporam's study. Seven trapped books were lying on the nearest desk in a stack.

I sat on a stool and started trying to free my hands. The door unlocked and opened. There was no one there. Then I saw two hands appear and pull aside a hood. It was Terthi in a hiding cloak. I mumbled something, but she must have understood me.

"I followed you. I've been following you in one of the cloaks my mother made for me. I wanted to know where they were taking you."

"Who else is here?"

"Some rebels. They all left, and I came in. It's my house, after all."

"I think these rebels are the ones who killed your father." Terthi looked up at the doorway. "I'll get your revenge, don't worry. I think someone else gave the order, though, and I have two guesses about who that might be."

She untied me, and I examined the trapped books on the desk. They were the real deal. I then went over to Chariporam's cheap copy of *Merovech in the Underworld*. "Help me with this, if you would," I said, and pulled out the first two volumes.

"When your father spoke about this story, I think he was trying to see how you felt about his actions. And he was giving you a clue about where he hid his work. It's just a feeling. I don't know if the runes are hidden inside these books or if there's some clue to their location. Just skim through them and look for any handwritten notes, loose pages, anything odd."

Terthi took volume two and started looking through it. I flipped through my volume quickly and then examined it in more detail. The binding was coming apart already. There was nothing hidden there. I found a small knife and slit open the cover, but there was nothing there, either. I felt the pages. One pair was already coming apart, so I pulled them open. On the inner side of the pages was more writing. "Terthi," I said, pulling the pages further apart.

She came over and looked at the writing hidden between

the pages of the cheap books. "Those are real," she said. "I can't carve runes, but I've seen the real ones often enough." I agreed. This first volume was on Suncalling, and I had seen one of those runes on my arms hundreds of times.

"I want you to promise me something," I said. I wasn't a Heartcaller, but I was certain Terthi would disappoint me. "Take these books to Sikich at The Weeping Cats. Can you do that?"

She nodded. "Why take them there? Why not show them to Lord Rakomech? I know he's been looking for them."

"I trust Sikich, and once he's seen them, we can talk about—"

We both jumped at the sound of the floor creaking above us. The rebels had returned. "Can you carry them all under your cloaks?"

She nodded. I looked at the pile of trapped books. "Is there any other way out of the house? Other than the front door?"

"No."

"Do you care about anything else in the house? Anything personal, anything of your father's?"

She shook her head. "I took everything I wanted as soon as I knew it had been robbed."

"Take these books, hide under your cloak and sneak out of the house, but stay nearby. When the fire starts, block the front door and flee."

"The fire? What are you going to do?"

"Something I wasn't hired to do. As soon as you block the door, get those books and take them to Sikich."

"If you're going to set the house on fire..."

She stopped and showed no sign of continuing. "Yes?" I prodded.

"They deserve it. If they killed my father... He thought some traitors among the rebels killed my mother as well. They set her workshop on fire. She lived four days, in the worst pain you can imagine."

I nodded. "Do you know who your real father is?"

"How did you—"

"You're a Beastcaller with a Threadcarver for a mother."

"He...Chariporam, he knew," she said. "He treated me like his own. They wouldn't talk about it. I don't know."

I picked up the rope that was around my wrists. "Tie me up again, loosely, and get ready to leave. Take the books to Sikich. We can show them to Lord Rakomech later."

"Thank you," she said, when she was done, and pulled the cloak back around her.

The cellar door opened not too long after that. It was open more than long enough for Terthi to get out. A dozen or so young people came slowly down the stairs. Leuvith was one of them. Another one, a young woman, pulled a stool over and sat facing me.

"Hi," she said.

I said nothing. I didn't look at her.

"You can call me Pertini. It's a shame this happened. Rikicio hired you to find out how the books were killing us. And you did that. He'll be happy. But I think you found more than that. I think you found his runebooks. Did you?"

"Runebooks? No, I never found any."

She looked dubious. From her expression and concentration, I suspected she was a Heartcaller. I'd have to stick close to the truth.

"But someone hired you to find the runebooks, didn't they?"

"Yes," I said.

"Who?"

"I shouldn't tell you. Surrogate's rules."

She frowned. "You're lying. You break that rule all the time. Not that it matters." She looked at me again, and I realized this whole thing wasn't her fault. She was just trying to do what was right. "You're a smart guy," she continued. "You know we need those books, and the one who hired you wants us to have them. Whatever they're paying you, we can pay more. You can retire. You must be tired. No more duels." She was right. I was tired. And they deserved the runes. I should tell them everything. I should try and keep Pertini happy. And I should recognize Heartcalling faster when it was being used on me.

Pertini felt the enchantment break and stood up, knocking her stool over. "Do you know what's at stake here? The King has no choice but to make sacrifices here and there just to keep the world together. With these runes, he could fix all kinds of things by just carving on himself. He can do that, you know. He heals almost instantly. And you're keeping him from getting the runes he needs. Don't you care about the days being too short or long? About the crops failing? About everything being out of season?"

"I do care," I said. "I just don't trust you. Or Ketes."

"You're stealing our future, everyone's future by keeping them to yourself. You know where they are. Tell me!"

She was using her Calling hard, forcing the truth out of me. "I can honestly say I don't know where Chariporam's runebooks are right now."

Pertini stared at me. Then she spit on me and left. Some of the other false rebels hit me, knocking me back down to the floor. A few more kicked me on the way out, but they shut the door and left me there. . I let go of the ropes and stood up. I had little time to waste.

I laid the trapped books against the inner wall just touching each other. Then I took one book and ripped the pages out. I made a path with the pages, careful to make sure there was plenty of overlap, towards the center of the room. Then I took the remains of the book, a dozen or so pages, and put them at the end of the trail. I touched a corner and flipped a page. I hesitated. That hot a fire, with me paralyzed...even if this was just one page...but it must be done. Remembering what Nurbusha said, I took off my tunic and found a bottle of wine. Then I reached as far as I could, turning my face away. I pressed my finger down and felt the rune connect. The page ignited instantly, the flames leaping up and burning my hand. I tried to pull my hand away, but I could not move. I knelt there, holding my hand stupidly in the fire. I couldn't even turn to see the rest of the books ignite. Even though I was looking at the floor, I was nearly blinded when the flames reached the full books.

When the paralysis wore off, I crawled across the floor as far as I could. I poured the wine over my hand until the flames stopped. It looked like a lump of coal and my first two fingers were gone. I couldn't feel my hand at all. Would it heal? I wasn't sure just how much I could heal as Remade. It didn't matter. I was stuck in the house along with the rebels. The world began to dim further and further. Everything was gray except my ruined hand, which glowed a bright blue. I turned what was left of my hand around and could see the Spiritcaller rune on the back burning blue.

I looked up. I could see the fire, consuming most of the far wall and half the ceiling, creeping across the walls and floor. But I could see through the flames, through the wall. The false rebels were panicked and running back and forth beyond it. "That's odd," I said.

"It is, isn't it," said a voice. I turned and saw the outline of a man sitting next to me.

"Who are you?"

He made a little bow. "Chariporam, at your service."

"Can you tell me who murdered you?"

He chuckled. "Of course. Not that it will do you any good. You'll be dead soon yourself. I knew how our benefactor thought. I studied him. I sent him word that my work was complete. He sent his most loyal traitors to pick the books up. Ergoveri did the actual stabbing. I spoke with him just yesterday." A small smile crept onto his face.

"Your benefactor, was it Rikicio?"

"No, no, Lord Rakomech. The traitors reported to Rikicio, but they were paid by Lord Rakomech."

It made a kind of sense. But I was probably going mad.

"How did you learn how to make Spiritcalling runes?"

"The theory was there to be built on. I put variants of the basic rune on each of my fingers, but they did nothing. Then Lord Rakomech crushed my little finger. He was trying to get me to tell him the secret of how to make Spiritcaller runes, only I didn't know the secret. And then Wiswi was there, a great comfort to me in my pain. She showed me the humor in the situation. Without Lord Rakomech's torture, I'd have never gained the knowledge he was torturing me for." He held up his own hand, missing three fingers. "I spoke with the gods again and paid the price each time. I convinced Lord Rakomech I needed money for research. My real notes after that point had to be carefully hidden."

I closed my eyes, and then I knew I was dying.

Before me crouched a man, or something like a man, far more solid than Chariporam's ghost. Two starving dogs sat obediently to either side. Two vultures perched, one on each shoulder. The man opened his mouth – wider and wider and wider – showing rows of teeth that looked like silver arrowheads. Behind him, even with my eyes closed, I could still see the fire, the room, Chariporam's ghost, and the rebels beyond. I could see out of the house, all up the road of this branch of Tailfeathers, all the people moving around, going about their lives, like little ghostly ants.

"Q...Qovith," I said.

"My step-son," replied the god of death, "you are long overdue."

"You are not silent," I said, and felt stupid.

"I am as dead as you should be," Qovith said. He pointed at my chest. I looked down and saw there were two of me, both faint and overlapping. I looked back up and saw most of the rebels were one person, but a couple had a sort of shadow or ghost of themselves.

"What are they?" I asked.

"Remade," said Qovith. "Your siblings, Spiritcaller. My murderer must not get the runes. When you are ready, kill your other hand. Kill your feet, your eyes. See me again."

I felt light, as if I were floating up into the air. I felt something wet and opened my eyes. I was lying on my back, in the yard behind Chariporam's house. It had just started to rain. The fire covered the house like a blanket, and it was already starting to collapse. The neighbors had made a bucket chain and were trying, not to put the fire out, but to keep it from spreading.

My hand throbbed with pain. I looked at the charred lump again. Burning ink was one thing. Growing a new hand...who knows? I had lost some of the best space for runes, but I was alive. Somehow I made it out of the house before the flames reached me.

I limped back to The Weeping Cats. A little man I knew only as a guard informant ran out the second I showed up. Sikich wanted to examine my hand. I told him about the Spiritcaller rune, and what I saw. He didn't think I was crazy. Terthi wasn't there and hadn't been there. There was only one place she could be.

I managed to convince Sikich I was better off than I was. I didn't have time to get a tattoo, but he drew a couple runes on me. They wouldn't last, but maybe they'd make it to Rakomech's. Maybe I could bluff with them.

Rikicio came in as I was about to leave. I told him a version of what happened at Chariporam's house and that the rebels were dead. He asked for proof and I laughed at him. "Maybe there's something in the ashes," I said. "You could hire a Spiritcaller." He didn't think it was funny. He asked what happened to the books. I told him they were fake and explained how the trap works. I said someone set them off, and it ended up engulfing the whole building. It was the truth. He asked me how I got out, and I said, just as honestly, that I didn't know.

I left, once more, for Lord Rakomech's estate. I had to lean against some walls on the way up the hill, but I made it. This time, I didn't bother with the gate guard or even try to sneak in. I just hopped the fence. I knew where Lord

Rakomech's study was and where the windows were. Through those windows I saw Lord Rakomech and Terthi poring over a stack of pages covered in runes. I lined up the wind gust rune. It worked well for one merely drawn, and the windows shattered, throwing glass into the study. I stepped over the windowsill.

Lord Rakomech smiled at me. Terthi opened her mouth and covered it with both hands. "Did your uncle tell you why he wants the runes?"

"My uncle? Who are you—" Terthi looked at Lord Rakomech, who was having trouble managing his expression. I couldn't say what emotions were struggling to get out, but they were big ones.

"Terthi," he said, "I have reason to believe my brother was your father."

"Is that why you hired me?"

"Partly. After my wife died, I wanted to see if you would be a suitable heir."

Terthi took a step towards him. "And the other part?"

A guardsman ran into the room, sword drawn. Lord Rakomech dismissed him. "No need," he said. "Wait outside for now."

"And the other part?" Terthi repeated.

"I needed these runes." He poked the stack of pages on the desk.

"I've heard a lot about these runes," I said, "and what they can do. Some people think they can defeat King Ketes."

"They can't," said Lord Rakomech. "You can't fight a man who can kill anyone with a thought."

"Others think King Ketes can use them to fix the seasons, the weather, all the things that have gone wrong."

"It took six gods," Lord Rakomech said, "to do that work. However great a man he is, Ketes is one man."

"If you're not giving the runes to Ketes or the real rebels, why do you want them?"

"We have to repeat Ketes' crime."

"And what was Ketes' crime?"

Lord Rakomech smirked and tilted his head back. "Don't you know? Ketes' family was dying. He used his Spiritcalling to trick Qovith. He killed the god of death and saved his children. The other gods objected, but using Qovith's power, he killed them all. The gods' remnants, their spirits, are still out there, but Ketes took something else from Qovith, so there are no Spiritcallers. We need to speak with the dead gods, use these runes, and take on their power. It is just waiting there for someone to grasp it. I will be a perfect god of the night."

"Did Chariporam know what you intended? Is that why you had him killed?"

Terthi drew in a breath and stared at both of us, wide-eyed.

"Who says I killed him?"

"His spirit," I said.

I heard a faint thundering outside. I thought it must be a storm.

"You spoke with his spirit? Then you found the secret. And you will tell me," he said with an easy smile. "Everything is falling into place. Guards! Take these two to the cellar."

Then Lord Rakomech surprised me. He drew a dagger from his waist and vanished. He was a Starcaller. I had no runes left, and no way to tell where Lord Rakomech was. Terthi was leaning against the far wall with her eyes closed and her hands bunched into fists. I picked up a chair and swung it in a wide arc. But I felt the familiar heat of a stab in my side and another in my leg, and I fell to the ground.

The thundering grew louder until a bull leaped through a broken window, tossed his head high, then shook it vigorously from side to side. Blood appeared on the bull's horn. More cattle leaped over the broken window into the room and trampled the middle of the room again and again until Lord Rakomech's crushed body appeared on the floor. Starcallers could hide from sound and sight, but rarely bothered to hide from scent. The rest of the herd milled about, agitated and calling just past the broken windows. The cattle in the room kept stomping on Lord Rakomech's corpse until I managed to croak, "Terthi! He's dead!"

She started and opened her eyes. The cattle calmed immediately and a few of them jumped back over the windowsill. Terthi slid down the far wall, her power spent. She held her knees and began to sob. The guards who had gathered just outside the door hadn't made it into the room in time. They seemed unsure about what to do. Lord Rakomech didn't have an heir, and apparently didn't have a second in command.

"Well," I said to Terthi, "I guess you won't be joining his family."

The cattle had scattered some of Chariporam's runes around the floor. It seemed hours before I was able to stand and gather them up with my good hand. When I found them all, I knelt down next to Terthi and whispered, "I'm taking these. Sikich will copy them. Once that's done, come see me. We'll discuss how and what can be sold. If you want to sell them. Or what can be returned to you. But Ketes wants them, and I convinced Rikicio that they were burned. It would be best if most people thought they were destroyed."

I returned to The Weeping Cats once again. I brought the pages to Sikich who uncreased them and laid them out carefully, caressing each sheet like a lover. He even wept over one of them. I felt I should leave it all in his hands. I wanted to be done with it, but when I slept, I kept seeing Qovith.

Sikich woke me again the next morning. "Thank you," he said. "These are beautiful. Beautiful work. Chariporam was more of a genius than even I knew. We have a chance now."

I shook my head. "Whatever it is, I'm done with this business."

"Let us see how fast your hand heals. I know a good Heartcaller. And then we will need to speak with the gods, starting with the god of death."

The End

Author Bio:

Douglas Goodall worked in the video game industry for twenty years. After a series of unbelievable events, he has to write fiction for a living. He lives in rural North Carolina with the smartest wife, cutest daughter, and softest cat.

Forth From Hell

Tim Hanlon

*France
1643 A.D
Outside the town of Rocroi*

José Moreno knew they were doomed when the mounts of the Dread Cuirassiers did not balk at the planted pikes but came on willingly. The 20-foot-long spears pierced chests, tore guts from bellies so that they trailed behind the beasts like streamers of gore, but the demon horses were undaunted by the havoc wrought on their hell-born bodies. In their eyes blazed a lust for blood that was not equine and their necks strained forward with a craving to devour human flesh.

The Spaniard raised his musket as a horse broke through the line. Ignoring its rider, he fired the heavy ball into the side of the demon mount's head, so close that the muzzle was almost resting on the stygian hide. It collapsed on that spot with a bone-shattering shriek and its careening bulk dug a furrow in the already bloody earth. The cuirassier leapt from the stirrups and rolled on the ground, coming to a crouch in a heavy crash of black armor. The rider's helmet was lost and its face was like old leather stretched over bones as if its flesh was consumed by a fire inside. The cuirassier's eyes were sunken and blazed with a desire for death even stronger than the beast it rode upon.

It turned on Moreno but, as the demon rider stepped forward, his comrade Gutiérrez lunged from the melee and rammed his broken pike through the growling maw of the Dread Cuirassier. The steel head burst through the back of the thing's skull with a spray of blood as thick and dark as pitch. The cuirassier stumbled as Gutiérrez bore it to the ground. The black blood hissed and boiled where it splattered the earth as the spitted demon thrashed and tore at the weapon skewering its face. The thing gave not a care for the steel spitting its skull, for only the need to kill boiled in its chest. The pikeman, Gutiérrez, stamped on the armored rider's skull and the bones cracked under Gutiérrez' foot like poor pottery.

'My thanks, Mateo,' said Moreno as he reloaded his musket from the charges bandoliered across his chest. His actions were smooth and precise, even in the tumult around him, for the *musquetero* had crossed the continent with that weapon by his side. Moreno reset his hat so that it kept his dark hair off his face and smiled briefly at his friend. He was a squat man, Moreno, big in the chest and shoulders, and he walked with the swagger of a member of the feared Spanish Tercios. He wore no armor but a buff coat and the bandolier of charges crossed from shoulder to hip. At his side rested a sword, straight of blade with a simple hand guard. It was a battle weapon, stout and deadly.

'I think,' replied Gutiérrez, 'that you will have plenty of opportunities to repay me today, my friend.'

'It has certainly gone to shit quickly.'

Gutiérrez laughed and his round face showed genuine pleasure. He was not a tall man either but his thighs and shoulders were at solid and hard as the ash wood of his pike. 'As it always does, Moreno. And that is when we Spaniards are at our best!'

'*Musqueteros*, form line!'

The call sent Moreno to the front of the Spanish square. The musketeers would fire a volley and retire through the line of pikes; one volley only, for the Dread Cuirassiers covered the ground swiftly and there would not be time to reload.

They were well armored, this demon cavalry brought from death to aid the French. Helmeted, with chest, shoulders, arms and thighs metal bound, the cuirassiers where a fearful sight as they hammered the earth under their fiendish mount's hooves.

Moreno watched the mounted troops thunder down the

hill below the French command post. The Demon Cavalry had appeared with the death of the French King Louis XIII and the ascension to power of Cardinal Mazarin as the new child-king's prime minister. There had been talk of a pact with the devil. Moreno had been fighting this religious war long enough to know that the leaders on both sides would do anything for ascendancy. Catholic against Protestant, Catholic against Catholic, pope against emperor against king; faith was a flexible thing when it came to power and evil knew this fact very well. Mazarin had opened the gates to hell and the Dread Cuirassiers and their demon horses had ridden forth.

The Spanish Tercios had not faced them before but the rumors had abounded of these demon souls in their black armor on their fierce, fiendish horses and Moreno could see that, for once, the gossip had been accurate. The Dread Cuirassiers were not of this world, or perhaps had once been and were now returned as something very, very different.

Moreno raised his musket as the command resounded across the ranks and prepared to fire. The musketeer sighted on a rider to his front and held his weapon ready as the image beyond his barrel bounced with the movement of the charging beast.

'Fire!'

The musketeer paused for the right moment then fired his heavy musket. Moreno knew that at that range he could put the musket ball where he wanted to and, as the smoke cleared, the m*u*squetero saw the cuirassier flick back in the saddle and slide from his horse. The black rider was trampled by those behind, his armor beaten into the churned earth. Still the dread charger did not veer away as a worldly horse would do and, as Moreno stepped calmly back through the corridor of heavy wooden pikes, he watched the beast draw its lips back and its teeth were sharp and as thick as a man's thumb.

The Spanish *piqueros* held their ground and their pikes wrought destruction on the charge but the demon cavalry came on and their long horse pistols cracked and flamed. The

Spaniards fell, their breastplates shattered by the enemy's rounds. Men cried out in pain and blood splattered the field outside the town of Rocroi and the riders, their black armor dark as the entrance to hell, broke through again.

The air was thick with the splinter of ash pikes, the snapping wood rippled sharp and loud like an unseen giant was cracking oversized knuckles. Tumbling daggers of broken pikes pierced skin and eyes and Spaniards fell back with hands cupping bloody faces. The demon horses trampled these unfortunates to the ground, their death-shod hooves without mercy.

Moreno fired at point blank range into the chest of a demon charger. Its right foreleg collapsed and the cuirassier was trapped underneath. An *arcabucero*, Serrono, blasted the rider in the face and its dark blood, thick and oily and putrid, covered the soldier's boots. The arquebusier stepped back as the gore steamed on the tough leather and swore as only a Spanish soldier could.

Moreno could already feel his own sweat slick under his buff coat but there was to be no respite under this sun as a Dread Cuirassier loomed behind Serrono and chopped his sword at the *arcabucero's* neck. The long blade cleaved through the man's chest and his upper torso collapsed sideways under the force of the stroke. They did not have technique, the demon riders, but their strokes were strong and difficult to turn aside.

Moreno abandoned his musket and drew his own blade and plucked his *main gauche* from his belt. The musketeer leapt forward. The broad-bladed dagger covered Moreno's sword hand as he thrust his blade at the demon's face. The cuirassier beat his blade aside and swung back but Moreno's parrying dagger checked the blow and the *musquetero* stabbed over the locked weapons and into the demon's throat. It shrieked like a crow caught in a trap for it could feel pain, Moreno saw that now, but it just did not stop them. The cuirassier's left hand swung up and grabbed his blade. Moreno tried to rip the sword sideways but the thing's gauntleted hand held fast. In desperation, Moreno rammed his main gauche into the cuirassier's torso, through the arm-holes in the demon's breastplate. The hilt slammed against bone. Demon blood spewed from the torn throat and ruptured chest and splashed Moreno's hand. The musketeer released the grip of his dagger as the dark ooze burned his flesh. He stepped back and his sword slid free of the demon's grasp. The Dread Cuirassier folded over the dagger as it slumped to the earth and did not rise again.

Moreno gathered his musket and quickly reloaded. A slight tremor took hold of his right hand but he gathered himself by squeezing a quick fist. Around him men lay, their bodies torn by the charge of the demon cavalry. Their comrades bent and tended to them as best they could and lay hands on their shoulders to say that they had done enough. Still, there was no escape on that field, no reprieve, so all but the most damaged regained their feet and took weapons in hand. The *capitan* stood in the centre of the square, his breastplate battered by the cuirassiers' blades. The officer raised his voice above the din.

'Stand to, my *soldados veteranos*,' he called, 'for our job is not finished yet. Stand to and we shall face these things from hell together and show them that now they come against an army of Spain and that we do not retreat. We do not break. We stand and we fight.'

The soldiers raised a cheer as they reset the square and it was stout and it was heartfelt. These fighting men of Spain, underpaid, overused, looked down upon by those they died for, held one thing sacred above all others; their courage in the face of shot and steel.

Moreno moved to the front and gazed over the fallen bodies before him. The Spanish square was shrinking as the battle progressed and the corpses of his comrades and the smouldering armor of the enemy spread out from the formation for dozens of paces. Some demon horses, broken but not dead, crawled towards the Spaniards and their red-stained jaws stretched with blood lust. Soldiers ran forward and speared them until the slavering beasts were silent.

A breeze rose and cleared the powder smoke and the *musquetero* could see on the ridge the French commander, the Duke of Enghien, and the leader of these battalions from hell. A figure in black armor upon a massive charger, the malevolent commander seemed to Moreno's tired eyes to suck all the light from around itself like an open grave. Beside the dark leader was another figure, spoken of with wonder by those who spread such stories. A small figure, no bigger than a boy, with flowing blonde hair cascading from his helmet. It wore armor as bright as the other's was dark, the antithesis of the funereal figure on the immense demon warhorse. Moreno's eyes were tired but they were still keen and the Spaniard watched the large, black armored figure's head turn towards its diminutive comrade. This had happened every time the musketeer had chanced to witness the pair. It stirred something in Moreno's mind that he could not make concrete. Perhaps it was simply that the two, it was said, were inseparable figures on the battlefield and where they stood death gathered.

'That is a pair straight from hell,' said Gutiérrez behind him.

Moreno turned to the pikeman. His friend had a flap of cheek hanging down so that the white of his jaw was visible but the other side of his face grinned. Gutiérrez held a pike at rest on his strong shoulder as he bound his face roughly and waited as calmly as a man in church.

'Shall we send them back there?' asked Moreno.

'When we have dealt with these black beetles and their nags, I will personally march up that hill and give them my boot up their demon arses!'

'I will carry your pike for you, old man,' said Moreno and the men around them laughed softly.

'You musketeers are not strong enough to handle

anything of mine,' declared Gutiérrez to more laughter. The bandage on his face was already stained red and a trickle of blood began to work its way down his thick neck. Gutiérrez lifted his eyes to the ridge as the thunder of demon hooves descended again. 'They do not tire of dying,' the pikeman said flatly as he took his place in the line.

The French artillery had ceased firing long ago nor did the cavalry units set their mounts to the battle. The French infantry had grounded their weapons and shared what food and water remained. The French flags were still raised and Moreno enjoyed the bright ensigns against the sky. The Dread Cuirassiers did not care for their own lives, if indeed they were really alive, so the Frenchmen stood in ranks and watched the demon riders descend like a black wave on the Spanish squares.

Moreno sent another rider back to hell and retired in good order to stand and watch the pikeman ply their trade. The long weapons lowered in perfect unison and the monstrous mounts ran into their mass of sharp edges. The wave broke to the cries of the beasts as the pikes tore through them. Moreno saw Gutiérrez lance a dark charger in the chest and the musketeer saw, too, how the rider spurred his mount on, so that the beast forced itself down the length of pike. The steel pike-head burst through the rear haunch of the beast and still it strained onward. Its jaws snapped forward and Moreno watched his friend's left hand recoil, blood spurting into the horse's face. Gutiérrez released his pike, for it was held fast in the evil beast's torso, and drew his sword with his right hand. The beast's flailing head knocked the weapon from his grasp and it tumbled into the mass of straining bodies.

The Dread Cuirassier raised his pistol at the injured *piquero* but Moreno was faster and fired first. His musket ball slammed against the rider's breast plate. It ran along the curve of steel and did not penetrate but incised a piece of dead flesh from the cuirassier's neck. The demon wobbled, unbalanced, and it was then that its horse finally died. They both crashed to the ground. Gutiérrez stooped quickly and gathered the long-barrelled pistol that the demon rider had released and fired into the cuirassier's helmet. The metal tore with the dull sound of a hammer dropped on rock and the demon's face burst from the front of the helmet. The thing did not rise.

There were more of the unhorsed cuirassiers within the square as the pikemen, beyond brave, turned their backs and closed ranks against the demon cavalry charges still flowing towards their front. Moreno picked up a discarded rodela and slipped the metal shield onto his left arm and drew his sword as a demonic horseman advanced on him. The Dread Cuirassier's jaw hung by a flap of leathery skin, torn off by a near-miss, and this piece swung to and thro with the demon's steps.

The thing from the depths raised his sword and cut at Moreno and the Spaniard swayed left and used the rodela to pass the cuirassier's blade to his own right. His side-sword swept forward and hacked the rider's leg, just below the hanging steel tassets of its armor. It was a fine stroke and the honed edge of this blade parted dry flesh and sundered the bone beneath and putrid black fluid flowed. The evil rider collapsed on to its hands but its head turned to Moreno with hate and the *musquetero* backhanded his sword into the ugly face. The fold of jaw flew away as the rotten blood spurted again and the cuirassier moved no more.

Men fell back against Moreno. The unhorsed cuirassiers howled in fury and lay about them with no regard for safety. A comrade went down, his arm severed and his legs slipping on the spilled entrails of the shrieking soldier beside him. Moreno charged and his metal shield knocked a demon to the ground and his sword went in low and impaled the rider to the earth. A pikeman, his weapon shivered, caved in the side of the cuirassier's helmet with the heavy pole and kept hammering until the demon was still.

The pikeman fell. A black beast, its back broken but hostility undaunted, lunged at the man and latched its thick jaws around his left thigh. Moreno heard the bone crack underneath the Spaniard's shrieks and he saw the blood gush where the demon horse's teeth sliced the vessel in the pikeman's thigh. An arquebusier jammed his muzzle into the beast's eye and the mount's head split apart under the force of the shot. Black blood splattered the *arcabucero's* boots and trousers but the soldier stood there unmoving, examining the devastation, his clothes sending small tendrils of smoke into the air.

The last of the Dread Cuirassiers within the Spanish square finally fell, bludgeoned to the earth by the short war hammer Gutiérrez had plucked from the ground. The heavy ridged head of the hammer seemed to leak dirty oil as the demon blood dripped from the smooth surface. The blood had found a large tuft of dry grass and smoke began to rise as the demon liquid burned. Gutiérrez stamped on the small fire without hurry.

Moreno saw the c*apitan* on the ground, for the man's red sash stood out amongst the black armor around him. The captain had fallen with a demon's sword thrust through his armpit and into his lungs and the handsome man lay now and blood coughed from his open mouth. Moreno knelt and took the captain's hand but the officer did not see him and the man coughed one more time and was still.

'Not a bad man, for a *hidalgo*,' said Gutiérrez.

Moreno thought the epithet covered all that needed to be said so he rose and left the fallen *capitan*. The attack had been repulsed again. A musketeer finished off a fallen horse that thrashed and twisted and struggled to reach the men around it with demonic fury unabated. The *veterano* stared at the dead beast for a dozen heartbeats as he reloaded his weapon then spat on the ground and returned to his place in the square.

The squares were compacted as the survivors formed smaller and smaller lines. To his left, Moreno could see the Spanish commander, Paul-Bernard de Fontaines, in the centre of his own severely diminished square, propped up in his large chair. The old man could barely stand through ill-health but waited now with his *soldados* and Moreno loved him for that fact. Moreno saw the aged commander looking their way so the musketeer raised his hat in salute. The soldiers around him joined in and their cheer was strong when de Fontaines raised his hand in acknowledgement.

'The old goat will be with us 'til the end,' Moreno said to his friend.

Gutiérrez tied off the bandage on his left hand with his teeth and ignored the pain from his damaged jaw. The war hammer swung absentmindedly in his right. Gutiérrez could not hold a pike now with only a couple of fingers remaining on his hand but the veteran was determined to go down fighting. His injuries did not deter him, for he was a Spanish fighting man and he would not flinch.

'Yes,' Gutiérrez replied, 'we can't ask much more from our betters.'

Then, as if the fiends on the hill had heard the pride in the pikeman's voice, the blonde head of the glistening demon turned towards the damaged square of de Fontaines. Moreno watched the dark rider's head turn too and the Spaniard knew what was going to happen. The Spanish commander's hand dropped to the arm of his chair and, in unison, the black demon spurred his horse forward and set it to the slope.

The men around Moreno called out in alarm as the Dread Cuirassiers fell in behind their own leader. The dark demon was the tip of a deadly spear forged from charging death on horseback. It was an unstoppable force as its black mount churned down the slope of the hill. Moreno watched the pikemen of the commander's square set themselves and the musketeers raise their weapons but they seemed pathetically few against what was storming towards them.

The Dread Commander raised its long pistols in both hands and fired quickly. Two pikemen fell. It was an inhuman shot from that distance and Moreno would have admired the skill if he had not had a sour lump of fear in his gut. The pikemen fell and the dark commander guided its beast into the small gap as it dragged his sword from its scabbard. It laid sweeping strokes left and right and the gap widened. And the square was broken.

The Dread Cuirassiers followed their leader and men died. Brave Spanish soldiers lunged forward with swords and shivered pikes but their deadly edges were turned aside by the obsidian armor of the hulking demon. Its broad sword took heads from necks, arms from shoulders, and the big black-clad demon churned a passage to the heart of the Spanish square. Moreno and his companions were silent as they watched the carnage.

De Fontaine's bodyguard set their feet as the Dread Commander hacked towards their charge. They were veterans all, soldiers who had not suffered defeat in a decade on the battlefield, and they wielded large, two-handed battle swords. The dark demon did not hesitate. Its fiendish mount lunged forward and lashed out with axe-blade hooves and a bodyguard went down, his head spilt in twain. Blood splattered the Spaniards but they did not give ground as the demon charger spun and kicked with its hind legs. It was a battering ram, that equine monster, and the veterans were flung, broken and bloody, to sprawl on the battle-ploughed field.

A Spanish bodyguard, his helmet gone, cut with his montante at the Dread Commander but it caught the sword stroke on the forte of its blade and turned the weapon aside. The demon horse latched its gaping jaws onto the man's head and the crack of bone was sharp and distinct even in the tumult of battle. The bodyguard's screams were muffled by the monster's maw as it swung the brave man in a circle, his legs free of the bloody earth. The beast let the Spaniard go finally and his broken body tumbled away, lost in the steel storm.

Paul-Bernard de Fontaines watched the dark demon's inexorable forward progress. The old man, sick of body but still with a fighting man's pride, stood on his trembling legs.

He dragged his sword from its scabbard and raised it into guard. De Fontaines face was grim in the sunlight but he did not let fear mar his countenance. The Dread Commander was at his front and the old man struck with his blade. It was not a strong cut and the demon ignored it as it rang off his armored shoulder. The Dread Commander thrust with his own blade and it skewered de Fontaines' withered chest. The old man fell back under the force and the sword blade sunk deep into the wooden back of de Fontaines' fighting chair. The dread commander released his trapped sword and galloped on and the old general was left there, pinned to the chair like nothing more than a petty insect.

The soldiers of Moreno's squared cried out again at the carnage. They watched struggling comrades be cut down by the Dread Cuirassiers and could do nothing. Moreno could stand no more and he stepped to the front of the square. Gutiérrez, knowing his friend, stepped in front and offered his shoulder as a makeshift rest. The pikeman covered his ear and turned his face aside as Moreno settled the barrel of his musket on his friend's shoulder. Moreno cocked the musket. He trained his weapon on the dread commander's face but it was a small profile, protected by the demon's helmet. Moreno offered a prayer to a god he no longer believed in and settled himself. He fired.

The men around him held their breath as the heavy musket ball sailed high and began to drop. It dropped and it struck the Dread Commander's head and the demon jerked sideways in the saddle. It jerked sideways and righted itself in the saddle and Moreno knew that he had missed. The dark-armored demon reined in his beast and examined the Spanish musketeer for a long moment. Then it set it spurs again and trotted up the hill to join its shining companion.

Men clapped Moreno on his shoulder, impressed with the shot even if the gesture came to naught. Moreno reloaded and stood with Gutiérrez by his side and he looked at the battlefield with a thought no longer to defence.

His friend lifted his chin to the enemy ridge. 'He may have been a miserly bastard at times, de Fontaine,' Guiterez said. 'But he was our miserly bastard. That does not sit well with me.'

Moreno followed his gaze. He saw the French commander on a beautiful bay horse and, beside him, the gore-splattered leader of the companies of the damned looking towards its small, blonde shadow. Moreno saw, too, the woods that fringed the battle field and how heavy and dense they grew. A man could hide in those for a long time. Gutiérrez caught his eye when Moreno looked back and his friend nodded his head.

'The broken command square,' said Moreno. 'Then the woods.'

Moreno removed his battered hat and used it to beat the dust from his buff coat. He replaced it and stroked his short beard with his right hand. Moreno looked at the veteran corporal who had assumed command with the death of the officers and called to the man in a voice that did not betray the twisting in his guts.

'Diego! Gutiérrez and I are going for a stroll in the woods. Perhaps see if we can get close enough for my friend to give them the kick up the arse he's been promising.'

The corporal smoothed his heavy moustache with a nonchalance that other men envied. He studied Moreno and Gutiérrez from under the brim of his wide hat. 'Go with God, José,' the man answered with a laugh as he doffed that wide hat. 'We will see you when all this is over. Wherever that may be. We will give you as much smoke as we can muster.'

The two friends raised their hands in farewell. Moreno slung the rodela on his back, for he liked the feel of it, and Gutiérrez thrust the hammer into his own belt.

'Where did you find that?' asked Moreno.

The pikeman settled the heavy lump of steel more comfortably. 'On the ground,' he said. 'I must have belonged to one of those *bastardos*. An old weapon, I think, but I like it.' Satisfied with the hammer's seat he picked up another musket. 'I will carry this for you.'

They crossed to the left of the square. Men nodded as they passed and some held out their hands to shake. No one thought that any of them would leave this field alive today; none seemed particularly worried by this either. Two men, the Alvarez brothers, stepped into their path and fell in beside them.

'We thought we would join you,' said Lorenzo, the older. Lorenzo was balding where his brother sported a full head of hair, but this was the only thing that set them apart. Although some years divided the brothers, they could have been twins. Moreno knew them for stalwart fellows.

Moreno nodded. 'We go now with the next volley. To the square. Then into the tree line and make our way up the ridge. When we get there, we will decide how to kill those *bastardos.*'

The group paused at the edge of the square and Moreno surveyed the ground. It was churned by the heavy beat of the demon horses' hooves and littered with torn bodies of this and the underworld. They waited and heard the command from the corporal and the Spanish guns fired. Smoke rolled across, sparse but perhaps enough, and the men ran.

The made the carnage of the First Square and dropped among the severed limbs and spilled entrails of their dead comrades. Flies, already feasting, rose in a disgruntled swarm and then settled on the prostrate men. Gutiérrez raised his head slightly and expelled air slowly. 'So far so good.'

With the sun dropping, an outline of what could have been a small defile was appearing, some hundred paces across the field. 'There,' declared Moreno with a small nod of his head. 'If we can make that then we might get to the trees.'

Gutiérrez turned to the ridge. 'They are set for their next charge. Let us go.'

The four men began to run. Moreno could feel the turf begin to vibrate under his feet as the death riders descended but he did not turn and look. It was just the cut in the earth ahead and his legs straining and the rasp of his comrades beside him.

The younger Alvarez, Héctor, turned without breaking stride and exclaimed, '*Madre mia*, they see us!' The Spaniards surged forward with fear and they gained the small depression in the earth. The men crouched, panting, and saw half a dozen or more of the Dread Cuirassiers galloping towards them. The black mounts stretched their necks with each stride, straining to sink wicked teeth into Spanish flesh. The four men hurried along the cut and the edge of the trees appeared but the last ten paces would be too many.

'Into the trees,' commanded Moreno.

He brought his musket up and fired at the first rider and the horse went down in a tangle of rattling armor and broken limbs. The cuirassier was caught in the stirrups and the beast's body broke its back as it rolled over the hard ground. Moreno had hoped that the tumbling beast would bring down at least one other but the riders avoided a collision expertly, one jumping the fallen charger in a brilliant display of riding. Moreno turned for the trees but he could feel the force of evil bearing down on him. The Spaniard looked behind as a looming cuirassier swung its heavy blade. The musketeer ducked instinctively and was thrown forward to the earth with a discordant clang like a broken bell falling from a belfry.

Moreno rolled across the grass and was up before he came to a stop. The black charger towered over him. It reared and lashed out with its front hooves. Moreno raised his musket in two hands to protect himself and the lashing limbs sent the weapon spinning out of his hands. In desperation, the Spaniard dove under the horse. A hoof caught his shoulder and the heavy shoe numbed his arm but he crawled like an injured crab and was free of the Dread Cuirassier for a moment. He lunged forward and was into the relative safety of the trees.

Gutiérrez beckoned him forward. The four men crouched behind a fallen tree in the sudden cool of the dense forest. It was darker within the trees, almost pleasant if one ignored the evil not a stone's throw away. The horsemen walked back and forth outside the forest perimeter as they decided what to do. In the background, the Dread Cuirassiers could be seen charging at the Spanish squares again.

'You owe whoever dropped that shield,' said Gutiérrez as he passed the musket to his friend.

Moreno worked the rodela from his back and drew his thumb along the dent made by the cuirassier's sword. His right arm was still numb but movement was returning. He opened and closed his hand several times as the nerves settled in place. 'I hope I get a chance to thank him,' he said. 'Let us go. Quietly now.'

The Spaniards moved low and they moved quickly. The rise was slight and not difficult for men on foot but the trees were close and they had to weave their way. It was quieter within the barricade of trunks and the air did not taste of spent powder. After some time, the sound of horses galloping cut through the trees and, to their right, disjointed flashes of dark riders could be seen moving quickly up the slope. Behind them, too, came the crash as more demon cavalry forced their way into the dark forest.

'They are trying to cut us off,' said Héctor Alvarez.

'It is what we would do,' replied Gutiérrez.

Moreno said, 'The trees will slow them. Let us get ahead of those uphill and they will waste their time searching for us here.'

They pushed forward, breath rasping now as the gradient increased. The cuirassiers behind were hampered as their mounts had to thread their way through the larger trees. In their rage the beasts trod over saplings and the Spaniards could hear these whipping upright like the forest was chasing them. A Dread Cuirassier called out in a language Moreno could not recognise and then pistol balls began to lash through the trees.

'Keep moving,' the musketeer grunted. He hurdled a fallen tree then slipped on the blanket of leaves beyond and fell on his bruised shoulder. He cursed under his breath but Morno was too busy trying to breathe to be creative. The others gathered around him in a crouch and their heads twisted about the gloom.

'We are fucked,' said Lorenzo Alvarez. 'They are too fast.'

'Just get me close enough so I can put a ball through that big bastard's skull.'

Uphill, Moreno watched the demon riders dismount and leave their horses at the edge of the trees. The cuirassiers began moving through the foliage on foot, armor dark and slick in the shadows of the tall trees. They had left their long-barrelled pistols in the saddle-holsters of their mounts but their swords were long and heavy and deadly. They were black predators in a dark green sea.

'It will not be done if we just sit here,' grunted Gutiérrez and he stood up. Behind the group the demon beasts sent up a howl more like hunting wolves than horses and the crashing in the trees increased. Moreno joined him and began to hurry up the slope as fast as he could, the group creating some distance from the struggling riders behind.

Ahead, the first dismounted cuirassier was cutting swiftly towards them. Moreno lent against a tree for stability and sent it back to hell with a well-placed musket ball into the thing's face. The cuirassier jolted backwards and his armor rang a metallic alarm and the demon's companions screeched in the silence after the shot. The dark riders fixed on the men and they came forward with death in their sunken eyes.

Moreno swivelled around the trunk and reloaded quickly. He turned back to see Gutiérrez engage a demon rider. The pikeman was fearless and he did not falter and as the cuirassier swung his sword, Gutiérrez ducked the slashing blow and powered his war-hammer into the demon's knee. It sounded like a branch but it was bone that cracked fiercely and the rider buckled. Gutiérrez turned quickly and his war-hammer caught a flash of light between the trees as the pikeman raised it high.

The force of the blow would have split an anvil in two and the Dread Cuirassier's head, helmet and all, shattered. The thick blood against the trees sent dark smoke rising to the canopy. The third came at the Alvarez brothers and Héctor ignored his brother's warning to clear the line of fire and charged. Lorenzo thrust the pistol back into his belt and drew his sword and followed. They pressed the demon back and their blades rang off the black armor but the cuirassier regrouped and came on again. It lunged the heavy point of its sword at the younger brother and Héctor was a moment too slow and the blade pierced his stomach and the shock froze the young man for a moment. His brother yelled and cut at the rider's head but the thing from hell had the young man by the shoulder now and it turned him into his brother's strike. Lorenzo's sword hacked into his brother's neck and the young man's head flopped backwards on severed muscles. Lorenzo shouted with the shock and he did not recover his blade quickly enough and the Dread Cuirassier, in a show of malevolent strength, picked up the younger brother's body and, the sword still embedded, rammed him against his sibling. It forced both men back and they stumbled across the forest floor, pinned together by the cuirassiers long blade. Lorenzo's shout was a cry of pain now as the demon forced them both against a large tree and the blade thunked into the trunk. The Spaniard strained to push his brother away and free himself but the solid hilt of the cuirassier's sword held them fast.

The demon rider grabbed Héctor's head and tore it from the remaining strands of flesh and, with this, Lorenzo's pain at the loss of his brother overcame the pain of his ruptured chest. The Spaniard drew his pistol again and with his brother beyond danger fired into the cuirassier's head. Lorenzo had aimed for the face but his strength was going and the heavy muzzle drooped. The pistol ball went through the demon's neck and it staggered back and collapsed into a low bush and its rotten blood settled on dry leaves and a small fire sparked and began to grow.

Other fires were growing from the fallen demons but Moreno left them. He met Gutiérrez beside the strung bodies of the Alvarez brothers. Lorenzo was dead, his face slumped forward on to the headless shoulders of his younger brother.

'Holy Mary,' declared Gutiérrez, 'that was not a good way to go.' The bandage that bound his face was red with blood but the pikeman did not notice.

'Ours will be no better if we don't kill those ugly bastards first,' said Moreno. He stripped the powder and shot from Alvarez and passed it to Gutiérrez.

Gutiérrez picked up the fallen pistol and tucked it under his left arm and began to reload. 'We stand here?'

Moreno nodded. 'It's as good as any. We cannot outrun them.'

They could see three Dread Cuirassiers forcing their mounts through the trees and they did not have long. Moreno pointed to where a fallen tree created a natural buttress and the Spaniards hurried there. The fire from the last fallen demon was growing stronger and might protect their flank. Moreno knew he could kill one in the saddle, so only two would remain.

Two fiends brought back from hell with no fear and no remorse.

Moreno slipped the rodela from his back and rested it beside him. Moreno's thumb traced the dent from the cuirassier's blade again and he shrugged his shoulders in answer to an unvoiced question.

'¡Fue sueño ayer; mañana será tierra!' muttered Gutiérrez as Moreno crouched beside him.

'de Quevedo?'

'He had a way with words,' said Gutiérrez.

Death was shifting between the trees and the air was filled with demonic calls and the grunts of the monstrous mounts as they forced a way through the surrounding brush. Moreno rested the muzzle of his musket on the fallen tree but he hesitated. His sight was not clear; the enemy was there, then gone, then there again. He did not know how many there were any more or if he was just looking at the same beast in his confusion. He waited and his shoulder ached and his throat was dry from more than the sting of spent gunpowder.

To Moreno's right, the low trees were flaming and he could feel the heat against his skin and see glowing orange embers sailing on the breeze between the trees. Reluctantly Moreno slipped his ammunition bandolier over his head and placed it under the fallen tree. One spark settling on the gunpowder across his chest and there would not be much of him left to mourn. It was a double-edge sword, that fire growing on their flank.

It came through that very inferno, the demon mount in a burst of flame and hate and its hide blazed like it was made of fire. Moreno twisted as the cuirassier fired its pistol and the trunk beside him flicked splinters into his face. The *musquetero* fired and the heavy ball slammed through the rider's shin and into the belly of the flaming beast. The Dread Cuirassier tottered but kept its seat as the horse snapped its distended snout at Moreno's head. He battered the fangs aside with the barrel of his musket and the demon beast stumbled on the forest debris, its corrosive blood hissing a line in the forest litter. Moreno drew his sword quickly and lashed the horse across its muzzle and it twisted aside, its shoulder knocking him to the ground. The musketeer scrambled away from the stomping hooves then coiled quickly back, every ounce of his strength in his thick shoulders flowing into the blade of his sword as he thrust it up and into the beast's chest. The black horse staggered to the side and the cuirassier's sword stroke was useless as the beast went down like an overturned cart. The death rider was trapped under its bulk by the broken limb and it screeched and howled as it tried to drag itself free. Moreno crossed to his rodela and slipped it on his arm then returned to the struggling cuirassier. His right boot stamped the thing's flailing arm to the earth and he raised the metal shield high and slammed it across the demon's throat. Its cries were wet now as the dark blood caught in its throat and Moreno smashed with the rodela again. He left the rider there to choke on its own foul fluids.

Another had set its mount to the barricade but a hidden branch, fallen in front of the trunk, clipped its front hoof and the demon horse stumbled and slammed against the downed tree. Gutiérrez raised his pistol but the rider fired first. Its aim was off due to the jolting of its mount but the cuirassier's ball clipped the fallen trunk, ricocheted, and struck the pikeman low in the torso under his breastplate. Gutiérrez grunted with the force but he held his mark and, as the demon beast spread its jaws to snap at him, the Spaniard fired straight into its open mouth.

The pistol ball exploded through the back of the horse's head and Gutiérrez heard it clang off the death rider's armor. Gore from the stricken mount covered the fiend's chest. The beast shuddered and collapsed against the barrier. The cuirassier fell, struck the tree and crashed to the earth. Gutiérrez dropped the spent pistol and grabbed for his hammer but pained clutched his insides and he doubled over. The demon rose and drew its sword and struck at the pikeman's head. Gutiérrez saw the flash of the steel in new bright firelight and he dropped to the ground. The big sword thunked solidly into the fallen trunk and stuck fast. Gutiérrez, his hammer in hand now and fighting the pain, smashed the head down onto the dead thing's boot. Bones cracked like a dry sticks and the cuirassier sprawled. The pikeman scrambled along the fallen demon's body, hammering as he went. A knee was pulverized, a thigh. The Dread Cuirassier tried to rise but Gutiérrez hammered it down with three powerful strikes on the thing's black cuirass. The pikeman placed his right knee on the armored chest and beat the demon's face with his heavy metal hammer until it was a black pulp, steaming in the air. Gutiérrez slide off the cuirassier's body but could not rise. He rested against the black armor of the thing that had killed him.

'I'm done for,' he said when Moreno joined him. The

musketeer stood next to his friend but he watched the last cuirassier across the makeshift barricade. The demon sat his evil steed but did not advance. Its sunken eyes returned the stare and nothing could be read upon its parchment face. Moreno crouched next to his oldest friend and listened to the wet suck of Gutiérrez' breath. He had seen enough wounds to know what this one meant.

'Yes, you are,' Moreno said quietly. 'Let go now, Mateo.'

After all the years and distance travelled, he could think of nothing more to say. He placed his hand on the dying pikeman's shoulder. Gutiérrez sucked in a breath and his face clenched. 'Send them back to hell, José,' he said quietly as he let a breath out. The fearless pikeman did not take in another.

Moreno moved Gutiérrez so that he was not touching the dead cuirassier and removed the hammer from his still clenched fist. Moreno crossed his friend's arms upon his chest. It was not much for such a man, thought Moreno, but he had nothing else at that moment. Moreno stood.

He could hear the battle continue to thunder beyond the trees, a storm of steel that his beloved *tercio* would weather until the last soldier fell. They had thought they would stop this army from the abyss, the brave Spaniards, but not from a fatal hubris. The *soldados* had tested themselves against all who had taken the field and never been found wanting. No, they carried the confidence of men forged hard by battle who had right on their side against an army brought forth from hell.

The *musquetero* looked towards the last Dread Cuirassier upon its demon horse and he thumped his sword against his steel rodela. It rang out above the din beyond the forest and Moreno did it again. The death rider stared at him. Its parchment face was impassive and this was in some way more terrifying than a shrieking banshee. It did not seem to care about anything beyond killing. Moreno raised his sword and sounded the steel shield again. He yelled at the thing upon the black beast, not words, but rage and sorrow. And fear.

The Dread Cuirassier slid from his beast. It did not draw

the horse-pistol from its saddle holster. Moreno wondered if there was some small vestige of human pride remaining that caused the demon to move forward with drawn sword only. If it was true, it was, to the musketeer, scant comfort. The fire crackled beside Moreno, beginning to turn uphill. Embers floated in the air, too beautiful for the death and destruction within that forest glade.

The demon placed its left hand on the fallen trunk and vaulted over. Moreno stepped out of measure to clear the sweep of its sword but then powered forward, protected by the large shield. He cut at the cuirassier's head but it caught his sword in a bind, pushing Moreno's sword to the side. The musketeer covered with his rodela and disengaged with a side step. He cut down at the demon's leg but the fiend stepped back and the blade passed by harmlessly. The Dread Cuirassier pressed in and its formidable sword strokes rang left and right off the steel shield. Moreno retreated and the force of the blows almost overwhelmed his reasoning but his training asserted itself and he disengaged with a step to the side. The musketeer thrust his sword point at the demon's neck, unprotected by armor, but the rider's gauntlet brushed the point aside. Moreno riposted quickly and the false edge of this side-sword scraped along the demon rider's forearm. The steel scoured a line along the black armor which squealed in protest but protected the decayed flesh beneath.

Moreno pressed forward and thrust for the throat again but he was offline and the dark armor turned the blade once more. The musketeer danced back as the cuirassier cut at him, down then twisting the edge and rising on the same line. Moreno tried to smother the blade with his shield but the strength of the demon folded his arm and he had to give way.

He was tiring, Moreno, for fighting for your life strained every muscle and sinew. His enemy was not, it seemed, and a demonic endurance spurred it onwards. The Dread Cuirassier held no expression, but its eyes still burned in the depths of its skull like a fire on a distant hill and Moreno could place any meaning his flagging body wanted in them.

The rider came at him and its long sword was hungry. Moreno blocked the first stroke with his rodela and his arm shuddered under the blow. It slashed again, backhand, and the shield folded around the blade under the force. Moreno twisted the rodela and moved the cuirassier's sword for a moment and struck swiftly at the demon's lower thigh. The death rider shifted back but Moreno's blade opened its dead flesh and the black blood began to flow. The cuirassier swung Moreno around by its trapped sword and Moreno's shield and the musketeer could not keep his feet. His arm slipped loose of the rodela and Moreno tumbled across the earth and into the fire. His buff coat gave some protection but Moreno's right sleeve caught and the flame lashed his right arm before he battered it out. Moreno came to his feet.

He watched the cuirassier stamp on his rodela until the shield slid loose of the demon's sword blade. Its black armored skirts rang as it raised its leg and Moreno's mind went back to his youth and the bells on the sheep when he would bring them down from the high country. Before his parents died of the sweating sickness and he made his mark and joined the army of the Spanish King. The musketeer smiled at the memory; the land severe yet beautiful, the people tough yet passionate. Moreno smiled and with that he knew that he would not die here today.

The demon rider struck and Moreno matched the cut and the blades bit. He thrust forward through that bind, knuckles up, his point aimed at the fiend's throat and the thing kept the engagement and pushed Moreno's sword to the left and offline. The musketeer felt the pressure and used the demon's pushing blade as a fulcrum and rotated his blade around the other sword and whipped his cutting edge at the cuirassier's neck. The demon flinched but Moreno's tip cut. It cut and the cuirassier reared back now to clear its opened throat from danger and Moreno's rear leg drew forward for power and the musketeer lunged. Moreno's blade bounded forward and the

Dread Cuirassier was too slow and the sharp steel found the hollow of the demon's throat and the dark blood gushed forth as Moreno bore down on his blade.

Moreno kept pushing and the rider stepped back and Gutiérrez' corpse was at its heels and the fiend went down. Moreno landed above it and his boot trapped its sword hand and it tried to rise but Moreno sawed his blade back and forth across its neck. The putrid blood burnt his thick gloves and its howl tore his ears but he did not stop until the Dread Cuirassier's head rolled free and the thing did not move any more.

Moreno stood and he wrenched his gloves free. Blisters covered his palms and the backs and it hurt to flex his hands. He stood and examined the skin and he did not know what to do for them and it was then that the Dread Cuirassier's demon mount vaulted the fallen tree and was upon him.

The *musquetero* fell back as its razor teeth lashed at him. The beast pounded the ground where he fell and Moreno squirmed away from the deadly hooves. He stood and a hoof caught him on the hip and he spun into the barricade as pain stabbed his lower back. Moreno dropped again and the ghastly horse snapped at him and gouged a chunk from the tree. He squirmed under the trunk in a desperate bid for safety and his blistered hand caught the bandolier he had hidden there and he knew what he had to do.

The demon mount reared and Moreno sprang forward, under the flailing limbs. He grabbed the saddle bow as the beast spun, trying to reach him, and held on. Around they went, then again, and the world was a green and orange blur of forest and fire. Moreno looped the bandolier of gunpowder around the horn of the saddle with hands that bled now and were slippery on the smooth leather. He let go and the demon horse's rump thumped him to the earth again. But, he was a Spanish soldier, Moreno, and when his mind was set he carried through to the ends of the earth. He came up with the rodela in both hands and charged at the beast like a *toro bravo* and the hellish horse stumbled on the uneven ground and Moreno charged again. He forced it back towards the fire as it snapped and bit at the rim of the shield but it was off balance now and falling. The flames welcomed the beast as Moreno turned and ran for the safety of the fallen tree. He was climbing over when the powder ignited and the green and orange world went black.

****

Moreno regained consciousness and the pain welcomed him. His hands and arm stung with burns and his right hip was both painful and numb at the same time. Moreno did not want to move but he could still hear the sounds of battle beyond the trees now that silence had fallen upon the forest. He had a job to complete and he dragged himself to his knees and then up to lean on the trunk.

The glade had been shorn by the fire and the explosion. Moreno pushed himself forward and he hobbled the area until he saw the glint of metal. He knelt painfully and gathered the fallen musket into his damaged hands. Moreno worked his way over the weapon but it seemed relatively undamaged, the woodwork scarred and pitted but not split. Importantly, the firing mechanism was operational.

Moreno had a musket ball in his pouch but no gunpowder. He leant against the fallen tree and the scorched bark crackled under his weight. He tipped his head back and looked at the sky between the trees and knew that the day was passing quickly. Moreno's head came forward and he shuffled to the body of his friend. Gutiérrez' corpse had been flung away by the force of the explosion but his front was undamaged and, tucked into his belt, the gunpowder bag remained intact. Moreno pulled the pouch free and, in a disjointed collapse, sat on the ground. The musketeer loaded his weapon as if there was no job on the earth of any greater importance.

He walked up the hill but it was slow and it was painful. Finally, Moreno reached the point where the forest arced towards the commanders and he went even more slowly. The foliage was dense and gave good cover and he came to the edge undetected. The *musquetero* found a thick trunk with a low branch perfect for a barrel rest and he carefully broke the limb to clear his sight. Moreno propped his musket in the branch and he looked down the barrel at the Dread Commander.

The dark giant stood upon its dark mount and its arm would raise and away would flow another troop of demon riders. If he craned his neck, Moreno could see the Spanish Squares. They were small now and his comrades grouped together in haphazard fashion as there were not enough men to form ordered ranks. In the centre, the Tercio flags were still raised defiantly. The Tercios would not surrender and the black cavalry would give no quarter.

Moreno sighted again. He had one shot left in him. The distance, he thought, was less than one hundred long paces and normally he could place a ball in a breast-plate size target at that range without thinking. Normally, too, his hands were not burnt raw and his hip possibly broken. Moreno settled into the weapon and his body took on the familiar form, perfected over years of training and battle. Many soldiers did not like the heavy, noisy muskets but Moreno had an affinity with the blend of wood and steel since the first time he picked one up.

The musketeer raised the barrel so that the ball would drop on target and placed his finger on the trigger. Across the barrel he could see the unholy pair and, as he watched, the small blonde figure turned its head towards him. Moreno saw the large, dark armored demon turn towards its companion then back in his direction. The Dread Commander turned his horse and touched spurs to flank and the big beast bounded forward. Straight towards where Moreno stood. It raised its arm and a squad of brute cavalry turned like a flight of swallows and joined the charge. Moreno's life was now counted in seconds.

His finger tightened but then he paused. Moreno's gaze flicked between the two demons, the dark and the light. He looked at the two and that nagging feeling nudged him again. It was an instinct, nothing more, but the musketeer had survived the storm of steel for too long not to trust that feeling. Then, with a mental shrug, Moreno sighted and squeezed the trigger and the musket roared and the ball of lead flew.

The musket ball flew and the dread commander and its fiendish cuirassiers thundered towards him and in the space between firing and impact Moreno found some peace. There was, now, nothing more he could do. He watched and he knew that his aim was true and he thought he could see the flight of the ball as it descended. It dropped and it struck and it sundered the face beneath the shining mane of hair and the shimmering thing from hell fell slowly from its horse.

It hit the ground dead. It died and the shining thing smouldered on the ground as its blood boiled. The towering demon in black turned sharply as its monstrous mount thundered across the earth and looked towards the bright armor. The dark thing which had seemed unstoppable crumpled suddenly like its bones had suddenly turned to so much chalk. Its mount went under it too and together the things from hell tumbled across the ground. A cloud of smoke rose from the pile of dark steel armor but the demon was no more.

The shining thing died and the Dread Cuirassiers died too. They crumpled on their mounts and the beasts from hell disintegrated with them and the field outside Rocroi rang with the crash of dark steel armor, empty now, tumbling across the earth. The field rang and around the churned ground the things from the abyss were consumed by their own demonic flames. The fires sparked and blazed quickly but they could not catch on the blood-damp ground and in a short time the slight breeze caught the acrid smoke and it drifted away.

Moreno left the musket beside the tree and walked from the woods. He crossed between the French and Spanish armies and it was a long painful walk. The musketeer joined his remaining comrades and stood there looking up at the mass of the French troops, untouched by the battle. He stood and men laid their hands on his shoulders or touched his arm in thanks but no one spoke.

The sun descended to the horizon and in the last light the French commander and his entourage trotted their horses down the hill. The Spanish sent men out to parley. The Tercios, or what remained of them, were silent as the soldiers returned and the order was given to retire.

The Tercios held their banners aloft as they watched the French army retire in orderly ranks. The Spanish soldiers held their heads high as they then marched in quiet ranks from the battlefield.

Only when the Spanish passed from view over the low hill was the field finally still.

¡Fue sueño ayer; mañana será tierra!

(Yesterday a dream; tomorrow dust!)
Nothing, just before; just after, smoke!
And I plot out ambitions, and can claim
not one point on the siege that circling looms!

An extract from a poem by Francisco de Quevedo y Villegas

Tim Hanlon has been a History teacher since the dawn of time. He tries to follow the tenets of Stoic philosophy but generally fails. Since he began submitting during the great lockdown of 2020 he has had some success with stories selected for anthologies by Specul8 Publishing, Sundial Magazine, 18th Wall Productions, DMR Books, Tule Fog Press, and Wicked Shadow Press. When not writing or reading, Tim enjoys banging on about craft beer with friends, boxing, and getting caught in the rain.

https://us.amazon.com/stores/author/B0BQKWYWLT?ref_=ast_author_cabib

On The Job Training

J.P. Staszak

Light from the streetlamps glinted off the silver Saint Micheal's Medal as he turned the modest pendant back and forth between his fingers. The memory of how proud his grandmother was the day he graduated from the Academy helped him to steady himself. He just hoped no one paid enough attention to him to see how nervous he was as the old riot van rattled along the Brooklyn streets.

"That ain't gonna help you Probie."

So much for that idea.

"These bastids don't give a damn what religion you are." Williams and another of the more seasoned members of their unit chuckled.

"Yeah, well, we all gotta have something I guess." He pulled the neck guard of his armor down as far as he could to tuck the Medal back into his shirt. The cool metal against his chest gave him some small measure of comfort as he stretched his neck to get the chainmail hood and body armor back into place.

"Yeah, sure. Mine's right here!" A hearty laugh accompanied an emphatic, if not suggestive, pat of the MP5 submachine gun that lay across his lap.

"Don't mind him, kid. He's just sore that's the only tool between his legs that works."

The whole unit laughed.

"Screw you Mickey! I didn't hear any complaints from Melissa last night."

A groan came from the other side of the cabin at the mention of Mickey's wife.

"That's 'cause you weren't there."

"Oh that's right, musta been your mom's house."

"Alright, save it for the bad guys." Their sergeant shut them down from the front seat before things got out of hand.

"Sorry Shep."

"Do we know what we're walking into?" Thompson leaned forward from where the groan had come from.

"Do we ever?" Williams laughed it off but, lack of proper intelligence was all too common when heading into the field, Terrance remembered that from one of the lectures he had. The instructor had said something about the difficulties of on-site communication, but Terrance wasn't convinced he had ever been "on-site". Often, people were just too scared to relay information properly and the particulars weren't discovered until they arrived in the field.

"It's the usual rundown," Shep called back, "Witnesses claim a woman was dragged into the basement of a residential building but no one actually saw the perp."

"And for *that*, they called us in?" Terrance could hear the annoyance in Williams' voice.

"That, and the fact that she was reported as floating through the air, the smell of rotten meat coming from the basement and the neighbors haven't seen any of the residents for a while."

"Good thing we packed the sulfur rounds, then." Mickey ejected the magazine from his shotgun to confirm the yellow shells were stacked within.

"The residence isn't anywhere near the R train, so we won't have to worry about crossover with the subway."

"What about the sewer?" The concern on Thompson's face was almost comical, "I don't wanna deal with no sewer again."

"Should be all dirt and rock underneath those houses."

"We're goin' *au naturel*, I like it." Williams laughed at his own joke.

Terrance frowned.

"You look disappointed kid."

"I was kinda hoping my first call would be one of the

Werefolk." He tried to make himself as small as possible after admitting his naive wish.

"The shifters ain't comin' this far into the city, gonna hafta transfer upstate if you want that kinda action." Williams followed Mickey's lead, checked the rounds for his rifle and slapped the mag back into place.

"We're here." Nowak announced from the driver's seat.

The back doors were flung open as the van slowed and with no regard for personal safety, they filed out before the vehicle stopped.

Someone called out for Sergeant Shepard and Mickey motioned for Terrance to join the rest of the unit next to the van. There was so much noise and flash photography on the street that part of him would have been happy to hop back in the vehicle and wait for his orders away from the public eye.

As he looked past the lights from the squad cars and cameras, he could see the signs held high by fanatics that had come out to watch them do their jobs all before the sun had even come up. A young girl stuck out immediately as she waived a vibrant pink poster with black letters and random swirls of glitter spelling out "Thank You Guardian Angels!". On the other side, the one that caught his eye was a man who yelled incoherently and violently shook a plain white piece of oak tag with the words: "All Beings Respected!" in bold red font.

"Oh look, 'Assholes Being Retarded' are here." To the amusement of the rest of the crowd, Williams flipped up his middle finger to the group huddled around the guy with the sign.

"You hear what they tried to do up in Yonkers?" Thomson started to laugh before he finished the question.

"Nah, what?"

"Dumbasses staged a protest in front of the City Clerk's office thinkin' it was one of our precincts."

"No fuckin' way." With eyes lit up like a kid that just found out where he could get free candy, Williams looked back and forth between the group of ABR members and Thompson.

"Imagine being some po' bastard tryna get your passport renewed and one of these knuckle-fuckers comes up to you yellin' about 'respecting ancient beings'?" The words filtered out through Thompson's cackle of laughter.

"Is it always like this?" Terrance tried to be discreet with his question as Williams went to taunt the ABR group.

"Oh yeah kid, especially after what happened in Philly last year." Mickey said through a smile as he looked out at the crowd.

"That's what they get for cutting the budget for their locals in half." Nowak joined them.

"You're not wrong." Mickey gave a slight wave to someone in the crowd, his boyish smile never broke as he spoke around it.

"Sucks for all those people that got stuck in the quarantine."

"We don't even know if there's anybody left behind the wall to feel sorry for, Probie." Somehow Nowak managed to sound ominous despite the lack of emotion behind the statement.

To hear them discuss the city like it no longer existed, and with such a casual nature meant that it wasn't so far outside the realm of normalcy for them.

Who knows what else these guys have seen and heard that doesn't get talked about.

"After thirty years, you'd think people would be used to this stuff by now." He unconsciously turned his back to the crowd.

"Hell no kid! People need heroes, and right now, we're it." Williams rejoined them and put a fist in the air like an old-school wrestler, the reaction from the crowd amplified him like a battle charge.

"And you might as well enjoy it." Mickey nodded toward the van, "Why else would we have this awesome backdrop for photo ops?"

A glance at the side of the van was all Terrance needed to see the overly stylish lettering emblazoned across it:

Mythic Police Department, New York City Division.

"Rack 'em, we're not waiting any longer." Shep slid the visor from his helmet down as he walked up to them with the local uniformed officer in charge. "Local unis have already cleared out this block and the next one over, we're authorized for S&D."

"Whoa, hold up!" the officer threw his hands out to his side, "You didn't say nothin' about that. We called you guys in to help get that lady back."

"No," Shep gave the local a joyless smile, "you called us in because you can't handle the situation you've been presented with. We can."

The uni had no response. It was difficult for most civilians to comprehend the world they lived in now, let alone the mandate that MPD had.

After a comms check and a brief nod of encouragement from Shep, the crowd erupted with cheers and whoops of excitement at the sight of the MPD unit as they charged their firearms and moved out.

They moved down the street to the alley next to the target building and Terrance was glad to be away from the disruptive crowd as they entered the backyard.

Shep signaled Thompson and Nowak to grab the steel doors on either side of the basement entrance. With a quick three-two-one countdown, the doors were yanked open. Mickey and Terrance moved forward to aim their shotguns down the steps and shine their lights into the darkness.

The warm smell of rot and filth hit them like a baseball bat to the face. Terrance did his best to fight down the sickness as it rose inside him, but the vomit was unstoppable. He was at least able to turn his head away from the steps and to his credit, he slid right back into his position with no mind paid to the chuckle from Williams.

"Happens to all of us Probie." Shep gave his shoulder a light pat to reassure him, "When you're ready."

With a sheepish nod, he descended the steps into the dimly lit basement. Mickey and the rest followed suit while he silently reminded himself that he earned the right to be there with this unit, at this moment. All his assessments from the Academy proved that he had what it took to fight the mythical monsters that had terrified humanity since their so-called reawakening.

The basement was warm and more damp than it should have been for the time of year.

"It's always the humidity that gets ya."

"Why the hell *is it* so humid?"

"Some of these guys like to keep things... *moist.*" Terrance could hear the amusement in Williams' voice.

Someone snorted.

"Shut it! Watch your corners."

Between the smell and the damp air, Terrance didn't know whether to breathe deep or shallow as he moved with slow, deliberate steps. He watched for a shimmer, a flutter, any disturbance in the air just as he had been trained to do. Despite his lack of experience with the unit, he had complete trust that the rest of them would check his sides and watch their six as they moved cohesively through the dark room.

"Burrow, ten o'clock." Mickey moved forward at a quicker pace and the unit followed.

The entrance to the Burrow was just a hole in the corner of the basement where the wall met the floor. Dirt, brick, and cement lay strewn across the floor like something had burst forth from underneath. Everything that made the basement intolerable had emanated from the hole in the floor and it was exponentially worse within.

"Party time gentlemen."

Everyone took that as their cue to put on their air-purifier masks and sling their weapons while Thompson secured a line for them to drop into the burrow. Mickey and Terrance were the first two down, followed by Shep and Williams with the other two members of their unit remaining in the basement. He didn't dare say anything, but he was concerned with leaving Thompson and Nowak behind since their two largest members would probably be a big help if they made contact.

The masks didn't block out any of the smells completely, but they at least made the hole about as bearable as the basement had been, for whatever that was worth.

Terrance was faced with two tunnels that had been dug out of the earth in the direction they had come from, each of them pitch black and uninviting. He didn't know which way to go. Did he even have to make that decision? What if he chose wrong? What if they split up?

He exhaled slowly and remembered the advice he got during combat training.

Focus, listen to your Sergeant, follow orders, it'll all wash out.

Mickey shined his light on a specific patch of dirt that looked like someone had dragged a garden rake through it.

"Looks like she didn't go easy." Shep pointed towards the tunnel the drag marks went down and this time Mickey took point, followed by Shep. "Williams at our six. Activate halos."

Terrance reached up and clicked the button to activate the built-in ring light. All four men were bathed in their own personal aura of ultraviolet light as the angled strip around the side of the helmet came to life.

"Take it easy Probie, fun's just gettin' started." He gave Terrance a slight nudge on the shoulder to get him on his way.

He had never been claustrophobic, but he began to understand it as they moved through a tunnel with a ceiling too low to stand upright and walls too narrow to travel in more than a single file. They staggered their paths so they could at least shoot past each other if need be but if they had to resort to a firefight in this tomb, they would probably be dead in short order no matter what they did. At least now he knew why the big guys stayed behind; Shep had plenty of experience and Terrance was right not to question him.

As they moved through the tunnel, Terrance could feel the gradient shift downwards and he had to wonder just how deep underground they would end up. They maintained a steady pace until it opened into a cavern, wider than the basement and twice as high.

The stench of death was so prominent that their masks were rendered useless in the face of it.

"Kill chamber." Shep whispered the warning and Terrance could feel his chest tighten.

This is it.

Mickey stayed low to maintain eyes on the ground and Terrance followed his lead while Williams and Shep scanned the cavern ceiling for any potential "hangers".

Their lights revealed a hellscape of bodies strewn across the ground in various states of decay. Some were obviously killed more recently than others, but all of them were locked in positions of anguish and torment.

As they moved through the chamber, their lights settled on a stone slab that resembled a dais. Like the dead bodies before her, the woman that laid on the platform was contorted in pain. Paralyzed by the toxin in her system, she melted from the inside while the creature that lay atop her perversely sucked her life away.

As the sickly pale skin of the parasite began to redden from their UV lights, its blood-soaked face detached from her neck. The limbs unfurled from the carelessly discarded meal as it stood to a full height of over seven feet.

A sense of dread crept up in the pit of Terrance's stomach as he examined the horrifyingly inhuman features that stared at them.

Its oblong head housed coal-colored eyes with ruby centers that glistened in the light and somehow took attention away from the fact that there were only two mucus-lined slits where a nose should be. The open mouth revealed viper-like fangs and a proboscis tongue that continued to slurp at the blood and liquefied organs that dripped from its face.

Terrance had seen all the photos in the academy and had read both witness testimony and detailed forensic explanations for exactly what he saw in front of him. He thought it had prepared him for this day but the tears in his eyes that mirrored those that flowed from the woman told him differently. He quickly came to terms with the fact that *nothing* could have prepared him for an encounter with a full-blown vampire.

He wanted to run as it flexed spider-like hands with razor-sharp talons, but he was frozen and felt light-headed, unable to think clearly as spindly arms were spread wide and a scream erupted from the creature's gullet. All four men buckled and instinctively reached to cover their ears as though that would stop the hypersonic scream that ripped through their ear protection into their very minds.

Terrance shook his head to try to clear the fog and pain that had been brought on like a shockwave.

"Stupid cheap-ass ear plugs!" He barely heard Williams' nonsensical complaint as the report of weapons fire echoed through the chamber and the new smell of garlic and rotten eggs filtered through the mask.

Mickey grabbed him by the vest and shook him violently. He heard him say "Snap out of it!" but it was like he had yelled from another room. He got dragged to his feet as the flash from the muzzle of Williams' sub gun caught his attention.

Time to go to work.

He brought his shotgun up and aimed in the same direction Williams had fired but the vampire was already gone. With a rapid sweep of his light, he looked for distortion in the air and found it as the creature shifted from gaseous to physical form right in front of Shep. With the force of a Mack truck, the vampire railed into the sergeant and the rest of them were left to helplessly watch as the man flew backwards. His halo flickered and died as his helmet bounced off the cavern wall.

Dirt sprayed into the air as bullets from Williams' short

burst went straight through the vampire that became more miasma than flesh. Not content to leave Shep knocked out on the ground, it rushed forward and lifted him into the air by his head.

"Check fire!"

None of them wanted to risk the shot as Shep dangled like a ragdoll in the creature's hand. Instead, Terrance and the rest narrowed their light beams to use them like lasers against the sensitive skin of the vampire. It dropped Shep back to the ground as it screeched in pain and phased again. The cloud of particles became little more than a shimmer in the air as it moved around the cavern with the speed of a tornado.

"Come on fuckstick! Land already!" In a strange twist of fate, it listened to Williams and materialized on the upper part of the far wall. It turned to hiss at them from its perch as though the height provided safety.

They know not to get shot but they don't understand what a gun is.

Williams let off a long burst while Mickey and Terrance moved forward and peppered the wall with buckshot. For a moment it seemed like it had lost its grip and was about to go into freefall but instead a mist burst away from the rockface.

The vampire gave away its next position as it collided with the wall behind them. It screeched rapidly and clawed at its leg, far more concerned with the painful reaction it had to the sulfur-infused bullet that had bitten into its flesh.

"Don't like that, do ya bitch?" Mickey pulled his sidearm and fired several rounds from across the chamber.

The sonic howl ripped through them again but not as powerful as the first one.

Terrance was able to clear his head more easily than the last go around, just in time to see the distortion in the air move towards him and begin to solidify.

He panicked, squeezed the trigger too early and the buckshot blew through the vampiric cloud like it wasn't even there.

"Check fucking fire Probie!"
"Jesus, shit! You good Mick?"
"Yeah. Get your head on straight kid!"
The air between them fluttered, Mickey was lifted off his feet and dropped like a hot potato.
"What the fuck was that?!?" Mickey groaned from the floor.
"Get him up Probie!"
Williams let off several quick bursts of cover fire through the chamber while Terrance ran to help Mickey to his feet, but he never made it to him.
His feet went out from under him, and he suddenly stared up at the floor of the cavern as he crashed into it.
The cavern went quiet.
"You two bumblefucks wanna get up and join the party?" Williams kept his head on a swivel as he scanned the chamber.
"Shut. Up. *Harry!*"
Back on their feet, they widened their lights to cover more area and spread out slowly.
"Get down kid!"
Without hesitation Terrance listened to Williams and took a knee as the vampire materialized behind him and then tried not to think about the bullets that flew over his head.
It screeched again when the reports stopped, and Terrance spun himself around on his knees to see a completely solid vampire that was fixated on Williams as he reloaded. He took aim and sent a single shell into the demonic face above him. The skull of the vile creature turned into a geyser of blood and bone fragments as the body collapsed into a gangly pile.
From the ground, he thanked his grandmother, Saint Michael, God, and whomever else just shined their grace on him as he stole a moment to catch his breath and lay his hand over the pendant beneath his shirt.
"Hell of a shot Probie! One in a million!" Mickey gave him a congratulatory slap on the shoulder and simultaneously pulled him back to his feet.

"Shep's hurt bad! We gotta get 'im outta here!"

Terrance was suddenly reminded of when he'd get to watch the races at the old Aqueduct Racetrack back in Queens while his father tended the grounds. The stadium floor would rumble when the horses galloped past him at full speed, and he thought it was the greatest thing.

The cavern floor did the same thing now and the memory of better days was stolen away from him as grisly sounds that no horse could make filled the chamber.

"Another one?!?"

Mickey shook his head rapidly. He knew it was a stupid question the moment it came out of his mouth since all reports he'd read had claimed vampires hated cohabitation.

They shined their lights around the cavern frantically and for the first time noticed the other tunnels as hairless, human-sized creatures rumbled into the chamber and scrambled towards them on all fours.

"Dhampir! *Run!*" Mickey pushed him towards the tunnel that was now their only source of escape.

Of course it had dhampir with it.

Williams dragged Shep ahead of them and they alternated cover fire at their six. The occasional half-breed fell to their blasts whenever they got too close, obliterated by the narrow spread.

The mutated humans may not have been as strong as a full-fledged vampire, but they were fast. Whatever they lacked was made up for in numbers that typically would have ensured a vampire's safety. Of course, without their master to guide them, these daytime guardians were nothing more than rabid beasts looking for a meal.

At their exit point, Williams quickly secured Shep so the other two could bring him up. Mickey and Terrance planted themselves at the mouth of the tunnel and squeezed off shots every time a mutated rat-like head came around the corner. The confined space ensured quick and easy kills.

"Break!"

They fell back to reload while Williams took their spot, controlled bursts rang off down the tunnel while magazines were exchanged and Shep was handled.

The rope was dropped back down, and Williams yelled for them to go. Without argument, Terrance quickly wrapped the rope around his forearm and the two human cranes struggled to bring him up into the basement without further injury.

Sarge definitely made the right choice; I wouldn't have been able to do that.

"Get Shep outta here!" Williams yelled between bursts of fire the moment he cleared the hole.

Thompson and Nowak carried their wounded leader as carefully as two men of their caliber could, while the other three continued to fire into the burrow.

"There's too many of them!" Mickey dropped back to slap his last extended magazine into his shotgun.

Without much thought behind it, Williams proceeded to grab a grenade off his belt, yank the pin, and with a sidearm throw that would have made any major league pitcher proud, he beamed it into the tunnel.

"FRAG OUT!"

Once the grenade left his hand, they all high-tailed it for the exit. Whether the tunnel collapsed from the concussive force or not was an afterthought as they launched themselves up the stairs and slammed the steel doors behind them.

Terrance collapsed onto the ground and ripped his mask off to catch his breath. Compared to the vampiric hellhole they had just escaped from, the city air was as fresh as a country meadow. He wanted to rip off the body armor as well but after an up-close observation of exactly what a vampire did to its victims, he might just get himself a set of chainmail pajamas.

"C'mon T, we ain't done yet." Williams helped him to his feet.

"What happened to 'Probie'?"

"Probies don't kill vampires, certified badass mother

fuckers do."

Terrance smiled in a way that gave away his youthfulness.

"Don't go gettin' all soft on me now." He gave Terrance a playful punch in the arm as Mickey shouted from the front of the house and waved them over.

"Shep has a cracked sternum, probably a concussion, they've got medevac on the way, plus three other units to work clean up." Mickey informed them as they made their way back to their van.

"Helluva day."

Terrance ignored them and got in the back of the vehicle.

"Poor little guy must be all tuckered out." Mickey smirked at the jibe.

"Not yet." Terrance came back around with his shotgun slung on his back, an MP5 in hand, grenades on his belt, and spare magazines in every pouch possible.

"Like you said, the fun's just getting started."

"I think I'm startin' to like this kid."

"He certainly has a bit of charm to him."

"Yeah, like a puppy or somethin'."

"Maybe one of those special puppies, you know, like the kind that go running into walls for no reason."

Terrance didn't really know what a "guffaw" was. He'd heard the word and read it a couple of times in books he'd been forced to read for school, but it wasn't until he heard the sound come out of Williams' mouth, did he understand it.

Mickey laughed along with him, and Terrance couldn't help but join in. The stress of their experience beneath the surface would be enough to make normal people whither into a blathering mess, but they cackled like immature children.

"We should probably get these people out of here." The dirt from the back of Mickey's hand smeared a line along his cheek as he wiped away a tear.

"How's the ears?" Williams removed his plug from the ear that didn't have the comm and Terrance noticed the dried blood that had pooled within.

He swiped out his own plug and looked down at the flecks of blood on the innocuous piece of foam.

"They hurt, but not as much as I thought they would." Suddenly the gravity of the situation became very real, and his hands started to shake uncontrollably. His breaths became shallow and rapid as he desperately looked to his teammates for some kind of guidance.

"Okay kid, relax." Willaims grabbed him and moved towards the back of the van to get him out of the public eye.

He set Terrance down and Mickey unbuckled his vest to relieve some of the pressure he felt in his chest.

"Terrance, look at me!" Mickey pointed to his own eyes with two fingers, "Right here buddy, okay? You're all right, deep breaths." He demonstrated the slow inhale through his nose and exhale through the mouth several times until Terrance caught on. "There we go, you're good man, everything's good."

"You did a hell of a job down there T, couldn't ask for better." Williams tousled his hair.

"My hands." He looked down at them as they continued to shake violently.

"Yeah, it happens kid..." for the first time since Terrance had met him, Williams looked somber, "It'll happen a lot more to ya, and it'll take a while for it to stop happening too. Just take a load off, you earned it."

He didn't want to let the team down, didn't want to remind them how green he was but he didn't have the drive to argue, and he had no way to stop the tremble he could feel straight down to his soul.

Thompson and Nowak jogged over to them and both burly men gave Terrance the same look of concern.

"You good Probie?"

"He's fine!" Williams nearly bit Thompson's head off, "He just needs a minute..." His tone softened and took on something that resembled pride as he added: "The kid took out his first vampire, he's entitled."

The two newcomers exchanged a glance and stared at Terrance in disbelief.
"No shit?"
"Y-yeah."
"It was young, but it counts." Mickey confirmed.
"Y-*young?*"
"Oh yeah kid, it only gets worse from here."
"Either way," Nowak gripped his shoulder, "We celebrate tonight."
Terrance forced a laugh.
"Go on, take whatever time you need." Mickey pointed to the inside of the van once he realized the crowd had all eyes on them.

On shaky legs he moved as far into the van as he could and sat heavily on the bench, his body curled in on itself as he closed his eyes and continued to breathe the way Mickey had shown him. He took his earpiece out and tucked his hands into his armpits to try to slow down the shakes, but it felt like it was a permanent part of him now.

Williams' voice carried into the van as he announced to the crowd that they had everything under control. The crowd exalted with cheers and shouts of thanks after Williams added that they had themselves a bona fide hero on their squad. Some part of Terrance found comfort in the reaction they got from the people, and it helped to calm him, but it wasn't long before his body gave in to sleep.

He became oblivious to the sounds of joy and celebration around him and never knew when they turned to screams of terror and pain.

The van rocked hard enough to jostle him awake. He shook off the sleep and realized the doors were closed now, possibly in consideration for his impromptu nap. Sunlight shone through the slats of the windows, and he checked his watch in disbelief as the number 10:34 stared back at him. A glance out the front window made him pause and something about the view made his neck tingle.

There was no crowd, no police, no movement at all.
That's not right.
He put his comm back in and tried not to panic.
"This is Brooklyn-One-Foxtrot to Brooklyn-One-Bravo, please respond, over."
Static.
"Brooklyn-One-*Charlie*, this is Foxtrot, please respond, over."
Static.
"This is Br-
"*Holy shit T, is that really you? We thought you were done for!*" Screams, gunfire, and dhampiric screeches could be heard in the background of Williams' transmission.
"What the hell is going on? Where are you guys?"
"*We're about fifteen, shit I don't know... Thompson, where the hell are we?... no motherfucker I got the kid on the line... well put your fuckin' earpiece in!*"
"Hey Probie, you know where the dealerships are at on Fourth Ave?"
"Yeah... I think so."
"*Well go to Fourth and then head North, ain't no way you'll miss us.*"
"Copy that!"
"*Head on a swivel T, those rat-faced fucks are everywhere!*"
"Copy, en route!"

As the adrenaline pumped through his body again, he quickly straightened his armor and grabbed the sub gun he had carelessly left on the deck of the van. With a chambered round, he knelt and pushed one door open slowly. With no immediate response, he eased his way out onto the street to get a better view.

Numerous fires raged, some out of storefronts, others from vehicles that included an overturned MTA bus. He could hear gunfire in the distance but there was no way to tell where it originated or who was behind it.

Before he could take a single step away from the van, he heard a guttural sound come from above him. With barely enough time to turn around, he found out what had rocked the van as a dhampir dropped off the roof and knocked him to the ground. Bloodshot eyes stared at him hungrily as he moved his head to keep the rancid saliva that dripped from overgrown razor teeth away from his face. The mutated human was stronger than him and easily kept him pinned as he used his forearms to keep the vermin at bay and silently thanked their armorer for the bracers he wore.

His only choice was to risk the bite and hope that his armor didn't fail him. His left hand groped at his belt to grab his sidearm but found the hilt of his knife first, he pulled it and awkwardly stuck it into the gut of the dhampir.

The hot breath that came out as it howled in pain made his stomach lurch. A sideways yank of the blade gave him a bath of intestines and bodily fluids as he scrambled back. With some space between them, he pulled his pistol and ended the life of the creature in front of him while it tried to rein in its own organs.

Except for his heavy breathing, it had gone quiet on the street. Now that his face wasn't in danger of being ripped off, he noticed that "it" was in fact a "she", not much older than his baby sister. This was someone's daughter, indiscriminately stolen from her family by monsters.

Just like mom...

He shook off the memory, clouded judgment was the last thing he could afford right now. Under protest, he forced his body to get up. He grabbed his sub gun to make sure everything was still in proper working order and headed towards Fourth Avenue.

Most of the streets were deserted but he could see people peak out from behind window curtains or occasionally over the edge of a roof as he double-timed it until he caught sight of a small group of dhampir up the street from him. He stopped next to a cargo van and lined them up in the red dot optical sight.

He steadied himself against the van as he screwed on his suppressor and clicked the selector switch to semi-automatic. With the leader of the pack lined up in the red dot, he exhaled and squeezed the trigger. The dhampir's head erupted onto the side of the building and its cohorts screeched in shock. The rat-like appearance of the dhampir fit their behavior and demeanor so well that Terrance somehow found them more repulsive than the pure vampires. As the vermin anxiously looked around, he lined up the second one and went through the motions again. The final dhampir recoiled in disgust as the gray matter of its companion splattered all over its face thanks to another clean headshot.

Despite these creatures being little more than animals, especially without their sire, they still seemed to know that they had kinship with one another. If he cared enough, he'd consider it interesting, his sister the zoologist might even call it fascinating but as far as he was concerned it just confirmed that they felt the same fear he did.

He lined up the last one as it stupidly looked around for where the assault came from. At the last second, it spotted him but never got the chance to even bare its teeth. Terrance squeezed the trigger one more time and sent a round straight through its left eye.

Very pleased with himself, he lowered his MP5 and ensured there were no other wanderers around him.

A scattered applause could be heard, and he looked up to see people on their roofs as they cheered him on. He felt his face get warm with the attention and he gave them a polite wave before he moved on.

As he neared an intersection less than three blocks away from Fourth Avenue, he heard hail or heavy rain but there wasn't a cloud in the sky. He continued until he caught something in the distance off to his left. A swarm of dhampir that resembled an ocean wave recklessly clambered over abandoned vehicles as they worked their way down the street.

Towards him.

"Shit."

As fast as his legs could carry him, he ran down the sidewalk away from the ocean of rabid vermin.

Out of pure instinct, he threw himself to the side and let loose two quick bursts as a half-breed jumped out in front of him from a shattered storefront window. With a tuck and roll, he sprung back to his feet and continued his mad dash.

All those damn burpees paid off after all.

Finally on Fourth, he could hear a hail of gunfire, screeches from dhampir, and shouts from good old home-grown American humans. Thompson was right: there was no way he'd miss them.

"Brooklyn-One-Foxtrot... coming in hot."

"*Oh take your time kid, we're here all day.*"

"Northbound on Fourth!"

"*We got ya T, come on in.*"

He ran straight down the center of the avenue; his lower body began to burn as his legs pumped like pistons once he saw the faces of the men from his unit. He had never been so happy to see anyone in his life. He slid over the hood of a police cruiser and landed flat on his backside between Mickey and Williams.

"Goddamn kid, that was a ballsy maneuver!"

"How the hell are you still alive?"

"Gotta... go." He forced out the words as he tried to catch his breath.

"Not today you ugly mother-" gunfire from Nowak's short-barreled SAW drowned out Thompson as he yelled at the half-breeds.

"Whaddya mean kid? We got a perfectly defensible position right here."

"More... coming."

"Well, bring 'em on!" Williams pointed at another group of shooters that held their own against the dhampir, "Even the gangbangers are gettin' in on the fun."

"No-no... too many."

Mickey risked his head for a quick scan and caught sight of a small group of vermin as it worked its way around a corner.

"Apf, that's noth-" his voice trailed off as the group continued to come around the corner. He dropped back down behind the car and quickly switched his magazine for a fresh one.

Williams caught sight of the flood and something he saw piqued his interest.

"Ho. Lee. Shit." He looked around and clicked his comms, "Hey yo Thompson, *Archie Bunker*, ten o'clock."

Thompson stopped his assault and Nowak covered him as he looked down the avenue.

"*Well. Ho. Lee. Shit.*"

"That's what I said!"

Terrance followed their line of sight to see a dhampir larger than the rest with a more prominent skull. It was just different enough from the others to be noticeable.

"That's the guy the big guy makes so that he can make all the other little guys." Is the way an archdhampir was described to him when he was younger. They were rarely ever seen, but they were still a known commodity.

The archdhampir, *Archie*, screeched and chirped at his smaller counterparts.

"*Is that motherfucker directing them?*"

"Can they do that?"

"*Apparent-fuckin-ly.*"

The avenue filled with dhampir as Archie perched himself atop a semi-truck.

"Alright, time to go!"

There was a chaotic sprint up the avenue, the gangbangers chose to split off and head west while the MPD unit continued North.

Terrance stopped dead in the middle of the street, his chest heaved from the sprint as he stared at the vehicle next to him.

One of his teammates yelled at him to keep moving and another questioned his sanity.

"What the fuck kid?"

Terrance pointed to the cigar-shaped truck with the name ExxonMobil painted on the side of it. Williams looked to the truck and when he turned back to Terrance, he was eye-level with a hand grenade.

The rest of the unit joined them and it didn't take long for them to realize what Terrance had suggested.

"I like it." Nowak nodded approvingly.

"Fuck it, let's tap this keg."

It wasn't long before the tanker had spilled its load of gasoline out onto the avenue. The team hurriedly moved to a safe distance and watched as the dhampir plodded into the small lake.

"Have at it kid."

Terrance pulled the pin and launched the grenade down the avenue. The team watched the small explosive sail through the air, hit the ground and detonate. Dhampir scattered away from it, but little else happened.

"Dammit."

He was about to ask if he should throw his other grenade when the gasoline went up. The flames spread instantaneously and sent the dhampir into a panic. When the first vehicle went up, bodies flew.

It was a slow chain reaction, but it was well worth the wait to see the street littered with dead and injured dhampir while the flames and explosions were enough of a deterrent to stop the swarm from advancing.

"Nobody's ever gonna call you 'Probie' again." Williams called out as he approached.

"At this rate, he can be called whatever the hell he damn well pleases." Thompson laughed.

"At this rate, we're gonna be calling him 'Sir'." By Nowak's standard, that was a joke but there was something there that the veterans silently acknowledged amongst themselves.

"How about you just tell me why the *fuck* you left me in the van?"

"It wasn't on purpose kid, I swear to you. We were clearin' out the civilians, got word about dhampir comin' up outta the sewers and then everything went to shit." Williams' eyes showed that he was apologetic.

"There was no getting back to the van, especially after they started popping up all over the city." Mickey stepped up to support his teammate.

"So what's the plan?" Terrance slumped his shoulders.

"We gotta get outta Brooklyn, hopefully we can regroup with another unit or the National Guard."

"Queens?" Mickey suggested.

"Hell no, too far." Thomson seemed adamant, "My dogs barking already."

"We're closer to the Varrazano anyway, we hoof it across there and down to Midland, borrow a ride from the precinct there and then up across the Bayonne and right back to HQ in Midtown."

Everyone stared at Nowak as they quietly picked apart the suggested plan and looked for a reason to argue against it but everyone came up short.

"Alright, I guess we're goin' to Staten Island."

They walked the abandoned streets of Bay Ridge slowly so as not to risk another run-in with whatever was left of the swarm. Thanks to a little professional courtesy from some of the local uniformed police at the other end of the Varrazano-Narrows Bridge, they bypassed a checkpoint and made their way onto the island.

By the time they reached the MPD precinct in Midland Beach, a station less than half the size of the headquarters in Manhattan, it was late afternoon with evening close behind.

There was a commotion of people throughout the building and all of them ignored the five men who looked like a group

of lost children that had gotten separated from their school trip.
"What the hell happened to you?" A young officer stopped in her tracks as they caught her eye.
"Brooklyn." They answered her simultaneously.
"You're gonna want to talk to the Captain then." She craned her neck and stood on her tiptoes as she looked through the bustling crowd. "Back there, by the conference room. Big guy, bald head, can't miss 'im."
The look on the Captain's face said more about their physical condition than any of them was willing to acknowledge.
"You're not going to headquarters."
"Sir, we gotta report back, we-" Williams being the most senior officer, spoke for them but could barely get a word in.
"You don't understand Officer, Manhattan has fallen."
They looked at each other and back at the Captain in open confusion.
"How long have you been out of contact?"
"All day."
"At approximately oh-eight-hundred hours this morning, a massive incursion took place, thousands of dhampir emerged in Greenwich Village and swept across lower Manhattan. By midday, there were tens of thousands moving north, as of an hour ago, there were so many new infected that the Governor has decided to blow all the bridges and collapse the tunnels to try to isolate the infestation."
"They're just turning people?" Mickey's brow tightened.
"Near as we can tell, yes."
"That's the same way things started in Brooklyn."
"And Philadelphia." The Captain remained stone-faced as they realized the implication he had made.
"Off the record, Brass thinks it might be the same bloodsucker directing everything. It's all too organized to be a random attack and all those dhampir had to come from somewhere."
"So, what about Brooklyn?"

"National Guard is being brought in to assist in containment but the infestation isn't spreading as fast there." The Captain looked them over again. "I can take a guess why."

"Do we know where the swarm is at?" Terrance was done with the conversation.

"We can find out..." The tentative answer didn't build any confidence as he looked Terrance up and down.

As far as he was concerned, rank and protocol were out the window, he wanted to get back out there, and his defiant stare let the Captain know exactly how he felt.

"What kind of ordnance can you spare?" Nowak stepped up next to Terrance, clearly aware of the tension that rose between the two men.

"Where do you think you're going?"

"Back to work." Williams smirked.

After a good haggle, some minor theatrics, and the revelation of the archdhampir in charge, the Captain authorized their return to Brooklyn via an aerial drop with whatever ordnance they could comfortably carry.

The swarm had indirectly wandered their way down through Bensonhurst and ended up in Washington Cemetery. Though they had been greatly reduced after the events in Bay Ridge, it was too much of a risk for the helicopter that chauffeured them back to Brooklyn to set down in the cemetery directly.

Fortunately, Gravesend Park was close enough that they could be offloaded safely, and they'd still be within walking distance. The pilot would also be close enough to fly over the area for a quick survey, as promised.

Mickey stared up at the dim autumn sky as the rest of them rechecked their gear.

"Anybody else realize we're about to go into a cemetery, at night, to fight a bunch of literal monsters?" Mickey didn't take his eyes off the sky.

No one answered.

"I'm just saying," he checked his magazine and charged

his weapon, "another time, another place, this'd make a helluva movie." He hefted his MP5 into position as he faced his teammates.

"Damn man..." Thompson looked down at the dirt, "We live in a horror movie."

No one spoke.

"Way to bring the mood down Mickey." Williams goaded.

"I'm just saying!"

"Yeah, yeah."

"We should get moving before it gets any darker." Nowak didn't bother to wait for them to acknowledge his suggestion, he just started toward the cemetery.

"*Brooklyn One this is Midland Aerial, it looks like most of the infected are down past 21st, you should have a quiet walk ahead of you.*"

"Roger that Midland, 'preciate the ride."

"*Anytime Brooklyn, good fuckin' luck, Midland out.*"

They strolled their way through the abandoned streets of Mapleton with less care than they should have. Whether it was exhaustion or arrogance that caused their lapse in judgment, the universe chose to remind them exactly where they were.

The screech came as the dhampir was already in the air and mid-fall onto Mickey's back. The two bodies tumbled along the pavement and the dhampir latched on. With its teeth sunk into Mickey's shoulder, it shook him back and forth like a dog with a new chew toy.

Terrance was the closest to him and didn't hesitate to run over. He slid on his knees, aimed at the side of the dhampir's head and fired once at an upward angle. It was a clean kill that garnered no noise from the creature and got the jaw loosened from Mickey's shoulder.

"Did it go through?!? Did it go through?!?" Williams ran over and frantically helped Mickey remove his vest.

"I don't know! Get it off! Get it off!"

Nowak slid in next to them and with far steadier hands

worked at the chainmail armor while Thompson and Terrance stood watch over the other three.

As far as they could tell, there were no other vermin around, but Thompson remained focused on their surroundings while Terrance foolishly backed up to get a look at Mickey.

With the vest and chainmail removed, Williams stared at the torn padded shirt underneath.

"Mick..." Williams hesitated.

Nowak pulled the shirt over to reveal the bare skin and a small cut on the flesh, barely bleeding.

"Is it bad? What's going on?!? I can't fuckin' see!" The panic in Mickey's eyes matched the desperation in his voice.

Williams pulled an antiseptic wipe from a pouch while Nowak grabbed the shoulder between his large hands. After a frantic wipe-down and a moment where no one dared to breathe, nothing happened.

"I think we're good."

Nowak let go slowly and Mickey exhaled like he had just run a marathon.

He stretched his back after they helped him to his feet.

"Damn, that was a close one." He laughed it off like it was no big deal that he could have suffered a fate worse than death if any dhampir saliva had gotten into his bloodstream. The retrovirus they carried would have spread throughout his body and twisted it into one of them.

"I keep telling you to wear your damn shoulder gear!" Williams picked up the chainmail by its hood and handed it to Terrance while Mickey got his tattered shirt back into place.

He couldn't help but be impressed by the way Mickey handled the situation despite his poor choices regarding his armor. But he never got to say how much he respected and admired the man.

"Three o'clock!" Thompson fired multiple rounds as Terrance and Williams turned to their right just in time to see a dhampir launch itself toward them and fold Mickey in half.

They slid a few feet and when they came to a stop Mickey was on his back with the dhampir clamped down on his exposed neck.

Williams yelled at the top of his lungs and Terrance felt his stomach drop as the dhampir ripped Mickey's throat out with a voluminous spray of blood.

Williams opened up with his sub on full auto as he moved toward his fallen friend. Bullets peppered the beast and its copper-colored blood spurted out of each wound as it fell over into the grass to twitch in its death throes.

He ran up to Mickey and held him with no regard for the blood that freely flowed from the massive wound.

"I got you bro! I got you!"

Mickey couldn't talk but desperately made a motion with his lips that resembled an "M".

"Don't you worry man." Williams stared at his friend with his best attempt at remaining calm, "I got her covered, just like we talked about, she ain't gonna want for nothin', I swear man." He fought the tears for Mickey's sake.

He tried to talk again but Williams just grabbed his hand.

"It's okay bro, it's okay..." his voice strained, and his face contorted in pain as Mickey just stopped.

A stifled groan came from deep within Williams as he began to rock slightly. He grit his teeth, squeezed his eyes shut and held his friend tightly one last time.

"We gotta go." Thompson gently prodded.

"Just gimme a minute..." He set Mickey down gently and ran his fingers over the eyes.

"Don't wanna be here if they decide to come running man."

"I said just gimme a goddamn..." he put his head in his hands and tucked into a near-fetal position on his knees before he got back to his feet.

The dhampir twitched as he stood and in an uncharacteristic fit of rage Williams brought his boot down onto the creature's head. With focused effort he ground his foot into the bone and soft meat to leave behind a pulpy mess where the head used to be.

"Let's go kill these motherfuckers."

"We're just gonna..." Terrance halfheartedly gestured toward what was left of Mickey.

"You want to drag a corpse all over Kings County?" Nowak turned away from his dead friend, "He's not the first squad member we've lost, won't be the last, we'll mourn later."

"Yeah... right." He jogged to catch up with Nowak after he realized the older man had already followed behind Williams and Thompson.

It was dusk by the time they hit the cemetery, and they turned on everything except their halos before it got too dark. They moved through the field slowly in a sweeping formation.

Stragglers popped up here and there but there were no major concentrations until they cleared 21st Avenue and saw what was left of the swarm that had torn through Bay Ridge.

Williams motioned for them to duck behind some gravestones to observe them like they were at some demented zoo. Without direction from their sire or potential food in front of them, they were almost docile. They lounged, casually loped around and a few of them looked like they played a game as they hopped from gravestone to gravestone.

Vanessa would love this...

"*Kid!*" If one could whisper and yell at the same time, Williams figured out how to do it as he got Terrance's attention.

With hand gestures, he signaled everyone to use their grenades. The first volley would be at the outer edges of the crowd to force them towards the middle where the second volley would land. In theory, the attack would yield maximum casualties with little effort.

With a countdown reminiscent of the one Shep had given them earlier that day, something that felt like a lifetime ago, they each yanked the safety pins and let loose with the modified smoke grenades.

They hit, bounced, and exploded with a cloud of curated sulfur that quickly debilitated any dhampir that were too close. Some clawed at their necks, unable to breathe as the severe allergic reaction closed their esophagus off. Others keeled over instantly as their skin blistered and formed lesions. The rest clustered in their panic and did indeed move toward the center of the group.

The second volley went out with the signal from Williams and the massive sulfuric cloud from four grenades going off at once took out a significant portion of the dhampir swarm.

"Let 'em have it boys!"

Bursts from their submachine guns rang out in the dying light as they picked off the dhampir that scattered across the cemetery.

Terrance dropped down to replace a mag as a staggered howl intermixed with clicks and chirps could be heard all around them.

"Sounds like Archie's back!" Thompson sounded excited. But Terrance was more worried about the eerie tone the area behind them had taken on. With a heavy exhale he widened the beam on his light and shined it into the field behind them to see substantial movement within the darkness.

"Behind us!" He didn't know if they heard him, but he did everything he could to make sure none of his new-found brothers got taken out from behind.

One of them eventually realized what was going on and joined him in cover fire.

"We're running out of ammo!" Nowak yelled around the reports.

"Where the hell are they all coming from?" He kicked himself mentally for the stupid question.

"Guess Archie went to round up the stragglers!"

"Who gives a shit? Just shoot the fucks!" Williams wasn't in the mood.

"We're gonna have to make a run for it!"

"And go *where* Thompson?"

"I don't know, higher ground maybe?"
"The Con Ed building is right there!"
"Fuck it! Let's go then!"
They took off at full tilt towards the building in question and managed to scale the vehicle gate with relative ease before the swarm caught up to them.
Terrance used his shotgun to breach the door and they secured it from the inside with anything they could move. Without delay, they made their way to the roof to look out over the cemetery and try to get a sense of how many more dhampir they would have to deal with.
"Man, you could see everything from up here." Thompson looked in every direction.
"We should've come up here to begin with." Terrance leaned on his knees to alleviate a crick in his side.
"Yeah well, you know what they say about foresight being twenty-twenty."
"Hindsight." Thompson corrected.
"What?"
"Hindsight is twenty-twenty, hind is back, fore is forward."
"Right, so I didn't think forward enough. That's what I'm saying, it's on me."
"No, but-" Nowak bumped Thompson's arm and gave him a quick head shake before he could try to explain the idiom to Williams again.
Terrance moved to the edge of the roof and watched as the dhampir that remained gathered outside the fence of the building they stood on.
"Goddamn, there's still a buttload of them."
"Exactly how much is a 'buttload' kid?" Williams joined him on the ledge and got the answer, but it certainly wasn't the one he wanted.
"We definitely didn't bring enough rounds."
"I mean, we made a dent." Terrance tried to find some kind of silver lining to their situation, until the big one showed

up. The rest of the sirelings deferred to him as he stalked through the crowd. Even at the distance they were, it was clear that Archie was highly interested in them.

Williams gave him a pat on the shoulder and walked away in casual defeat.

"So what's next?"

"There is no 'next' kid, we wait for the National Guard to show up and maybe we live to see tomorrow." He plopped himself down on the roof and laid back to stare at the night sky.

Terrance looked to the other two men for an alternative but they both looked as exhausted and completely out of ideas as Williams did.

He looked down at how large the building was and it hit him.

"What if we lure them inside?"

"And then what?" Williams threw up his hands.

"We blow up the building."

He sat up and stared at Terrance incredulously.

"And how much C4 did you bring with you today?" The sarcasm in his tone was palpable.

"Enough."

Everyone looked to Nowak.

"You've got C4?" Williams got to his feet, trying to stifle a groan as he did so.

"Cap said whatever we could carry."

"Well hell, now we just gotta get the little rat-faced assholes inside."

"It'd probably be better to utilize that." Nowak pointed across the street at the Mobil sign.

"Man, those people are gonna hate us." Williams snickered. "You think we can pull off the same thing twice? And isn't that a little, I dunno, unimaginative?"

"I'm just working with what we have available."

"So we funnel them through here," Williams gestured at the roof, "make them follow us across the street, and-"

"And we havin' a dhampir cookout." Thompson smacked Nowak's arm.

"Basically." A hint of a smile passed over Nowak's lips.

"Who's our fastest runner?" Terrance could feel a bit of excitement even though this was an act of desperation.

Everyone looked at Thompson.

"Really? Wow."

"Hey, you're the one always talkin' about being from the same place as Usain Bolt."

"I said our *families* are from the same place you son of a bitch. I'm from Jamaica *Queens*."

Terrance snickered and even Nowak chuckled.

"It don't matter, either way. These things might be dumb but they ain't stupid."

They all stared at Williams and waited for him to elaborate.

"We're not gonna get that whole swarm to follow one person."

"So we attack again."

"And hope they take the bait."

"Well, Archie seems like he wants to get to know us."

"More like he wants to get to know *you*." In response to the confused look Terrance gave him, Nowak pointed to another spot on the roof, "Just walk over there, and Williams, watch the big guy."

They tentatively followed Nowak's instruction and through his scope Williams made a noise of amusement.

"Yeah, he sure is watchin' you kid."

"Why *me*?"

"Maybe he knows about the vampire."

"How in the fuck could he *know*?"

"I have no clue, but that sonofa bitch wants him a piece a your ass."

"That's not fucking funny." He could feel his heartbeat start to pick up and he moved away from the edge of the roof so Archie couldn't see him.

"Relax kid." Williams grabbed him in an almost fatherly manner. "We're almost out of this. Let's see if we can't fuck some shit up, yeah?"

They moved through the first floor and mapped out exactly how they would get Archie and the swarm into the building and where they would go from there.

"I think we're all clear on what we're doin'... ain't no sense in waitin' any longer." He hit the button on the automatic roll up door and they made their way out to the fence.

Terrance hefted the pair of bolt cutters they found and waited for the signal to cut the lock on the gate.

"All right you miserable knuckle-draggin' cocksuckers... you want some? *Come get some!*"

With the shout from Williams, Terrance pressed down as hard as he could while the other men opened up on the swarm through the chainlink fence. The plan had been to roll the gate open, make some kind of commotion to attract their attention and lead them through the gate.

Archie had his own plan.

The signature clicks and screeches they had ascribed to the archdhampir once again filled the night air and the sirelings climbed the fence.

"Of-fucking-course!"

They continued to fire into the swarm, bodies of dead and near-dead dhampir were trampled on and pushed into the chain-link indiscriminately by their brethren as more made their way up the two-story fence.

"Hey kid! It's time to go!" Williams called out as Thompson and Nowak ran into the building and fired from the doorway.

The fence began to bow under the weight of so many dhampir as some made it over and began to rain down into the lot.

Terrance provided cover fire as Williams made his way into the building. He kept an eye out for Archie as he cross-stepped his way to his teammates.

Where the hell did he go?

As though he could hear Terrance's thoughts, Archie leaped up to get onto the fence. His added weight was all the metal poles needed to collapse.

"Move your ass Terrance!"

The voice in his ear jarred him enough that he took off for the open delivery door, he hit short bursts from his sub the entire run as the fence came down on those dhampir that had already cleared it.

"We'll hold 'em, go!"

Thompson and Novak ran for the exit while the other two men picked off as many of the vermin as they could.

"Fall back! Fall back!"

They backed their way through the building as the dhampir started to filter in.

"Reloading!" Terrance took a knee while Williams looked over him. The back of his neck tingled as Archie announced his presence in the building.

"Standing!" With a fresh magazine in place, Terrance hopped up after he got the all-clear from Williams only to see Archie stalk his way in. He charged his weapon and took aim at the archdhampir, but as he fired Archie grabbed one of the sirelings and used it as a meat shield.

"We should definitely go."

They continued to back out toward their exit and took full advantage of the pinch point the door provided. Bodies piled up not just from their assault but from Archie's continued use of the smaller ones as defensive tools.

Through the door, they sprinted across the road towards the other members of their unit as Nowak finished his set up.

"We good?"

"About as good as we're gonna be."

The door burst open, and the swarm came through the door with no regard for how many of them could fit through it at once. Screeches of pain and frustration echoed across the avenue and Terrance raised his sub to increase his kill count.

"Whoa kid!" Terrance felt Nowak's bear-like grip on his elbow. "Gas station."

"Right…" He took his finger away from the trigger as he looked for the C4 charges.

The dhampir ran towards them and violently skidded to a halt as Archie seemed to bark orders at them. He moved hesitantly across the street, like any other wild animal would as it approached the unknown and then stopped to look at the company logo.

"There's no fuckin' way he recognizes the name." Williams muttered.

"Then why ain't he movin'?"

He turned his attention back towards the team and looked each one of them over slowly. Eyes so red they seemed to bleed settled on Terrance and Archie hissed at him.

"What the hell is that supposed to mean?" he could hear the fear in his own voice but he was too terrified of the death stare he was in to feel embarrassed.

"I think he's offended." Nowak's tone reminded him of his sister every time she would work out a problem for school, it was that same quiet intelligence.

"*Offended?!?*" Williams did his whisper scream again.

"We tried to do the same thing twice."

"I fuckin' told you!"

Archie screamed at Williams but did not pass the row of shrubbery that separated the gas station from the sidewalk.

"Well fuck you too, asshole!" Williams leveled his sub at Archie's head, "Enough of this back-to-school bullshit!"

Several dhampir screeched as they stared down the street. All four men, Archie, and the rest of the vermin turned to see what the stupid things had screamed at.

They saw the headlights before they heard the engines of the Humvees as they barreled down the road towards them.

The drivers of the two military vehicles slammed on their brakes at the last minute and the rubber screeched along the pavement as the .50 caliber mounted machine guns went to work on the dhampir, some of them were vaporized instantly while Archie and the rest made the smart decision to run away.

The gunner of the closest Humvee turned to them and smiled.

"And where the fuck have *you* been?" Williams approached the Humvee more aggressively than he should have.

The gunner's smile was quickly replaced with a look of dissatisfaction as several well-armed soldiers filed out of the armored vehicles and aimed their weapons at Williams.

"Gonna need you guys to identify yourselves." The one in charge stepped forward.

"We're MPD you *dope*." Williams was officially done with everything.

"What the hell are you doing here?" Another soldier walked up.

"Holding the line." Nowak said all that was needed.

"Sure." The first was apparently ignorant of all that had been going on in Brooklyn beyond the fact that there was a secondary dhampir infestation.

"Look, National Guard base camp is set up in Marine Park if you want to head back there while we continue on."

Williams looked over the guardsmen in their uniforms still clean and freshly pressed. Then he looked down at himself and the state of his team.

"I think we could do with a shower." He suggested to his brothers instead of the soldier.

"I could eat." Nowak counter offered.

"Italian?" A smirk came to Williams' face.

"Fuck you."

"So we're gonna walk *all the way* to Marine Park?" Terrance gave him a look of complete disbelief.

"Sarge, I could drive them back and return with additional personnel since it seems like we're going to need it." A third soldier who looked like he was too young to shave and too short to drive spoke up.

"My boy, if you can do that, I will personally make a man out of you."

The kid stared at Thompson in literal fear.

"He's mostly kidding." Terrance managed to force out the words.

"I don't, right, yeah, sure, I knew that."

"Go ahead and take them Sparky, and hurry back."

They piled into the Humvee after they stowed their weapons in the back, content that their lives were now placed into young Sparky's hands.

Sandwiched between Nowak and Thompson in the back, Terrance watched the streets that they drove along while the two larger men chose to go to sleep.

Many of the buildings and abandoned vehicles were intact and showed no sign of the devastation that had been left behind in the western part of the city. While there was a distinct possibility that no one would say it, he knew that everyone and everything in Brooklyn that survived was a result of his unit's actions. It was hard not to feel proud about that.

It was also a struggle to reopen his eyes after they closed involuntarily. There wasn't any room for him to change his position and in no time at all he drifted off without any energy to stop it.

There were no dreams of monsters or desperate escapes. Nothing at all came to him as he slept.

And then his face hit the pavement.

There was no pain as he gasped for breath and slapped at the blacktop wildly in his disoriented attempt to grab a hold of something. Like a newborn deer, he struggled to get his legs underneath him as he attempted to get his bearings.

The Humvee was on its side, one of the doors was ten feet away on the ground and the driver's was open at an angle the manufacturer never intended. The machine gun was still on its mount and seemed to be intact, as far as he could tell from a distance. It was too dark to see if anyone was still inside and he didn't see any other bodies on the street, so he hobbled his way back to the vehicle, hoping to find his brothers.

Three steps forward and it felt like he had been hit by a car as everything moved rapidly to the right.

He was back on the pavement and his side was on fire as he haphazardly rolled onto his back as quickly as he could. Thoughts of what happened to Mickey and his new fear of his neck being ripped out was a great motivator.

The night sky of the city didn't allow for many constellations to be seen, only the brightest were ever viewable with the naked eye but the one the Terrance always looked for was Orion's Belt. Unless it was an overcast night, he found those three stars every chance he could and found comfort just in their existence.

He found them now, and for a brief moment, he found the same solace in them that he did when he was a child.

Of course, the moment was ruined as the repulsive face of an archdhampir entered his field of vision and blocked out anything behind its obtuse head. In the back of his mind, he knew he wasn't about to get out of this, but he still attempted to back away despite the scream from his ribs not to move.

Archie hissed and cocked his head at Terrance as he looked for the best part of him to bite. The mutated hand Archie placed on his chest to hold him still set his ribs on fire again.

Not only did the archdhampir seem to take pleasure in the pain inflicted in its prey, but it wanted more. It narrowed its demonic eyes, put its hand on his right shoulder and pushed down like Terrance was an open can of paint.

The sound of his shoulder as the bone separated was not a loud thing but it felt like thunder throughout his body.

He opened his mouth to scream but the only sound that escaped him was a raspy groan.

Fangs flashed in front of his face again in what must have passed for a dhampiric smile and he realized it was over.

"Get away from him you piece of shit!" A high-pitched

voice that cracked halfway through its shout broke the silence and was punctuated by two quick shots from what sounded like a pistol.

Terrance followed Archie's line of sight to see the young soldier he knew only as Sparky, larger than life and ready for a fight.

Not over yet.

A high-pitched whine took the place of any actual sound as an enraged screech blew out what remained of his right ear drum.

Whole damn right side is cooked.

Archie pushed off of Terrance and galloped towards Sparky. To his credit, the kid stood his ground and fired again, the rounds were enough of a deterrent that Archie leapt out of the way and hit Sparky with another screech and a cat-like spit.

Nothing wrong with your legs, get up!

His whole life became pain as he tried to get up, failed, tried again, and failed.

Darkness crept in at the edges of his vision, a threat to take him away from the conscious world.

Sparky screamed and let off two more rounds.

Terrance finally reached for his own pistol only to find an empty holster.

Goddammit. Get. Up!

"Oh shit!" Sparky started to run as Archie clicked at him.

The sonofa bitch is playing with him.

"Getupgetupgetup!" Sparky's voice was shrill as he worked through his fear, but it had the desired effect.

"You heard the runt, *get up!*"

With a glimmer of hope in his heart he looked up to see Williams as he dropped himself onto the pavement. Blood trickled down his face from a head wound and his left hand looked like he had shoved it in a garbage disposal, but he was *alive!*

"Come on T! Get your ass up and help me with this damn gun!"

There was no choice to make. It didn't matter that he couldn't stand up straight as he dragged himself along, or that his entire core felt like an inferno, or that his arm felt like it was going to fall clean off of him, or that his lungs felt like he was about to drown.

He pushed on.

When he made it to the Humvee, he slipped on something slick that spun him around and caused him to fall back against the roof of the car with not a single ounce of grace and a metric ton of pain. He coughed up blood and felt pain throughout his body.

"What the fuck is this, oil?" His voice sounded like a gravel road.

"Nah kid, it's blood... don't look in the truck, just fuckin' focus." He leaned back on the hood; the words were a struggle for him to get out. "You need to prime it first, then we'll take it off the mount."

Terrance looked at him like he was crazy.

"You've got one good arm, I've got one good arm, stop fuckin' lookin' at me like that." His knuckles were white from the grip he had on his left wrist and his face had lost color.

"Come on, before Archie gets tired of playin' with the new kid." Even as his breaths became labored, he was able to find something to smile about.

Terrance was barely able to get his left arm up and onto the mounted gun. He fumbled around for the charging lever and pulled as hard as he could to prime the weapon.

He couldn't get it back far enough.

"I... can't..."

"Yes you fuckin' can! Don't gimme that shit!"

The darkness worked its way in again and his head rolled down. The sound of Williams as he yelled at him to wake up faded into the darkness with him.

It was over.

"Oh my *GoOOOD!*" The scream from Sparky and the subsequent impact of both him and Archie as they collided with Williams and the hood of the Humvee gave Terrance just enough adrenaline to prime the weapon and level the machine gun at the archdhampir as it sank its fangs into poor Sparky.

Williams was pinned between Archie and the hood that was now caved in and wrapped around them.

"Get outta there!" He yelled at Williams and instantly regretted it as Archie turned his attention toward him.

"Oh no you don't mother fucker!" Williams wrapped his arm around Archie's neck and held on with everything he had left. "Shoot it, T!"

Archie clawed at the bracer pressed against his throat.

"Get outta the way!"

"I'm already gone kid, shoot!"

He couldn't see.

His eyes began to tear up and he squeezed them shut to say a silent prayer to anyone that would listen.

They focused as he opened them, and he lined the machine gun up with his target.

"Say goodnight you son of a bitch." With everything he had left, he kept the gun level at the beast as he squeezed the trigger. He roared as Archie and Williams disappeared into a cloud of blood.

His hand slid off the weapon into his lap the moment he released the trigger.

The pain was gone. It was time to rest.

Helluva day.

The darkness enveloped him.

The next time he opened his eyes it was almost as painful as the walk to the Humvee had been. LED lights on a stark white ceiling blinded him as he tried to get up to see where he was and instantly thought better of it.

"Yeah, you might want to take it easy there young man." The voice was familiar.

He let his eyes open slower this time around and blinked rapidly to get them to adjust to the light that saturated his vision.

"Welcome back to reality," Shep gave him a polite smile, "such as it is."

"Hospital?" His throat felt like sandpaper.

"Absolutely."

"How long?"

"Little over three weeks." The smile faded, "You had one foot in the grave when they found you, concussion, three broken ribs, a punctured lung, and a separated shoulder... still, that's better shape than the rest of the team." The corners of Shep's eyes tightened as he held back his emotion.

Silence hung between them.

"They were good men." He could hear the strain in his own voice.

"Yes, they were." His somber nod said all the things that he didn't. "And apparently, so are you, *Officer*."

Terrance couldn't look at Shep the way he wanted to but his confusion came across.

"If it wasn't for you, *all* of you, taking on that swarm of dhampir the way you did, we would've lost Brooklyn too."

"So, Manhattan...?"

"Military carpet bombed the whole island for two weeks straight." He shook his head. "Just so we don't leave things on a completely sour note: yes, you are definitely getting promoted and you've got enough medals coming your way to cover at least one side of a horse."

"Thank you, Sir."

"Don't thank me yet." He smirked, "The media is calling you 'The Savior of Brooklyn' and there's a lot of baggage that's going to come with that."

"Understood."

"We'll see." Shep tapped the railing of the bed with his knuckles, "For now, rest. Get better. I'm going to need a hand breaking in a new team."

"Will do, Sarge."

Shep left Terrance to heal and ruminate on the information he'd given him. Despite the deaths of his team, the destruction of Manhattan, and his new celebrity status, the only thing he could think of was something one of his instructors once told him at the academy:

"No matter how much information I give you here, no matter how many case files you read, nothing will stack up to the education you're going to get on the job."

The End

Author Bio:

J.P. Staszak is a Yankee by birth and a Southerner by choice. A proud husband and father, he spends his free time building worlds to play in and tell stories about personal growth and the proliferation of liberty.

Links:

https://www.facebook.com/profile.php?id=61550788058842&mibextid=hIlR13

https://substack.com/@jpstaszak

The Historians

K.M. Sykes

The not so distant future...

I'd seen the video I don't even know how many times, if you've been on the jury in the last ten years or so where the guy pleaded not guilty to a felony then you've probably seen it too. You know the one, where that guy that was famous like twenty years ago comes on and explains what's going to happen, how Looking Glass works.

"Looking Glass will transport you to the time and place just before the crime takes place, and you will witness exactly what happened. I'm sure you have lots of questions, but don't worry, I'm here to answer them.

"To start, you won't be able to change the course of history. You may be able to interact with objects, such as doors, but you will only be able to return them to their original position. Don't worry, you can't cause any problems, the laws of physics simply won't allow it. For instance, if you open a door and try to leave it open, it will eventually close itself. This is part of what physicists refer to as the universe's "rubber band principle", which prevents history from being altered.

"Although it's unfortunate we can't prevent these crimes from happening, it does prevent unknowable consequences that could arise from tampering with the timeline.

"When you arrive at your destination, it is normal to feel some disorientation and discomfort. You may find that the temperature, air pressure, and other environmental characteristics may be different. For this reason, the transportation room slowly adjusts its internal atmosphere to what is expected in order to ease the transition.

"Now unfortunately, you will likely see some very disturbing things as you witness the crime. The United States Department of Justice apologizes for the discomfort you may feel, but reminds you that it is your civic duty as a juror, as outlined in our United States Constitution.

"Should you have any further questions, a representative from Sylph Company will be happy to answer."

The video comes to a stop, the jury moves into the transportation room, they watch some guy do something awful to some other guy, and the legal system marches on. For better or for worse, I have to go with them each time to ensure that the prosecution doesn't try to taint their opinions with any nonsense.

See, I'm a defense attorney. My job is try and defend people against the justice system, which has gotten really difficult when there's a machine that lets prosecutors and juries go back in time to watch my client do it. Back in the day my client would plead, "not guilty", I'd point out how shoddy the evidence is (and it is often very shoddy if you know what you're looking for), and we'd establish reasonable doubt. And if you've got reasonable doubt, you can't convict. But these days there's no reasonable doubt, the jury gets to watch the defendant do it right before their eyes.

So now my job is to argue technicalities, and try to get lesser sentences. Now admittedly this has long been a major part of the legal system. Take the case of *State of Florida v. George Zimmerman*, for instance. Looking Glass wasn't needed, there was no one disputing the events. No one was disputing that George Zimmerman shot Trayvon Martin, no one disputed the events leading up to the shooting. The question was whether or not he was justified in shooting Trayvon Martin, the crux of which was whether or not Trayvon Martin was justified in attacking George Zimmerman. That's the sort of thing I deal with these days; some guy indisputably does a thing, but were they allowed to do that thing? And if they weren't allowed, how do I get the judge to show some leniency?

In this particular case, I did not win. My Guy insisted on pleading not guilty, despite me watching him smash a drug dealer's brains out with a crowbar. And as his defense attorney, I have to watch that shit over and over, combing over the footage to try and find something. There wasn't jack shit, My Guy did it, and that was that. I did my best to try and plead it down to a lesser charge, tried to get leniency. I'm damn good at what I do, so I managed to get a few years shaved off on account of arguing that my client was a redeemable member of society.

But still, I vowed then and there; no more, "not guilty", types. Plead guilty and let me do my job, or chance it with the public defender. And let me tell you, I went to law school with the head of the public defender's office, the guy is only there because the prosecutor's office doesn't like to hire regular customers.

Thing about being a defense attorney is that we all go into the business wanting to be either Atticus Finch, or Johnnie Cochran. Met a lot of assholes in both camps over the years, though the Johnnie Cochran types were usually a more annoying kind of asshole, albeit with better suits. The unfortunate thing is that you may go in wanting to be Atticus, but you end up playing the role of Johnnie. God damn waste of talent a lot of times. Conversely, the guys that go in wanting to be Cochrane never play the role of Atticus Finch, which is another waste of talent.

Me, I was a guy that went into the business wanting to be Atticus, but now I was playing Cochrane. Paid well, but you know, there's stuff that makes you not sleep so well at night. I firmly believe that everyone, and I mean absolutely everyone, is entitled to a competent legal defense. Had I been alive then, and had he not decorated the ceiling with his brains, I'd have defended god damn Adolf Hitler at the Nuremburg trials without any hesitation.

Sounds horrible that guys like me are trying to get guilty

people off scot-free, but without bastards like me a lot of innocent people also get convicted. Remember, the court of public of opinion is one made up by flagrant dumbasses. Just because the public knows for certain that someone did it doesn't mean shit. Take the Central Park Five case. Everyone and their mother knew they were guilty, but turns out they weren't. Everyone and their mother was a fucking idiot. Hence the reason defense attorneys will defend anyone. Not that we like defending the worst humanity offers, but because it's necessary to protect the innocent.

At least this is what I explained to my usual audience later that evening. My typical hang was a joint called the Automat; yeah, named after the Edward Hopper painting. Joining me for that lecture were the Professor, the Banker, the Mechanic, and the Bar Owner Himself. They were pretty good about humoring me, probably because I tended to buy rounds. Hey, being the modern day Johnnie Cochran might be soulless, but it pays well enough to buy rounds for your drinking buddies.

Next morning I rolled into the office, my Paralegal looked to have been there a while. Coffee was going, she looked fully awake. I checked the clock, I technically wasn't late by the standard I'd set, but she still had a way of making me feel like I was late to my own funeral. She reminded me that I had an appointment with an important prospective Client. I'd honesty forgotten about it, this was why I'd hired the Paralegal. Well, that and her ability to do research; you know, the normal shit you hire paralegals for. But I paid her more than the average salary on account of having a more diverse skill set than average.

Got some coffee, took some aspirin. The Bar Owner Himself likes to do shots with his regulars, always makes it a rougher night than I intend. Got myself presentable just in time for the Client.

He shows up, immaculately dressed, but just a little bit off. Like, nothing is wrong per se, but something is off, and you can't quite put your finger on it. No matter, I've dealt with stranger. Guy looks to be around my age, says he's from the Themis Foundation. Never heard of them, I made a mental note to have the Paralegal check 'em out. Never know in this business, after all, I deal with a lot of criminals. On purpose.

Client tells me, "I'd like for you to represent (the Defendant)."

I tell him, "Ah yeah, heard about that one, was wondering if or when that'd come my way." With everyone accused being guilty, there's a lot less crime these days, I hear about most felony cases in Alameda County.

Alright, real case, pretty high profile. The guy's from a foundation, so they've probably got a good amount of money. I go ahead and step behind my desk to the minibar and offer him a drink. He takes his pour neat, we toast, and get to business.

I explain to him that based on what I heard, no guarantees, but I can probably get a reduction in sentence with a guilty plea. Fewer prisoners these days, but prison is still expensive. No one wants prisoners staying long term, costs too much. The Client explains to me that the Defendant plans to plead, "not guilty". Fuck me, I just vowed the day previous that I wasn't taking on any more of these assholes unless they had a really good technicality I could work with. Everyone deserves a competent public defense, but at the same time I'm in my 50's, I've got my health to look after.

I tell the Client I'm not interested. He decides to press his luck, and you know what, I ain't got shit going on this morning. I'll humor the bastard. He tells me that the Looking Glass was ran, and shows my client shooting some poor bastard in the face. Shows me the footage, and it looks pretty cut and dry. Arguing not guilty is fucking suicide, perhaps literally with the California legislature debating a bill to bring back the death penalty, and not the nice kind where you just get to peacefully asphyxiate. The Defendant could fry, and I'm not looking to be the first defense attorney in a decades to let a client ride the lightning.

He's still got about half his pour of Jefferson's Reserve left, it's a good whisky, no man with any god damn taste would leave that behind. I really need to stop offering people a drink until after I commit to the case, now we're just stuck in my office. He tells me that funny thing about the Looking Glass showing the Defendant shooting a guy in the face, autopsy shows the victim shot in the chest. Okay, yeah, that's pretty fucking weird. But I've been a defense attorney for a hot minute, I've seen weirder shit than this. I tell the Client that the cops or coroner or whoever probably fucked up. Autopsy reports probably got mixed up or some shit. Occam's Razor says that the simplest explanation is usually true, and the simplest explanation is usually incompetence.

Client says he saw the body himself, positively identified them as the victim that was in the Looking Glass footage. Definitely shot in the chest, nothing to the face. They've even got permission to exhume the body if need be. Alright, even weirder, but mistakes happen. I'd have to follow up to say for sure, but I don't have time for that. I tell him that things happen. Could've well been twins that got shot the same night, drug deals sometimes go bad like that and weird shit happens. Client mentions that there's no evidence of the victim having a twin, they double checked all the paper work, did their due diligence; blah, blah, blah. I've heard it all, everyone and their mother is convinced they've got Looking Glass beat.

But remember what I said earlier about everyone and their mother.

Finally the man finishes his drink, gets up, buttons his suit jacket. Very prim and proper type, something still feels off about his dress and mannerisms. No matter, just need for him to leave. As he's about to leave, he turns back and gives this look, like he's just casually mentioning something, and asshole says, "Say, before I leave, you heard about [the Coach], yeah?"

I don't say anything. Yes I know the Coach, anyone that's seen the news lately knows about him.

He says, "If you hadn't heard, he was recently given the death penalty in the Philippines, they brought it back when the public heard what he had done. At least a dozen victims, really grisly stuff. I'm sure you're familiar with what he does."

I'm familiar with the Coach. Never convicted in the United States of so much as double parking.

Client says, "Word is he confessed to a number of crimes here in the US, and the FBI used the Looking Glass. We suspect he's hoping to be extradited back here. Supposedly they confirmed that he did in fact kill a young boy. Fifteen years ago to this day in fact."

He's not wrong, it's April 14th.

I tell him, "[The Crackhead] was convicted of that crime not long after. Looking Glass confirmed it."

The Client says, "So I've heard. I heard you used to be part of the ACLU until that case. Then had a change of heart, disagreed with their opposition to Looking Glass and left."

I sip my whiskey, tell him to get the fuck out, and pour myself another. And another. Paralegal eventually comes to bug me about something, she tells me I'm drunk and it's time to go home. Can't argue with that, but wasn't ready to go home. So I go to the next best thing, it's back to the Automat. The Bar Owner Himself sees me walk in and pours my usual, man is a consummate professional. I down it quicker than usual, have another, and things go from there.

At some point I pull open my phone and text a Contact of mine in the FBI. And by Contact, I mean the fucker owes his continued employment by the United States Government to me. The man owes me. If I tell him we're having drinks, then we're having drinks. Sometimes being a Johnnie Cochrane kind of motherfucker has its advantages.

My Contact swings by the Automat after work. I ask him what the hell's going on with the Coach. Contact is being cagey, no matter, I change the topic to sports. We talk about proposals to bring the Raiders back to Oakland where they fucking belong. This continues on, the Bar Owner Himself plays his part by continuing to bring shots, there's a reason I tip so well at this place. Finally it's time to press the advantage, I ask the Contact about the Coach.

He's still cagey, but the defenses are weak. Finally admits that he heard some guys in his office checked out the Coach allegations, seems to be some truth to it. He can't confirm or deny the case that happened 15 years ago. He resists, I tell him that was my son.

I'm not lying.

He folds, he saw the footage. He watched the Coach kill my son in cold blood. I order something stronger, this can't be fucking real. The Looking Glass showed the Crackhead doing exactly that. Looking Glass even showed the Coach doing shit in his little office at the time. Coach was fully exonerated.

I think back to the case. I watched the footage probably hundreds of times. I've watched my son be killed in a horrific way more than all my other cases combined. I don't need to watch it again, it's burned into my memory. How in the fuck can the Looking Glass show two different men perpetrating the same crime?! I tell him that as the father, I have the right to see the footage. I'm not making that up, the Looking Glass Viewing Rights Act Of Fucking Whenever says so. Tell him I'm a lawyer, I know. Contact says the footage has been deleted, they won't be viewing the event again. The Coach isn't being charged with anything in the United States.

Word is he's getting hammered in the Philippines. The United States Department of Justice is providing Looking Glass footage of the shit he's done over there. Not very common, DOJ usually only does that for foreign crimes if it impacts the US, or if the current president happens to be cooperating with the International Criminal Court on something. Killing poor brown kids usually doesn't pique their interest unless a documentary gets made. Someone wants this guy put away for a long time, or potentially executed, just not in the United States. I ask who. Contact doesn't know. I press, and I mean press.

Contact says he discreetly looked into it. He's the curious type, it's how he got in the sort of trouble I had to save him from in the first place. Good on him, we need people like him in government. Says he's pretty sure it came from someone in the United States Attorney General's office.

Okay, that's some major shit. Start thinking I might want to take out a good life insurance policy if I want to push this any further.

I thank the Contact for his time, buy him a goodbye round. We have the round, then the Bar Owner Himself interjects with another goodbye shot. Contact is pretty well shitfaced, and I notice that he left his wallet on the bar, but never actually paid.

I settle up his tab, and tell the Bar Owner Himself that I'll return the wallet.

Next day I'm pounding water and Advil as I'm riding to Sylph Company's Looking Glass facility in Mountain View. It's one of their oldest facilities, built near their original headquarters. Sylph started off in the Silicon Valley, a startup created by some former SLAC researchers who realized they were on to something and decided to privatize it before the Department of Energy swooped in and patented everything.

I'm going to break into the place, and illegally access their machines.

I've been to this place many times, defense attorneys had to keep the prosecution from pulling any funny business with the jury while doing the viewing. So I have a pretty good sense of what the security is like. I've also defended a lot of B&E cases, even helped one of my clients setup a security company so he could use his experiences in a more lawful manner. A lot of people think that break-in's are done at night by guys dressed like ninjas.

That's one way of doing it, but it's hard to do in a well secured facility. A place like this has cameras all over the place, and I don't have the expertise to go about disabling them. Besides, as soon as they realize someone broke in, they'll just use Looking Glass to identify the intruder and follow them back home. Looking Glass is why you don't hear about people breaking into museums or banks anymore. These days theft is done almost entirely on paper, white collar crime is where it's at. Of course, that's been true for a long time before Looking Glass.

Instead I'm going to use the approach that my clients tended to get away with for much longer; go in broad daylight and act like you're supposed to be there. Turns out this is remarkably easy if you're dressed in coveralls and carry a ladder. All we had to do was get in the door, which is where my FBI Contact's ID badge came in. Pro tip: Never leave that kind of shit in your wallet.

Joining me on this intrusion is my Paralegal. I was initially going to go on my own, but she insisted I'd get caught without her, and I couldn't argue against that. There's a reason I pay her well above average. We get in without trouble, and make our way to one of the Looking Glass machines.

I've seen the machines operated enough to have a good sense of how to use them; after all, detectives used them, so they had to be idiot-proofed. I dial in the time and place; my son's elementary school, fifteen years and some hours ago.

God this is fucking horrendous, I can't believe I'm watching this again. But I have to see, I have to do this without someone else operating the machine. I have to see this first hand, rather than footage. I'll spare you the details, but I just watched the Crackhead do what I've seen him do hundreds of times. No change.

But something is nagging me, I ask my paralegal to go to the same time and place. Doesn't have to watch the whole thing, just has to tell me who approaches my kid. She goes in, and reports back shortly afterwards. Tells me it's the Coach. I ask her to go back, confirm some things. She can't find the Crackhead anywhere nearby, and the Coach definitely does it. The recording she takes confirms what she's saying.

What the fucking hell is going on here?!

Alright, time to try something. I go back to my own home, that very morning. I set the location to outside. The key in my pocket still works on the front door, I go in. This is the first time I've ever gone back in time and seen myself, it's fucking weird. But I don't remember seeing myself at breakfast, so I guess that confirms that you can't actually see the viewers. I confirm that I had coffee and Froot Loops. Yeah, I know, old guy breakfast. Next I send my paralegal to the same time, but start her off in my kitchen. She tells me I had Fruit Loops.

I'm well aware that viewers at the same time and place can't see each other, but I was curious about objects. Never seen it happen, but never thought my about it. Her footage never shows the front door opening. That's interesting, can't see viewers, and can't see viewers making any changes to the environment. I guess maybe it's the same incomprehensible laws of time travel that prevent the current residents of that time from perceiving viewers.

Again, what the fucking hell.

I've been working cases with Looking Glass for decades, never thought about this kind of shit. And unfortunately the eggheads that build these things are notoriously tight lipped, real nasty NDA's. I've read them and even I can't find a way out of them that isn't painful.

Alright, one last case before we get interrupted. Let's go back to the Defendant, the one the Client wants me to defend. May as well humor him. I go back, the murder happens on the campus of UC Berkeley, broad daylight. Lots of witnesses, lots of cameras. Guy gets shot in the face.

I send in the Paralegal, she doesn't know anything about the case yet. Same time, same place, guy gets shot in the chest. Something's up. Alright, time to bounce.

We slide on out, no one says so much as a word to us. If we'd shown up in our usual suits and ties, at the very least we'd get a, "good morning". But show up in coveralls and you're totally ignored. Says a lot about our society, but whatever, it got me what I needed.

Later back at the office we're combing over footage, and I'm thinking. Thinking about things more than I ever did before with Looking Glass. I've got an idea, and I take a look at the Paralegal's footage from my place. See, I'd drunkenly had this idea the night prior, and stopped at the store so I could test it the next day, on the off chance I still had the balls to pull off that stunt when I was sober.

Look over the Paralegal's footage, and there it is, a box of Fruit Loops on my kitchen table. Only problem is that it's supposed to be spelled Froot Loops. No really, look it up. I check my footage, and it's Froot Loops. I took pictures before I left in the morning, and its Froot Loops. My Paralegal is younger than me, her generation didn't come up on high fructose corn syrup for breakfast. She's never had Froot Loops, easy mistake for her to make. The question is why her camera is making that mistake.

Alright, I already knew shit was weird. It's been quite a day, I call it early and head to the Automat. Sometimes talking to your drinking buddies over a nice whisky helps process things. Go in, the FBI Contact is there waiting for me. Understandably pissed that I took his wallet, I should've called him today, exactly what you'd expect. I tell him I was kind of drunk when I took it, totally slipped my mind.

He then asks why I showed up on security footage at Sylph Company. Uh… fuck. For the first time in a long time, I don't have a good answer. I'm a defense attorney that can't even defend myself. Well, actually, to be fair I usually have a lot of prep time to make my arguments. Still, not a good look for me.

He's not a field agent or anything, but he's still with the FBI. He's with law enforcement and he's more or less accusing me of a crime. Time to go back to legal defense 101; shut the fuck up. Don't say a god damn thing about, you will never beat the cops with cleverness, largely because they're too dumb to affected by cleverness. Anything you say can and **will** be used against you in a court of law, all that jazz. I tell

all my clients, shut the fuck up. Looking Glass might prove you're guilty of something, but saying too much might cause them to suspect you of shit they didn't before. Minimize how much they use Looking Glass by not giving them anything to go off of.
The Contact is hella pissed now. This guy could absolutely fuck me. Trespassing is an easy one to argue down, but unauthorized use of Looking Glass, that one has some severe penalties attached. I'm fucked. I go against what I just told myself, shutting the fuck up isn't going to help. Even if I somehow manage to beat jail time, unauthorized use of Looking Glass will absolutely cause the Bar to pull my license to practice law. And I mean the state bar that governs lawyers, not the place I drink at. Though to be fair, the Bar Owner Himself is well connected, I'm willing to bet he could get someone's license pulled if he made the right calls. But I digress, I'm about to get fucked. Right in the ass, no lube. Not only is this about to be an unlubricated fucking, this is about to be a fucking with an extra-large dildo covered in sandpaper.
I've got to throw a Hail Mary here. Time to do what I tell my clients not to do, I try to get the guy to feel sorry for me. I tell him that after what I've heard, I had to see it for myself. Had to know if the right guy went to prison for what happened to my son. Had to know that justice was served. And now I don't know. I wasn't just saying that to get out of trouble, I fucking meant it. Every word.
Contact says he hasn't said anything to anyone, he had a feeling that's what was up. Tells me that we're even now, that's fair. I buy us pours of Yamazaki 12 year to celebrate a debt settled, that puts him in a better mood. We commiserate, he warns me to never pull shit like that again. I keep buying the rounds. Part of it is to keep my ass out of trouble, but also because I haven't gotten everything I wanted. I still need answers, and I can hold my drink better than he can.
I casually mention the Froot Loops. He seems a bit uncomfortable, but I press. I press carefully, but I still press

him on it. He tells me that the Mandela Effect isn't exactly uncommon. If you're not familiar, the Mandela Effect is when a lot of people remember something wrong, and in a specific way. The name comes from a phenomena where a lot of people were pretty sure that Nelson Mandela died in prison back in the 80's, which made them awfully confused when the news reported him dying in 2013. But it also happens with stuff like people remembering Berenstain Bears as Berenstein Bears, the Fruit of the Loom logo having a cornucopia, the Monopoly guy having a monocle, or... Froot Loops being spelled Fruit Loops.

Contact tells me that its usually overlooked, but if you know what to look for, it happens more than you'd think. Him and some of the other techs have a list of known common Mandela Effects, and they see them pretty often actually. No fucking clue why it is, but doesn't seem to effect anything.

Well I tell him that two different people being shown raping and killing a child is a pretty big fucking deal. He admits it's not the first time he's heard of this happening. Fucking seriously dude?! This technology is producing wildly different results, and we're still using it? How are they determining which version is accurate? He tells me he doesn't know, it's a very rare occurrence, and the decision always comes from higher up.

I ask if there's any commonalities. I've already got a really good guess as to what's happening, but I want him to confirm it. He confirms it. It happens when someone with little to no knowledge of the case does a second viewing, unaccompanied by anyone with familiarity. Thing is, that scenario doesn't happen very often. Looking Glass is so accurate that you have no need to review it. The evidence is never disputed, so it's not like anyone gets sent for a second viewing on an appeal. Hell, you rarely even get appeals when Looking Glass provides the evidence.

I tell him that in three out of three cases I looked at, I found noticeable differences by using an unfamiliar second viewer. And in one of those cases, it produced an entirely different perpetrator. Seems really sketch to me. Contact shrugs, says that one's above his paygrade.

But then he reminds me, Looking Glass has completely changed society for the better. Pre-meditated violent crime has dropped to near zero, even the crimes of passion have dropped dramatically with people knowing they can't get away with it. Most felony crimes have dropped to record low rates. Police have less to do, so cities are able to reallocate tons of money elsewhere. In the last Oakland city budget before Looking Glass was introduced, the police ate up 45% of the city's budget, the city attorney made up another 2%. We're talking about nearly half the budget dedicated to dealing with crime. Nowadays the police and city attorney budget is closer to 3% in Oakland. All that money they're not spending went into shit like infrastructure and social programs. Quality of life in Oakland is leaps and bounds ahead these days. One of America's formerly most dangerous cities is now so safe that few people lock their doors.

Contact makes a valid point. Still, I'm starting to wonder how many innocent people are in prison. Contact points out that it's probably actually fewer than it was before Looking Glass. Says they didn't exactly have the best record back then, and he's not wrong. I started well before Looking Glass, I remember how it went down. Evidence was often shoddy, if you were accused then it largely came down to whether or not you could afford a private attorney like myself. Public defenders are a great idea, but they're always purposely underfunded. Cities and counties do not like acquittals.

Not long after, Contact has had too much, he's got to call it quits. This time he makes sure he's got his wallet, I catch the bill. Winds up being an expensive night, but still, cheaper than losing my license to practice my livelihood. And besides, never know when I'll need that dude's help on something again. People often underestimate the importance of maintaining relationships. Now don't get me wrong, if a relationship is bad for you, then fucking get rid of them. But my personal feeling is that good friends and contacts are hard to replace, don't let them go too easily.

Next morning I'm pounding water and Advil again. But this time I skip my office, and go straight to the Foundation to see the Client. Whole place feels off, just slightly so, and it's hard to explain why. Luckily the Paralegal did some digging, she's gotten me answers on the Foundation. Now I know why the Client feels so off, I know why this place feels off.

This is a religious organization.

It's like if you're old enough to have had Mormons come to your door. If you weren't aware of Mormons, it'd be hard to put your finger on what's so off about their dress, but deep down inside you'd know something's off. You might not be able to consciously recognize that no one wears short sleeve all white shirts anymore, regular people have another color or pattern. No one wears ties with short sleeves. No one buttons that very top button. You know something is off, but can't quite say what. But once you know, it's obvious.

Your run of the mill religious person isn't all that unusual. 99% of religious people forget that they're religious 99% of the time. But people that work in religion professionally, they've got appearances to keep up. They live it, and their behavior changes accordingly.

Now you've got to be really careful about representing respectable types. See, the less respectable types don't have to try and justify anything beyond survival. They know what they're doing is wrong, but they're not looking to starve. The respectable types, you know, your priests, politicians, businessmen, coaches, those types; they'll spin all sorts of wild justifications. And they think they can win based on that. They'll do something horrible and try to make you think they're being persecuted.

An experienced criminal that's had brushes with the law knows to shut the fuck up, and they know to listen to their attorney. Experienced criminals are easy to work with, they know what's up. Respectable types are wild cards, never know what kind of lunacy you're going to get out of them. I'll have to tread carefully here. But I've got a good idea of what they're after. I walk right by the receptionist, *fuck* setting an appointment. These guys withheld a lot of information from me, as well as engaging in some severe emotional manipulation. Granted, it was my decision to go off the rails and break into a secured facility to access highly controlled machinery. But all the same, dick move on their part. Fuck these guys.

I sit down across from the Client's desk, and he greets me politely. I'm less polite, and get down to business. I explain that my Paralegal dug up what these guys are all about. On the surface the Foundation is all about opposition to Looking Glass based on legal and constitutional grounds, the sort of thing that gets sympathy from people like me. Not so much the average American Idiot, but the ivory tower liberals eat that shit up. Well, at least until they've got a personal stake in it, I know how that goes.

But the reality is that their entire board, and most of their employees, are religiously affiliated. And not just Christianity. This foundation is a coalition of Protestant Christians, Orthodox Christians, Catholics, Jews, Muslims, Hindus, Buddhists, even a Zoroastrian in HR. And most of them have been publicly arguing against the further development of Looking Glass.

See, Looking Glass has limitations to how far back it can go. Your standard machine operated for routine use can safely send a group of people back about fifty years, though they're restricted to forty years for a little extra safety. Size of the group doesn't matter, the amount of time what does it. You send people back any further, and they might not come back. And given that experiments with eating and drinking in the past haven't been promising, the whole inability to permanently change things, most likely they die of dehydration within a few days. There's probably a good few intangible corpses floating around right now.

And interesting thing about Looking Glass is that a human being has to go in. Can't send a drone on its own, can't send a monkey, has to be at least one human. The reason why is unknown, lots of theories about it, most of them are total crap.

But more advanced, more powerful machines can go back further. Sylph Company has been using those machines to conduct historical research, solving questions ranging from the Kennedy assassination, to exonerating Mrs. O'Leary's cow. And they keep developing machines that can go back further and further. They just did a paper about the Battle of Bunker Hill. Well, this historic tourism got the attention of the religious types when Sylph sent an expedition to Manchester, New York in September of 1827. It's not entirely clear why they mounted this expedition, but the results were disastrous for the Church of Latter Day Saints.

The reason it happened to the Mormons first is because they're a more recent religion. The older religions know that it could happen to them, it's only a matter of time. Eventually Sylph will make machines capable of going back to the time of Muhammad or Jesus, and it's going to be a shit show when that happens.

Problem is that there's too many contradicting religions. If someone goes back and proves that Muhammad was not a prophet, that's going to cause problems for the Muslims. If they go back and prove that Muhammad was indeed a prophet, that'll be a problem for pretty much everyone else. Not to mention, any depiction of Muhammad would be sacrilegious, which would on its own cause tons of issues. There's no way these religious expeditions are going to go well.

These religious groups know this. They're all tempted to go back and see their religions proven correct, but even the faithful among them know that it might not pan out that way. They also know that the societal upheavals and religious fighting that could result would be catastrophic, and in no way worth it.

I share all of this with the Client, and he brings up another point I hadn't considered. He tells me that the point of religion isn't the mythology. The mythology being the events and the characters and all that. He tells me that as a Christian, it doesn't really matter all that much to him if Jesus actually walked on water. If the expedition goes back and finds that Jesus actually got soaking wet, it won't change things, because the purpose of Christianity is to make us better people. Personally I like that outlook.

He explains to me that if the mythology is proven, say we get a firsthand view of Jesus legit walking on water, it'll change religion for the worse. It'll be about the mythology, and not the beliefs and behaviors. People will forget that it's about Jesus telling us to party on and be excellent to each other. They'll just focus on the supernatural shit. That's not what the Client and his friends want for the world.

Alright, I get that. Even when I was actively practicing I really only went to church for Easter, I'm not a religious authority.

I then get into where I come in, the Client doesn't deny it. See, they know that the march of technology is unstoppable. Perhaps the most feared technology on the planet besides Looking Glass is the nuclear bomb. So the United Nations devised the Nuclear Non-Proliferation Treaty, which limited nuclear weapons to the five countries that had them at the time. Since the treaty came into effect, we've seen the number of nuclear weapons holding nations triple. There's just no blocking the spread and development of technology in the long term. And the Foundation knows it. Eventually, even if it's not Sylph, someone will make a Looking Glass that can go back far enough to see their major religious events. And eventually that machine will fall into the hands of someone that will use it for a religious expedition. It's inevitable.

What they need me to do is not to prove the Defendant

innocent. That's not possible, nor is it really within their interest. What they need me to do is discredit the technology. It won't matter how much it spreads or what they see if everyone knows that it's a crock of shit.

Specifically, what they need me to do is show that the killing happened in a way different than what Looking Glass shows. I don't have to keep the Defendant out of prison, I just have to show that Looking Glass is fallible, which is different. And they need me to do it a way that's public, high profile, and exceedingly well documented. We all know that my case won't overturn Looking Glass derived evidence on its own, it's not like the courts are going to allow it to go all the way to the US Supreme Court. But it'll get people talking, and doubting, and looking into it. I'm not meant to bring an end to Looking Glass on my own, I'm just expected to start the conversation.

I just have two questions. The first, is why me? The second, is why this case?

Client tells me I'll have to ask the Defendant, the Foundation is just paying my fees.

Having gotten confirmation of my suspicions, I file the papers to take on the Defendant, and head to Marin County. There's so few dangerous suspects these days that the counties don't even maintain jails with the security needed to hold them. Everyone arrested for a violent crime in California just gets sent to San Quentin, it's where they'll end up anyhow.

I get access to the guy, and we chat in a room set aside specifically for lawyer-client discussions, the prisons have enough room for that these days. The Defendant was undergrad at MIT, PhD in physics at Berkeley, got hired on by Sylph just out of school. Same deal with the Victim, they'd been friends since sophomore year. When that sort of relationship breaks down, it's usually over a romantic interest, though occasionally business. Weird thing was there's no evidence of any romantic interest, no evidence of any business dealings gone sour, no evidence of any kind of falling out.

Everyone that knew the two was baffled. Looked at the security footage, seemed like the Victim wanted to be shot. Just stood there, peacefully as the Defendant raised the gun. Not a damn thing about this case was normal, but it was all starting to come together.

I ask the Defendant to confirm my suspicions. He tells me that him and the victim drew straws, victim won. Neither wanted to live with having killed their best friend, but they knew it had to be done. The plan was pretty simple. They had previously made an AI generated video of the event showing the Defendant shooting the Victim in the face. Next they get together, Defendant shoots the Victim in the chest. End result is the same, dead is dead, but it's an easily verifiable difference.

As soon as the shooting happens, the video gets posted all over social media. Gets sent to the news agencies, everyone. The video gets watched by the detectives before they ever see the body, or pull security camera footage. They don't even examine the body, that's not standard procedure. Autopsies take time and money, it's quicker and easier to just fire up Looking Glass. They've already seen video of the guy being shot in the face. They go into Looking Glass, see the guy shot in the face.

Case closed. Or is it?

What the cops hadn't taken into account was that the Defendant and Victim had visited the Foundation, told them to keep an eye on the situation, said it would benefit them immensely. Left a sealed letter detailing what they planned to do, with instructions and a copy of the Victim's will. An autopsy was to be requested, and Foundation was to get the security footage pulled, and gather witness statements. Now there was indisputable evidence of the Victim being shot in the chest. The will even said to exhume the body if there was any doubt, cremation was strictly forbidden.

And then, the Foundation was to hire me. I ask the Defendant why they chose me.

He tells me that it's because of my history with Looking Glass. Fifteen years ago when he was working for Sylph, I was considered a major thorn in the company's side back then. The Client wasn't wrong about me working for the ACLU. I was one of their staff lawyers back then, one of their best. I'd spent my days tearing police and prosecutors new assholes over Looking Glass evidence. I got Looking Glass evidence tossed out on constitutional grounds, I campaigned against its use.

And then, my son was taken from me, and there wasn't a lot of evidence pointing to a perpetrator. See, back then, Looking Glass wasn't used all that often. Only so many machines to go around, they were only used for really high profile cases. FBI had most of them constantly running counter-intelligence on Chinese spies, it was tough to get them for one kid back then. Sylph heard what happened to my kid and got an idea. They allocated one of their research rigs to my case, and turned over the evidence. Crackhead is shown doing it, goes to prison.

I stopped opposing Looking Glass after that. It brought some justice for my son, how could I argue against it? Wasn't too long after that the ACLU pulled an about face and started advocating for Looking Glass. They said they were sufficiently satisfied that it met constitutional muster, and that everyone deserved justice. I never went back to them, but all the same, the damage was done. Opposition to Looking Glass crumbled.

Well, the Defendant and the Victim happened to be well aware that my case likely had the wrong guy, they knew Sylph was going for a victory that'd shut me up. It was one of many cases in which someone who was totally unfamiliar with the case got a totally different result. They'd try blowing the whistle to reporters for years, never got taken seriously, never got anywhere. They knew that fixing our justice system would involve a very high profile case, that would have to be argued by someone that had experience in arguing against Looking Glass. I was their guy.

So after hours they'd use the machines to investigate the Coach, found out he was committing all sorts of crimes in the Philippines, quietly and anonymously forwarded it to the authorities over there. They couldn't quite use it as evidence, but it was enough to get them investigating. They investigate, find their own evidence, the Coach squeals. Tries to confess to crimes in the United States in hopes he'll be extradited over. Knows that prisons are way nicer over here, and knows that even with Looking Glass, the death penalty is not a fast process. Figures he'll take his chances in the American justice system.

FBI checks it out, and boom, they've got evidence it was the Coach that killed my son. Sylph knows this because they control the machines, they've got logs of everything. They make some calls to the Attorney General, Sylph used to donate to his campaigns when he held elected office, and they'll contribute to his run for senator in a few years. He tells the FBI to delete all their footage, provide Looking Glass evidence for the Philippines case, and not to press charges for any crimes committed in the US.

But the Defendant and Victim already have what they need. They tell the Foundation, and go about their plan. Defendant has no idea I'll go so far as to break into a Sylph facility, he figures I can undermine Looking Glass just by demonstrating without a doubt that the Victim was shot in the chest rather than the face. Which is good, that evidence I got from using Looking Glass would be inadmissible, as well as getting me into a lot of shit.

I just have one more question for today. What's the cause of these differences in Looking Glass? I've gathered that familiarity with the case impacts it, but why? As far as I know, Looking Glass works by getting magnets to divide by zero or something, I've never really understood the tech. Sylph is real quiet about the exact mechanics.

He doesn't know. Sylph has been studying that one for decades, no solid answer. But there's a hypothesis that's popular among the company's physicists. They're pretty convinced it's not a time machine, that'd violate all kinds of laws of physics. Instead they're pretty sure that it jumps people over to alternate universes where the Big Bang happened later. And because multiverse theory holds that there must be a universe for every possibility, there must be some in which people don't notice the visitors for whatever reason, no matter how unlikely that reason is.

For instance, say you open a door and leave it open. Well in that universe, that was already predestined to happen. But so is the breeze that shuts it. Or maybe it's a gravitational anomaly that shuts it, who the hell knows. But the universe you jump to is one in which you can't make any major changes, because of predestination and all that.

Thing is, the multiverse is theoretically infinite, and it's impossible for a computer to select from infinity. Just can't do it, computers are based on math, and the math just doesn't jive when you introduce infinity. Instead, the computer tries to shunt you into a universe that's as close to ours as possible. Only problem is that it has to account for your thoughts. Because remember, thoughts aren't just this supernatural intangible thing. Thoughts are made of electrical signals, which physically exist. So to get the dimension to line up, you get shunted into one in which your subconscious biases are correct. If that means shunting you into a universe in which Froot Loops are spelled as Fruit Loops, then that's what the machine will do. Or if you've got a preconceived bias that the Crackhead killed your kid, because the respectable Coach said so, confirmation bias is going to drop that detective into a universe where the Crackhead did do it.

After all, why else would black men make up around 6% of the population, but 32% of prisoners put away by Looking Glass? It sure as hell isn't reality doing that.

None of this is multiversal stuff is proven of course, but that's the working theory. Makes more sense than anything else I've heard. Guessing we'll probably never know, and I'm okay with that. What matters is that I've got evidence that Looking Glass does display a bias. Hell, I was arguing the numbers back when I was with the ACLU. But now we can prove it with more than just statistics. Now I've got a case in which Looking Glass is indisputably mistaken. The Defendant knows I can't keep him out of prison. Given what he's had to do, he doesn't really want to escape the consequences anyhow. Can't say I blame him. He's going to martyr himself, and it's my job to make sure it's not in vain.

Some years later...

I'm about to walk into a federal courtroom in San Francisco, and I feel more alive than I have in years. I think about my son, I think about the Defendant, and all the people that were denied justice. I look back on what's happened since I took on that case.

For starters, the Coach has his sentence commuted down to a series of life sentences. That was at the request of my ex-wife and I, we wrote a letter to the appeals judge. The important thing is he'll never be able to harm a child again, and revenge isn't going to bring back my son. Actually worth mentioning that the death penalty came back in California for a short amount of time, but got repealed when we started proving that the evidence against most of death row was a steaming pile of shit.

As for the Defendant, it went about as expected. There was no chance of getting him off, even without Looking Glass there was too much evidence, that was by design. And despite conclusive proof of Looking Glass having fucked up, I couldn't get that evidence thrown out. The prosecution dazzled the jury with bullshit, and the judge kind of went with it and evaded my arguments. Far from a fair trial, but that was to be expected, I was trying to upend the legal system in a big way, they weren't going to make it easy. And of course, the appeal got denied. They cited the other evidence, no one was really interested in putting Looking Glass on trial.

All as expected. But I did my part, I started the conversation. It got a lot of people talking about Looking Glass. Other whistleblowers started coming forward and being taken seriously, the ACLU began advocating a full investigation, a handful of politicians started asking questions and forming committees, scientists started expressing their skepticism in public. The really big kick in the pants that got people freaking out was when the Chairman of the Joint Chiefs of Staff admitted the reason the military never adopted the tech is because is they knew from the get-go that it was unreliable. The whole process has been slow going, eventually I got it before the US Supreme Court again to reevaluate, and they ruled that Looking Glass evidence is inadmissible. It's not total victory, but it's a hell of a start.

And for what it's worth, I did get a few years knocked off the Defendant's trial on account of it having been a voluntary death. I'm currently working a package to try and get the incoming governor to commute the sentence down some more.

As mentioned, the ACLU got their shit back together, and I started working with them again, at least part time. They were the ones that helped me eventually get a lawsuit all the way to the Supreme Court. Still not looking to join their staff again though, I like having my own firm, but I do work with them a lot these days.

That's actually the really big news.

Right now I'm headed in for day 1 of the what's going to be the largest class action lawsuit in the history of the United States legal system. The ACLU put me in charge of a whole team. Not only are they all motivated, they're damned good, wouldn't have let them on the team otherwise.

This is going to be big.

We're naming everyone that we can prove was complicit in a massive conspiracy to deprive numerous individuals of their freedom based on evidence provided by a system that they knew to be flawed. The list of people we're suing is extensive. The plaintiff list is even bigger, we opened it up to everyone that was ever wrongfully convicted based on Looking Glass evidence, which is a lot. This case will probably drag on for years, and in all likelihood it probably won't pay out enough to help all our plaintiffs start their lives over. It won't return the time they spent imprisoned on false evidence, and it won't bring back the hundreds that were executed.

The ACLU has also been involved in a massive project to try and get appeals for everyone that was imprisoned based on Looking Glass evidence. Not all of them should be released of course, many of them are in fact guilty, but they still deserve a fair trial all the same. Everyone does, that's what this is all about.

Between the class action lawsuit of epic proportions, appealing sentences for former clients of mine, and all the people that now have a legitimate shot at being acquitted, I'm busier than a one legged man in an ass kicking contest these days. I can't handle all of it on my own of course, so I've had to bring on some help. I paid out of my own pocket to send the Paralegal to law school, she graduated top of her class at Stanford (I needed her close by for her talents), and now she's my law firm Partner. And we've also taken on a lot of other junior lawyers, and a bunch of especially talented paralegals. It's not just that my firm needs the extra manpower, it's also that the justice system needs good defense attorneys. There's not many of us left, and I'm getting old, so I've got a duty to pass on what I know before I retire or kick the bucket. That knowledge is needed more than ever as our justice system returns to the old ways.

My hope is that some of these guys leave to go be public defenders. Believe it or not, I'm even hoping a few go become prosecutors. It's gotten a lot harder to prosecute people, but there's still a lot of bad guys out there, people that need to be put away. It's a tricky balance for sure, but you've got to have both sides.

Now in the interest of fairness, I had better address the

fact that crime did in fact spike in the United States. We're currently undergoing the worst crime wave since 2021, but it's still lower than it ever had been since before Looking Glass. As much as people have freaked out about how much higher the rates are without Looking Glass, smarter people are asking why it's not as high as before we had the system. A lot of social scientists are saying its because we shifted a lot of the criminal justice money into social programs, and it's made people not want to kill, rape, or steal from each other as much.

Don't know if that's the case, but it makes sense to me. Can't say I ever had a client do what they did because they were just outright evil. It was usually about survival, if survival gets easier than it follows that crime would come down.

But still, it's a big adjustment for a lot of people. Now they lock their doors, CCW permit applications have gone through the roof, and everyone constantly looks over their shoulder when they're in public. People are afraid in a way that many of the younger crowd never experienced before. Some of us old timers were already used to it from back in the day, but some got comfortable over the years and can't go back. So I get it, it's not the world I was ever hoping to go back to.

I have to acknowledge that I played a major part in that. I sparked the conversation. I'm not entirely to blame, but I do bear a lot of responsibility for what's happened. And I accept that responsibility. I'll never deny it, and I'll always own it.

But to be clear, I don't regret what I've done, I don't regret any of it. If I were to actually go back in time, I'd tell myself to do it. Maybe I'm just old and sentimental these days, but that whole liberty and justice for all spiel still means something to me.

Look, I get that things are scary now. For the first time in my life I carry a gun on me damn near everywhere I go, the Automat excluded of course; guns and alcohol don't mix. It's terrifying at times just to leave the house. But here's the thing, people always had the power to get rid of crime, well before Looking Glass. All we ever had to do was give up our civil rights, it worked pretty well for China. Scrap the middle part of the Bill of Rights, and we could've eliminated crime overnight. But back then we didn't, because we knew better than to take that Faustian deal.

People often get this idea that they're not surrendering their rights, they think they're giving up other people's rights. But it always comes back to bite us in the ass. Any power you give is a power that will be abused, every time. It was only a matter of time before it was used for political persecution, it looks like that may have already been the case in a few instances. The truth is, Looking Glass did nothing new, it just put a shiny technological sheen on abuses as old Hammurabi's Code. For those of you who mourn its demise, fret not, some other means of stripping the rights of your fellow citizens will come along any day now. Maybe it'll be a shiny piece of technology, maybe it'll be a set of vile words written on paper, but it'll come. It always does.

And you know what, I probably won't be there to fight the next round. But I'm preparing the next generation to fight the good fight. We'll win some, we'll lose some. That's just how it goes, history is a never ending struggle between freedom and tyranny. Always has been, always will be. All we can do is play our parts to try and keep the pendulum swinging towards freedom in our time, and setup the next generation.

Now if you'll excuse me, it's a long road to justice for a lot of people, and I'd best start marching towards it. Liberty and justice for all, motherfuckers!

Author Bio
K.M. Sykes has many interests and enjoys writing about them. **https://www.facebook.com/KMSykesWriting/**

The Rescue of Captain Guttierrez

John M. Campbell

Chapter One

It was midnight, and I was locked in a pod the size of a shoebox in the belly of a remotely piloted drone flying over the mountains of Afghanistan. A rogue group of terrorists had captured a US Army captain on a United Nations peacekeeping mission in neighboring Tajikistan. The CIA brought together a team to plan a rescue. Because each soldier in harm's way had a GPS locator chip implanted in their armpit before heading into country, the CIA had a fix on the captain's location. According to the plan, I would get in and out while flattened into 2D in a top-secret stealth suit. When I got there, I'd rotate into 3D, locate the hostage, stuff 'em into a stealth bag, zap 'em into 2D, and carry 'em out to the extraction point. The CIA always kept their plans simple so we grunts could understand 'em.

Inside the drone, I listened to periodic progress reports from Base voiced by Captain Patricia Cooper over our encrypted voice channel. I needed someone back at base who understood the technology I was using, and Patricia was the obvious choice. Not only was she the first female to receive the Darby Award in her Ranger training class, she and I were part of the inaugural class of Quantum Astronauts. When Patricia announced, "Approaching target. Prepare for release," things started to get exciting.

The release from the drone was clean. "Parachute deployed. Beginning descent," I reported. *Now for the fun part.*

Although I was still in 2D, the pod's sensors provided starlight and infrared visual modes on my helmet display. At this altitude, I operated in starlight mode with a map overlay.

From my vantage point I could make out the mountain stream at the edge of the town, which would be my escape route. Based on images from surveillance drones, the target location had an outer wall that set it apart from the surrounding buildings. My immediate destination was a nearby house with a rooftop garden where I could land and conduct my initial reconnaissance of the area.

With the pod's actuators, I manipulated the paraglider control toggles to steer the canopy over a mountain ridge and turn right to enter the valley as I descended. Trees in the village began to obscure the target from my view. The HUD traced a red line on my display to indicate the pre-planned glide path that would allow me to avoid the trees and come in at the proper trajectory. However, more wind than expected was rolling off the mountain and pushing me down into the valley, so I was tracking short of the desired path. I flared the canopy slightly to flatten my flight path and maintain my altitude.

I juked left to avoid the first tree and carved right around another. My landing destination came into view. As I lined up the canopy with the rooftop, the wind pushed me off to the left. Steering right to stay on course reduced my airspeed, so again I was bleeding altitude too quickly. At the current rate, I'd miss the roof and land on the road in front of the house. Light spilled from the front window of the house across the street. I decided on a fancy maneuver.

I eased up on both toggles, slightly more on the right side. The canopy dipped to the left, and my airspeed climbed. I was flying fast and low. I pulled on the right toggle to go into a swoop toward the near corner of the target building. Then I pulled hard on both toggles, which tipped the canopy up sharply to simultaneously lose speed and gain altitude. I cleared the rooftop ledge just as the canopy stalled.

The canopy slipped back, and the pod hit the rooftop harder than I intended. It crashed into the leg of a table and spilled a potted plant. I hit the control to open the pod and triggered the laser to rotate myself into 3D. I'd created quite a clatter. If I were discovered, there went any chance of saving Capt. Gutierrez, and the odds of my returning alive would sink to the level of a scratch-off lottery ticket.

I unzipped the hood of my infiltration suit and poked out my head. The pod lay under me, and the half-filled canopy billowed off to the side. I rolled to my feet and seized the canopy lines to pull it into my arms. I stuffed it into my suit then grabbed the empty shell of the pod and shoved it in after. The suit fit over standard fatigues, and it was loose-fitting enough to accommodate the pod and canopy. I scrambled to the ledge opposite from the shattered pot and sat down in front of a bench on which more flower pots sat. I zipped the suit up over my head and rotated into 2D.

My suit flattened into the plastic square formed when the "labels" mounted on the front and back collapsed together. I lay out in the open on the rooftop, so I used the curl-and-push maneuver inside the suit to bend the plastic square and slide it backward under the bench. My HUD displayed the edge of the bench above me. With another push I reached the shadows underneath it.

Outside, I heard footsteps on the stairs that led to the rooftop, followed by a cry of dismay from the owner as he discovered his broken flowerpot. Some choice words in Persian were followed by quick steps. I imagined the person looking over the edge of the roof ledge to see if anyone was around.

My radio received a transmission. "Base to Major Knight. Are you there, James?"

I was late checking in. "Knight to Base. I've reached the roof, Patricia, but it was a bit of a hard landing, so I had some cleanup to do. I'm currently hunkered down to avoid detection."

"Roger. Report back when you're clear."

In the meantime, I heard the man grumbling, along with the scrape and clink of pottery shards being gathered up. In a few minutes, a door slammed, followed thereafter by the wind rustling the leaves in the trees.

I waited another half hour before I moved. I wanted the occupants of the house asleep. As I waited, I opened a satchel-sized QMI bag and stuffed the parachute and pod into it. Then I shrank it down and tucked the resulting plastic label into my pack. As I listened to the rush of the wind through the trees, I stepped through the mission in my mind. Finally, I slid out of my hiding place.

As I emerged from under the bench, the sky appeared above me through my sensors. I rotated into 3D, unzipped my hood, and removed my helmet to see the Milky Way with my own eyes. The lack of light pollution and the clear mountain air made for excellent viewing. It was breathtaking—or maybe it was the icy wind that took my breath away.

Enough sightseeing. I radioed in as I peeled off my QMI suit and put it away in my pack. "Knight to Base. Roof is clear. Beginning recon."

I made my way to the roof ledge. I took my infrared scope out of my pack and scanned the egress route I planned to take through the town to get to the stream. The green image showed no heat sources that would indicate humans or animals out and about. I focused on the path to the house where our hostage was located. Again, nothing to worry about.

I used a drainpipe to climb down off the roof, crossed the street, and slipped between two homes. Across an alleyway stood the target house behind a nine-foot-high brick wall. Over the wall I glimpsed the second story of the house. No lights shone from the windows.

"Knight to Base. I've reached the target location. Beginning infiltration."

"Roger, James," replied Patricia. "Be careful."

I took a few quick strides across the alley and jumped. My hands caught the top of the wall, and I did a pull-up to peek into the space between the wall and the house. Our surveillance drone showed no sign of a guard dog or any other security outside the house, but I had to make sure. All I saw was a manicured garden space, with flowers surrounding a paved area that featured a patio table and chairs. I hoisted myself up and rolled over the wall in one continuous motion to minimize my silhouette while I was on top. I landed softly and stayed in a squat to see if I'd attracted any attention. The house remained silent and dark.

The back door had a small concrete landing with steps down to ground level. To the side, more steps led down to a basement level. I advanced in a crouch and checked my GPS tracker. It indicated the source of the signal was below ground level. I proceeded down the steps.

At the bottom was a door with no window. I'd be entering blind. Pressing my ear against the door, I heard nothing. I tried the doorknob. Locked. I pulled out my lock picks. Once the lock surrendered, I opened the door a crack. No light or sound originated from inside. I edged in and shut the door behind me. My heartbeat kicked up as my adrenaline flowed. I took a deep breath and let it out slowly.

A hallway stretched before me with closed doors on either side. At the end, a stairway led up to the ground floor. I checked the GPS, and it indicated the source was five meters ahead and to the left. The second door on the left fit the bill. Before I went in there, I had to clear the rest of the rooms.

The nearest doors were unlocked. One room was storage for household junk. The other contained exercise equipment suitable for the healthy terrorist. I proceeded to the second door on the right. Inside was a chair and table, along with a cot. The clothes hanging on the chair and the boots beside the cot told me the room was normally in use. I exited and quietly shut the door. Where was the occupant?

The room directly across the hall was where my tracker indicated I'd find Gutierrez. I tried the doorknob. It was locked. At the top of the stairs was a closed door. I padded up the steps to see if I could lock out anyone who might come down. No such luck. I had noticed paint cans in the storage room, so I went back and gathered as many as I could carry. I took them to the top of the stairs and arranged them in a haphazard pattern across the first few steps. It would serve as a poor man's security alarm.

I returned to the last room. I lay on the floor and pressed my ear against the gap under the door. I definitely heard noises—no conversation, something more guttural. Dim light leaked out from under the door.

I removed the QMI suit from my pack, put on the helmet, and pulled on the suit. Laying down, I zipped the hood over my head and triggered the laser to rotate into 2D. I engaged the lowlight optics in my HUD so I could see in the room as I slid under the door. I emerged to see candlelight flickering against the ceiling. The noises also became more distinguishable. I didn't like what I heard. I warped the suit label to point my visual sensors into the room. Nearby were the sock-covered soles of a man's feet. Beyond the feet a blanket heaved, its movement timed to the grunts and gasps.

I rotated into 3D and unzipped the hood. A man was on top of a woman, holding a knife to her throat. Her chin strained up and to the side to avoid the edge of the blade as her body shook with the thrusts. A cold fire ignited in my gut as I gained my feet.

Chapter Two

The back of her assailant's head was clear of the blanket. I lunged in with my right hand and grabbed the wrist holding the knife. I yanked his arm away from her throat and hooked my left arm around his neck. Arching my back, I pulled him off the woman. As we toppled to the deck, I locked my legs around his waist and wrenched his wrist backward. The knife clattered on the floor. I released his wrist and used my right hand to clamp my left arm around his throat, closing his carotid artery and cutting off his air.

He began to struggle. He grabbed at my arms, and his fingers scrabbled against my helmet. He flailed with his legs, trying to find purchase against the floor, but he couldn't break my hold.

I caught sight of the woman. She pulled on her fatigues then scrambled past me to grab the knife. Her lips pulled back in a snarl. She stepped forward and buried the knife in the man's chest, up under his ribs.

"Go rape your virgins in hell!" she rasped.

His movements lost their energy, and the tension left his body. She jerked the knife out. I rolled to the side and let go of the body. I checked for a pulse. Nothing.

As I removed my helmet, she grabbed a fistful of his shirt and wiped the blood off the knife. She looked over at me. "He's been at me nearly every night." She had fire in her eyes, and it wasn't a reflection from the candle.

"The bastard deserved it," I said in a low voice. "I'm Major James Knight. You are Captain Gutierrez?" She nodded. I recognized her from her photograph, but her cheeks were hollower, and her shirt hung loosely from her shoulders. "I'm getting you out of here. What can you tell me about hostiles in the house?"

"Two more men, plus the wife of one of the men. They all sleep upstairs." I heard little trace of an accent, but the dark hair and eyes left no doubt of her Hispanic heritage.

I began peeling off the QMI suit. "Are they armed?"

"Yes, AK-47s and pistols."

"Does this guy sleep in the room across the hall?"

"Not anymore."

Her deadpan sarcasm showed me she was mentally engaged. With the suit off, I removed my pack. "Does another guard relieve him during the night?"

"Yes, another one opens the door to check on me, usually an hour or two after he leaves. At some point before dawn, the woman brings me breakfast and a bedpan."

I checked my watch—2:30 a.m. We should have some time before the next guard arrived. "Are you hurt? Do you need any medical attention before we travel?" As soon as the question left my mouth, I kicked myself for asking. What rape victim didn't need medical attention?

She frowned. "I just want to get the hell out of here. But I need boots and a coat."

"I brought them. I don't have time to explain the details, but I'm going to zip you into a bag and carry you out on my back."

Her eyes opened wide upon hearing this.

She hesitated, then said, "Whatever you say, sir."

I took an old-style "body bag" label from my pack and laid it on the floor. I zapped it with my laser pointer. Captain Gutierrez drew in a sharp breath as the bag appeared from nowhere.

"This is new technology. It's a special kind of sleeping bag. Once I zip you in, I can shrink it down small enough to fit in my pack, but you won't notice anything from inside." Her eyes took on a skeptical look. I held her gaze with mine. "You can trust me, Captain. I know what I'm doing."

I unzipped the bag and took out a rebreather mask. It had four air canisters attached.

"Put this over your face and pull it tight, like a gas mask. It has enough air for twenty-four hours. You'll need it while you're in this bag." She did as I said. "There's an indicator for the amount of air left. Do you see it? Your coat and boots and a flashlight are packed in the bottom of the bag. Okay, now I'll zip you inside and carry you to the pickup zone. We should be home in three to four hours."

Her eyes showed concern, but she acquiesced. I helped her into the bag. I locked eyes with her through the faceplate and gave her a squeeze on the shoulder. Then I zipped her up and zapped her into 2D.

I manhandled the suit label into my pack. With her in it, the label weighed a hundred twenty pounds or so. I paused to shrink my own QMI suit and helmet and put its label in with hers. I lifted the pack onto the cot, squatted down, and slipped my arms through the straps. I leaned forward to take the weight on my hips and used my legs to push myself to a standing position. All the weight training I'd put my body through would now be tested.

The door was locked, so I squatted down to search the dead body and found the keys. I was headed for the exit when I heard footsteps above. I hurried down the hall to the back door. As I opened it, paint cans clanged behind me, followed by a shout and the sounds of a tumbling body. The poor man falling down the stairs had set off my alarm.

Chapter Three

I ran up the steps to the back yard and around the side toward the front of the house. With the extra weight I carried, I didn't trust I could scale the wall. A shaft of light shot out of a window. I ducked under it without breaking stride. A gate loomed ahead. A padlock hung from the latch, but only screws attached the latch to the wooden gate. I kicked it open and sprinted across the road. At this point, speed was more important than stealth.

I aimed for the nearest dark patch—a bush next to a house. I squatted behind the bush and looked back. One man exited the front door of the house I'd just vacated, followed immediately by another through the backyard gate. Both carried AK-47s. They exchanged words and moved in opposite directions along the road. There went my planned escape route. I was now officially improvising.

My best option was to move perpendicularly away from them and then circle around to the stream. I turned and threaded my way between houses while keeping hunched over. None of the houses showed any source of light, either external or internal, so I rapidly put distance between myself and my pursuers. I reached the edge of the village and found cover in a gully. The gully led downhill to where I hoped it emptied into the stream that would take us to the extraction point.

The gully took a steep downturn ahead. I crept to the edge, peeked over, and found a sheer drop. To my right was higher ground, which got steeper farther into the hills. To my left the ground leveled out, leading to the village. Although flatter, that terrain still exhibited a downward slope toward the stream.

I peered through my infrared scope to see if I could identify a route that provided cover from an observer in the village. I saw some patchy vegetation and rocky outcrops. Not perfect, but perfect was the enemy of good enough. I set out in a crouch to my first waypoint, a rock thirty meters away. As I ran, I glanced at the nearest buildings but detected no movement.

At the outcrop, I measured the route ahead to a patch of scrub. I took off again, and as I reached the scrub brush, I dove down prone. With the extra weight in my backpack, I landed harder than I expected, knocking the air out of my lungs. For a few endless seconds, I was in high school again, the little fullback who'd just been crushed by the hulking linebacker. Finally, my lungs began to fill in ragged gulps.

Fortunately, there was still nothing to worry about in the direction of the village. The gurgle of the stream sounded louder. My next goal was a tree near the edge of another drop-off to the water. I'd be covering a long expanse of open ground to get there.

I started off at a good clip, but halfway there I caught a glimpse of something. Rounding the corner of a building a hundred meters away came a guy with an AK-47. I had no choice but to try to get to cover. He raised his weapon and fired a burst when I was ten meters from the tree. I dove and scrambled on all fours to take cover behind it, this time taking my weight with my arms and legs instead of my ribcage.

I grabbed the sidearm holstered on my hip. I peeked around the tree trunk and located the shooter. He approached my position with the rifle trained ahead of him. I squeezed off two rounds. Unhurt, he dove to the ground. I hadn't expected to hit him at that range, but I needed time to assess the situation.

The sloping terrain leading to the stream below was littered with large, sharp-edged stones. Once I started down, I'd have to pick my way through the rocks without much cover, an easy target for shooters up on this ridge. These terrorist goons were notoriously horrendous shots, but even my eighty-year-old grandmother could hit someone my size from this ridge.

I fired another round to keep the shooter's head down. His buddy had started edging around the corner of the building, but once he heard the shot, he halted to ponder his next move. I took the time to look further to the left. I saw a possible path to the water. I extracted my QMI suit from my pack, zapped it into 3D, and put it on, along with the helmet.

I squeezed off another round to keep them guessing. Out of a shirt pocket I extracted the label of a satchel-sized QMI bag. I laid it on the ground and zapped it to 3D. Inside was a miniature raft, currently uninflated. A special bracket locked it onto the front label of my infiltration suit. The idea was to walk into the water, inflate the raft, and rotate myself into 2D. The raft would carry us to a pool five miles downstream for pickup there. According to the CIA, it couldn't be simpler.

The raft on my chest was made of Kevlar, and once inflated, it would provide a circle of body armor from my crotch to my chin. I counted on the noise of the inflation to be something they never expected to hear. I zapped the satchel to 2D and tucked it back into my pocket. Then I gathered my feet beneath me and pulled on the cord.

The raft inflated with a blast of flatulence. I sprang out from behind the tree, turned my torso to face the shooters, and fired rounds at both targets as I ran. They began to return fire as I reached the path heading down.

At least I'd thought it was a path. It was more of an overlook, complete with a bench, for viewing the pool that formed below. At the far end, the stream continued downhill in a cascade.

I made a snap decision. I accelerated three steps and launched myself from the cliff. I let the pistol go, and with that hand, I pulled the hood over my head and zipped it shut. With the other I activated the laser to go into 2D. I held my breath.

The raft struck the water, weighed down by the combination of my mass and that of Captain Gutierrez. From inside 2D, I sensed the impact on the water, but the techies who designed this raft must have gotten the calculations right because we didn't sink to the bottom. I let out a grateful sigh. The bobbing motions told me the current in the pool was carrying us toward the cascade, but judging from a couple of shocks, we floated in the pool long enough for our pursuers to reach the overlook and spray shots at the raft. Fortunately, the Kevlar protected us, and we sustained no apparent damage before entering the rapids.

For the next few minutes, I experienced shakes and bumps as the raft bumbled along, carried by the stream. I tried the radio. "Knight to Base. I have Captain Gutierrez. We are in the raft proceeding to the pickup area."

"Base to Knight. Copy you have Gu—*static*—peat your status?"

"We are in the raft and proceeding to the pickup area."

"*static*—not reading—*static*"

The raft obscured my front view, but I got a view from the back. Water sloshed over the label as the rapids carried us downstream, not enough to sink us but enough to interfere with the radio.

Patricia knew I had the captain. She'd be monitoring our channel. The drone would be circling and ready to come in for pickup at a moment's notice.

The mission planners estimated we would reach the target pool in two hours. I wasn't sure how they'd arrived at that number. It wasn't as if they'd dropped a stick in the stream and timed it going down to the pool. I checked my watch. It was almost four a.m. I relaxed and tried to monitor my progress on the HUD. The terrain map displayed a red circle to indicate where we were. It showed where we entered the stream, then more sporadically it plotted our location as the water sloshed away and momentarily uncovered the GPS transceiver. Each new point showed us at a location farther down the valley.

If we were getting our GPS coordinates, then Patricia was, too.

Chapter Four

We'd been on the water for nearly two hours when we went into freefall. We landed with a splash, but we managed to lose enough water from the raft to get a good fix on our position. It was a quarter to six, and we floated in a small pool less than a kilometer from our destination. From my back camera, the sky was a lighter shade of gray than the rocks and vegetation around the pool.

We drifted awhile, but I expected any minute we'd be pushed by the current into the cascade again. After ten minutes, we were still in the pool, but an occasional rolling motion made me think we were progressing. After another five minutes, I decided to rock the raft. Shifting my weight from side to side, I watched the back camera, and with each roll I caught a glimpse of the problem. A tree branch blocked our way downstream.

I had little choice but to act. The terrorists had seen the raft heading downstream, and although the terrain around the stream was rugged, they knew the area. They'd be taking the fastest route after us. We'd been stuck here for too long, and we wouldn't get moving again unless I did something. I activated the laser and rotated into 3D.

Bitter cold penetrated through my suit. The streams in this area were glacier fed. I'd come out face down with the raft under my chest. I kicked my legs so I could orient myself upright to see where I was. I unzipped the hood, keeping my helmet on. Water leaked into the suit down my chest and back. The cold was a knife slicing my flesh.

The muscles in my back and abs seized up. I clenched my teeth to keep from chattering and hooked my arm around the tree branch. Kicking with my feet and pulling with my arm, I got my head and neck above the water. I zipped my hood up to ear level to stanch the flow into my suit. I paused to catch my breath and fight off the shivers.

Dawn was approaching. I glanced around the pool. Sitting on the bank was a boy of nine or ten with a fishing pole. He viewed me with a mixture of fright and curiosity. I raised my hand and gave him a friendly wave. That gesture broke his trance. He dropped the pole and ran up the bank. I could only imagine what he thought I was, but it couldn't have been good.

To the side, I saw the current pressing debris against the branch. The entrance to the cascade was two meters farther along from where we'd come to rest.

Pins and needles of cold pricked my feet as I pulled myself along the tree branch toward the current. I planned to climb over the branch and launch us down the cascade while rotating into 2D again. As I moved along the branch into the current, I began to sense the power of the rushing water. Before I could react, I lost my grip, and the current sucked me under.

I was in the cascade again, and the water sped me downstream on my back with the raft pushing my chest under. I flailed my arms at the water, struggling to lift my head out to take a breath. My rear end scraped over the edge of a rock, and freezing water lacerated my rump. The suit had been slashed.

I flipped myself over to get on top of the raft intending to bodysurf my way down the cascade. I used my arms and legs to keep me centered in the current and away from the rocks, but the water tossed me on my back. I struggled to flip over again, only to have the current launch me off one rock and face down on another.

My faceplate cracked but didn't shatter. I tasted blood. I kept trying to fend off obstacles with my arms and legs, but I had lost all feeling in my extremities. The shock traveled to my shoulders and knees, and there was no telling what damage my hands and feet were sustaining.

After an eternity, I slipped into a rather large pool. I paddled to the side and crawled onto the bank. Shivering, I pulled the hood over my head to get warm. I had to call in to Base. Hopefully, the radio still operated.

"Knight to Base, come in." My voice strained as I attempted to speak in spite of the shivers.

"Base to Knight. Great to hear from you, James. What's your status?"

"We ran into pro-problems on the trip down the river. Ca- can you tell me where I am?"

"We have you located at the extraction point. Are you ready for pickup?"

"Let me check my equipment." I concentrated on pronouncing my words, but my tongue felt clumsy. "I'll let you know."

"Roger, James. Standing by."

The little finger on my right hand stuck out at an odd angle, but I didn't feel any pain. I used my left hand to straighten it out the best I could. I fumbled with the straps to open my pack. My fingers weren't working right. When I finally got it open, the contents appeared undamaged. I mumbled a prayer of thanks.

I found my laser pen and zapped a satchel to 3D. Inside was the balloon with the helium canister attached. A carbon-fiber cable three hundred meters long attached the balloon to a basket, which is where we needed to be for the evacuation. The balloon had two purposes. One was to act as signal buoy, and the other was to lift the cable high enough for the drone to snag. I moved along the bank of the pool to the upstream end, carrying the balloon and basket with me. The drone would be flying in through the valley, approaching from upstream. When it snagged the cable, the basket would be pulled downstream, so it swung out over the water as the winch pulled it up. This extraction point was selected for having the fewest obstacles downstream.

"Patricia, I'm ready to deploy the balloon. Let me know when you're set." The balloon was a bright orange color to allow the drone pilots to use it to target their flight path. Unfortunately, the balloon would also signal our position to anyone looking for us, a situation I wanted to delay for as long as possible.

"Roger. Drone is eight minutes out. We will let you know when it is three minutes away."

The drone had enough power to winch up our weight, but the payload bay on the drone was too small for full-size passengers. I slid the 2D package containing Captain Gutierrez out of my pack and hefted it into the basket. I peeled off my damaged QMI suit. There was no way I could use it to rotate into 2D now. I had a missing fingertip on my left hand from a previous mission to remind me of that fact, and I was lucky that was all I was missing. I reached into my pack and took out the only remaining "body bag" suit. Although not appropriate for walking around, it would work fine as a lifeboat to get me home. I wadded up the damaged suit and stuffed it into the backpack.

I removed my helmet and sat down with my back against a small boulder. I zapped the bag into 3D and pulled it over my feet. My lungs took in a deep breath of pine-scented mountain air, and my eyes took in the view down the valley. Above the burble of the stream, a pair of birds exchanged songs. As the adrenaline in my system dissipated, I became aware of the battering my body had taken. It made me wonder if I was still cut out for this life. For sure, I loved being a Marine. I enjoyed the camaraderie and the exhilarating rush of the missions. I felt good about protecting my country from those who would harm her. My only regret was my career seemed incompatible with finding a woman to love and start a family with—to enjoy for myself the life I enabled for others. I was happy Captain Gutierrez would have a chance at that life.

I felt drowsy, so I may have nodded off. Something told me the birdsong had stopped. I opened my eyes and registered movement on the ridge on the opposite side of the stream. Against the brightening sky was the silhouette of a man with a rifle—and then another. I hunkered down behind the rock. The early morning light hadn't yet reached this side of the canyon, so I didn't think they saw me.

I reached for my pistol and found the holster empty. Then I remembered—I'd ditched it when I dove off the overlook. Inflating the balloon would present my adversaries with a juicy target. Without my pistol, the option to stay and provide cover for Gutierrez with a few well-placed shots wasn't viable. Plus, a crosswind had come up, and heavy cloud cover was rolling in. Deploying the balloon now would likely drag the basket into the trees. That risk to Capt. Gutierrez was bad enough, but facing two men with AK-47s was worse.

I pulled on my helmet. "Patricia, I have hostiles across the stream, and I am unarmed. Any suggestions?"

"Roger. Sit tight." Then ten seconds later, "James, we have three targets on infrared approaching your position. Can you confirm?"

Three? I took a quick reconnoiter around the rock. I observed two men with rifles in the canyon and a third on the ridge above. They must have picked up another guy during the pursuit. I ducked behind the boulder, but they'd spotted me. They opened fire, and the rounds carved granite splinters off the rock above my head. "I confirm three hostiles across the river from me. Sixty meters and closing."

"Roger, James. Take cover. We're coming in hot!"

Seconds later a Griffin missile set the opposite side of the canyon on fire. The explosion engulfed the area where I'd last seen the three men. Pressure knifed into my eardrums and left them ringing. Hot air rolled over my position, bringing welcome warmth. Then bits of blast debris showered on me, signaling the end for this rogue terror cell.

Chapter Five

My feet and hands tingled as the blood flow returned. I was unfolding from my fetal position when the radio crackled.

"Come in, Major Knight. Over." I heard concern in Patricia's voice.

"Roger, Patricia. Nice shooting. We're good here."

"Glad to hear it, James. You need to evacuate your position immediately. We've lost visual cover, and that smoke plume's going to attract attention. We recommend you head to the backup site for pickup."

"Roger. I concur." My mind was a bit fuzzy. "Can you remind me where that is?"

"Sure, James. It's ten klicks northeast of your current position."

Windborne sleet tapped against my faceplate. To the east, a forest-covered mountain rose steeply above the pond.

"Roger, Base. I'm moving out."

"Godspeed, James. We'll continue to monitor your position and keep in touch by radio."

I wrestled the 2D package out of the basket and laid it on the ground. Was it heavier than I remembered? I packed the uninflated balloon into the satchel along with the cable and basket, zipped it up, and zapped it into 2D. I was ready to slide the package containing Gutierrez back into my pack when I had second thoughts about hiking up the mountains carrying an extra hundred and twenty pounds. I pointed my laser at the 2D label and rotated it to 3D. I unzipped the suit, and Captain Gutierrez sat up.

"Are we home?" she asked before she looked around and saw we weren't. Her gaze darted over to the conflagration on the other side of the canyon.

I removed my helmet. "Sorry, Captain, no," I began.

She stripped off her faceplate. "What the hell happened there?" she asked, the pitch of her voice rising. Anger laced her dark brown eyes.

"It's okay. We ran into some trouble getting here, but we made it to the extraction site. We were ready to evacuate, but the weather kicked up. Some hostiles followed us, but they're toast now." *Burnt toast*, I thought, and I started giggling.

She looked at me, then glanced at my helmet. It had a star-shaped crack in the visor where it had struck the rock on the way down the stream.

"Are you injured?" she asked.

"I'm okay. Just a bit of a headache." I had trouble focusing on her face. And there was something important I needed to tell her.

"We better get away from that fire." She stood up and stepped out of the bag. She wore the boots and jacket that had been packed inside.

That was it! "Right, we need to go east to the evac-swashun point."

"Which way's east?" she asked. I gestured vaguely uphill.

"Okay, let's pack up and move out."

We stuffed her faceplate and my helmet into her body bag. I kept the radio headset on. After patting a few pockets, I noticed the laser pointer was still in my hand, so I zapped the bag into 2D and put it into my pack. I tucked away the laser pointer in my pocket. Gutierrez reached over and zipped my pocket closed.

The wind was swirling, and I was mesmerized by the snowflakes that spiraled around us. Gutierrez took my elbow and led me into the forest.

****

I tensed up, hearing a voice in the distance. Then I realized the voice was a friend, and I relaxed.

"I recognize the symptoms," the voice said. "Aspirin or ibuprofen?"

The answer was swallowed by velvety silence.

"We should be okay here for the night. The snow covered our tracks. Any idea how long the storm will last?"

More velvet.

"We'll manage. I found some rations in one of the shrink-bags."

The voice came closer.

"Okay, Patricia. I'll keep in touch. Maria out."

That was the friendly voice. I opened my eyes. Light filtered in over a mound of snow. I lay on my back under an overhanging rock. A movement in my periphery caused my eyes to move toward it. Pain stabbed through my head, and I gasped.

"Easy, Major. You've got a concussion. Try not to make any sudden movements." Gutierrez tore open a foil packet. "Here, take these. They'll help with the headache."

I took the tablets with a swig from a water bottle and laid my head back down on the pack she'd put there as a pillow.

"Thanks," I might have said.

****

I had a dream where I sat under a tree overlooking a pond and watched a little boy fishing. I had the impression he was *my* little boy. I was relaxed and happy, with the sensation of a woman's body against my back, her arms encircling my torso. It might have been my wife, sometime in the future. She rested her chin on my shoulder, and her hair grazed my cheek. I smiled and pulled her arms tighter around me.

I woke during the night with warmth on my back and arms encircling my chest.

The next time I woke, faint light filtered into our shelter from the entrance. I couldn't tell if it was dawn or dusk. I heard a rustle and looked cautiously in that direction. The movement didn't exacerbate the dull pain in my head. Gutierrez was watching me.

"Good morning, Major. Is your headache better?"

"Call me James. I'll live. How long have I been out?"

"Most of yesterday and all night. I'm Maria."

"Did I hear you talking to Patricia?"

"Yeah. The weather's too gnarly for a pickup."

I glance around our bivouac. "I see you learned how to use the laser pen." All the QMI bags had been zapped into 3D.

"Yeah. You've got some fancy tech there. I had no idea we

had it."

"It's been kept under wraps."

"I can understand why. If terrorists ever got it—"

"It would be a disaster, yeah. Lots of people could die. Did you eat? I expect you found the water and rations."

"I'm good. Are you hungry?"

"I'm hungry, but I don't know if my stomach can take it. I'll try a bite." She handed me something dry and crunchy. I took a nibble. "Are you cold?" I asked her.

"I'm okay."

"You did well to find us shelter. I couldn't have been much help."

"I've had cold-weather training. It's not so comfortable, but we'll survive."

Her words triggered a pang of regret. "I'm really sorry I got you into this mess."

"It beats the hell out of where I was before." Her voice turned husky.

"You deserved three-hots-and-a-cot by now. Instead, you got this."

She laughed. Her laugh was delightfully melodic. "If that's what I expected, I chose the wrong profession."

The laugh echoed through my head, erasing the pain along with it. Then the dull ache behind my eyes returned. I needed to find a way to hear her laugh again.

"By the way, did I feel you against me last night or was it a dream?"

"You must've been delirious from your head injury." She gave me a mischievous smile.

"Hey, I'm not saying I didn't appreciate the extra warmth."

"Yeah, well, it's not like I was going to ignore the big heater in the room." Her eyes crinkled at the edges as she smiled.

"Sure, I get it," I said. "I've spent many a cold night in bivouac spooning with my buddies to keep warm. It's why I love being a Marine."

That laugh warmed me again. "I always knew there was something strange about you Marines," Maria said.

Chapter Six

A few hours later the snow had stopped, but angry clouds still presented a low ceiling. I was on the horn with Patricia. "Do you have any projection of how soon it'll clear up?"

"There's another front close on the heels of this storm system. We may have a window of a few hours tomorrow afternoon. Between now and then, expect more snow."

"And how far are we from the pickup site?"

"You're still eight clicks away."

"Eight kilometers of rugged country, uphill through the snow," I replied for Maria's benefit. "Okay, give us a minute."

"So how's it look?" she asked.

"Another storm's coming, with maybe a break of a few hours tomorrow afternoon when they could get in for the pickup. The pickup site is above the tree line."

She frowned. "I think we need to go now, while we've got daylight, and get as far as we can. We can find shelter again before dark."

"I agree." I got back on the radio. "Okay, Patricia. We're moving out."

"Roger, James. Good luck."

We packed up the satchels and zapped them into 2D before stowing them in my pack. I surveyed the area around our cave with my binoculars. Our bivouac provided a good view downhill, and I detected no movement of any kind. I ventured out to check the three-hundred-sixty-degree picture. Same result, so I motioned Maria to come out.

The area was blanketed under a foot of snow, with drifts three or four feet deep in places. The hillside was generally wooded with outcrops of stone. I took the lead, selecting a meandering route to avoid the deepest drifts while still heading uphill in roughly a northeast direction. The pickup site might be eight kilometers away, but we'd have to traverse twice that distance to get there.

At this altitude, I was soon huffing great billows of vapor, which didn't help my headache. Maria didn't seem to be affected as much. I stopped every fifteen minutes or so to catch my breath, making a show of checking the area with my binoculars. Judging from the amusement in her eyes, Maria didn't buy my act, but she played along. At least the exercise kept me warm. When I stopped, however, the sweat soon sent a chill through me, so it was a mixed blessing.

After a few hours, the snow started up again, gently at first, then heavier. We took a break, and I unpacked the meager rations.

"Sorry about the lack of food," I told Maria. "I didn't anticipate the mission taking this long."

"I was meaning to go on a diet, anyway," she deadpanned.

I smiled. "I wasn't going to say anything."

She smiled back, with her eyes and nose crinkling in a pleasing way.

Despite the snowfall, I found a rhythm I could sustain, so we continued our slog at a slow but steady pace, hour after hour. We'd just crested a ridge when my boot skidded on a patch of ice, causing me to lurch sideways. Something buzzed by, followed immediately by a crack.

Gunfire! Both of us dove to the ground and scrambled to take cover on the other side of the ridge. I glanced at Maria and saw concern in her eyes. She hadn't found any weapons in the 2D satchels. She must've seen the same concern reflected in my eyes, since the only pistol I'd brought with me was at the bottom of a pool of water.

I edged my scope over the ridge and took a quick scan in the direction of the rifle shot. The snowfall obscured the view, and I didn't see anything heading toward us. I shifted my position a few meters and repeated the scan using infrared. A hot spot showed up some distance below us. I ducked under the ridgeline and crawled over to Maria.

"I've got a hostile maybe six or seven hundred meters

away."

"One of the terrorists?"

"I doubt it. I think the Griffin took them out back at the primary pickup site." My mind raced. Could it be a hunter out for deer? No, our trail in the snow was clearly human footprints. "But they're definitely after us."

"Is there more than one?"

"I only saw one on infrared. Let me check again." I moved up to the ridgeline and peered over again. Still one hot spot, which suddenly flared. I ducked, and a bullet struck the rock above me. The rifle shot echoed.

"We've got to get moving." In the fading afternoon light with the snow falling, a seven-hundred-meter shot wasn't possible with an optical sight. This guy had infrared optics on a high-powered sniper rifle. The game had changed. We weren't facing wannabe *jihadis* with AK-47s anymore. This guy was a professional.

We ran directly away from the ridge, both of us in a crouch. I banked on the shooter approaching the ridge with caution, expecting a possible ambush. We had no hope of covering our tracks in the snow, so we had to put as much distance as possible between him and us. But I was the weak link. After a few minutes of running, I was in oxygen debt.

I looked behind us. The ridge was out of sight among the trees, so I vectored us back in the northeast direction and slowed to a walk. Maria joined me.

"What's the plan?" She searched my eyes.

I decided to verbalize my thoughts. "We've got no weapons," I grabbed a breath, "except my knife and the one you took." Two more breaths. "We've got another half-dozen kilometers to the pickup site." Two breaths. "It'll be dark soon, and our bodies show up on infrared."

"So what's the good news?"

"You tell me."

We walked in silence for a minute. Then she said, "There are two of us and one of him. We know where we're going, and we have a head start. He has to proceed slowly for fear of an ambush. If we can get to the pickup site with enough of a lead, we can make it out of here."

I liked her optimism, but I didn't share it. He could track us all the way, and the timing would have to be perfect for us to reach the pickup spot just as the weather cleared enough for the cavalry to arrive. Plus, the pickup spot was above the tree line, making the sight lines much longer due to the lack of cover.

"We've got something else," I replied. "The stealth technology. I just need to figure out how we can use it in our favor." I'd finally caught my breath, so I settled into a pace I could maintain as I considered our options.

****

The snow grew heavier and the wind stronger. I used my knife to cut branches from a fir tree, and Maria and I dragged them behind us. We hoped to obliterate our footsteps enough for the snow and wind to cover our tracks. In the early afternoon, the light was failing. I had Maria scout out our next bivouac as I used the infrared scope to check for our pursuer. No hot spots showed up, but that fact didn't guarantee we were safe.

Maria found a combination tree well and rock outcrop we could fit into. We ducked into the depression and pushed the snow out to fill the entrance so no heat signature would betray our location. As we packed the snow into the opening, the wind outside reduced to a steady whisper. I took out my flashlight, opened my pack, and brought out the QMI bags. I zapped the two body-bag suits into 3D. We wrapped ourselves in the suit fabric to keep warm. Then we shared the last of the rations.

"Tomorrow, we're gonna have to lure him in and kill him," I said.

"I know that might become necessary," Maria replied, "but

I think we have other options."

I was open to any ideas. "What are you thinking?"

"First, the storm may cover our tracks enough to lose him. If we get to the evac site before he picks up our trail again, we're home free."

"Only if the weather is clear enough when we get there. But you're right, we shouldn't rule out that possibility. What else?"

"We could hole up here until the weather clears then make a dash for it. Maybe he goes off somewhere else or gives up looking when he can't find us."

That idea might work. "So that option assumes the snow covers our tracks well enough that he can't trace us to this den. Also, it assumes we can dash through heavy snow to the pickup site in the window between storms before he catches up to us."

"Right, but during that window, we'll have air cover to protect us."

"Good point, but what happens if the window closes before we get to the evacuation site? We'd be trapped for days out in the elements without any food and with the sniper on our ass." My pessimism must've shown because Maria's expression fell. "But having air cover could be crucial for a shorter sprint. Let's keep that option in our playbook."

Maria nodded, but she had something else on her mind. "Since we've only got knives, why would the sniper let himself be lured in? Wouldn't he keep his distance and try to pick us off?"

"It's possible he wants you alive."

Maria frowned. "I'd rather die than go back to that hellhole."

"And I'd rather die than let that happen. Unfortunately, we're carrying—or rather, I'm carrying—something more valuable than both our lives."

She raised her eyebrows, and then realization dawned on her face. "Damn it," she said in a low voice. "The stealth technology."

"Yeah. Like I said before. I'm real sorry I got you into this. But this technology is a weapon *we* have. So I'm going to teach you how to use it."

Chapter Seven

I gently pushed the pod out of our den along the top of the snowbank, displacing the snow until the electronics got a view outside. With my helmet on, the HUD displayed what the infrared optics detected. Even with the snowfall, the sniper's heat signature would shine through. Using the pod instead of my own scope to look outside, I avoided revealing my own heat signature. I took the first watch while Maria got some sleep. We would alternate four-hour watches until dawn. At first light, we'd be off again.

We'd devised a plan of action, and we'd briefed it to Patricia. She had given us the latest updates on the weather and downloaded to my HUD the most direct route to the pickup site, given the terrain. She was concerned about the hostile tracking us and promised to have continuous UAV coverage available to take advantage of any breaks in the cloud cover. In the worst-case scenario, she could use our GPS position plus some offset to target a Griffin missile.

My head had begun to throb again, so I took another couple of ibuprofen tablets. I spent a few minutes silently cursing myself for screwing up what should've been a routine extraction, as if I ever expected a CIA operation to come off without a hitch. I glanced over at Maria. She'd fallen asleep in seconds. She had to be exhausted, and now in repose, her gaunt face reminded me of how malnourished she'd seemed when I first encountered her. Not only was she tired, she had to be hungry, too, yet she'd never voiced a hint of a complaint. She was one tough specimen.

I'd seen her pack some snow together and slip it into the front of her pants. She'd caught me looking and explained she had some chafing, but I knew it was worse than that. I'd witnessed the last assault she endured and was ashamed I hadn't considered earlier what she'd been dealing with. Despite her own trauma, she'd stepped up and taken control when my concussion took me out. Stranded in the wilderness with an invalid, she'd kept us both alive. She was a helluva soldier—a helluva woman.

Now it was my turn to step up. We had to get to the evacuation point alive tomorrow. If I were the sniper in this situation, what would I do? I had to get inside his head.

The woman slows them down and is probably a distraction, so I have the advantage of speed. Against the cold background, my infrared scope will work best. By now, I know the general direction of travel, even if I don't know the exact destination. I'll continue in the direction my quarry is headed, hoping either to pick up the trail in the snow or to see them on infrared. The weather keeps their allies away, but as soon as the weather clears, they'll swoop in. They'll need treeless ground to land, perhaps a meadow. I must get to them before the weather breaks, when I'll be vulnerable to an attack from the sky.

Our best bet was to get to the evacuation point with as big a lead as possible. That meant we had to keep pushing forward—and pray for the weather to clear.

****

We left our den the next morning when it was light enough to see where to step. Thankfully, the snow and wind had obliterated our tracks from the day before. An unbroken white blanket spread over the landscape below our bivouac. My scope showed nothing in the infrared spectrum, so we started out. The snow presented an exhausting slog. We paused frequently to catch our breath in the thin air. I scanned behind us at every stop, and nothing appeared on the scope. Good news, but both of us knew we must keep pressing forward.

By late morning, the snow tapered off, and the sky brightened. Unfortunately, the trees were thinning, providing less cover. The map on my HUD showed us under two kilometers from the pickup site when a bee stung my left shoulder—and we heard the rifle crack from somewhere above us.

We both hit the deck and scrambled back behind the ridge we'd just crossed. I fingered the hole in my jacket sleeve. Blood coated my fingertip.

"Are you hit?" Maria saw the blood.

"It just grazed my shoulder."

"Do you have a first aid kit?"

I shrugged off my pack.

While she opened the kit, I took out the satchel containing the pod and my helmet and zapped it into 3D.

The bastard had gotten ahead of us. I donned my helmet, pushed the pod to the top of the ridge, and looked for a heat signature in the direction of the shot. Nothing showed up, so I reached up to rotate the pod to the right. There he was four hundred meters away. I'd just taken my hand off the pod when it exploded into splinters.

I rolled away from the flying debris and landed on my injured shoulder. Pain stabbed down my arm. I sat up to take the pressure off my arm and left a bloodstain in the snow. It gave me an idea. I took off my helmet and pulled my damaged suit out of the pack. I removed my jacket and squeezed my shoulder so the blood dripped onto the suit. It needed to look like my dead body.

I explained to Maria what I had in mind.

She started to protest, but I interrupted.

"This could be our only chance," I said as she applied the bandage to my shoulder. "We don't have time to argue. You take the helmet and the pack. The helmet controls will allow you to rotate your suit to 3D and back. The HUD will show you the path to the evac point. When the weather clears, if I'm not there, deploy the balloon and shrink yourself down into the basket. The UAV will winch you up. If you need to, call in a Griffin to provide cover."

"What are you going to do?"

"I'll keep him occupied while you get away. Then I'll follow your tracks to the pickup. Now move out, using that ridge for cover." I pulled on my jacket.

She hesitated—and grabbed me in a hug.

I hugged her back with my good arm then said in her ear, "Get going. That's an order, Captain."

She strapped on the helmet and hustled away, crouching under the cover of the ridge. I stuffed snow into the damaged infiltration suit until I had it filled out, and I zipped the hood closed. I pushed the dummy's head to the top of the ridge then pulled it down a few seconds later. I moved to the side and repeated the maneuver. A bullet zinged off the ridge where the dummy's head had been, and a puff of snow settled on me. I waited a minute then repeated the maneuver at different random positions, like I was peeking over the ridge to see where he was. Maria had long since left the ridge and turned the corner out of sight some sixty meters away. I was determined to play this cat-and-mouse game for as long as possible.

Twenty minutes later the sniper hit his target. The force of the bullet tore the suit out of my hands and left it lying a few feet away. I let out an incoherent noise like I'd been hit. I was now on the clock. I took off my jacket, tore off the bandage, and used it to smear blood around the hole the bullet had made in the hood of the suit. I squeezed the hood until snow protruded out to simulate blood-soaked brain matter. Dragging it to a cliff I'd seen earlier, I laid the suit onto the onto the snow and pushed it down the slope. It left a trail of red behind before disappearing over the drop-off.

I followed in Maria's tracks, taking care to leave only one set of footprints behind. I searched for the right location. There it was. The place out of sight of the shooter where Maria had turned right and surmounted the ridge. When she turned, her foot had slipped, leaving a jumble of footprints as she regained her balance. I took the body-bag label out of my pocket and zapped it into 3D. I stepped into the bag and took a last glance back.

From this angle, I spotted the QMI suit where it had fallen onto a jumble of granite rocks. The suit's arms and legs splayed in unnatural positions. I donned the rebreather mask and zipped the bag shut over my head. Bending my knees, I launched myself into a backward dive as I pushed the laser pointer button to rotate into 2D. My suit shrank down, and the label buried itself into the soft snow below the ridge.

Chapter Eight

With no way to see outside, I had to rely on my judgment when to rotate into 3D. In the darkness inside the bag, the throbs in my shoulder marked the seconds. At last, the luminous numbers on my watch indicated half an hour had elapsed. I zapped myself into 3D. The body-bag suit expanded to its full dimensions.

I inspected the trail of footsteps that led away from my location. My plan had worked. The two sets of tracks before me meant I would come up from behind the sniper. The tracks also meant Maria was on her own against a guy with overwhelming firepower—unless I got to him first.

I jettisoned caution overboard. I had to rely on the fact the sniper was focused solely on Maria and wouldn't look backward. Maria had a head start of almost an hour on me and up to thirty minutes on the sniper. Even if I cut fifteen minutes off her time, the sniper would likely catch up to her before I would, but I still had to try.

I followed the tracks at the maximum speed I could manage in the uncertain footing. The pounding my joints had taken in the trip down the rapids now came back to haunt me. The weakness in my knees and ankles caused me to lose balance several times, and I fell. I set myself in stubborn Marine mode, rose to my feet, and plowed ahead, one step after another. In thirty minutes, the trees were all but gone, replaced by scrub. Forty minutes on, I heard the first shot. I scrambled ahead at double-time, my lungs burning, and another shot echoed ahead. I crept over the next rise. Footprints curved around a large, flat-topped rock. I climbed the rock for a better vantage point. On the top, I flattened onto my stomach and edged forward through the snow.

Below me was a depression. Maria's footsteps led down into the depression and up around a boulder. Beyond the boulder was another ridge. A trail of footsteps led halfway up the rise to the ridgeline, but haphazard marks in the snow indicated a scramble back to the protection afforded by the boulder. The sniper had Maria trapped, with sightlines covering all her possible exits.

A furtive movement to my right corresponded with the crack of another shot. I spotted him lying prone behind a bush. His rifle pointed at Maria's location. I surveyed the terrain between him and me, looking for the shortest route for me to take him from behind.

Suddenly, an explosive inflation sounded from behind Maria's boulder, and the balloon leapt into the air. The graphite cable spooled out behind it.

My first thought—*the rescue is on!* The sniper must have thought the same. He fired at the balloon. My next thought was, *oh, no, it's too dangerous!* The winds aloft buffeted the balloon, which caused the sniper to miss, but any attempt to hoist Maria up with a sniper on the ground was foolhardy. The question became moot when the next shot brought down the balloon.

I glanced at the shooter. He got to his knees and then to his feet. I scanned the area ahead of him. The quickest way to Maria would take him directly under my rock. He needed to get to her before the rescuers arrived.

I reached for my knife. The sniper ran in my direction

heading into the depression. I remained motionless until he passed out of sight, approaching my position. I sprang to my feet in a crouch. Over the edge, I located the top of his head and timed my jump. His head tilted up, and his eyes met mine as I crashed down on him.

He turned and hunched his shoulder to take the blow. My arm hooked around his forehead instead of his face, and my stab hit his side rather than his neck. My blade bounced instead of penetrating. He wore body armor. The weight of my fall took him to the ground, and I redirected my stabs to his legs and lower abdomen. He grunted in pain but twisted in the direction of my momentum, throwing me free. He stood.

Rolling to my feet, I re-engaged before he could grab a gun or his own knife. I outweighed the guy, so I bulled my way forward with kicks and knife thrusts. The wounds in his legs slowed his reactions as he parried my blows. I faked with my knife at his wounded leg. He pulled it back, and as he put his weight on the other leg, I crashed my boot against that knee. He crumpled to the ground with a scream.

I lost sight of his right hand for an instant. When I glimpsed it again, it held a pistol. I dove on top of him, trying to pin the weapon against the ground, but it sank into the snow. My hand lost its grip, and the gun rose out of the snow bank. I slashed his ear as I rolled away. The gun went off beside my head.

I went deaf in that ear, but the bullet missed. I rolled back, blocked his gun hand with my left arm and kneed him in the groin.

His fingers gouged my eyes. I turned my head away. He worked the gun free again. I ducked under as he fired. The bullet struck the boulder next to us, and a granite splinter raked my forehead. Blood seeped into my eye.

I kicked at the gun and tried to pin his arm, but it came free again. I slashed his face, and he raised his arms to ward off another blow. He fired again in desperation. I aimed a thrust at the exposed arm hole of his vest and buried my knife into his chest.

I lunged across him with both hands to immobilize the gun arm. I pried the pistol out of his fingers and held it under his chin as I searched his body for more weapons. I confiscated a knife.

The vapor from his nostrils turned pink. I'd punctured a lung. He was bleeding out, with only minutes to live. The right side of his face was burned, with part of his beard singed off.

I leaned over to face him nose to nose. "Who do you work for?"

Rage filled his eyes. He said something, but the words came out as a gurgle. He spat in my face. I swiped off the blood-specked spittle with my glove and smeared it on his jacket. I got to my feet and retrieved his rifle from the snow. When I returned to him, he'd stopped breathing.

"Clear, Maria!" I shouted. "I got him!" With all the gunshots, I'd half-expected her to have run down with her captive's knife to give assistance, though I was glad she hadn't. Too many random bullets had been flying around.

She didn't answer. I followed her trail of footsteps in the snow. I rounded the rock where she hid.

She wasn't there.

Behind the rock, a small alpine pond filled a depression, most of it covered with snow and ice. The trampled snow between the pond and the rock indicated she'd taken shelter there from the sniper fire. I glanced around but didn't see any blood. The footsteps I'd seen from afar only went halfway up the ridge before turning back. Water from the pond carved a runoff channel into the rock where it emptied over the cliff. The channel would've provided some cover from the sniper if she'd crawled on her stomach.

I followed the channel toward the edge. I noted a ricochet mark in the area where I'd seen movement from my rock. Something in the channel caught my eye. I squatted down. It was a button from the jacket she wore. I looked to the edge where the channel emptied into space. The trickle of water from the pond had coated the rock with a sheen of black ice.

335

A lump formed in my throat. The ice would've been impossible to see in the flat light we experienced earlier. Once the balloon had been shot down, she might have decided this escape route was her only option.

I imagined her plunging over the edge. A wave of grief and self-loathing rolled through me.

No, no, no, no! I scoured the area again to find something I'd missed. I caught sight of the basket. I leapt forward, hoping to find her suit label nestled inside, awaiting pickup. The basket was empty.

The adrenaline high I'd ridden after fighting for my life with the sniper now plummeted into an abyss. Against long odds, Maria and I had defeated the enemy, but with her death, it all meant nothing.

I collapsed to my knees in the snow and wailed to the sky.

Chapter Nine

Eventually, a ray of sunshine pierced the clouds and prompted me into action. I trudged down to where the sniper's body lay. I took the body-bag label from my pocket and zapped it into 3D. I rolled the sniper into it and shoved his rifle in with him. I zipped the bag almost all the way shut, leaving enough room to put my hand inside and grasp one of the handles sewn into the corners that allowed us to warp the plastic square while in 2D. Using the handle, I dragged the bag over the snow up to the pond.

I sat down heavily, facing the pond with my back to the boulder. There wasn't much more I could do except wait. Maria had the HUD and the radio. The balloon wasn't repairable, so UAV extraction was a non-starter. My fate was out of my hands. Either Patricia came up with something, or I was fucked. At that point I didn't much care.

My vision blurred as my eyes again filled with tears. I wiped them with the back of my hand, and the edge of the pond came into view. Something about the scene crystallized in my mind, but I didn't immediately understand what. Finally, my subconscious thought wrestled its way through to my conscious mind.

A small area of open water existed at the low end of the ice-covered pond where it trickled into the channel. The ice at the edge of the water traced a smooth arc—except for one segment, where it formed a perfectly straight line, as if sliced by a knife.

I crawled to the edge. *It might be.* The length of the line was right.

I leaned over to peer into the water, but the light didn't penetrate to the bottom, even though it was only a few inches deep. I pulled off my gloves and eased my hands into the water. Near-freezing cold engulfed my fingers. I'd only have a few seconds of feeling before they went numb. I explored the rough surface of the bottom, reaching back toward the frozen crust. The texture changed to smooth-as-glass, which could be silt, but, no, there was an edge, then two edges meeting at a corner.

Straddling the end of the tiny pool, I worked my fingers underneath to get a grip and used my legs to pull the hundred-twenty-pound plastic label from the water. I wrestled it off to the side, took out my laser pointer, and pushed the button to trigger the return frequency. The suit appeared on the ground. I knelt beside it and unzipped the bag. Out popped Maria's head wearing my helmet. She raised a knife, ready to plunge it forward.

"James!" She ripped off the helmet. "Where is he?"

I reached out a hand to her. "I got him, Maria, we're safe."

Her fingers enclosed over mine. "We're safe?"

"Yeah, we're safe," I said softly, pointing to the body bag lying in the snow.

She peeked at the bag, then back at me. Relief flooded her face. She flung her arms around my neck and kissed me hard.

I pulled her up against me and kissed her back.

After a minute, she tilted her head up to look at me.

"You're bleeding," she said, reaching up to touch my forehead.

"It's just a scratch."

She kissed me again, this time longer and more softly.

I loved the way she felt in my arms.

****

Eventually it occurred to me we might want to get rescued before the next storm came in. I smiled at Maria. "I think we better contact Base and see what they can do to get us outta here."

"The Osprey will be here soon," she said, then smiled at my expression. "With us out here all alone facing a sniper, I thought it would be better if Patricia sent in a special-ops unit. Once they agreed, I kept heading for the rendezvous point, until the sniper pinned me down behind this rock. Things weren't looking good, so I sent up the balloon to keep him occupied and shrunk myself into 2D to hide in the water until help arrived."

Her initiative and ingenuity was a marvel. "What gave you that idea?"

"The rebreather gear reminded me of scuba, and I figured nobody would look there. How'd you find me?"

I pointed at the straight line in the ice. "The label must've grazed the ice as it fell into the water."

I told her how deploying the balloon had allowed me to locate the sniper and set up an ambush. I unzipped the bag and exposed his face. "Was he one of your abductors?"

"No. Never seen him before. Any idea who he might be?"

"Not really."

"How'd he get those burns on his face?"

"He must've been the one on the ridge when the Griffin took out the other two back at the primary pickup point. He got burned but survived."

"What the hell was he doing out here?"

I shook my head. "It's hard to say. Maybe he was involved

with your capture, or maybe it's something else. We'll bring him back with us and see if we can identify him."

"How convenient that you brought a body bag with you." She gave me an impish smile.

I smiled back. "And it has these handy built-in grips. You can help me drag him to the extraction site."

****

Patricia was in the Osprey when it landed. Along with the other soldiers, she jumped out with a carbine at the ready. She exchanged hugs with both of us, and then we boarded.

On the way back, I insisted they follow our footsteps to retrieve the QMI suit I'd slid off the cliff. While the massive rotor blades held the Osprey in a hover, they lowered a commando on a rope to snag the snow-packed dummy. Patricia and Maria understood why, but one of the troops questioned my reasoning for taking the risk to retrieve some clothing.

"We leave no one behind," I said. I think the bandage the medic had applied to my head wound convinced him I was delirious. Either that, or he didn't expect a major to make much sense anyway.

END

John M. Campbell spent thirty years in the aerospace industry building computer systems in support of the armed forces and intelligence agencies. Short stories of his have appeared in Compelling Science Fiction (Issue 12) and Writers of the Future (Volume 37), as well as other anthologies.

For a complete list of his publications, visit his website at www.JohnMCampbell.com. His Amazon author page is https://www.amazon.com/author/johnmcampbell, and his Facebook page is:
https://facebook.com/JohnMCampbellSciFiAuthor/

Cannon Publishing is the premier Indie Military, Sci-Fi and Fantasy publishing company, bringing you stories that range from elves fighting tanks to modern PMC's conducting lighting corporate raids. But mostly damn good characters and stories.

www.cannonpublishing.us

Made in the USA
Middletown, DE
24 May 2024